W9-CHN-994

HIS MAJESTY'S U-BOAT

Douglas Reeman

A BERKLEY MEDALLION BOOK
PUBLISHED BY G. P. PUTNAM'S SONS
DISTRIBUTED BY BERKLEY PUBLISHING CORPORATION

For my mother, with love

Library of Congress Catalog Card Number: 73-78604
SBN 425-02779-1

BERKLEY MEDALLION BOOKS are published by
Berkley Publishing Corporation
200 Madison Avenue
New York, N.Y. 10016

G. P. Putnam's Sons
200 Madison Avenue
New York, New York 10016

BERKLEY MEDALLION BOOKS ® TM 757,375

Printed in the United States of America

G. P. Putnam/Berkley Medallion Edition, MARCH, 1975

CONTENTS

Author's Note

The Allied invasion of Sicily in 1943 proved to be the turning point in the Second World War. Too many setbacks and retreats had left Britain and her Allies almost beyond hope, and the proposed invasion, the biggest amphibious operation ever planned, needed to be a success, perhaps more than any previous undertaking. Over the years, that first combined stab at Europe's underbelly has been overshadowed by other events, and greater invasions, but none was more vital at the time.

My story is fiction, but most of the background is based on what actually happened. A German submarine, U-570, was in fact captured by the British and used against her previous owners. The then unknown secret weapon, a radio-controlled bomb which could be launched and directed by an enemy aircraft, may seem to us almost antique in this age of nuclear weapons, but in 1943 it was a threat which almost tipped the balance against us.

Had the Germans discovered our intention to invade Sicily, instead of through Greece and the Balkans, it is almost certain that those deadly bombs would have broken the back of our sea forces before a landing could have been completed. As it was, several cloak-and-dagger ruses were successfully used. A dead body dressed as a Marine officer was found on a Spanish beach with supposedly secret details of an Allied invasion through Greece. Other schemes were employed to make the enemy believe in this idea, so that when the attack began his forces were wrongly deployed to repulse it.

Two months later, when the Allies struck at the Italian mainland and hit the beaches at Salerno, there were many who realised just how thin the margin of success had been.

The Germans, then prepared and ready, brought those radio-controlled bombs into immediate use. Many men were lost, and fine ships put out of action. Among the latter were famous veterans of the Mediterranean campaign, including the battleship *Warspite*, the cruiser *Uganda*, and the American warships *Philadelphia* and *Savannah*.

1 A Good Catch

IT was nine o'clock on a February morning when His Majesty's Submarine. *Tristram* edged against the greasy piles at Fort Blockhouse, Portsmouth and her lines were taken by the waiting shore-party.

In the forepart of her conning tower Lieutenant Commander Steven Marshall watched the wires being dragged to the bollards along the pier, felt the steel plates beneath his boots vibrating uneasily, as if, like himself, his command was unable to accept that they had arrived safely.

In the early morning, while they had idled outside the harbour until the tide was right to enter Haslar Creek by the submarine base, he had studied the land as it had grown out of the gloom, searching his thoughts for some sensation of achievement. Now, as he glanced briefly at the curious faces along the wall and below on the pier he could sense little but anti-climax. Even his men looked different. It did not seem possible. For fourteen months they had lived together in their own confined private world within this hull. From one end of the Mediterranean to the other, with each day bringing some fresh challenge or threat to their very existence.

There had been a few new faces during that time. To replace the dead and wounded. But for the most part they were the same men who had assembled fore and aft on the *Tristram*'s casing when she had slipped out of Portsmouth to join the war and seek out the enemy.

"All secure aft, sir."

Marshall turned slightly and glanced at his first lieutenant. Robert Gerrard, tall and thin, with the slight stoop brought about by service in this and other boats. Even he seemed strangely alien in his reefer and best cap. For months they had seen each other in almost anything but regulation dress. Old flannel trousers and discarded cricket shirts. Shorts and sandals in kinder days. Dripping oilskins and heavy boots when the Mediterranean showed its other face, the one never seen on travel posters.

"Thank you, Bob. Ring off main motors."

He turned back to watch the busy working party on the pier. There were two Wrens sheltering below the wall on their way to some office or other, their arms crammed with files and papers. One of them waved to him, and then they both scuttled out into the wind again and vanished. A party of new trainees was being mustered on the rampart above, a petty officer no doubt pointing out the finer points of a returning submarine. Few appeared to be paying much attention, and Marshall could guess their feelings at this moment in their service.

From the periscope standards above his head flew their Skull and Crossbones which the coxswain had cared for so proudly over their long days and nights at sea. Sewn above and around the grinning death's-head were their recorded battle honours. Bars for vessels sunk, crossed guns for those hair-raising attacks on ships and coastal installations alike, stilettos for the *cloak-and-dagger* jobs, landing agents on enemy shores, picking up others with valuable information. Sometimes they had waited in vain for these brave, lonely men, and he had prayed their end had been quick.

The new intake of seamen at the submarine base would see the flag, would picture themselves and not his men on the scarred casing.

The deck gave a quick shudder and lay still. They had officially arrived. This part at least was over.

From aft a generator coughed into life and a haze of exhaust floated over the hull. Marshall thrust his hands into his pockets, momentarily at loss. There was nothing to do. Soon the boat would be taken to the dockyard. Stripped out and refitted from bow to stern. He sighed. God knows, she needs it. The silent recruits would also be seeing the submarine as she really was. Pitted from continuous service in all conditions. There was hardly a square yard without a dent or a scar of some sort. Splinters from shellburst. Buckled plates below the conning tower from a very close depth-charge off the Tunisian coast where they had stalked the Afrika Korps' supply ships. The deeper furrow across the bridge itself was from a burst of cannon fire from an Italian fighter outside Taranto. It had killed the lookouts even as the boat had dived deep. A cruel justice, if you could see it that way. They were the ones who should have seen the danger to themselves, and therefore to all those under their feet who depended on their constant vigilance. They had died because of that hair's-breadth between life and oblivion which every submariner should recognise.

A wooden brow was being hauled out from the pier now. He saw the captain of the base and some other officers with oak leaves around their caps waiting to go through the formalities. He did not recognise many of them. It was hardly surprising. A lot had happened in fourteen months, and not only in the Mediterranean.

"Dismiss the hands, Bob. I'll——" He faltered, suddenly unsure. "I'd like to speak with them before they shove off on leave."

The words came out at last. These men, his company of fifty officers and ratings, would be scattered to the corners of the British Isles. To share their leave in their own ways. With parents and wives, girlfriends and children. Merging for just a few weeks in that other world of rationing and shortages, bombing and pathetic determination.

When the leave was over they would be sent to other boats. To form a hard core amongst men like the recruits on the wall. To crew new boats which were being built to replace those strewn across the beds of a dozen disputed seas.

He shivered, feeling the wind cold and clammy across his face. 1943 was now a month old. What, when his own leave was over, would it have for him?

He leaned over the screen to watch his men hurrying gratefully for the main hatch. In white caps, their hands and faces deeply tanned, they looked out of place. Vulnerable against the grey stone, the cruising wavecrests of the Solent, the rain-haze across Portsdown Hill. He sighed again and climbed out of the bridge and down to the casing.

The base captain was genuinely welcoming, his handshake hearty. Other faces moved around Marshall, a pat on his back, more handshakes.

The captain said, "Good to see you, Marshall. By God, it's a tonic to read what you've done out there. Just what the doctor ordered."

Another officer suggested swiftly, "Now, if we could go to your office, sir?"

Marshall was tired, and despite a clean shirt and his best uniform felt dirty and unkempt. You did not shake off submarines merely by walking ashore. They all said that. The smells seemed to get right inside you. Diesel and wet metal. Cabbage-water and sweat. And that wasn't the half of it. But he was not too weary to notice the brief exchange of glances. A sense of urgency.

The captain nodded "Fair enough." He touched Marshall's arm. "I expect you'll find things have changed a bit since you've been away." He walked to the brow and returned the trot sentry's salute. "Heavy bombing all round here. Terrible." He forced a smile. "But the Keppel's Head is still standing, so things can't be too bad!"

Marshall fell silent as he walked through the familiar gates, allowing the conversation to flow around him almost unheeded. Even out of the wind he felt chilled to the marrow, and wondered how long it would take to get away from this unexpected gathering. He saw young officers marching to instruction, others sitting in a classroom where he had once sat. Gunnery and torpedoes, first lieutenant's course, and then finally the one for command, the *Perisher* as it was guardedly called. Fort Blockhouse seemed to have altered little. Only he seemed an intruder.

Into a large office, where a fire burned invitingly in its grate beneath a picture of a pre-war submarine lying in Grand Harbour, Malta. He found himself studying it intently, recalling the setting as he had last seen it. Rubble and dust. Endless bombing, and a population eking out their lives in cellars and shelters.

A steward was busying himself with glasses at the far end of the room, and the captain said cheerfully, "Early in the morning, I know. But *this* is special."

Marshall smiled. He remembered this room well enough. The base captain of the time had had him here on the carpet. Had given him the most severe dressing-down over some lapse or other. Later, that same captain had called him to tell him his father had been lost at sea. The two extremes of that particular captain seemed to sum up the whole submarine service, he thought vaguely.

Glasses filled, everyone turned expectantly towards him as the captain said, "Welcome home. You and your people have done a fine job." His eyes dropped to the breast of Marshall's reefer. "A D.S.C. and bar, and damn well earned."

They all raised their glasses, and it was then that Marshall caught sight of himself in a wall mirror behind them. No wonder

4

he felt different. He *was* different, from these officers anyway. His dark hair, unruly at the best of times, had grown too long over his ears. There had been no time for a haircut during their last stop in Gibraltar, and anyway the starboard motor had been playing up. Again. He had noticed only that morning while he had been shaving that there were tiny flecks of grey in his hair. Very small, but they were there all right. And he was twenty-eight years old. He smiled briefly at his twin in the mirror, saw the shadows below his grey eyes momentarily vanish, the mouth twitch upwards, so that he was young again, for just a moment.

The staff officer who had hurried them to this room said, "The maintenance commander is ready to have *Tristram* moved to the dock area, sir. As soon as her crew are paid and have got their ration cards and travel warrants they can be sent on leave." He swivelled his eyes to Marshall. "Unless. . . ."

Marshall raised his glass to his lips for the first time. It was neat whisky. He could feel it searing his throat, stirring his insides like a returning confidence.

He said quietly, "I will speak with them first, if I may."

The captain nodded. "Of course. It must be quite a wrench after all this time, eh?"

"Yes," Marshall emptied the glass and held it out to the hovering steward. "It is."

He was behaving badly but could not do anything about it. They meant well. Were doing their best to make him welcome when most of them probably had a hundred jobs to do.

Quite a wrench.

Perhaps it was the way the urbane staff officer had written off his command already. Just so much steel and machinery. Material of war. He wondered if some of the *Tristram*'s company were feeling as cut-off and lonely as he was right now. Would they be able to talk about what they had faced and endured? The chilling suspense of a depth-charge attack. The nerve-grinding tension of stalking their prey, the order to fire, the ticking seconds before a tell-tale boom of a torpedo finding its target.

Tristram's return was special, the captain had said. In one way he was right. Five other boats of the same class had left Portsmouth for the Mediterranean. With many more they now littered the sea-bed, their companies sealed inside them.

The captain said evenly, "I was sorry to hear about young Wade."

5

"Yes, sir." The whisky was like fire. "He was due to come home the week after it happened." He did not notice that the others had fallen silent as he continued in the same unemotional voice, "We did our *Perisher* together, and even when I got *Tristram* he was given *Tryphon*. We were always running into each other."

A new voice asked, "How did it happen?"

The captain shot the man a fierce stare, but Marshall replied, "We were on the bread-run." He gestured vaguely. "Taking food and ammunition to Malta. Nothing but a sub could get in. Even then we had to lie on the harbour bottom during daylight to avoid the bombers. *Tryphon* left Malta before dawn that particular day. She was never heard of again." He nodded slowly. "A mine, I expect. God knows, there were enough of them about."

Even as he spoke he could recall exactly the last meeting. Bill Wade with his black beard and huge grin. The drinks and the ancient Maltese playing a piano in the next room. Almost his last words had been, "Never thought we'd make it, old man. I guess we were just meant to survive." Poor Bill. He had been mistaken about that.

The base captain glanced at his watch. "I think we'd better get things moving." He nodded to the others. "I'll just put Lieutenant Commander Marshall in the picture."

The officers filed out of the room, each pausing to murmur a word of congratulation or welcome, and finally the steward, who closed the door noiselessly behind him.

"Sit down." The captain moved to his desk and squatted comfortably on one corner. "Did you have any plans for leave?"

Marshall rested his arms on the sides of the chair. The whisky and the warm room were making him drowsy. Detached.

"Not really, sir."

It was easy to make it sound so casual. No plans. His mother had died before the war after being thrown from a horse. She was a beautiful rider, a superb horsewoman. But she had died nonetheless.

His father had been axed from the Navy some years after the Great War, but had been recalled immediately when the Germans had marched into Poland. After his mother had died, Marshall's father had withdrawn into his own private world, so that they had drifted very much apart. Some of his old spirit had returned when he had been recalled to the Navy, even though he

6

was to be employed in merchant ships. As commodore of a westbound Atlantic convoy he had been attacked by a U-boat pack. His own ship and several others were sunk. It was a common enough story.

"I thought as much." The captain seemed to be hesitating over something. Playing for time. "Fact is, there's a job waiting for you, if you'll take it. I'd not be so blunt about it if there was more time. But there isn't. It could be dangerous, but you're no stranger to that idea. It might even be a complete waste of effort. But the appointment demands every ounce of experience and skill." He paused. "It needs the best man available, and I think it could be you."

Marshall watched him gravely. "You'd want me to decide right away?"

The captain did not answer directly. "Ever heard of Captain Giles Browning? *Buster* Browning they called him in the last war. Got the Victoria Cross among other things for taking his submarine into the Dardanelles during the Gallipoli fiasco. A real ball of fire to all accounts."

Marshall nodded. "I read about him somewhere." It was not making any sense. "Is he involved?"

"He was out of the Service soon after the war. Axed, like your own father. He came back to do various jobs, training depots and so forth, but now he's been landed with some special appointment in Combined Ops." He smiled. "It's all very vague, but it has to be."

Outside the thick walls a tug hooted mournfully, and Marshall pictured *Tristram* resting at her moorings. Soon she would be empty, with only a few damp and tattered pin-ups, the pencilled doodlings around the chart table where the navigator had controlled his nerves during each attack to mark their passing.

Why not? There was no point in spending a whole leave going from one hotel to another, visiting friends, or. . . .

He said suddenly, "But I'm not to be told what it is, sir?"

"It's a new command." The captain was studying him intently. Searching for something on Marshall's impassive features. "If you accept, I'll have you whistled up to Scotland tomorrow morning where you'll meet Captain Browning." He grinned. "*Buster*."

Marshall stood up. His limbs felt strangely light.

"I'll have a go, sir." He nodded. "I can but try."

"Thank you. I know what you've been through, so do all

those concerned. But you, or someone like you, are what we need." He shrugged. "If things change, you'll take your leave, and there'll still be a command waiting for you. You might even get *Tristram* again if the refit works out all right."

The staff officer peered round the door. "Sir?"

"Lieutenant Commander Marshall has agreed." The captain added softly, "You'd better send for Lieutenant Gerrard and brief him."

The door closed again.

Marshall turned sharply. "What has my first lieutenant got to do with this?"

The captain eyed him calmly. "He will be *asked* to volunteer to go with you." He held up one hand. "Your company will be mixed. Some new, some old hands. But we *must* have a perfect team at the top."

Marshall looked away. "But he's married, sir. And he's due for a commanding officer's course at the end of his leave. Because of me he'll be pitchforked straight into another boat after fourteen months in the Med."

"I know. Which is why I did not tell you about him first." He smiled sadly. "But I'll let him have a couple of days at home before he follows you up north." The smile faded. "Can't be helped. This is important."

"I see."

Marshall thought of Gerrard's face as the early daylight had found them in the Solent that morning. Like a child seeing a Christmas tree for the first time. It had been an intrusion just to watch him.

But as the captain had said, nothing could be done now. It had probably been decided days, even weeks ago that this was going to happen. A new command of some urgency. Maybe an experimental boat full of untried equipment which might shorten the war, or blow up the lot of them.

He picked up his cap.

"I'd like to go and see my people over the side, sir." He faltered. "They've been a good crowd. The best."

"Certainly." The captain frowned as a telephone started to ring. "There's a new class of sub-lieutenants going through here at the moment. Would you care to dine with them this evening? The sight of a real veteran might broaden their outlook a bit."

Marshall shook his head. "Thank you, sir. But no. I've a couple of people to see. Some letters."

"Very well. Take yourself off and relax for a bit. I'll see you before you go tomorrow."

He watched him leave and then picked up the telephone. When Marshall had been suggested for the appointment he had had no doubts at all. His record, his list of sinkings and other operations spoke volumes. The fact that he had survived was proof enough. But now, having seen him, he was no longer sure. Yet he could not put his finger on it. Marshall was good all right. On paper, the best man for the job. But there was something missing. He sighed deeply. *Youth.* That was what Marshall had lost. Somewhere back there in *Tristram*'s wake. It had been ground right out of him.

He snapped tersely, "Yes?"

The voice was complaining about supplies and spare parts. The captain tried not to think of Marshall's eyes. Lost? **Desperate? He pushed it from his thoughts and concentrated on** the voice in his ear.

After all, it was no longer his affair.

If Marshall harboured any doubt as to the urgency of his secret appointment he was soon made to think otherwise. With first light little more than a grey blur over Portsmouth Harbour he was accompanied by the base captain in a staff car to a Fleet Air Arm station a few miles inland.

Once strapped into a seat aboard a noisy and apparently unheated transport plane, he turned up his greatcoat collar and considered his experiences of the previous day. For the most part they had been disappointing, even fruitless. It had all begun badly with his farewells to *Tristram*'s company. Despite being so close for so long, the mood of sentiment and parting seemed to elude them all. It was often so in the Service. Embarrassment perhaps at showing true feelings. Eagerness to be away and to find what awaited them at home.

He was still not too sure what Gerrard thought about the sudden change of plans. He seemed more worried about what his wife would think than anything. Of his proposed command course he had said nothing, which had surprised Marshall. Gerrard was a good submarine officer, and as the base captain had remarked, they made a comfortable team together.

When the last man had hurried ashore and the dockyard workers had clattered on to the deserted casing, Marshall had taken a last look round. It was stupid to give any boat character. Maybe that staff officer's attitude was safer. Steel and machinery. Spare parts and fuel. *Men* made a submarine work. It was a weapon, not a way of life.

And yet, as he had hesitated inside the tiny wardroom, had glanced at the stained curtains on each bunk which had given them their only brief privacy, he had found such reasoning hard to accept. The footsteps on the casing above had seemed muffled, remote, so that the boat had appeared to be listening, like himself. For those other familiar voices. The mixed accents and dialects which made up her company. The wits and the hard-cases, the dedicated and the ones who looked upon work as a disease. Separated, or seen as individuals in some peacetime street, you would not have noticed more than a handful. But bound together within *Tristram*'s toughened steel they had become an entity, a force to be reckoned with.

Having discovered where he was to sleep that night, and arranged to be called in time for the ride to the air station, he had gone ashore. A rare taxi had carried him to the house on the outskirts of Southampton, and each mile of the journey he had wondered what he was going to say to Bill's widow, the girl his best friend had married just two months before they had sailed for the Med. He remembered her well. And so he should. Small and dark, with the vitality and wildness of a young colt.

What had he gone to tell her? That he had seen Bill before he had slipped out of Malta? That they had shared drinks together in a bar the night before?

He had almost decided to order the taxi back to Portsmouth and forget the whole idea. He need not have bothered. The house where he had spent many hours in the past had been occupied by total strangers. She had moved away. No, they did not know where. Nor care, by the sound of their voices.

Perhaps she had gone back to her parents. Or maybe she had just immersed herself in some sort of war-work to keep her hurt from familiar faces and voices from the past.

Either way, he had returned to Fort Blockhouse feeling tired and depressed. When he had passed the pier he had stared with something like disbelief. *Tristram* had already gone, her berth taken by another boat. For the first time in so many months he

10

felt at a loss. It was unreal, disconcerting. He was being flown to Scotland in the morning, but nobody could or would tell him where or why. His command had been spirited away as were her company, and he was completely alone.

He had gone to his room, avoiding familiar faces in the wardroom bar, open stares from the new intake of sub-lieutenants, like a man with some terrible disfigurement or guilt. It was ridiculous, and destructive, and he told himself so again and again.

The old naval pensioner who tended over his needs required no explanation. He had seen too many like Marshall come and go. He brought him a bottle of gin, watched him sign the chit, and left the room without a word. Not even about the weather, which was surprising in England.

The flight north to Scotland was a bumpy one. The February skies were thick with cloud, and the aircraft sounded as if it had known better days. The journey too seemed like a dream sequence. Even the handful of passengers were unusual. A pale-faced seaman handcuffed to an escort being taken back to his ship to face charges of desertion. A young Wren officer who fell asleep immediately on take-off and did not stir until the plane touched down outside Rosyth. A lieutenant with a terrible twitch who looked as if he was on the extreme brink of a breakdown, and a sergeant of marines who repeatedly massaged one ankle as if it was hurting him. In fact, he was trying to see up the Wren officer's leg.

The bottle of gin had not helped Marshall to face the uncomfortable flight. His mouth was like raw flesh, and he was grateful for the coffee and sandwiches brought by one of the aircraft's crew.

At the airfield a harassed R.N.V.R. lieutenant ushered him to yet another plane. A small, single-engined job with a pilot who seemed too young to be out of school

North and still further north. On their shouted conversations over the intercom Marshall was able to glean a little more of his destination.

The pilot bellowed, "Just south of Cape Wrath, sir!"

It was far enough. Much more and they would drop into the Atlantic.

Despite the base captain's caution, Marshall had still expected to be going to Holy Loch. Submarines did a lot of working-up there, as well as sailing on operational patrols. But

11

Cape Wrath was the north-westerly tip of the British Isles. He could not imagine what they could have up there.

Occasionally he caught sight of humped hills and rain-washed roads through gaps in the cloud. The Mediterranean was drawing farther and farther away with each turn of the prop, and not merely in distance.

Eventually the pilot shouted, "Coming into the field now, sir!"

The *field* proved to be little more than a strip of tarmac surrounded by mud, a couple of dismal looking Nissen huts and a wind-sock. If the flight had been overtaken by darkness, Marshall doubted that either the plane or its occupants would have survived.

Some oilskinned figures emerged reluctantly from one of the huts and ran towards the plane, their bodies bowed to a steady drizzle which looked as if it had come to stay.

As they gathered up Marshall's luggage, a burly marine provost sergeant squelched across to meet him and threw up a stiff salute. Despite his rain-spattered waterproof cape, muddy boots and leggings he still managed to make Marshall feel crumpled and untidy.

"'Tenant Commander Marshall, sir?" The eyes moved ... .uy from top to toe. "Identity card, if you please, sir." He took it and held it beneath his cape. "Fair enough, sir. Now we'd better be off." He gestured towards a dripping Humber car. "Not far. Good 'ot meal waiting for you, sir." He swung on his heel, barking at the men with the luggage to "*get a bleedin' move on*."

Marshall turned to look back as the small plane taxied round and began to lurch along the shining strip of tarmac. The youthful pilot had already forgotten him. One piece of freight safely delivered. Now back to the field, and probably some girl.

Marshall smiled into the drizzle. Good luck to him.

The sergeant called, "Now then, sir, we don't want to be late, do we?"

Marshall climbed into the car and held to a strap as it churned noisily across the furrowed ground.

The sergeant squinted through the windscreen and said, "Loch Cairnbawn, sir. That's where we're 'heading." He swore as a sheep ambled across the narrow track. "If we're spared!"

Marshall relaxed slightly. He was allowed that piece of information now that he was safely inside the car and the aircraft gone. What would this sergeant do, he wondered, if he ordered him to drive back to the airstrip? Pretend not to hear, probably.

It was all but dark by the time they reached the loch, but after the savage jerking motion and the sergeant's constant swearing, albeit under his breath, Marshall hardly cared. Faces and flashlights loomed against the side windows, barbed wire and armed sentries slid away into the gloom as they continued more smoothly between a line of huts.

"This way, sir." The marine held open the door and snapped his fingers to some more anonymous figures to collect the luggage again. "There's a launch waiting to take you out to the depot ship. You are expected."

"I should bloody well hope so after getting this far!" Marshall was surprised at his own anger. "Thanks for looking after me, sergeant."

The marine watched him walk towards a small police light at the end of the pier and chuckled indifferently.

More barbed wire, and once again his identity card was scrutinised, a torch flashed across his face.

A lieutenant came out of the darkness and said apologetically, "I'm sorry about all this, sir. Security's pretty tight here."

Marshall nodded, half-blinded by the torch. He could see no sign of any depot ship.

The lieutenant waved his torch towards a small motor boat which had been swaying and pitching a few yards from the pier.

"The old *Guernsey* is moored out in the loch, sir. The buoys were laid especially for her."

Marshall watched the motor boat as it came alongside. The *Guernsey* was not unknown to him. Nor any other submariner who had been aboard her. A very old depot ship, coal-fired, and extremely uncomfortable, she rarely appeared anywhere these days, except as a temporary accommodation vessel.

The boat's coxswain stood in the sternsheets as Marshall climbed into the small cockpit. Marshall watched him as he waited for the luggage to be loaded forward and found some small sense of belonging. The familiar tally on the man's cap, *H.M. Submarines,* showed that even up here on this desolate, freezing loch there was a world he could understand.

It did not take long to reach the moored ship. As the boat plunged and dipped around her outdated stern Marshall saw two submarines tethered alongside, but that was all. The boat swung to the opposite side, and after a snarl of churning propeller came to rest against the accommodation ladder.

The Officer of the Day, shining brightly inside the square of the entry port, saluted smartly and said, "Nice to have you aboard, sir."

Marshall removed his cap and shook it on the deck. With the screens dropped across the entry port again he was conscious of being swallowed up. The start of a new process.

He heard rapid pistol shots, the sound of thundering horses.

The O.O.D. grinned. "There's a Western in the ship's canteen, sir. They've all seen it before, of course, but up here there's not much else to do."

"I see that you have a couple of boats alongside."

The lieutenant looked past him. "Did you, sir?" He did not go on. Instead he said, "Captain Browning left strict orders that you were to be given your cabin, a good meal and anything else you need immediately." He glanced meaningly at the bulkhead clock. "He will see you at 2100."

Marshall felt the same unreasoning anger returning. It was like being a raw trainee.

He snapped, "Is it all right to be told what's on the menu?"

The lieutenant flushed. "Cottage pie, sir." He dropped his eyes. "I'm only obeying orders."

A steward led the way down two companion ladders and into a neat panelled cabin. Probably first-class originally when the *Guernsey* had begun her long life as a cruise ship.

A piping hot bath, a change of clothes and what proved to be a very good cottage pie helped to ease some of his resentment. The meal was laid at the end of the long table and he was served by at least three stewards. There was not one single officer present, and he pictured them elsewhere, maybe watching the Western.

He leaned back in the chair and sighed. Poor Gerrard would get a shock when he joined him again. It was more like a monastery than a submarine depot ship.

"I'd like a glass of port."

The steward glanced at his watch. "Beggin' yer pardon, sir, but I don't think you've got the time just now."

Marshall twisted in his chair. "*A glass of port!*" He saw the stewards exchanging unhappy glances. "And I may want another!"

14

Outside the sealed scuttles he could hear the wind getting up and rain slashing against the ship's tall side. He thought he heard a motor boat chugging abeam, and wondered if it was some sort of security patrol, or maybe a night exercise. While he sipped his port he thought about Gerrard and wondered what he was doing. In his wife's arms. Or still explaining why he was being sent away again so soon.

He glanced at his watch. He was five minutes late for his meeting with Captain Browning. He smiled despite his previous anger. *Buster*.

He could almost feel the stewards sighing with relief as he rose and left the table.

The captain's office was below the main bridge superstructure, and in a small outer compartment Marshall was confronted by a bespectacled lieutenant seated at a desk. He had white cloth between his gold stripes.

He snapped severely, "I'm Morris, Captain's secretary." He seemed about to remark on the time but said, "He's *waiting*."

The inner office was very large and ran the whole width of the superstructure. Like much of the ship, it was panelled, and held an air of shabby opulence.

Captain Giles Browning stood with his back to a steam radiator, eyes fixed on the door as Marshall entered, his hands hanging at his sides like huge chunks of meat. He was not tall but extremely broad and full-bellied, so that he appeared to be leaning backwards to adjust the weight.

He waited until Marshall had crossed the room and thrust out one large hand. "Glad to have you, Marshall." His voice was thick and resonant, his grasp hard. He gestured to a chair and then crossed heavily to a decanter and glasses.

Marshall watched him warily. Browning was bald, with just a few tufts of grey hair above his ears which joined sparsely at the back of his collar. But his bald pate was very tanned and freckled, and he decided that with hair it would somehow seem wrong on the man. The face too was interesting. Crumpled and uneven, and he guessed he had been a boxer or rugby player in younger days.

The captain offered him a glass.

"Nice drop of port." His eyes fixed on Marshall's. They were ice-blue and very clear. "I gather you enjoy it," he added dryly.

Marshall sipped it slowly. An apology was pointless. And

15

any man who took pains to find out what he had been drinking at dinner would see through it in a flash.

Instead he said, "I understand I'm to take command of——"

Browning interrupted him curtly, "All in good time. Drink your drink and relax. I know a lot about you. Now I want you to know a bit about me." He seated himself carefully in a big chair. "I admire professionals. Always have. And you've been damn good to achieve your record. I was good myself once, but I could no more take a submarine into action now than speak Yiddish. And it doesn't follow that *you're* any use for what I want!"

Marshall came up in the chair with a jerk.

But Browning held up one of his massive hands. "Keep calm. I speak my mind. And as I'm far senior to you, I can speak mine first, right?"

A grin spread very slowly across his battered features. Like sunlight on some old ruin, Marshall thought vaguely.

But he found himself smiling. "*Right,* sir."

"Good. This job is ve y hush-hush. Has to be. Hence me. Hence you." He reached or the decanter. "You've been a long time in the Med. You kno\ the picture out there. It's been a hard struggle, but now the Geri ans in North Africa are on the run. With our Eighth Army pus ing from the east and the Americans from the west, Rommel wi be out of Africa by the spring."

Marshall leaned back in hi. chair again. Browning spoke with such calm assurance that it was fascinating.

"The next thing will be an Allied invasion of Europe." The blue eyes vanished in a crinkle of lines. "That's a secret, too! But one thing is certain, we'll need many more troops than we have available now. They'll come from America and Canada, and round the Cape from Australia and New Zealand for such a massive operation."

Marshall glanced at the Victoria Cross ribbon on Browning's jacket. It was not all that hard to picture him in his own boat.

Browning asked sharply, "Do you know what a *milch-cow* is?"

Marshall started. "Yes, sir. The Germans have several of them. Big submarine supply boats. Well over two-thousand tons each, or so I hear."

"Good lad. You probably know their function as well as I do. The average U-boat can cover 7,000 miles on an operational cruise. Now even with their French coast bases they lose 4,000

16

miles just getting out to mid-Atlantic and back home again. That only leaves 3,000 miles to do any damage, right?''

Marshall nodded. He could find no connection between events in North Africa and U-boat operations in the Atlantic.

"So these *milch-cows*, as they call 'em, can meet their U-boats at prearranged billets. Supply 'em with food and fuel, torpedoes, letters from home, almost anything they need. They can treble the time that each boat can stay at sea and therefore attack our convoys. Before, just to keep, say ten boats operational off the American coast, they required thirty. The supply boat has cut their problems, and so far we've not been able to track down any of 'em. If one of our killer-groups gets anywhere near 'em they merely have to dive and poodle on the next arranged billet. Easy as falling off a log." He took a deep breath. "In the next month or so we can expect huge troop convoys from the States if we are to exploit the North African successes. If we can bag a couple of their *milch-cows*, or even one, it would make all the difference. It might take weeks for the Germans to realise what's happened. Valuable weeks when half of their U-boats are creeping home or running out of fuel and supplies before more aid can be sent to them."

Marshall gripped his glass more tightly. So his new command was to try and run a *milch-cow* to earth.

He said quietly, "I still don't see what hope we have of finding one, sir."

Browning smiled happily. He was enjoying himself.

"If anyone can do it, I *think* you can." The smile faded. "Anyway, I believe it's worth a bloody good try."

He heaved himself upright and moved restlessly to his desk.

"Last month, a U-boat outward bound from Kiel to the Atlantic developed trouble in her motors. She was not a new boat, but her crew were. Green as grass. The weather was foul at the time, blowing a Force Ten and black as a boot. The U-boat's skipper decided to run for shelter to carry out repairs. He chose a fjord on the east coast of Iceland. He took a risk but it probably seemed a good idea. I expect others have done it before him. God knows, the bloody Icelanders have no love for us and the Americans since we occupied their country!" He studied Marshall for several seconds. "Fortunately, the skipper of a clapped-out Asdic trawler had had the same idea. They met eye to eye, so to speak!"

Marshall stood up without knowing he had moved.

"And you've managed to capture her rendezvous codes for their supply submarine?"

Browning walked over and grasped his arm, his eyes dancing.

"Better'n that, boy. We've got the bloody U-boat!" He pointed at the side of the cabin. "She's out there now."

Marshall stared at him.

"God Almighty!"

"Indeed." Browning smiled gently. "And now we've got a captain for her, right?"

Marshall slumped down in the chair again. He forced a smile.

"*Right*, sir."

Browning beamed. "Thought you'd like the idea. Right up your street." He seized the decanter. "So have some more port, *Herr Kapitan!*"

2   Confrontation

OVERNIGHT, the rain had passed inland, and the wind, although as sharp as ice, had fallen away considerably.

After a hasty breakfast in his cabin, Marshall hurried on deck where he found Captain Browning and two of the depot ship's officers in deep conversation by the guardrail.

Having breakfast in his temporary quarters had been another of Browning's *suggestions*. It seemed as if he wanted to isloate Marshall completely from all distraction until the chosen moment of confrontation. The previous evening, and long into the night, Marshall had stayed with him, saying little, and content just to hear the other man outline the plan he had envisaged for so long, and which might now become reality.

Capturing the U-boat had been a whole series of lucky incidents as far as the British were concerned. Once faced by the sheltering Asdic trawler, the German commander had tried to scuttle his boat, only to discover that the strong gale had driven him further into the fjord than he had intended. With her tanks flooded, the U-boat had come to rest on a hard shoulder, her periscope standards still awash.

Caught in the trawler's searchlight, and with a few warning cannon shells whining dangerously overhead, the submarine's crew decided to surrender without further trouble. Her captain and first lieutenant were old campaigners, but the majority of the company were, as Browning had described, green as grass. Otherwise it was unlikely they would have given in without some show of fight.

The news was flashed to the Admiralty in London, and within hours an expert salvage team was on its way by air to Reykjavik with orders to save what they could. Long hours of darkness, thick snow and a raging blizzard greeted the party when they finally reached the isolated fjord. Two divers were drowned, and several of the men received severe frostbite. But despite all this they got more than a few useful relics, they raised the U-boat and at the first easing of the weather had her in tow, *en route* for Scotland.

While Browning's team of experts worked round the clock to put right the U-boat's damage and install what replacements they could lay their hands on, others kept a ceaseless radio and intelligence watch, waiting to hear that the U-boat had either been able to signal her predicament before capture, or that some agent ashore had seen the Navy's jealously guarded prize. To most people's amazement nothing was reported.

Browning confessed that there was still a possibility. A leak of information, or some additional safeguard which the German Naval Staff at Kiel had had prepared for some such emergency.

But as the days wore on he had gained fresh confidence that all was well. Command of any submarine was an independent role. And that of a U-boat stalking the vast wastes of the Atlantic was the most independent of all.

A bugle blared, and from aft the White Ensign rose curling and flapping to its staff to mark the official beginning of another day. Against the leaden sky and dull, mist-shrouded land along the loch it looked unnaturally bright.

Browning turned as the "carry on" was sounded, and saw Marshall framed in the screen door. He grinned.

"Morning!"

He was glowing with health, and it was hard to believe that they had finished the decanter of port just a few hours ago.

Marshall saluted. "Well, I'm ready, sir." He shivered in the wind. God, it was bitter.

Browning introduced his two companions. Both were commanders, and each had been responsible for preparing the unexpected addition to the fleet for sea.

One, a bearded man called Marker, said cheerfully, "We've

had a lot of the gear re-labelled. Metres into feet and so on, for the benefit of the simpler souls aboard! But most of the technical equipment is as before, so don't forget the fact if you go into a crash dive.'' They walked out into the wind and he added gravely, ''Naturally we're not in the habit of stocking spares for German subs. You'll have to make do with what you've got. In the meantime I'll get my people to rummage discreetly around the stores. You never know. We may need them later.''

During their long discussion Browning had hinted as much. If Marshall was successful they might be able to use the U-boat in another unorthodox operation. It explained Browning's connection with Combined Operations, a fact which had puzzled Marshall since the captain at Fort Blockhouse had mentioned it.

If Marshall was not successful, then of course there was no point in bothering further. It was assumed, if not stated, that he and his crew would be on the bottom. For good.

He leaned over the outer guardrail and stared down at the boats alongside. The inner one was a small H-class submarine, a survivor from Browning's war.

The captain murmured, ''We use her for training, and as a guinea-pig. She also helps to make inquisitive eyes ashore think we're just doing normal instruction.''

Marshall did not hear him. He ran his gaze very slowly along the outer craft, feeling a strange sensation in his stomach, a mixture of excitement and uncertainty. Although her conning-tower was crudely masked by painted canvas as an additional precaution against prying eyes, there was no mistaking the outline and design. About two hundred and fifty feet from a sharp, raked stem to her partly submerged stern, the U-boat was exactly as he had expected she would be. A few overalled seamen were working at the open forehatch, and others were training and elevating the powerful-looking gun on her casing and slapping on grease where it mattered.

Browning said, ''Vicious looking beast, eh? Her skipper was Korvetten Kapitan Opetz. He got the *Ritterkreuz* after his last cruise.'' He added bitterly, ''Put down twenty-two ships. One hundred and five thousand tons. The murdering bastard!''

Marshall tore his eyes away and stared at him with surprise. Often when he was ashore he had heard similar views. He found them both illogical and disconcerting. As a submariner he saw the underwater battle quite differently. He hated to read of all the much-needed ships which were sent to the sea bed, of the suffering and death caused by each attack. At the same time he reacted against those who trotted out remarks like Browning had just made. It was war, and there was no difference between a German torpedo and a British one when it found its mark. Not to those on the receiving end. And Browning, as a submariner, should have been the first to respect an enemy's skill, if only to use such knowledge to destroy him.

Browning said, "We'll go down. They should be ready for you now."

He led the way along a steep catwalk without saying more. Perhaps he sensed Marshall's reaction to his outburst. He did not seem easily fooled by anything.

Across the deck of the H-boat and then a brief pause while Browning initialled a signal pad for another officer.

Marshall stood quite still with only his feet moving to the little boat's gentle motion. He looked up at the U-boat's conning-tower where a seaman was putting finishing touches to a newly-painted ensignia.

The officer called Marker said gently, "Thought it best to invent a new badge for the boat. Just in case Jerry knows he's lost her."

The ensignia was of a prancing black bull, with steam shooting from flared nostrils and bright green eyes which stared forward as if to see some possible victim.

The commander continued, "The painter got the idea from a Walt Disney film." He grinned. "What better to catch a bloody *milch-cow* than that, eh?"

Browning turned. "Your new company has been training aboard for two weeks. It was all the time we could afford. But you can rub off the rough edges while you're on passage to the rendezvous area. After all, I'm not expecting you to start looking for trouble. Just the targets we talked about." The blue eyes hardened. "No heroics beyond the job."

Marshall nodded. If only he could control his limbs. Even his teeth were chattering so badly he imagined the others must have noticed. Cold, nerves, or just the plain apprehension of going straight back into the melting-pot without a break. It might have been all or none of them.

They scrambled across a creaking brow and then Marshall reached out to grasp the rail around the U-boat's conning-tower. It was merely for a few seconds, and yet. . . . It even *felt* different.

A sentry saluted as they climbed up the straight ladder to the bridge, and Marshall wondered how much, if anything, they all knew about his arrival. Within days he would know that sentry's face and what lay behind it, probably as well as the men he had said good-bye to in Portsmouth. He threw his leg into the bridge and hesitated. That was only two days ago.

Another pause as he looked around him. It was unlike *Tristram*'s bridge. Narrower and longer, while just abaft the conning-tower he saw a deadly looking Vierling gun mounted on a bandstand. Four barrelled, eighty-eight millimetre cannon with a tremendous rate of fire. He knew that much already.

Then they were climbing down, the smells and sounds rising to greet them, until at last they were all assembled in the well-lit control room. Browning stood aside to watch his reactions.

Marshall knew they were studying him but ignored them. It was his ability which mattered now. Once at sea there was not a dockyard man or a depot ship mechanic who could help him.

It was well laid out. More spacious than he had expected, and he noticed that, unlike British boats, there was a section in the control room entirely for the engineer officer. So he would be in here w........ .... It was excellent to be in close contact with a man so vital to the boat's safety and performance. On the other hand, he would feel his eyes on him throughout each attack or flight from danger, gauging their chances, seeking out his skill, or lack of it.

Browning said, "I've cleared the boat of all but essential personnel. Thought you'd like to get the feel of things unhampered."

"Thanks, sir."

He saw printed instructions had been pasted over German wording on many of the gauges and dials. One brass plate remained on the forward bulkhead, unmarked. A reminder.

U-192. Krupp—Germania, Kiel—1941.

Despite his excitement he felt a chill on his spine.

Half to himself he asked, "Can we have the main periscope raised?"

A stoker applied the switch, and as he stooped to seize the handles, watching the great periscope as it hissed from its well, he had a sudden picture of those who had gone before him.

He swung the periscope slowly in a small arc, seeing the depot ship's spindly funnel, some gulls diving and wheeling in

22

the hopes of food. Further still. Across the choppy waters of the loch he saw the nearest land, a cluster of small houses nestling against some trees. He twisted the right handle towards him, making the same houses leap forward, astonishingly clear and close as he brought the lens to full power. He watched an old woman standing in the open door of one of the houses, her body crouched against the cold. She was waiting for a cat to make up its mind. To go inside or stay out. He smiled and clicked it back to normal power.

With the left handle he swivelled the top lens upwards, towards the dull sky. Where the prowling aircraft would be. Waiting and noiseless for a submarine to surface. The most vulnerable moment.

Browning must have seen his quiet smile as he had studied the little scene ashore, for he said, "You seem happy with her. Got the *feel* already, eh?"

Marshall looked at him gravely. The captain's guard had momentarily dropped. It was all there on his battered face. Pleasure, pride. But most of all envy.

Envy. Poor old *Buster,* he thought. He's been left too far behind to understand.

"Something like that, sir. I'd like to do a full tour of the boat and then compare my notes with your fitness reports."

The other officer said, "As you know, she mounts six tubes forrard and two aft. She carries twelve spare torpedoes inboard and nine more on the after casing in pressure-tight compartments."

Browning said quickly, "A total of twenty-nine tin-fish, eh?"

They all looked at him. Marshall realised with a start that Browning was already feeling out of things. His scheme, his plan to pull off the impossible, had been made to give way to the real professionals.

He said quietly, "Not like *your* last command, I expect, sir?"

Browning beamed. "Too true. Even that little H-boat alongside would have seemed like a liner to me then!"

The one called Marker said, "The diesels are excellent. Will give you eighteen knots on the surface. The electric motors can do eight submerged."

Marshall asked sharply, "You're not so happy about those?"

"My people have stripped them down and they *seem* fair

23

enough. But they probably said that when she left Kiel. You'll have to watch 'em.''

They moved forward through the pressure bulkhead and past the main switchboard where three artificers were crawling amongst a complex of wire and gauges. There was a gentle hum of power, a sense of some latent energy which made the hull feel alive.

Marshall saw a door marked ''*Kapitan*'' and faltered. In *Tristram* he had shared the wardroom with his officers, had been made to display his confidence and doubts off duty as well as on. Here at least he would have somewhere to be alone, no matter how briefly, with his thoughts. Be able to shed his outward mask of assurance, have no need to shield his anxieties.

A quick glance inside. The shelves of the bulkhead were already filled with British publications as well as the original ones.

Browning called from the passageway, ''You will have one officer who speaks fluent German. Two of your telegraphists are also hand-picked for their work with enemy codes and transmissions.''

''That was thoughtful, sir.''

He hid a frown. What was the matter with Browning? Was he worried about his ability to command, or his own problems in getting the boat prepared? To have trained operators and an officer who was equally versed in German was obvious. Or should have been.

Occasionally men squeezed past them as they carried on with their inspection. Marshall saw their glances. The *word* would soon get round. The new C.O. was aboard. What's he like? Wait and see. You never know with officers. And so on.

And here was the wardroom, where he would meet his officers. Assess them, as they would him.

Petty Officers' Mess and past the refrigerator compartment where a supply officer was engrossed in checking his lists against those pasted on the door. Every inch of space must be used. Every item checked. And then checked again.

Forward into the torpedo stowage compartment, the long, gleaming *fish* in their racks. Here, most of the seamen would also live as best they could, sharing their daily meals and off watch relaxation with these sleek killers.

24

A glance above to the forward escape hatch. A quick look down into the Asdic compartment and through the watertight door to the tube space. Six gleaming breeches, and lashed close by a great crate of tinned milk. That too had to share the boat's most precious commodity, room to live and breathe.

Once or twice he made quick notes on his pad as he allowed the submarine's shape and area to form in his mind like some mental blueprint. His throat felt dry, probably the stink of diesel and new paint. Also the smell of previous occupants. Even the other aromas and the boat's brief flooding had not erased it completely.

He could imagine the scream of the klaxon, the commander's eye glittering in the periscope lens as it broke surface. All the world of attack and target being drawn through the small aperture into one man's pupil and brain. For translation into action, and death.

He shivered again. God knows, he had seen that sight often enough himself in the past months. The untidy cluster of ships swimming across his vision in their alien, silent world. Selecting the right one for attack, watching her as she moved so inevitably until she was caught enmeshed in the crosswires of his sights. Around and beneath him the boat would have been alive with quiet murmurs, the click of valves and instruments. Another quick glance. Where was the escort now? Had she detected their presence? The feeling of ice water on the spine. The decision. *Steady. Steady.* Ignore the muffled pounding of screws as another escort swings dangerously through the convoy. *Now. Fire One!*

"Are you feeling all right, Marshall?" Browning's face moved into his vision.

"Sorry, Just thinking of something."

Browning chuckled. "I can imagine."

Marshall looked away. What was happening? Perhaps he was already overstrained. Written off like so many he had known. To survive was not always enough. There were other considerations.

He heard himself say, "I think that does it." He glanced at his watch. They had been aboard for two hours, yet it seemed like minutes. He looked at his companions, wondering how they felt about it. About him.

Marker said, "If we go back aboard *Guernsey* I can fill you in on the latest reports."

Browning added, "Then you can get the check-up over and meet your new people, eh?"

"Check-up?" Marshall faced him.

Browning shrugged. "You know how it is. After your last commission it has to be done. The P.M.O. will just make sure that all your limbs are still in the right place. Flag Officer Submarines would have my guts for garters if I didn't go through the motions!"

Nobody laughed.

Marshall nodded. "Yes." That's all I need now. To be found unfit. Be given some shore job, or end up like Browning. Watching others go off to fight.

They climbed up the shining ladder from the control room in silence. How smooth the rungs felt. How many men had run blindly into the sunlight for a gun-action, or to catch that first sight of home at the end of another patrol?

On the bridge again the keen air drove some of his apprehensions away and he was able to look along the U-boat's upper deck without flinching. It would be a new start. Not just another patrol on top of all he had done so far. He *must* think of it that way. Poor Bill had said, "*Never thought we'd make it.*" And *Tristram* had outlasted all of her consorts. He had to see this as something quite fresh and different. Not as one more weight on the scales of survival.

They had reached the depot ship's steamy interior and Browning asked, "D'you know a chap called Roger Simeon, by the way?"

Marshall frowned. "Slightly. He was first lieutenant of an S-boat last time I saw him."

He got a brief mental picture of a square, reckless face. Short fair hair. A man who would excite any woman's attention.

"That's the one. He's promoted to commander now, of course."

Marshall waited. *Of course?* What did that mean?

"Bright lad. He's been heavily involved in Combined Operations, too. First-class brain, and a real goer. You'll be meeting him shortly."

Marshall darted a quick glance at him. You hate his guts, don't you?

Aloud he said, "I never knew him other than casually at Fort Blockhouse."

"Er, yes." Browning waited for the other officers to move

away. "Lieutenant Commander Wade was a good friend of yours, I believe? I heard all about his boat being lost last year. Damn bad luck."

Marshall watched him warily. 'We were pretty close."

The captain seemed to be wrestling with his thoughts. "You'd better hear it from me then. Get it over and done with. Wade's widow married Commander Simeon last month." He looked uncomfortable. "Best to get it out in the open. This job is hard enough without——" He did not finish it.

Marshall turned to stare through a nearby scuttle, his mind cold. He tried to recall exactly what Bill had said in those last days. Had he been the same? Or had he just discovered about his wife? Christ Almighty, it was bad in any sense of the word to con a submarine out of Malta through those minefields. A captain, already worn out with combat and endless watchkeeping, would be strained to the limit. If Bill had her on his mind, had been thinking of what he would do and say when he reached England again, it would be more than enough. It only needed seconds. Those few precious moments when a lack of vigilance brought oblivion.

He controlled himself with an effort, but when he spoke his voice was flat. Hard.

"I think I'd better get on with my check-up, sir. Then we'll know."

He saw the crestfallen expression on Browning's face. In the reflected light he looked suddenly old and tired.

He added quietly, "But thank you, sir. I'm glad you told me."

Browning removed his cap and ran his hand over his bald head. "Rotten business. The war has spoiled things for a lot of——" But when he turned he realised Marshall had already gone.

He sighed and unconsciously touched the Victoria Cross ribbon on his chest. He could understand. In war you got very close to some people. Even now, after all these years, he could still remember.

He clapped on his cap and barked, "Muster the new company in the recreation space at 1100!"

The quartermaster, who had been eyeing him with mild curiosity, saluted and watched him leave the lobby. Poor old sod, he thought, as he reached for the tannoy speaker. Past it. Then he switched on the microphone and raised his silver call.

The pipe squealed from a dozen speakers throughout the ship. The sound even reached the outboard submarine with its fierce-eyed bull glaring towards the bows.

A stronger gust sent an eddy of cat's-paws along her broad saddle tank and made the mooring wires creak and jerk as if to break away.

Whatever mere men had to contend with, U-192 was eager to be away. Back to the killing-ground. The only world she knew.

For the next three days at least Marshall found little time to think of anything but the job in hand. With only brief respites for meals or ironing out unsuspected faults, he absorbed himself completely in putting his command through every situation he could envisage. From the moment he had completed his medical check-up and had confronted his new company for the first time he had realised that his task was going to be harder than he had imagined. Submarine crews were always allowed plenty of scope to work-up together, to get the measure of their new boat and each other before setting off on a patrol. This time, although no actual date had been announced, there was obviously going to be very little opportunity except for the most basic tests and trials.

In some ways that was good, Marshall decided. Too much freedom to brood might lessen their chances of success. In addition, security was paramount, and every hour alongside the *Guernsey* seemed to offer a new threat to secrecy. Loch Cairnbawn was a good choice for their preparations. It had seen many experiments in the past, including the training of the midget submarines which had made their hair-raising attack on the German battleship *Tirpitz*. The location was not the real problem. It seemed to Marshall that too many people were becoming involved, and each day brought fresh faces to inspect his progress, be shown around the boat like so many visitors on peacetime outings. Two Members of Parliament, a couple of admirals and a whole trail of lesser fry. And it all took valuable time as well as adding to the real risk of a security leak.

Curiously enough, his medical check-up had been the easiest part so far. The P.M.O. had been more interested in asking about his experiences in the Mediterranean than testing his qualities for this new role. There had been something unhealthy about the man. He reminded Marshall of the person who sits for days at the Old Bailey just to listen to the gruesome details of a murder or to watch the faces of stricken witnesses and those under sentence.

During the forenoon of the fourth day he was sitting in his cabin aboard the U-boat, re-reading the notes which had grown since his first inspection to a pad the size of a bulky novel. Gerrard was due to arrive that afternoon, and he would need to have every last detail at his fingertips so as not to confuse him when he began his own briefing around the boat.

The submarine's mood had certainly changed. It no longer felt like a floating schoolroom. It was filled with stores, ammunition, fuel and, above all, men. As he sat at his bulkhead desk he could hear the constant movement all around him. Feet on the casing above, the scrape of mooring wires and the clatter of metal from another session of gun drill. More bodies moved back and forth past his closed door, and in the wardroom nearby he heard the steward rattling crockery in readiness for lunch.

He found himself thinking about his officers. Apart from himself and Gerrard, there were four of them. A mixed bunch, and still hard to see as a team.

Lieutenant Adrian Devereaux, the navigator, would be a key member of their little community, yet he seemed vaguely out of place, and Marshall suspected it was largely his fault. Handsome and well-bred, with the easy drawling tone of one who could be slightly contemptuous of those around him.

Lieutenant Victor Frenzel, the engineer officer, was a complete opposite. He had served in submarines since before the war and had worked his way to commissioned rank by the hardest route, and had first served as a lowly junior stoker. But despite his beginnings in life and his frequent use of crude language when getting the engineering staff to accept his set standards, he possessed a real charm. He had dark curly hair, a broad grin, and seemed totally unimpressed by the job he had been given.

The other two were temporary officers. Lieutenant Colin Buck, the torpedo officer, had been a garage manager and secondhand car dealer. Sharp-featured, cold-eyed, he would be a difficult man to know. Unless he wanted you to, Marshall thought. The wardroom's junior member was Sub-Lieutenant David Warwick. As gunnery officer, and the one picked to deal with German translations, he had the outward innocence of a child. Fresh-faced and with almost delicate features, it was difficult to picture him as a man of action. Yet from his documents Marshall knew that after leaving university to enter the Navy, Warwick had passed his submarine and gunnery courses at the top of the list. So there had to be more to him than was instantly recognisable.

The rest of the company were equally mixed. Some were old hands, like Starkie, the coxswain, or Murray, the Chief E.R.A. Others were straight out of the training school with the captured U-boat as their first-ever operational submarine. Perhaps they were better off. Only when they were sent to other boats would they find trouble. They would have to re-learn their basic training all over again.

Marshall had seen very little of Browning since the day he had met his company aboard the depot ship. The captain had been kept busy with his own preparations, but there were other reasons for his staying away.

Marshall blamed himself for what might show later as a rift between them. But as the U-boat was now his responsibility he had to begin in his own way. He had sensed that Browning was going to make some sort of speech to mark the occasion. In the depot ship's recreation space Marshall had watched the assembled officers and ratings, seeing them studying him while Browning introduced him as their new commander. Had the speech been made to civilians, or spoken over the radio to those not involved in actual warfare it would have had the desired effect. It was rousing and patriotic, but at the same time seemed totally out of date and remote from their surroundings. Browning had spoken of loyalty and keenness, when Marshall knew such things were taken for granted. They had to be. When U-192 finally slipped her moorings there would be fifty souls crammed within her toughened hull. Men who would *need* to rely on each other, have to know what to do if they became separated by accident or by the hideous necessity of slamming a watertight door to save the boat from destruction, but at the same time sealing a best friend in a steel tomb.

He had been thinking along those lines when he had realised that Browning had turned to face him, that the whole of the assembled men were looking towards him. Waiting.

He had let his glance move slowly along the uneven ranks, had heard his own voice like a stranger's.

"Some of you already know me. I have met you in other boats at other times. Most of you are as new to me as you are to the

Service. I am only sorry we have not the time to alter that state of affairs before we begin our work." He had turned slightly so as not to see the hurt on Browning's face. "There are just a few things I want to make clear. This is *not* some sort of game, nor is it an heroic escapade to boost morale. We are here to learn about this boat. To use it as a weapon and destroy part of our common enemy. We can trust nobody outside the hull. Ours may be one of the loneliest tasks ever undertaken at sea. It will certainly be one of the most dangerous." He had seen some of the older hands nodding grimly, the startled exchanges between the newer men. "Forget the fact that you volunteered or were *hand-picked*, such terms mean nothing once we are away from here. What you can do as a team, what you can endure when you have passed the margins of endurance are what count." He had paused to watch the effect of his words. Too blunt? Too brutal? It was hard to tell. "If we are successful, we will have done well. Very well. But again you will be unable to show your pride openly, for if we are to extend and exploit our worth then so must we hold our secrecy. Otherwise we and not the enemy will be the hunted." He had lowered his voice slightly, suddenly aware of the tension in his own limbs. Was it that he was trying to regain something in himself? "You will have one prize, however. One which you will be able to share amongst yourselves. The knowledge that you, and you alone, have taken the war amongst the enemy. On his own ground, by his own code. I will expect much from you, just as you will rightly expect the same from me." He had felt drained. "That is all. We will go to general drills at 1400."

There was a tap at the door. It was Lieutenant Devereaux, his face devoid of expression as he announced, "Captain Browning is approaching, sir." He held out a signal pad. "From the S.D.O. Lieutenant Gerrard has landed at the field. A car has been sent for him."

"Thank you, Pilot." Marshall stretched his arms and stood up. Browning was coming to make peace. Or otherwise. "Your department all buttoned up?"

Devereaux shrugged elegantly. "Quite, sir."

Marshall smiled. The navigator was giving nothing away yet.

Together they climbed to the bridge and met Browning as he heaved himself over the rim of the conning-tower.

He looked at Devereaux. "Are you O.O.D.?"

"Yes, sir."

"Good. Go aboard *Guernsey* and clear all your people off. I want 'em mustered and accounted for within the hour, right?"

Devereaux opened his mouth and then shut it again.

As he hurried down the ladder Browning murmured, "Pompous prig. Still, he has a good record."

Once in Marshall's small cabin he shut the door and said, "Sailing orders." He shook his head gravely. "I *know* what you're about to say, and I agree. But something's happened. I've had a signal from A.C.H.Q. in Iceland. They have confirmed that one of this boat's original crew has escaped from the temporary prison camp. He may be dead, frozen stiff somewhere. He could be hiding out or searching for a neutral ship to carry him off the island. But we have to assume that he might be able to contact some unfriendly bastard and blow our secret to the winds."

"I see, sir."

Marshall walked to his cupboard and took out a bottle and two glasses. It was pointless to mention that Gerrard would arrive shortly with no knowledge of the boat in which he was first lieutenant. That they had not even done a dive together, and many other factors brought about by this unexpected flaw in the plan. Browning would have thought of them all.

Browning watched as he poured out two full glasses of Scotch. Then he said, "Sorry we got off badly when I made that stupid speech." He sighed. "I was very much like you at your age. But time puts a rosy glow on things. Takes the pain out of bravery."

Marshall held out a glass. "I'm the one to apologise." He forced a grin. "Anyway, you said we'd have to rub off the rough edges as we went along!"

Browning swallowed the whisky and added fervently, "By God, I wish you were taking me with you!"

"So do I." Marshall was surprised to find that he meant it.

Browning sank down into a chair and stared moodily around the cabin. "Makes you wonder about the chaps who've sat here, doesn't it?"

Feet clattered on the casing and he said abruptly, "You can slip at 1630. It'll be all but dark then. I've laid on the armed-yacht *Lima* to guide you out. She'll stand by for your test dive." He sounded tired. "After that, you'll be on your own. My people have prepared a complete up-to-date intelligence pack. Everything we know, and a lot we're only guessing." He

32

looked steadily into Marshall's eyes. "But it's your affair, your rules."

"Thank you."

Marshall poured two fresh glasses. In his mind's eye he could see the men filing into the hull, checks being made, nicknames emerging to wipe away the first reserve and uncertainty. They were getting the feel of their new situation. Only their captain had yet to prove himself.

There was a tap at the door and Lieutenant Frenzel poked his head inside the cabin.

"We were wondering if you would join us in the wardroom before we get busy, sir?" He grinned at Browning. "And you, of course, sir."

Marshall nodded. It was beginnning. "Thanks, Chief. That would be fine."

Surprisingly, Browning stood up and said, "Sorry. Lot to do. But I'll watch you leave, and I wish you all the luck in the world."

Frenzel nodded. "I'll pass it on, sir." He looked at Marshall. "In about ten minutes then?" He vanished.

As the door closed Browning said harshly, "I couldn't sit there drinking with him as if nothing had happened." He thrust one hand into his pocket and pulled out a crumpled signal. "Came just now. Frenzel's wife and kid were killed in an air raid last night. If I told him it could do no good, and might put the whole mission in jeopardy." He reached for his cap. "But I couldn't sit there acting like a clown, knowing all the time. . . ."

Marshall watched his despair. "He'll understand. It *is* the only way."

They shook hands gravely, and Browning said, "When you get back. I'll tell him then. My responsibility."

They walked out into the passageway and towards the brightly lit control room. Apart from the duty stoker it was deserted, and Marshall knew that, like himself, Browning was seeing it as it would be in a few more hours. The nerve centre. The place which would draw together all the fibres and the strength of the boat to one man. The captain.

He followed Browning up to the bridge and watched him until he had disappeared aboard the depot ship.

It was like the cutting of a wire, he thought. It was all his now.

He looked down at the wet casing where the sentry stamped

his feet noisily to keep warm, and beyond the raked bows towards the end of the loch. It was hard to find any pattern in what they were doing. Bill had died even as his wife planned to deceive him and leave him for another. A woman and her child lay buried in the rubble of their home while their man poured drinks in the wardroom for his captain, ignorant of this necessary deception. And in Iceland an anonymous German had triggered off yet another chain of events, one which would send all of them to sea and an unknown challenge.

Strangely, Marshall found that he was no longer afraid of what lay ahead. Perhaps after all it was the land which had created his apprehension, and like the boat which stirred uneasily beneath his feet, he was glad to go, no matter what awaited him elsewhere.

3   Only The Job In Hand

AFTER all the tension and the brittle tempers brought about by last minute checks and frantic preparations, the actual moment of getting under way was almost a relief. The weather, perverse as ever, had worsened, and a stiff wind lashed the waters of the loch into a confusion of short, vicious whitecaps. It seemed as if every available man aboard the depot ship was lining the rails to see them off, and close by, her rakish hull rocking uncomfortably in the wind, the armed-yacht *Lima* lay hove-to to guide them clear of the anchorage and out to the open sea.

Marshall stood high on the steel gratings in the forepart of the bridge, craning over the screen to watch the second coxswain, Petty Officer Cain, as he pushed his wire-handling parties into their various positions of readiness. Known as the Casing King, he was a good petty officer, and Marshall knew he was too experienced to let anything slip past him. Beneath his leather sea-boots he could feel the grating trembling and thudding to the powerful diesels and pictured Frenzel at his control panel, his eyes on the dials and his men nearby.

Marshall was wearing an oilskin over several layers of clothing and had a thick towel around his neck. Even so, he was cold and could not stop his body from shaking. Nerves. He shouted, "Stand by!" Below him a lookout repeated his warning into the voicepipe, and he heard a brief squeak above his head. Probably Gerrard taking a glance through the periscope. Getting his bearings. He had looked very tired when he had reported back from his short leave. He never had been much of a talker but was always a good man to be with. Reliable.

A seaman yelled, "Three minutes to go, sir!"

"Very well."

There had been no time at all to ask him about things at home. Just "How's Valerie?" "Fine." Or, "What did she say about your leaving so soon?" Reply, "Not a lot." Poor old Bob, she must have given him a rough time.

He turned slightly to watch as Sub-Lieutenant Warwick strode from beneath the conning-tower to speak with the Casing King. Against the thickset P.O. and the shining black shapes of the other seamen he looked even frailer than usual.

A few figures were on the little H-boat's casing alongside, waiting to let go. One shouted, "Good luck, mate!" Another, "Get some sea-time in!"

Despite the familiar shouts, encouraging or derisive in their normality, Marshall could feel the strangeness all around him. Pointing away towards the tossing whitecaps he saw the U-boat's forecastle like a long black arrowhead, the jumping-wire making a thin line across the skudding clouds and darkening sky.

A light stabbed from the depot ship's bridge and a few cheers echoed above the pounding diesels and insistent wind.

Lieutenant Buck climbed up through the hatch and groped his way to the gratings, his pointed features very pale against the dull metal.

"All ready, sir." He had a faint South London accent. "I've checked the list you gave me. I don't think we've missed a thing."

Marshall waved his hand. "Let go forrard!" To Buck he added, "Too late now if we have."

He felt the deck lift slightly as the wind edged the submarine's bows easily away from the other boat. A wire splashed alongside and grated on steel as Cain's men hauled it hastily inboard.

"Let go aft!"

More scampering feet, a man slipping and cursing in the wet gloom.

"All clear aft, sir!"

Marshall said sharply, "Make certain of that!"

He saw Buck leaning over the rear of the bridge, knowing it would be all right. But to wrap a wire round one of the screws would put paid to their sailing on time. A bad start. Unlucky, some said.

Buck reported, "All clear, sir."

Marshall nodded and turned to watch as the strip of trapped water between the two hulls widened still further. Faces on the other boat were already blurred, and on the depot ship it was impossible to distinguish men from fittings.

"Slow ahead together."

He listened to the immediate response from the engines. Throaty, deeper than before, the screws lashing the water into bright froth astern before settling into a steadier pattern.

"Steer two-nine-zero." He waited until the order was passed down the voicepipe and added, "Tell Number One to train the periscope on *Lima*. She'll show her stern light in a moment. He can con the boat on that."

How quickly it had all happened. The boat was sliding away from the moorings, her sharp stem throwing up feathers of spray, while the bow wave sluiced aft along the fat saddle tanks.

He heard one of the lookouts whispering excitedly to his companion and said, "Keep silent! Watch your prescribed areas and save the chat for later!"

Buck called, "First lieutenant reports all well in the control room, sir."

"Good."

A cluster of gulls floated abeam, clucking irritably, trying to decide if it was safe to remain on the surface. In the fading light they looked like a discarded wreath.

He shivered. The engines sounded very good indeed. He watched the armed-yacht turning steeply to lead them clear. She was beautiful. A millionaire's plaything in happier times. Probably kept in the Med in those times. Warm nights. Tanned bodies and soft wine.

He stooped over the voicepipe. "Watch her head, 'Swain. There'll be a stiff cross-current in about fifteen minutes."

"Aye, aye, sir." Starkie, the coxswain, sounded miles away.

He was unusually small. Like a leathery ferret. What was he thinking, Marshall wondered? Starkie's previous boat had been sunk by a dive bomber off the Hook of Holland. He had somehow survived with three others until picked up by a M.T.B. more dead than alive. Now he was back. Perhaps his wiriness had saved him. It was a fallacy that fat men survived better in the water.

Marshall trained his powerful glasses and watched it for several moments. One of Browning's security boats. Making sure.

"Well done. Disregard it now and carry on with your sweep."

"Yessir." It was the lookout he had previously choked off for gossiping. But his voice sounded slightly mollified by the brief praise.

On down the loch, with the swell growing more noticeably as they ploughed towards the sea.

Gerrard seemed to have no difficulty in holding the yacht's sternlight in her periscope. It would be good practice for him. Start with something simple.

Warwick's round face appeared above the bridge screen shining with spray.

"All wires secured and stowed, sir!" He sounded breathless.

"Very well." And there they will stay until we tie up again in a home port. Unless . . . He said, "Fall out your people and send them below." He hesitated. "Then check the fore hatch again, Sub."

The boy vanished and Buck said, "I think he's enjoying all this."

Marshall glanced at him. "Probably. What about you? You've been eighteen months in submarines, I understand."

Buck sifted through his answers and settled on, "Makes a change, sir."

Feet scraped on the ladder and a man tried to struggle on to the bridge even as the first of Warwick's casing party crowded over the rear of the conning-tower.

Marshall snapped, "What the *hell* are you doing?"

Buck said, "He wants to be sick, sir."

The seamen from the casing, already cold and sodden with spray, stared at the wretched man unfeelingly. One said, "Shove over, Ginger, and let the real men get below!"

Marshall added, "Send him down. If he wants to be sick he'll use a bucket."

He heard the man retching and bubbling as he dropped from view. He bit his lip. He had been harsh with the luckless seaman. But once at sea, with just the officer of the watch and his lookouts on the bridge at any given time, one such incident could cause disaster. A sudden attack, the need to crash dive, and men could be struggling in an open hatch even as the boat plunged under. Gerrard, who was in charge of the control room, should have known better.

Warwick came on to the bridge and shook himself like a puppy emerging from the rain.

"All secure, sir." He grinned. "Really."

Marshall smiled. Perhaps he had been like Warwick once. He must have been. It hardly seemed possible.

"Right. You can go below."

Warwick asked shyly, "Can I stay here, sir?"

"Of course." Marshall raised his glasses and watched the yacht lift and stagger across the first of the inshore swells. "But hold tight."

He tried to picture the land which was sliding into the darkness abeam. Nobody would see them pass. Somewhere above the clouds an aircraft droned faintly until it was lost in the noise of diesels. Marshall thought suddenly of Frenzel as he had been that lunchtime. Cheerful, confident that his department was ready to move. Above the engineer's bunk Marshall had seen a picture of his wife and small son. That had been a bad moment.

"Captain, sir!" It was Gerrard on the voicepipe.

"What is it?"

"Coming on to new course now. Two-seven-zero, that is if the *Lima* has checked her own compass properly."

"Very good." He waited, knowing there would be more.

"Sorry about that seaman, sir. Stupid of me."

"That's all right, Bob. I expect you've got your hands full."

A chuckle. Relieved. "Enough, sir. But the lads seem to be able to manage her. She handles very smoothly. Touch wood."

Marshall stood upright again. Gerrard's personal worries could be almost anything. War or not, mortgages to be paid, bills met even if there was precious little to buy. His wife, Valerie, would be alone once more. He wondered if she was wearing the shawl Gerrard had bought her in Malta.

Warwick asked, "Do you think we'll get really close to them, sir?"

Them. "The Jerries, you mean?" He shrugged. "Could be. You'll have to be all about if that happens."

Warwick murmured, "I'll try sir."

Buck said dourly, "He'll look a right little *kraut* when he gets his gear on!"

Marshall nodded. They had a selection of German uniforms on board. If they got close enough to need them, Warwick would have to be good indeed.

Buck added suddenly, "You'll be okay, David, don't you sweat!"

Marshall said nothing. Buck's change of attitude had told him plenty. He was not quite the unfeeling man-of-the-world he often seemed to portray.

Warwick relaxed slightly. "It's all right for you. Bloody great torpedoes. They don't need *any* language."

The bridge lurched steeply and brought a curtain of spray dousing over the persicope standards. It was getting wilder, and on either bow there was no longer even a shadow of land.

The blue sternlight was pitching in all directions, and he guessed that aboard the yacht things must be getting very uncomfortable. Her skipper was probably praying that the next two hours would pass without incident so that they could watch over the U-boat's test dive and then scurry back to shelter.

Marshall considered the prospect of diving. It would be an unhurried affair. The last time they would get to test their ability. After that. . . .

He pushed it from his mind and said, "Change the lookouts. And tell the steward to send me something hot to drink."

Throughout his command he could imagine his men sitting or standing at their stations. Watching their gauges and levers, listening to the engines' pitch and the steady beat of screws. Others, as yet unemployed, would have more time to think, to examine their own feelings as each minute took them further and further from home. In a few days everything would be as familiar as any other boat. Well, almost. But he must not let it become too familiar. That could be equally dangerous. Fatal.

"Able Seaman Churchill requests permission to come to the bridge, sir." The lookout could not restrain a grin.

Churchill was a torpedoman, but also acted as wardroom steward. It was a difficult name to have in wartime.

"Very well."

The man squeezed through the hatch carrying a jug and mugs against his chest.

"Kye, sir." He poured some of the thick cocoa into a mug

and squinted outboard at the tossing whitecaps. "Strewth!"

Marshall held the hot mug against his face. "How are things, er . . . Churchill?"

The steward eyed him curiously. "Great, sir." He was a Cockney, with an accent you could cut with a knife. "Cookie's got a smashin' 'otpot for later on."

Marshall watched him slither into the open hatchway.

One of the lookouts whispered, "Give our love to the War Cabinet!"

Churchill's head quivered in the hatchway. "Get knotted!"

Buck said, "I hope the torpedoes won't let us down. I've checked them over until I know each one by name. All the same, I hear Jerry has a fair share of duds." He shook his mug on the deck and added, "I'll go forrard now, with your permission, sir."

"Yes." Buck's arrival in the fore-ends would shake up his torpedomen. Keep them from pondering too much.

When he had gone below Warwick asked, "Was that right, sir?"

Marshall lowered his glasses. "We have our share of duds, too. Nothing you can explain. It just happens sometimes." He craned over the voicepipe. "Watch your revolutions. The yacht is making hard going of it. We'll overtake her if we're not careful."

He heard Starkie's terse acknowledgement and pictured Gerrard and Frenzel translating his advice into action. Devereaux would be leaning on his chart table. Very little for him to do at present. Just watch everyone else, his handsome face set in a cynical smile.

Warwick said, "There's a lot to know, isn't there, sir?"

Marshall looked at him. "I suppose there is. I hadn't thought of it like that. It sort of grows on you."

Warwick was still watching him, eyes filling the pale shape of his face. This would not do at all. It sounded like some sort of awe. The birth of hero-worship. But Warwick had to be independent. Stand on his own two feet.

He changed the subject. "Did you have any outside interests at university, Sub?"

"I was a pacifist, sir."

Marshall grinned at his confusion. "No comment!"

As the submarine pushed further and further from the land the motion became worse, the noise of wind and sea louder even than the engines. In uncomfortable, swaying silence the four men on the open bridge withdrew into their own resources, gripping the wet steel, bracing their aching legs against the steep, dizzy plunges.

Marshall watched the blurred sternlight across the bows until his eyes watered with strain. It would be better once they could clap on more speed. A U-boat was designed principally to run on the surface. To chase her quarry and overreach it. Then dive and await the kill. He could feel his stomach tightening to the boat's antics and guessed that many of the new hands would be in real torment.

At long last they arrived at the arranged position, and as the *Lima* rolled drunkenly in the steep troughs Marshall said, "This is it." He spoke into the voicepipe; "Everything ready below?"

Starkie called back, "Standing by, sir. Control room clock reads 1900."

Marshall straightened his back. "Signal the *Lima*." He waited until Warwick had picked up the small lamp. "Am about to carry out trim dive." To the lookouts he added, "Clear the bridge." He felt strangely calm. Detached.

A light stabbed across the water, and he thought he heard the yacht's siren give a quick squawk.

Warwick hurried to the hatch and Marshall was alone. Slowly and deliberately he snapped shut the cocks on the two voicepipes and took a last glance around him and at the faint outline of the yacht. Then he lowered himself through the hatch and spun the locking wheel into place. Unhurriedly down the polished ladder where a seaman waited to slam shut the lower hatch. It made a dull thud, like someone banging an oil-drum under water.

After the stinging wind and spray his cheeks felt flushed in the ordered world of the control room. He handed his dripping oil-skin to a messenger and ran his gaze over the men around him. Starkie, small and intent at his wheel. The two planesmen, heads tilted to watch their dials. Gerrard, arms folded, standing just behind the coxswain, a slide-rule projecting from one pocket. Devereaux by the chart table as he had expected. Frenzel leaning on his control panel, face alight in the reflected coloured bulbs.

"All set, Number One?"

Gerrard turned towards him, pale despite his tan.

41

"Ready, sir."

Marshall crossed to the forward periscope and swung it gently until he had found the *Lima*'s vague outline about a cable clear.

"Turn out the foreplanes."

He depressed the periscope lens and watched the forward hydroplanes opening outwards from the hull like two pleading hands. The after pair were submerged. But everything must be checked, if only this once.

"Test fore and aft planes, Number One."

Again he watched them, moving from rise to dive positions before returning to their horizontal trim. Beyond the periscope he caught a glimpse of a young stoker. Watching him like a mesmerised rabbit. He gave him a brief smile but the youth showed no change of expression.

He glanced around the control room again. It looked comfortingly warm in the glowing lights, the jerseys of the occupants still unsoiled by grease or dirt.

"Hydroplanes tested and found correct, sir."

"Ready, Chief?" He saw Frenzel nod.

He turned back to the periscope. The moment had come. How quiet it was now that the diesels' heat had given way to the electric motors. Restful almost.

"Group up. Slow ahead together. Open main vents. Take her down to fourteen metres!"

He concentrated his gaze on the foreplanes as they tilted downwards like fins. They were easy to see against the frothing bow wave. It was a fascinating sight and never failed to excite him. The bow dropping, the sea surging up the casing towards him while the deck tilted below his feet. The casing had gone now, and he saw spray leaping at him, so that as always he was tempted to hold his breath as if to avoid drowning. A distorted but silent sea, engulfing all of them as the boat continued to dive.

"Down periscope."

He stood back, bracing his body as he looked quickly over the depth gauges and hydroplane tell-tales. Gerrard was doing well. Nice and smooth. He watched the big needle edging round, steadying.

"Fourteen metres, sir. Periscope depth." Gerrard sounded hoarse.

"Up periscope."

Again a quick circling inspection. No sign of *Lima,* but he

42

could hear her ragged engine beat without difficulty.

"Down periscope." He clapped home the handles.

"Twenty metres."

He waited, hearing the crackle of reports over the intercom and voicepipes as sections contacted the control room, half listening to the ping of the echo-sounder, the smooth purr of motors.

Gerrard said, "Twenty metres, sir." He wiped his face with his forearm. "No reports of leaks."

Devereaux remarked casually, "*That's* good news."

Nobody replied.

They maintained the same depth and speed for the prescribed half hour. The hull felt as steady as a barrack square, and the reports from the various departments were equally encouraging.

Marshall said at length, "Stand by to surface. We will signal *Lima* that all's well and then lay off our new course, surfaced."

Gerrard said, "She seems fine."

Marshall nodded. "We will dive before first light. Make sure all the watchkeepers know the standing orders *thoroughly*. They'll not get a second chance."

He looked at the men around him. "We are in business." He smiled gravely at their mixed expressions. "Under entirely new management!"

Marshall opened his eyes and stared for several seconds at the curved deckhead above his bunk. He knew immediately by the background of silence that the submarine was still dived, that breakfast had not yet begun. His reading light was on, and he realised he must have fallen into a deep sleep, and saw his notebook lying across the blankets. There was no gap between sleeping and being awake, his past experiences had done away with such luxury. But as he stared at the curved steel overhead he was aware that the sight no longer confused or surprised him. They had been at sea for eight days, and you got used to a lot in that time.

He looked at his watch. It was six in the morning. Since leaving the loch they had spent most days submerged and every night running on the surface, charging batteries and checking the inflow of signals which filled the darkness with the affairs of war.

In eight days he had got to know a lot about his command and her new role. While they had driven westwards into the Atlantic, avoiding the main convoy routes and watching for friend and foe alike, he had gone over his intelligence pack again and again. Browning's staff had done a good job in translating the German logs and codes, and he knew almost as much about U-192's previous life as his own. She had been based in the French port of Lorient, and had been employed in the Atlantic against Allied shipping for the whole of her lifetime. Then, needing a big refit, she had returned to her real home, Kiel. There she had been overhauled and her crew scattered to other, unseasoned boats, new from the shipyards. The pattern was almost exactly like his own. Like *Tristram*, U-192 had been ordered to sail on an independent patrol, to work her company into a proper team on actual operations. Afterwards, if she survived, she would return to Lorient and rejoin her old consorts. Again the similarity was very clear. For although her crew had been mixed and only partly trained, she had an experienced and hardened captain and first lieutenant. It was almost unnerving.

He twisted his head to look at the German cap which hung behind his door. The one he might have to wear if every other ruse failed. It had a white top, the mark of a U-boat commander. He had tried it on just the once. The effect had been startling.

He licked his lips, tasting the diesel in his throat. It was a pity they had been made to dive overnight, but safety came first. The submarine was now about a thousand miles south of Cape Farewell, Greenland and a similar distance east of Newfoundland. Out here the enemy was not only made up of men. There could be ice about, and it was best to run deep and avoid the risk.

Feet padded past his cabin and he thought he heard the clink of cups. Breakfast. The one real occasion when he faced most of his officers at once.

The passage to the first rendezvous area had been busy for all of them. All the usual teething troubles. Faulty valves and inexpicable failures in wiring which had to be traced with the aid of Warwick or one of the telegraphists to translate the German handbooks.

After the first day or so many of the company seemed to get overconfident. It must have been a strange experience for everyone. Dodging their own patrols, diving whenever an aircraft was heard or sighted. It gave an air of *cloak-and-dagger* which helped to mask the grim reality of their mission.

Being forced inwards on their resources was bound to have its other effects, too. Small irritations grew into open arguments. A man who was minutes late on watch was met with something like hatred by the one he was relieving. It was unreasonable as it was natural. Only when they had something from without to test them would they finally draw together as a unit, irritations or not.

There had been a quick spark of anger between Gerrard and Devereaux, for instance, which he had quickly quenched. It had started because of something he had done himself. Three days out from the loch the weather had moderated, the Atlantic smoothing its grey face to a long succession of humped rollers. Marshall had decided on a deep practice dive, something they had not yet done together. It was always a tense moment in any boat, let alone this one.

Three hundred and fifty feet. It was nothing like the depth the boat was built to withstand, but you always felt uneasy. As they had sunk deeper and deeper, with Frenzel and his E.R.A.s creeping about the hull in search of faults and leaks, several men must have considered the fact that boat's skin was less than an inch thick.

Gerrard had handled deep dives in *Tristram* on many occasions, and had been busy with his slide-rule and calculations before the actual moment of taking her down. Each hour of the day the boat's trim had to be watched and checked. As fuel was consumed the weight had to be compensated. Food and fresh water, even the movement of large numbers of men at any one time, such as going to diving stations, had to be allowed for. A bad first lieutenant had been known to let his submarine's bows flounder above the surface at the moment of firing torpedoes, merely because he had not compensated for their sudden loss of weight.

Every so often there had been a sharp squeak or groan, with attendant gasps from the inexperienced men aboard. For even at a mere one hundred feet there was a weight of twenty-five tons of water on every square yard of the hull.

As the depth gauges had steadied on one hundred and five metres Gerrard had asked, "Shall I take her up again, sir?"

Devereaux had remarked, "Getting worried, Number One? I *am* surprised!"

For those brief seconds Marshall had seen the hostility between them. Maybe Devereaux had expected the appointment

45

of first lieutenant, especially as he had been in the U-boat since her capture. And perhaps Gerrard really was rattled after his last commission in the Med. Either would be easy to explain.

He had said calmly, "Check all sections." He had waited, listening to the negative reports flooding through the intercom. The Kiel dockyard workers had done a good job. Right at that moment there was a total weight impinging the pressure hull of some 80,000 tons, the displacement of the *Queen Mary*.

But it had not settled anything. Everyone had to trust him and the boat. Know that together they could survive. Also he had needed to fracture that barrier between his two lieutenants as they eyed each other like strangers.

He had snapped, "Three hundred and eighty feet, Number One."

Gerrard had nodded jerkily. "Very good, sir."

More groans, and a few flakes of paint which had drifted down like snow as the hull had taken the strain. As she levelled off Marshall had made another comparison. The surface was now the height of St. Paul's Cathedral above their heads. Nothing happened, and when Frenzel had ducked through the after bulkhead he was quite satisfied with both hull and machinery.

Marshall had said to the control room at large, "Now we all know."

But if it had given the company more confidence, it had done little to ease the tension between Gerrard and the navigator.

Churchill opened the door and stepped gingerly into the cabin.

"Mornin' sir." He placed a cup of coffee beside the bunk. "You want to shave today?"

Marshall sighed and stretched his limbs. Encased in heavy jersey and stained sea-boots, he would have given anything for a hot bath, a shave and change of clothes. But outward-bound it was too wasteful.

"Just coffee. How are things?"

Churchill rubbed his chin. "All quiet, sir. Nice'n steady. Twenty metres when I come through the control room. Let's see now, 'ow much is that in *feet?*"

Marshall grinned. "Sixty-five. You'll soon get the hang of it."

Churchill moved away. "Why can't the bloody Jerries use civilised measurements like wot we does?"

Marshall let the coffee explore his stomach. That at least was better than the previous owners had had, he thought.

"Captain in the control room!"

He was off the bunk and running the short length of passage-way before the cup had rolled across the cabin floor.

Buck was officer of the watch, his pointed features anxious as he said, "The hydroplane operator reported propeller noises at Green four-five, sir. Very faint. Lost it almost immediately."

Marshall brushed past him and leaned over the operator who was crouching in his little compartment like a man at prayer. He tapped him gently on the shoulder.

"What d'you think, Speke?"

The leading seaman leaned back and moved one earphone aside.

"I'm not sure, sir. It was just a blur. Thought it was a shoal of fish for a minute."

Marshall looked at Buck. "Sound the klaxon." He saw the lieutenant's eyes sharpen. "Jump about!"

The scream of the klaxon brought the off-watch men charging to their stations. Gerrard, paler than ever, arrived panting in the control room, his thin body bowed below the overhead pipes and valves.

"All closed up at diving stations, sir." Starkie sat loosely in his steel chair, his fingers easing the brass spokes of the wheel, giving no sign that he had been fast asleep thirty seconds earlier.

Marshall looked at his watch. It would be daylight of a sort.

"Stop the fans. Absolute silence throughout the boat!"

Gerrard asked quietly, "What do you think, sir?"

He shook his head. "Could be mistaken. But we'll take a look."

Gerrard nodded. "Periscope depth."

Marshall crouched beside the periscope, listening as the com-pressed air pounded steadily into the saddle tanks. *Easy. Don't take her up too fast.*

He snapped, "Raise the periscope." He held out one hand. *"Slowly!"*

He crouched right down, almost on his knees, flipping open the twin handles as the periscope slid gently from the well. It felt warm, as indeed it was, to prevent the lenses from misting over.

"Easy!"

He saw the glimmer of grey through the lens, the froth of bubbles as it cut above the surface.

"Periscope depth, sir." Gerrard's voice was a whisper.

47

Crablike, Marshall edged round the well, blinking as the spray doused the lens. Nothing.

"Raise it completely."

He straightened his body with it, feeling the others watching his face, hearing them murmur as he halted his slow inspection.

"It's a ship. Motionless."

He clicked the lens to full power and held his breath. It was a medium sized freighter, listing badly, with a gash in her hull you could drive a bus through.

The petty officer who was recording the bearings on the periscope ring called, "Ship bears Green three-five, range——"

Marshall interrupted him. "She's sinking. There are two boats in the water alongside."

He held the small drama in his eyes, unable to let it go. The heaving grey sea, the tiny scrambling figures sliding down falls and nets into those two pitiful boats. A straggler from a convoy, her crew must have given up the fight to save her. He thought of all the miles before they could reach help or safety. It looked like the beginnings of snow or sleet across the lens. He stood back.

"Take a look, Number One."

She was a British ship. Old and worn out. Probably dropped from an eastbound convoy to effect repairs. Then, out of the blue, a torpedo.

He heard himself say, "That H.E. you heard, Speke. Most likely the U-boat. She must have been hanging around just in case another ship came to help." He looked at Gerrard's bowed shoulders. "Two for the price of one."

Gerrard asked thickly, "What'll you do? About *them?*"

"The U-boat may still intend to stay in this area. If we surfaced she'd be on to us in a flash." He said in a quieter tone, "It's no go, Bob."

There was a sudden silence, and even Starkie turned on his chair to look at him. As if they had all been frozen by his words.

Devereaux exclaimed, "You're not going to leave them, sir?"

Marshall took the periscope handles and made a quick all-round search of sea and sky. Cold, bleak and empty. When he looked again at the ship he saw her rusty stem was already lifting clear of the sea, as if being raised by invisible hawsers.

He slapped the handles inwards. "Down periscope." He crossed to the chart. "Take her down to twenty metres again and alter course to two-four-zero. We'll increase speed in an hour and make up what we've lost by this alteration." He listened to his own words. Cold, flat, without feeling. How could he do it when every fibre was screaming to surface and drag those poor frightened wretches aboard.

Devereaux began, "But, sir, if——"

He swung on him. "No *ifs* or *buts,* Pilot! D'you imagine I'm enjoying any of it? *Think,* man, before you start playing the bloody hero!"

A rumble sighed against the hull. It was followed by a drawn-out scraping sound which seemed to go on and on forever. A ship breaking up as it took the last plunge.

Gerrard's eyes met his. He understood. Better than any of them. It was all there in his eyes. Sadness and shame. Pity and awareness that no one else could take the responsibility.

"Fall out diving stations." He walked past them, the silence following him like a cloak.

4 "Start The Attack!"

MARSHALL entered the wardroom and pulled the curtain across the doorway behind him.

"All right, make yourselves comfortable."

He waited for the four officers to seat themselves and for Warwick to weight down the corners of the chart which he had laid on the table. Beneath the solitary deckhead lamp their faces looked strained and tense, their movements lethargic.

Beyond the gently vibrating curtain he could hear Buck's sharp tones as he reprimanded one of the planesmen, but otherwise the boat was completely silent, and with her motors reduced to an economical four knots could have been hanging motionless in the water.

He glanced round at their faces again, trying to gauge their feelings. Their doubts.

Twenty-nine days. He could see where each one had left its mark in their guarded expressions. The excitement of leaving the loch and following the armed-yacht to the open sea. The tension of the first dive, even the sick horror of having to leave the sinking freighter to its own pitiful resources had dulled and merged into an overall frustration and disappointment. It was like being completely severed from the rest of the world, shut off from reality.

Whenever they had gone to periscope depth or had cruised on the surface they had listened to the constant flow of signals, Allied, enemy or neutral, yet felt no part of any of them. Distress calls from merchant ships under attack, homing instructions from the German submarine headquarters to wolf packs deep in the Atlantic, and garbled snatches of countermeasures from warships and aircraft. It never stopped, but as day followed day Marshall found himself wondering if his own role had already been overreached. Perhaps the German High Command had somehow changed its plans for refuelling U-boats at sea, or had discovered that there was an enemy in their midst. If the latter were true, there might even now be extra U-boats hunting for them, changing their role to that of victim.

The air throughout the boat was stale and dank, so that clothes clung to their skins like dirty rags, adding to the general depression, the uncertainty of waiting for something to happen.

He looked down at the chart. The submarine was steering in a south-westerly direction, her present position some two hundred miles south of the Bermuda Islands, a thousand miles east of the Florida coast. It was hard to reconcile their appearance and listless movements with the other picture he had seen an hour earlier when they had gone up to periscope depth. The sea's face had been unbroken by any wave, had stretched away on every bearing in a glistening panorama of pale green, catching the sunlight and lancing through the periscope like a million bright diamonds. There had been a low mist too, betraying the heat and nourishment that everyone aboard so desperately needed. But for nearly three days they had stayed submerged, listening and watching as mile by mile the boat had made her way across the rendezvous area. And it was their second attempt so far. The first time had found them two hundred miles to the south where after a careful search they had revealed nothing. Reports had been picked up of a heavy enemy attack on a convoy to the east, and Marshall guessed that the *milch-cow*, if indeed she was still in the area, had taken herself a position where she would be more greatly needed. To *this* area, he had thought. Now, he was no longer optimistic.

He said, "I've called this conference to put you all in the picture." He watched Gerrard's fingers as they tapped soundlessly against the chart. "To hear your views."

Devereaux glanced up at him. "It looks as if we've missed this one, sir." He picked up a pencil and laid the point on the opposite side of the Atlantic. "Now, according to our information, the second supply boat is operating here. Off Freetown." His eyes flickered to Marshall again. "Why not go for him? Better than losing both, surely?"

Gerrard said swiftly, "It's not that easy. We've been a month at sea. If we cross to the other side to hunt for the other boat and fail to make contact we'll barely have enough fuel to reach home, let alone run back for another rendezvous with this bugger."

Devereaux smiled gently. "I realise that, Number One. I do the navigating, remember?"

Marshall said, "Nevertheless, I agree with you, Number One. We could be dragging from one end of the Atlantic to the other chasing shadows. If we remain in this area we still have a chance of making a strike."

Frenzel, who had so far remained slumped against the bulkhead, leaned forward and placed both hands on the table.

"I'm not happy about this enforced diving, sir. We need to ventilate the boat and charge batteries. Later, if we run into trouble, we'll need all the power we can get." He looked bleakly at the solitary lamp. "I've shut down all the heaters, lights and fans I can without driving our lads berserk. I can't do much more."

"Yes."

Marshall straightened his back and tried to think clearly. It was his responsibility. But to do what? Had they been engaged in actual operations things would have been very different. But this was enough to crack even a hardened submariner's reserve.

A week back they had sighted a neutral, and to break the boredom he had carried out a mock attack on her. It had been during the night, and as he had studied the ship through the periscope he had marvelled at the other captain's confidence. The big Swedish flag painted on the hull had been well lit, and her upper decks and cabins aglow with glittering lights. Was it possible for people to move without fear like that? Even as he had listened to his men going through the motions of an attack he had sensed something else, too. A sort of wildness which he could even feel in himself. Had he pressed home a real attack and ordered Buck to fire his torpedoes, he felt they would have done so. In war it was hard to stop acting in the manner which had become your daily life.

He said, "We'll surface tonight, Chief. It's the best I can do. I know we're pretty safe from Allied patrols out here, but I daren't risk surfacing anywhere in the rendezvous area until I'm sure of contact with the supply boat. If we get entangled with another U-boat, or worse with a whole bloody pack of them, we'd be hard put to explain our intentions."

Surprisingly, Warwick grinned. He said, "We could say we were lost, sir!"

Marshall smiled. Warwick at least seemed able to keep his good-humour.

He looked at his watch. Nearly noon. The supply boat would make her brief homing signal then at short-range. Just enough for the rendezvous, not sufficient to be detected and fixed by the powerful beacons on the American mainland. Always provided she was actually in the area and that her captain was satisfied about his own safety. It could be no joke to cruise about the ocean in what amounted to one giant bomb.

He heard Devereaux ask, "Look, Sub, are you quite sure you've checked your log of signals? The W/T office does a good job, but in the end it all falls on your plate." It sounded like an accusation.

Warwick replied quietly, "I've treble-checked. If the Germans are using a different system I can't find it."

Gerrard added, "Leave him alone, Pilot. None of *us* could do it, so there's no point in rattling him."

Marshall tensed. There it was again. The rift.

He snapped, "If we *all* do our jobs and——"

Buck's voice cut through the tension like a saw. "Captain in the control room!"

With the others close on his heels Marshall thrust through the curtain and ran for the one brightly lit compartment in the whole hull.

Buck said crisply, "Asdic reports faint H.E. at two-five-oh, sir."

Marshall kept his face impassive and strode to the shielded compartment where the operator was crouching over his controls.

"Well?" He watched the man's face, gauging his assessment. It was Speke again, the senior operator.

The leading seaman shrugged but kept his eyes on the dial by his fingers. "Very faint, sir. Single screw. Diesel."

Marshall said, "Keep listening."

He tried to hide his disappointment. Whatever it was, it was certainly not the big supply submarine.

Behind him he heard Warwick say uncertainly, "Damaged U-boat. I'll bet it's one from that convoy attack. Coming to another for help."

Marshall swung round and stared at him, seeing the youth fall back under his gaze.

"What did you say?"

Warwick swallowed hard, suddenly pale as the others watched him like strangers.

"I only thought——"

Marshall reached out and touched his arm. "You're young, Sub. Young and fresh." In a calmer tone he continued, "And you could just be right."

Warwick flushed and shifted his boots on the steel deck. "Gosh!"

Marshall looked at Buck. "Bring her round to intercept. Then sound the alarm. Complete silence throughout the boat after that." He held up one hand to restrain him. "But remember this. All of you. If this is a damaged U-boat and she is making a rendezvous, it'll mean we will have to act all the faster. Neither of them can be allowed to break W/T silence." He looked at Buck. "So the attack team must be perfect."

Buck nodded, his sharp features mellowed slightly by the beginning of a beard. "Right."

"Steady on two-five-zero, sir." The helmsman sounded hoarse.

"Very well. Klaxon, please."

As the men came running through the bulkhead doors, their faces still heavy with sleep, from trying to relax in the unmoving stale air, Marshall could feel his own weariness falling away like a feverish dream.

Gerrard reported, "All closed up, sir."

Marshall looked at the control room clock. Five minutes to noon.

"Periscope depth, Number One. Easy does it."

He saw a brief smile on Gerrard's lips. Perhaps like himself he was recalling all those other times. The same pattern but all different.

Then he forgot him and crouched beside the periscope well,

testing his own reactions, the steadiness of his breathing, the even beating of his heart.

"Fourteen metres, sir."

"Up periscope." He glanced at the stoker. "Slowly."

He bent double, his forehead pressed against the rubber pad, watching the sunlight probing down towards him, the swirl of silver bubbles, the sudden blinding flash as the lens broke the surface.

"Hold it there!"

Easy now. Take your time. He edged round the well, watching the misty sunlight playing across a long shallow swell, turning into living green glass. He could almost feel the warmth across his face, taste the clean salt air on his lips.

Without removing his eye from the lens he asked, "How is the bearing now?"

"As before, sir. But still very faint." Speke sounded unruffled. Which was just as well.

"Full extent."

He straightened his body as the periscope slid smoothly from its well. A quick glance above. It was unlikely there would be any aircraft. They were needed elsewhere, and the long haul from the American mainland made any danger of attack remote. But you had to be sure. There might be a carrier, or some seaplane off a heavy escort. He brought the periscope to full power and steadied it towards the hidden bows. But the haze was too thick. Like steam playing across the gently heaving swell.

"Down periscope." He stood back and rubbed his chin. It felt like sandpaper. "Increase to seven knots, Chief. We'll miss this chap if we're not careful."

Even as the periscope hissed into its well Warwick shouted, "W/T report the signal, sir!" He had his handset pressed to his ear, but was peering at the faces around him, shouting as if they were all deaf.

From the attack table Buck snarled, "Bearing, for Christ's sake?"

Warwick gulped. "Approximately the same as this other boat. Sorry."

Marshall crossed to the chart. They could only just hear the damaged submarine's remaining screw, and as yet Speke had heard nothing of the big supply boat. *We must make more speed.* The *milch-cow* was probably lying directly ahead of their own course, with the damaged boat somewhere in between. He smiled grimly in spite of his tense nerves. Just like it said in the folio. True Teutonic precision.

He snapped, "Group up. Full ahead together. Twenty metres." He was thinking aloud. "We'll get as close as we can to the first boat. Then we'll surface. We must make more speed, but in any case the supply boat would be suspicious of any of her brood approaching submerged. She'd dive and be away, no matter how much trouble the other chap's in."

He saw Frenzel stooping over his panel, his dark features set in concentration. Calculating. Understanding.

At their maximum underwater speed it took about fifteen minutes to travel two miles. A lot could happen in that time.

"Twenty metres, sir. Course two-five-zero." The coxswain looked very relaxed. Maybe like his captain he was glad to be doing something again.

Marshall gripped the edge of the chart table, trying to remain relaxed. It was hard to keep from looking at the clock. Watching the seconds becoming minutes. Matching them against heartbeats.

Speke said, "The range must be about six thousand yards, sir. It's hard to tell. The one diesel sounds pretty dicey."

Three miles. But for the mist he would have sighted the other boat. Even so, it was still too far to begin an attack. He must not think of this one, limping target. It was quite close enough. One fanned salvo and he could send her to the bottom. They would never know what had hit them. But the other submarine was something else entirely. They must be sure. Exact.

"Diesel's stopped, sir."

"*Blast!*"

Marshall moved to the periscope well and back again. The damaged boat probably had the *milch-cow* in sight. He could picture all of it in his mind. The relief, the weary lookouts numb with thanks as the massive hull hove in sight. And aboard the supply boat all the busy preparations to pipe fuel across to the battered survivor from some attack or other. Food and fresh clothing, expert mechanics waiting to send over spare parts. There would even be a surgeon aboard to care for the sick and wounded.

He heard himself say, "Stand by to surface. We will continue on electric motors, but be ready to switch to main engines as soon as we're spotted. If we make a boob of this one we'll not get another chance."

He looked around their intent faces.

"Sub, you can muster your gun's crew. See that they're rigged out in German caps and lifejackets." He saw Churchill hovering by the attack table. "Fetch my cap."

He knew his words had sunk in. That it was going to be close and quick. Dangerously so.

As Churchill scurried away he added quietly to Gerrard, "If we catch it on the surface, Bob, take her deep. Don't try and save the deck party. Just get the hell out of it."

Gerrard nodded, his eyes grave. "Right."

"And forget the other rendezvous. If we blow this one they'll have every U-boat from here to Calais waiting for you." He slung his glasses closer around his neck and took the white cap from Churchill, touching the salt-stained eagle, the swastika in its claws. "Ready?"

"Yes." Gerrard ran his eyes along the control room. "As we agreed. Surface attack with six tubes. Gun action as a last resort." He nodded firmly. "God, what a way to earn a living!"

Feet clattered below the conning-tower hatch and he saw Warwick and his gun's crew, some of them grinning sheepishly as they adjusted their German caps and slipped into the bright orange lifejackets which were always worn by U-boat deck parties. He must miss nothing. Not even the smallest detail. Warwick looked younger than ever, if that were possible, and so much might depend on his nerve and intelligence.

Marshall said calmly, "Prepare your gun as soon as we surface. After that keep your people hanging around. Casual, but close enough to move like quicksilver." He raised his voice. "That applies to the machine-gunners, too. Any surfaced U-boat would have its defences ready, but not obviously so."

They were all staring at him, suddenly moulded together, the strain showing on each unshaven face.

He said, "Periscope depth again."

He waited as the deck tilted very slightly, the compressed air pulsing into the ballast tanks. He wondered what Browning would have made of all this. *Buster.*

"Fourteen metres, sir."

He licked his lips. Throughout his command every man would be waiting to act. The bearings to be set on each torpedo.

Everything. Thank God the Germans had perfected the fan method of firing. A British boat had to be aimed at her target or swung at the moment of releasing her torpedoes. Every U-boat was fitted with a device which allowed each shot to be fired individually on varying bearings while the boat's course remained constant. It was to be hoped that all Buck's training and drills would use this to good effect.

"Up periscope."

He waited, counting seconds. He let his breath exhale very slowly. There she was.

He heard Buck intone, "Range four thousand yards, sir."

Marshall ignored him, watching the other U-boat's conning-tower as it swam and lifted in the drifting haze as if detached from any hull or foundation. Smaller than this one. Dirty grey in the filtered sunlight. With full power on the lens he could see the rust and slime on the plates, a length of brokern guardrail as evidence of her earlier encounters.

"Down periscope." He strode to the ladder. "Open the lower hatch." He started up the smooth rungs, the gun's crew crowding up behind him, their breathing very loud in the narrow tower.

He reached for the locking wheel, feeling the moisture running down his wrists like rain. Some one had hold of his feet. Just in case. It was not unknown for a captain to be plucked out of the hatch before the build-up of pressure adjusted itself. He saw Warwick's hand on the ladder by his hip. Small and pale. Like a woman's. He took a deep breath.

"*Surface!*" It had started.

Seconds later, he heard Gerrard's voice far below, and with all his strength he swung the locking wheel, feeling the ice-cold water dash into his eyes and mouth as he heaved open the hatch and dragged himself on to the bridge. The gratings were only just free of water, and some still gurgled and sluiced through the scuppers as with her hydroplanes at full elevation the boat lurched into the sunlight. Marshall ran to the forepart of the bridge, seeing the foam seething away from the shining ballast tanks, laying bare the gun and casing, the dripping jumping-wire beyond which he saw the other U-boat almost broadside on to their approach.

He trained his glasses on the haze-shrouded conning-tower, saw the flash of sunlight below the periscope standards as someone levelled his binoculars on their sudden appearance. He could imagine in those flashing seconds what the Germans were thinking. Sudden panic at their rapid surfacing, fear giving way to relief at the realisation it was no enemy but one of their own.

A lookout snapped open the voicepipes and he heard Gerrard call, "We have the first target in sight, sir. She appears to be slewing round."

Marshall kept his glasses to his eyes. He should have realised. Should have checked. The damaged U-boat had not stopped merely because she was awaiting help. Her last diesel must have packed up. She was rolling heavily in the swell, her after casing awash where some seamen gathered below the conning-tower. He heard Warwick calling to his men, the click of metal behind him as the machine-gunners mounted their weapons on either side of the bridge. Further aft on the bandstand feet slithered on slime-covered steel as other men brought the Vierling to readiness.

He moved the glasses very slowly from bow to bow. Nothing. The supply boat might be visible to the damaged one, but as far as he was concerned she was invisible.

He snapped, "Tell the Chief to switch to main engines. Begin charging and ventilate the boat."

Frenzel must have been waiting, for as the diesels coughed into life he felt the air being sucked down the open hatch like a strong wind.

"Slow ahead together."

They were rapidly closing with the other boat. They must hold back until the *milch-cow* showed herself. The diesels would help make conversation difficult. It might also ease any remaining suspicion of their arrival.

A light stabbed across the milky water and Petty Officer Blythe, the yeoman of signals, acknowledged it briefly with his handlamp. At his side one of the telegraphists translated breathlessly, "He's asking your number, sir."

"Reply, Yeoman. One Nine Two."

God, how quickly they were closing the other boat. Even the haze was drifting clear, lifting and curling in a soft breeze. He could see the scars on the rounded hull, the uneven casing to mark the nearness of an exploding depth-charge.

He added, "Make the coded challenge."

He gripped the screen until the pain steadied him. Down below his feet Gerrard would be peering through the small attack periscope, watching for some sign that things had gone wrong, ready to dive deep in an instant.

This was the moment. The wrong code, a false acknowledgement, and. . . .

Blythe murmured, "Reply, sir. U-One Five Four." He ruffled his small book. "Fair enough so far. Not one of this boat's mob from Lorient."

The light was flashing again. Slowly and uncertainly as the other boat staggered and rolled drunkenly beneath the German signalman's feet.

"Requests that we take her in tow, sir. Has too much drift to——"

He broke off as a lookout said sharply, "There she is! Fine on the port bow!"

Almost simultaneously Marshall heard the voicepipe intone, "Target in sight, sir. Bearing Red one five. Range five thousand yards. Closing."

At first Marshall could see nothing and cursed as he lost valuable time to wipe moisture from his glasses. When he looked again he saw the great supply boat edging out of the haze like some vast, impossible creation from a nightmare. She bore little resemblance to a normal submarine, and her upper hull and casing were much like those of a partly completed surface craft.

Blythe hissed, "Jesus, she's a big un!"

Marshall darted a quick glance over the screen. Warwick was leaning on the guardrail waving his cap towards the damaged boat while some of his men pointed and gestured like old comrades. He noticed that Leading Seaman Tewson, the gunlayer, had remained by his seat, one hand resting on the brass wheel, the other gently dabbing spray from his telescopic sight.

Gerrard's voice again. "All tubes ready, sir."

Marshall replied slowly, "You must carry out the attack from the control room. We're too close for comfort. If those bastards see me using the bridge sights——" He did not finish it.

He heard Gerrard shouting his orders, fought the desire to run below and resume control. The ranges and bearings were being fed into the *fruit-machine,* as it was casually called, the results passed forward to the torpedo compartment.

"Bow doors open, sir."

"What shall I reply, sir?"

Marshall glanced at the yeoman. He had almost forgotten the German's request for aid. But if he sheered off now the supply boat would know immediately what was happening.

"Very well. Make to them that we are going to cross their port bow. Stand by on the fore casing with heaving lines." He ignored the slow stammer of the morse lamp and shouted to Warwick below the tower, "It's all yours, Sub! Make it look as if we're trying!" He saw Warwick wave and the Casing King dragging a spare wire and bending it to a heaving line.

He forced himself to concentrate. To ignore the nearness of the swaying boat, the waving arms and faint shouts from the other crew.

"Range now four thousand five hundred yards, sir." Gerrard sounded very cool. "Tubes one to four ready."

Marshall bit his lip. The damaged boat was barely two cables clear now. It would have to be soon. At any moment the Germans might notice something, or call him up by name. He swore silently and deliberately and turned his back on the enemy. Why *should* they? The challenge and acknowledgement were perfect. The Germans had their own troubles, and probably looked upon them as an additional aid in their predicament.

He saw the machine-guns swaying on their mounts, their long belts of ammunition trailing down through the open hatch like twin snakes.

Gerrard called, "We can't hit the damaged boat, sir. The explosion would finish us, too."

"Yes. Thanks, Bob, I had noticed." He beckoned to a lookout. "Pass the word to the gun crews. Rapid fire on the damaged boat when I give the word." He added harshly, "*Walk,* man! You're supposed to be among friends!"

The yeoman grimaced. "Some bloody friends, sir!"

The other lookout said, "The Jerry's got a megaphone, sir! He's gettin' ready to chat when we gets a bit closer!"

Marshall nodded, his eyes again towards the *milch-cow*. She was moving very slowly, like some great slab of grey pier, her upper deck alive with tiny figures, the sunlight glinting on the brass nozzle of her fuel pipe.

He saw the lookout reach Warwick beside the gun, watched his message make the youth step back as if he had been struck.

A voice echoed tinnily across the heaving water, almost drowned by the mutter of diesels, the hiss of spray against the hull.

Very slowly he removed his cap and waved it towards the other boat. It seemed to do the trick. The other captain spread his arms and pretended to hurl the megaphone overboard in disgust.

"*Sir!*" The lookout's voice made him freeze. "Smoke! On the starboard quarter!"

He dare not turn and look at it. The other boats had not seen it, and it was probably masked by his own conning-tower.

"Control room! This is the captain. Smoke on the starboard quarter. Check it with the main periscope."

An agonising pause and then a voice called, "One ship, sir. On the horizon."

He could not place the voice. Probably a spare seaman. But they had had so little time. . . .

He barked, "Start the attack!"

The voicepipe went dead, as if everyone below had been struck down by some invisible force. Then he heard Buck's orders being passed unhurriedly across the intercom. No panic, no emotion. It could have been a mock attack on another neutral.

"Fire One!"

Marshall felt the steel screen kick gently against his chest. Pictured the first torpedo as it shot from its tube.

"Fire Two!"

On the fore casing one of the seamen was whirling a heaving line round his head like a film cowboy, one eye towards the bridge as he played out the long, dragging seconds.

"Fire Three!"

Again the little kick. Like a conspiratorial nudge.

Marshall shuddered and snapped. "Get *ready*!"

"Fire Four!" A pause. "All torpedoes running, sir!" The last two in the bow tubes were to have been for the damaged boat. But she was near enough now to hit with a brick.

The lookout called, "Ship on the starboard quarter is closing, sir. One funnel. Probably destroyer."

Marshall nodded jerkily, unable to drag his eyes from the murky outline of his target. On, on, on. He pictured the four torpedoes streaking through the water, working up to some forty-five knots as they fanned out in a deadly salvo.

Blythe muttered, "Christ, we've missed the bugger!"

The first explosion when it came was like a thunderclap. In that split-second Marshall saw the forward portion of the enemy's hull burst open and upward in one great searing orange ball of fire. Ringed with black smoke and whirling fragments of metal it seemed to spread in size and brilliance so that the next torpedo's detonation was all but lost in the devastation.

Despite the terrible power of the noise and fire Marshall saw several tiny details, as if all of them were happening consecutively instead of the twinkling of an eye.

A seaman on the casing running aft and staggering as the shockwave swept over the hull in a scorching wind. Cain, the Casing King, kicking the spare wire over the side and yelling soundlessly to his deck party to take cover. The gun's crew moving jerkily like robots around their breech with Warwick's head and shoulders glowing bronze in the reflected inferno.

More terrible explosions, and Marshall felt the hull jerk and buck as if it had been hit by a submerged wreck.

On the damaged U-boat the first striken horror had changed to a wild scramble of running figures, some of whom had already reached the deck gun where an officer was dragging out his pistol and firing blindly across the narrow strip of water.

Marshall ducked as something clanged into the tower and shrieked away over the sea. A bullet or some fragment from the supply boat, he did not know or care.

He punched the nearest machine-gunner on the arm. "Open fire! Clear those men from the casing!"

The gun stammered into life, the thin line of tracer licking up and over the German's periscopes before steadying and ripping sparks from the grey steel.

When he looked again Marshall could see nothing of the *milch-cow*. Just a huge pall of drifting smoke against the sky, a spreading pattern of oil and bobbing flotsam to mark where she had made her last dive.

He yelled, "Full ahead together! Port ten!"

He watched as Warwick's crew brought the gun's long muzzle round across the rail, following the other boat as it appeared to career drunkenly on their mounting bow wave.

"*Shoot!*" The gun bucked back on its springs, the shell exploding far beyond the target in a cloud of vapour and bursting spray.

"Down one hundred!" The breech clicked shut. "Shoot!"

The conning-tower shook violently and a tall waterspout rocketed skywards some half-cable from the side. Marshall swung round, knowing the answer even as the lookout yelled, "Destroyer has opened fire, sir!"

The voicepipe called, "Other boat is trying to transmit!" A gasp as another shell whined overhead and exploded abeam.

A savage glare lit up the bridge and he turned to see the other boat's periscope standards and radio antennae reel apart as Warwick's gunners found their mark. Smoke billowed from the broken bridge, and he saw some of the German gunners running aft towards the tower. It was futile, for without engine power the U-boat was helpless. It was training and instinct, the relentless code which even in the face of death the U-boat's men could not break.

The Vierling crackled viciously, the four barrels cutting down these same running men with the ease of a reaper in a field. The officer, isolated and alone, was reloading his pistol when some of the shells smashed him into oblivion, leaving a bright smear to mark his brief passing.

Another shell slammed into the exposed ballast tank, and above the din of engines and yelling gunners it was possible to hear the truimphant surge of inrushing water.

Marshall had to clench his jaw to speak steadily into the voicepipe. "Break the charge! Out both engine clutches!" Before the sound of the diesels had died away he cupped his hands and shouted, "Secure the gun! Clear the bridge!"

Gerrard's voice, suddenly loud in the stillness. "Bridge! Both engine cluches out! Main motors ready!"

Men tumbled past and into the hatch, dragging with them the machine guns, one still smoking as it vanished blow. Wild eyes and brief, breathless voices, until only Marshall and the last lookout remained. The latter looked at the approaching destroyer, the hull of which was almost hidden behind her massive bow wave as she tore into the attack. Her skipper probably imagined he had caught two surfaced U-boats in the act of sinking some unidentified ship.

Either way, just one of his shells would make the score three instead of a pair.

Marshall nodded to the seaman. "Off you go."

He crouched over the voicepipe as a shell screamed low overhead, the shockwave hitting his shoulders like a man's forearm.

"Dive! Dive! Dive! Ninety metres! Shut off for depth-charging!"

He closed the cock and paused momentarily to peer abeam. The stricken U-boat had almost gone, her stern poking out of the seething bubbles and escaping oil like a crude arrowhead.

Then he jumped into the hatch, feeling the hull falling steeply, hearing the sea surging along the casing and against the conning-tower as Gerrard took her into a crash dive.

He slammed the hatch and locked the wheel tight. Down the ladder and into the control room, the familiar smells, the enclosed world of their being.

The lower hatch banged shut and he heard Gerrard call, "Group up. Full ahead together." He turned from peering over the helmsman's shoulder and met Marshall's gaze.

"Done it, sir."

Marshall clung to the ladder, his chest heaving, his lungs feeling like raw flesh. He managed to nod. Then he replied, "Not too much time in hand." He could hardly get the words out.

"Ninety metres, sir." The coxswain twisted round, his face set in a fierce grin.

"Was there *ever* enough time, sir?"

Marshall looked at him and shook his head. He felt completely spent and sick. *In the twinkling of an eye.* Two submarines and some hundred and fifty men. Wiped out. Written off. Just like that.

Somewhere overhead he heard the thrumming beat of the destroyer's racing screws. She would drop a few charges, but with luck they would be well clear before her captain got an echo on his Asdic. If there were any survivors from the second U-boat, which was unlikely, they would be gutted like herrings in the depth-charge explosions.

He swallowed hard, tasting the bile in his throat. He hoped that Browning would be satisfied. Mission accomplished.

A depth-charge exploded far away, like a muffled drum in a tunnel. The destroyer's detection gear had probably homed on to the sinking submarine.

He glanced at the faces all around him. Lined and set as they listened and then understood.

They were safe and that was enough. It was all they had.

5   Home Is The Sailor

FOR some unstated reason U-192 was not required to seek out the second German supply submarine. Two days after their successful attack, their avoidance of the American destroyer, they had received a brief signal from the far off Admiralty in London. In their own, special top-secret code, which had probably been dictated by Browning himself. *Return to base forthwith.*

At the time the submarine had been on the surface steering south-east towards the Freetown rendezvous beneath a velvet sky where the stars had appeared to reach from horizon to horizon.

As Marshall had sat in his cabin with Gerrard reading the decoded signal he had been aware of his own confused feelings. The sudden recall might mean that their deception had been revealed to the enemy, so that they were needed for some different scheme without delay. Browning's staff would have been following their progress by using a duplicate set of codes and rendezvous-boxes, and would have realised they had either been successful with their first attack or had been sent to the bottom.

For the first time since quitting the secluded Scottish loch he made a signal, equally brief, but one to let Browning know they were at least alive. He had pictured the radio operators and coding experts, both Allied and German, who might have picked up their crisp acknowledgement. But whatever anyone might suspect, Browning would know for sure. One of his plans had been carried out, and his brain-child would be given due credit.

Throughout the boat the news had been recieved with surprise. Nobody in his right mind had been looking forward to a second clash with the U-boat *milch-cows,* but once the new course had been laid, the tubes reloaded and batteries charged, most of the company had made the best of it. With the announcement of a recall the reactions had been as mixed as Marshall's.

The first part of the return passage had gathered something like a holiday atmosphere as the boat had headed north-east, avoiding shipping lanes and spending most of the time on the surface.

Whenever possible men were allowed to take turns on deck, sunning their bodies, laying naked on the casing as if on a pleasure cruise. Once, when Frenzel had requested him to stop the boat so that divers could inspect the port screw, Marshall had permitted swimming parties, although never more than a few yards from the hull. It was not usual, but then neither was their role.

When they had drawn nearer to the convoy routes and into the range of patrolling aircraft they had been made to realise that their brief freedom in sun and warm seas was likely to be their only reward for their achievements.

Few bothered about what the Germans might or might not do. As day followed day, the R.A.F. and the American land-based bombers were cursed with more feeling and anger than any enemy.

Twice they were faced with disaster. The first occasion had been while they were surfaced, charging batteries, making sure they were fully prepared for the final leg of the journey home. From nowhere, or so it had appeared, a fat Sunderland flying-boat had plunged out of low cloud, machine-guns hammering, depth-charges dropping from either wing as the U-boat had dived frantically for safety. Off the coast of Ireland they had been caught again. This time it had been a twin-engined fighter, streaking out of the mist barely feet above the water. The bullets had clanged across casing and bridge, and one had passed through Devereaux's oilskin between his arm and his side. He had drawled, "Some bastard must have it in for me!" But he had been badly shaken, nevertheless.

For two whole days they had idled back and forth west of the Outer Hebrides, following their instructions, awaiting the right moment to make their approach and meet their guide, the armed-yacht *Lima.* To attempt to make an independent land-fall would have invited disaster. What with minefields and hidden booms, the chance of being caught on the surface by some prowling aircraft or armed trawler, they had to wait their turn if they hoped to continue their work in secrecy.

During those last days Marshall had had plenty of time to watch his companions. Daily he had found it harder than he had believed possible to meet Frenzel's eye, to join him in casual conversation, or worse, to be left alone with him. What would he say? How would he feel when Browning broke the news about his wife and child? And Gerrard seemed to grow more restless and less inclined to share his confidences as hour by hour they crawled back and forth, rising occasionally to periscope depth to make a fix, check a bearing, or merely to take a quick glance at some passing vessel. Because of his concern for the two officers who were perhaps closest to him, Marshall spent less time that he would have liked with young Warwick. He had changed most of all. In the two months they had been at sea he had altered from a boy to a hollow-eyed stranger. Marshall was fully aware of the reason, but knew that to interfere at this stage might push him over the edge. He had seen him in the control room when they had headed away at full speed from the destroyer's depth-charges the sounds of the damaged submarine breaking up as she plunged to the sea-bed. Shaking uncontrollably, his face like chalk, he had been staring at the side of the hull as if he had expected it to cave in on all of them. But it was not fear of dying which had changed him. Marshall had heard Buck saying quietly to Gerrard one night, ''What can you expect, Number One? He's just a kid, seen nothing, knows nothing but what he's got from books. Then it all became real and nasty and he's made to kill. The gun crews were too busy yelling and pulling triggers. But *he* had to stand there like some bloody executioner making sure they cut down every last living Jerry, when seconds earlier thay had been waving at each other like mates.'' There had been a pause and Buck had added harshly, ''Me, I don't give a sod for any of 'em. I've seen what those bastards have done. I'd gun down any Jerry given the chance. But young David's not like us. Not yet anyway.''

It was to be hoped that some shore leave, being able to mix with ordinary, everyday people would make a difference. Otherwise, valuable or not, he would have to recommend that Warwick be transferred out of submarines for good. Like many others had been. Too much depended on each of them. They needed one another's strength, not despair.

At the arranged time, as dusk had eased some of the hostility from the sea's face, they had turned towards the land. The sound of a small charge being detonated under water had told them their guide had arrived, and firing a smoke float to the surface they had gone to periscope depth again, had picked out *Lima*'s blue sternlight and had followed her towards the shore.

Surfacing for the last haul along the loch, Marshall stood on the gratings, leaving the conning to Gerrard and the mooring preparations to Buck. Loch Cairnbawn seemed exactly as before. It was April now, but the air was as keen as a knife, the choppy water just as dark as when they had left the place with the same stealth as now. So unlike his other patrols, he thought. No welcoming signals or cheering ships' companies lining the guardrails to watch them pass, their Jolly Roger showing some new conquest or successful attack.

He touched his face, thinking of the bath and change of clothes he would get once they had reached the old *Guernsey*'s side again. He had shaved an hour or so earlier, but it was not the same. He felt dirty and unkempt. That at least was normal enough.

A motor boat chugged out of the gloom and turned easily to run parallel with them. He found himself wondering how those men would have reacted if the enemy had captured a British submarine and were now escorting her right into their own base.

He saw the swift exchange of signal lamps, a show of lights close to the water where the mooring parties were ready and waiting.

"Slow ahead together." The motors thudded uneasily and some spray burst above the bridge screen like hail. "Port ten." He watched a torch revolving slowly, saw it reflect against the tall side of the depot ship. "Midships." He heard Buck calling hoarsely at somebody beyond the bows but kept his eyes on the torch for the last few yards. "Slow astern starboard." She was swinging nicely, and he saw the heaving lines snaking across the torch beam, heard the shouts from the waiting seaman, the grate of mooring wires.

"Stop together." The hull gave a quick shudder and he felt the bridge begin to roll as the loch's uneasy waters took charge.

"All fast forrard, sir!"

More shouts, the sounds of padding feet along the small H-boat to which they were making fast. He wondered if she had been out while they had been away.

"All secure aft, sir!"

"Very good." He lowered his face to the voicepipe. "Ring off main motors." He waited until Gerrard had passed his orders and added, "Home and dry, Bob. Send some extra hands up to help rig the awnings around the conning-tower. Just in case we're still on the secret list."

He tried to recapture some of the old feeling. Elation, pride at getting his command, his men back without loss.

Buck clattered on to the bridge banging his hands together. "Permission to open the forehatch, sir?" He jumped as the generators rumbled to life. "Hell, I'm getting edgy!"

"Yes, carry on. The depot ship's people will be giving the boat a going over at first light. Might as well get our gear moved."

More feet on the casing and a head appeared over the rim of the bridge. It was the bearded commander, Marker.

He thrust out his hand and said, "Bloody good to see you!" He peered down the oval hatch, his eyes glinting in reflected lights below. "No trouble with the engines then?" He dropped his voice. "Captain Browning is waiting for you, but he wants to see your engineer officer first."

"Yes." Marshall knew Buck was listening and said slowly, "Tell him, will you?"

The commander turned away. "What a rotten welcome for him."

Marshall watched him running his hands along the bridge screen. You're more excited about getting your toy back than caring about Frenzel's family, he thought bitterly. And why not? Marker had become hardened. Watching boats go out and never return. Seeing the empty seats in this and other depot ship wardrooms. Nobody ever mentioned the missing. They were made to disappear. As if they had never been.

Frenzel thrust himself through the hatch, he was still wearing his stained boiler suit, and asked, "What's all this, sir? I've a lot to do before those depot ship loafers get their hands on my engines!"

Marshall said quietly, "Get along over to Captain Browning. Your chief E.R.A. will watch things till you come back."

Frenzel opened his mouth and shut it again. After a pause he replied, "Very well." He looked at the commander but did not seem to see him. "I'll be off then."

Marshall watched him go. *He knows. By God, he's guessed already.*

The commander cleared his throat. "Now, if you'll come with me, old chap, I'll get down a brief report." He dropped his eyes. "While we're waiting."

Marshall walked to the voicepipe. "Control room. This is the captain. Inform the first lieutenant that I'm going to the depot ship." He snapped down the cover, feeling the smoothness of the brass despite being so long under water.

Had things turned out differently it would be a German's hand closing the voicepipe now. Another harbour, another set of rules.

He took a quick glance at the men working by the forward hatch. But the same bloody war.

Marshall walked into the big cabin below the *Guernsey*'s bridge and heard the commander withdraw behind him, closing the door very quietly. Browning was standing by the desk, his eyes empty as he shuffled a pile of signals with one of his huge hands. Then he turned and studied Marshall with something like surprise.

"Sorry. I must be getting old." Some of the burden seemed to slip away and he strode across the carpet, both hands outstretched. "I can't say what it means to see you back safely. And you've done well. Damn well."

Marshall watched as the other man moved heavily to the decanter and glasses on the small table. Browning wasn't joking. He looked ten years older.

He was saying, "I saw Lieutenant Frenzel. Told him as best I could."

"How did he take it?"

Marshall took the proffered glass, noticing the stains on his faded reefer. Against the bluff captain he looked like a tramp.

"Didn't say much." Browning turned the glass round in his fingers. "I think he knew why I'd sent for him." He raised the glass. "Well, here's to you anyway. I'm bloody proud of you."

It was whisky. Neat and fiery. After two months without so much as a sniff of it Marshall could feel it going to his head like a drug.

They both sat down opposite each other, momentarily separated by their thoughts of Frenzel, what it might do to him.

"I expect you're dog-weary, so I'll try to get things moving." Browning seemed unwilling to begin. "You'll be wondering about the recall." He swallowed some whisky. "Well, the second supply boat was sunk in harbour. Never made it to the rendezvous. She and a sister boat in the same dock.

The R.A.F. laid on a big raid. Lost twenty planes there and back, but did a fine job. It'll keep the Jerries hopping for a few months. And now you've bagged the main one, which the enemy'll be relying on still. We've heard nothing to suggest they know you sunk her." He shook his head. "And you caught another U-boat for good measure." He sounded bewildered. "Marvellous."

Marshall listened to the wind sighing against the hull. Despite the cabin's steamy heat he felt cold. He needed to bathe and change. Adjust his mind to an absence of danger and fear. But something in Browning's attitude worried him. Playing for time, as he had when they had first met.

Browning said suddenly, "Fact is, the Admiralty has required us to hand over the captured codes. Escort group commanders, hunter/killer frigates and the rest will use 'em to full advantage and be able to exploit what you've started. Their lordships insist that for the next month or so it will do far more good than individual operations like yours."

Marshall let the whisky burn across his tongue.

"I expected that, sir. But of course it will mean that the enemy will realise what's happened just that much sooner. The codes will be changed. Maybe the tactics, too." He saw again with stark clarity the mounting orange ball of fire as the supply boat had gone up. Tons of fuel and ammunition. Torpedoes and men. A cameo from hell. He sighed. "And what of us? Do we become *His Majesty's U-boat* and take a conventional place in things?"

Browning looked at the carpet. Where Marshall had been standing were two small oily marks from his boots. Like little horseshoes.

He did not smile. "Well, not exactly. It is felt that you can do a lot to help in the same unorthodox way as before——"

He broke off as the door opened and a voice asked crisply, "All right to join the party, sir?" He did not wait for permission but strode into the cabin, a brief-case under one arm.

Marshall made to rise but the newcomer waved him down. "Not to bother. You look bushed." He smiled, showing very even teeth. It was a smile without warmth.

"This is Commander Simeon." Browning sounded unusually formal. "He's been running our liaison with Intelligence and the S.O.E."

71

Marshall eyed Simeon thoughtfully. Much as he remembered. Square face, neat fair hair. Well-pressed and impeccable. The man who had married Bill's widow.

Simeon said swiftly, "Just read part of the report you gave to Marker. Good stuff. The very thing to make the top brass take notice." He chuckled. "Try hard enough and you eventually get through even the thickest skull at the Admiralty."

He unlocked the brief-case and flicked open the top in one movement. Well practised, Marshall thought. Like everything else about him. He did not seem the sort of man who would ever act wastefully. Deed and effect.

Simeon was saying, "Captain Browning has told you about the captured codes, I imagine? But I'm not sorry. We've got a perfectly good U-boat at our disposal. It would be a tragic waste to employ her on dreary, everyday patrols, eh?"

"I've never found them *dreary*." Marshall could not hide the bitterness.

Simeon regarded him calmly. "No. Maybe not. However, when I explain. . . ." He glanced at Browning and nodded. "I'll take a glass if there's one going." He showed his teeth. "Sir."

Marshall darted a quick glance at the elderly captain. It was sickening to see the way he shambled over to get a drink for a man who was officially his subordinate.

Simeon removed a pink file from the case and opened it, one hand outstretched for the whisky. "Cheers," he said. "Here's to us, then."

Marshall watched him coldly. No wonder Browning was in awe of him. Simeon was going somewhere, no matter who got in his way. It was written all over him. Clear mind, quick grasp of events. A man with his own destiny very much in the forefront of things.

Simeon frowned and ran a finger down the file. "Strange how luck comes into even the best-laid plans. That Jerry who escaped from the Icelandic camp, for instance. He was found half-dead with cold less than a quarter of a mile from the place. But the fear of his escape was enough to get things *moving*. To send you off to sea double-quick, when if the brains in Whitehall had had any say in it, you'd have been rotting here in the loch for weeks."

Browning said, "I was doing my best. They couldn't have stopped U-192 from sailing for much longer anyway. The enemy would have got wind of it. Marshall might have run slap into a trap!''

Simeon turned on him. "You think that would have moved them? Their idea of warfare is watching films made twenty years ago!'' He brought back a smile just as quickly. "But as I just said. Luck stepped in. U-192 proved what a submarine can do when not required to slam tin-fish into merchantmen who can't hit back, eh?'' His eyes came round to Marshall. "No offence to you, of course.''

Marshall tried to relax. "I did wonder.''

Simeon nodded. "That's the ticket. Keep wondering. That way we'll get on like a house on fire.'' He looked at Browning again. "By the way, sir, I've asked Marker to lay out U-192's report. He has it in the operations room. I think he'd like your—'' he paused as if searching for the right word, "—your opinion.'' He walked to the table and picked up the decanter. "About now, I think, sir.''

Browning walked to Marshall's chair, his face heavy with suppressed anger. "I'll see you later. Damn good to have you back.'' He did not turn towards Simeon as he added hotly. "To see a real submariner again.'' He strode to the door and slammed it behind him.

Simeon shook his head. "Pathetic. Nearly four years of war and we're still bogged down with fogeys like him. I often wonder if Admiral Dönitz is plagued with old-age pensioners, too!'' It seemed to amuse him.

Marshall sipped his whisky, his limbs suddenly relaxed. Simeon was trying to provoke him through Browning. Or something very like that.

He replied evenly, "Not too many pensioners about with Victoria Crosses, I'd have thought?'' He smiled. "Sir.''

"Possibly.'' Simeon took several more seconds to study the file. "But I'm not here to discuss him.'' He was momentarily confused. Off balance. "The important thing is that I, that is *we* have another job lined up. I've been burning the midnight oil for weeks with the Intelligence boys, waiting to hear that you'd sunk that supply boat and were ready for recall. Personally, I'd have requested that Browning's plan be cancelled from the start. U-192 might have been destroyed, and we'd have lost a valuable commodity with her. As it worked out, we gained. The brass were impressed, and we have been given more scope perhaps because of their inflated optimism.''

Marshall said bluntly, ''Captain Browning's idea will have saved many lives. Troopships which might otherwise have been sunk will now stand a better chance of reaching harbour. Escorts with the new knowledge, and until the Germans discover otherwise, will catch more U-boats than they would without it.''

Simeon sighed gently. ''I can see that Buster's been talking to you!'' He smiled. ''No matter. Hear *me* out now.''

Somewhere overhead feet moved restlessly on the bridge gratings and a tannoy croaked, ''Chief cook report to the gally!'' So U-192's men were coming aboard now. To their first good meal for weeks.

Simeon continued. ''To lose a troopship, or any vessel in wartime, is a bad business. But if we threw in the towel after our record in disasters we'd have been polished off years back.'' He leaned on the desk, his eyes very bright. ''But this is the year to change all that. For the first time the Atlantic battle is on the turn. More U-boats sunk, more convoys getting through. In North Africa the Germans are on the run. By next month the Afrika Korps will be forced to surrender or get out of the fight as best they can. Their own Dunkirk, if you like. After that the Allies will have to take the plunge. Force an invasion in Europe.'' He lowered his voice slightly. ''And it will have to be *perfect*. The top-secret label is on this, of course, but we're going into Sicily and up through Italy.''

Marshall remembered Brow.....g's enthusiasm when they had first met. Almost his own words.

Simeon added, ''Our people will try to make a secret páct with the Eye-ties, of course, so that as we advance they will come over to our side. Leave the Germans on their own.''

''They're not going to like that.'' He watched Simeon's quick movements. The unruffled confidence. He could still not see what Gail had found in him. Had made her turn her back on Bill.

''An understatement. And *that* is why this invasion must go like a clock! All over Europe the occupied countries will be waiting and watching to see how we get on. Another Crete, another Singapore, another anything, and our chance of invading Northern France and bashing on to Berlin will be set back for years. May be forever.''

''I still don't see———''

Simeon raised one hand. ''You will. You must. For years we've had agents in every occupied country. Working with the

Resistance, forming new groups, supplying anyone who can pull a trigger or place a dagger in a Jerry's ribs. These groups, partisans, patriots or bloody bandits, call them what you will, are the ones who can help us. If they lose confidence it will be a long hard slog all the way, that is if our men even get off the beaches. I have been told that within two months of the German surrender or retreat from Africa we will launch our invasion on Sicily. Think about it. It could be just three months or so from this moment.'' He paced rapidly back and forth across the cabin. ''All the waiting. Seeing old friends die because of stupid unpreparedness, dull minds at the top, the sheer bloody waste of it all. This time we will pipe the tune!''

Marshall asked, ''Where do I come in?''

''Where you have the best chances of continuing with deception, using it as a weapon no less deadly than bomb or torpedo.'' He paused, his face flushed. ''I want you out in the Med. again. You know the stamping-ground well. You're at home there. Top security as before, but that's our problem, not yours. You will operate whenever and wherever you can do the most good. From what I've heard, you have a facility for causing chaos. Together we can give the enemy a real foretaste of what he has coming.''

Marshall rubbed his chin. ''Landing raiding parties and that sort of thing?''

Simeon smiled. ''Later. First tell me what you think of the prospect?''

''I've already done several cloak-and-dagger operations.''

Simeon twisted his mouth. ''Acting as a ferry-boat. Taking extra risks, of course, but without actually doing anything to hurt the enemy.''

Marshall eyed him coolly. How much time had Simeon been at sea since he had first met him in submarines, he wondered?

''I can see the possibilities. But it would put a double strain on my crew. It's no joke being hunted by your own ships and aircraft.''

''Who are you kidding?'' Simeon grinned broadly. ''Things can't have canged that much since I was doing patrols. I seem to recall that one submarine returning from her billet off the Hook of Holland made a signal which said she was coming home to base, *friendly* aircraft permitting!''

Marshall smiled despite his caution. ''Agreed. The boys in airforce blue can be hasty with the bomb switch. But this last job taught me what it's really like to be an enemy of both sides."

Simeon seemed content for the present. "Good. That's settled then. I'll have a talk with your people. Secrecy, keeping mum and all that rot. I think they'll see the sense of it. Their own lives will be depending on good security."

"What about leave?"

"Leave? You have to be joking. Don't forget you were recalled earlier than expected. Anyway, most of your chaps have been ashore for months, training and so forth. Bit of sea-time'll do them good." He allowed his face to become grave. "That does not apply to you and some of the others of course. It's asking a helluva lot from you. I know it. But we simply can't afford to spread our resources too thinly. Nor can we allow the grass to grow under our feet." The gravity vanished. "Go in and sink. Hit and run. That's going to be your job, and you can do it!"

Marshall stood up. seeing himself again in the bulkhead mirror. Tousled hair, oil-stained sweater and this worn reefer. Against Simeon's sleek image it was like a "before and after" advertisement.

"I'd like to tell my officers in my own way, sir."

"Certainly. Might be able to wangle a couple of days leave for a few special cases. Your Number One, for instance. Can't promise of course." He consulted his watch. "Good. I must be off. No rest on this appointment." He was groping vaguely through his brief-case when he asked, "I believe you knew my wife at some time in the past?"

Marshall watched him. "Yes."

"Splendid." He was being very casual. Relaxed. "I've got a commandeered house a few miles from the loch. You must drop in before we start jumping again. Have a bite to eat. Get the smell of diesel out of your belly, eh?" He swung round, his eyes searching. "How about it?"

"Thanks," He paused. "It was bad luck about Bill Wade."

"Wade?" Simeon smiled distantly. "Oh, yes, it was. Still, these things happen." He looked at his watch again. "Hardly any of the old crowd left now. Frightful waste. Could use a few of their sort at this stage, I can tell you." He snapped the brief-case shut and locked it in two quick actions. "See you tomorrow. Soon as you've had breakfast. Suit you?"

"Yes."

He watched him stride to the door. For just those quick

seconds he had seen through Simeon's guard, that façade of efficiency and self-control. Hostility or guilt, or it could have been the harboured resentment that he had known Gail even before Bill.

He picked up his cap and left the cabin. When he reached the entry-port where the quartermaster was lounging and yawning against his little desk he asked, "Are all my people off now?"

The seaman lurched to attention, his eyes moving over Marshall's crumpled uniform.

"Yessir. 'Cept the engineer officer. 'E's still aboard."

Marshall nodded and thrust aside the heavy canvas blackout curtain, feeling the chill wind across his face, the smell of the land nearby.

He clambered down a ladder to the catwalk and across the deserted H-boat to where the duty officer from the depot ship was checking mooring wires with a torch. Over the small, unsteady brow and then hand over hand up the ladder beside the wet conning-tower.

A muffled sentry mumbled something as he lowered himself through the oval hatch which in weeks had become so familiar to him.

He found Frenzel in the wardroom, still in the filthy boiler-suit, his hair over his forehead as he stared at the glass between his fingers.

"All right, Chief?" Marshall's voice was soft, but in the empty boat it sounded like an intrusion.

Frenzel stared up at him, his eyes dull with fatigue. And loss. "You *knew*, didn't you, sir?"

Marshall nodded. "Yes. I'm sorry. I had to agree. Now I'm not sure."

Frenzel reached over his head and without looking pulled another glass from a locker.

"I'd have done the same in your shoes." Frenzel's hand shook badly as he slopped neat gin into the glass. "Join me?"

Marshall sat down slowly. Feeling the man's hurt. His complete despair.

"I think I can arrange leave for you, Chief. Before we shove off again."

Frenzel drained his glass, some of the gin running down his chin like tears.

"Off again? So soon?" He nodded stiffly. "I guessed that would happen. Only way." He seemed to realise what Marshall

77

had said. "Leave? Thanks, but no. Her father did all he could. The grave. That sort of thing. Going there won't bring them back. This way I can hold on to something. . . ."

Marshall looked away. "Come over to the *Guernsey*, Chief. To my cabin if you like. I'll send for some food."

Frenzel said vaguely, "Shoving off so soon, eh? That's good. What I like about the sea. You get lost in it. You forget."

He stood up and carefully removed the photographs from his bunk. As he laid them in his wallet something dropped across them. This time it was not gin.

Marshall switched off the wardroom light and together they walked in silence towards the conning-tower hatch. On the open bridge Frenzel paused and gripped the screen and stared up at the sky. The clouds were moving fast but had thinned considerably so that it was possible to see the stars far above them.

Frenzel said quietly, "Don't worry about me. I'll be all right."

"I know." Marshall groped for the ladder. "I never doubted it."

They reached the depot ship and then Frenzel added. "I'll turn in, I think." He tried to smile but it would not come. "There's always tomorrow. That's what they say." He lurched against the quartermaster's desk and then headed away towards the cabin flat.

The same O.O.D. came through the screen, rubbing his hands and stamping his feet to restore the circulation. He glanced after Frenzel and grinned.

"Home is the sailor, eh, sir?"

Marshall faced him calmly. "One of these days," he saw the young officer flinch, "I hope that just *once* I shall hear you say something which is neither stupid nor childish." With a curt nod to the quartermaster he strode towards the companion ladder.

The O.O.D. turned away, blushing with embarrassment. What the hell had he said? Who did Marshall think he was?

He glared at the quartermaster's cheerful face and snapped, "Don't stand there gawping! Do something!"

"Aye, aye, sir!" The seaman could hardly keep from grinning. "At once, sir!" He watched the lieutenant hurry away. Bloody officers, he thought. Didn't know when they were well off. The O.O.D. would be in a foul mood for the rest of the watch now. He chuckled. It had been worth it to see the sub's skipper hack him down to size.

Very carefully he opened the gangway log book and eased out his last letter from home.

Throughout the moored depot ship Marshall's men prepared to settle down for the night.

With the hot water almost touching his mouth Lieutenant Devereaux lay full length in a bath, his mind drowsing and reawakening as he thought of the bullet which had clipped through his coat, missing his heart by inches. In his cabin Gerrard sat with a half-finished letter to his wife. Not knowing how to complete it, or whether he should first find out about the chances of leave. In the adjoining cabin Frenzel lay face down on the bunk, still in his boiler-suit, his legs outstretched as he had fallen. He was not asleep. Nor did he want to. He was afraid of losing the mental picture. As he had last seen them. Waving to him as he had gone to catch his train. Once he twisted his head to listen. In the next cabin he could hear young Warwick pacing back and forth like a caged animal. Three paces this way. Three back again. Poor little bastard. But with luck he'd get over his brief moment of horror. Whereas. . . Frenzel buried his face in his pillow, his shoulders jerking violently to his grief.

In another part of the ship, in a large cabin which they shared together, the chief petty officers sat around a table in contemplative silence while Starkie, the wizened coxswain, refilled their mugs with hoarded rum.

Keville, the chief electrical artificer, swilled the rum around his mug and smacked his lips.

"Well, 'Swain, what d'you think?"

Murray, the chief engine-room artificer, was lolling forward, his eyes almost shut.

"Wot about?"

The coxswain regarded them both with a thin smile.

"I *think* we'll have another tot all round, right?" Keville shook his head, the action making him wince. "No, I mean about the last patrol."

Starkie sighed. One more swallow of rum and he would go under. He had it timed almost to the spoonful.

"I never think about the last one, matey. Nor the next one neither. I just think of *now.*"

He pushed the bottle to safety as Murray's head came down on the table with a dull thud.

Keville eyed him blearily. "You *worried* then?"

" 'Course I'm bloody worried!" Starkie gave a relaxed grin.

79

"This silly sod might have broken our bottle!"

Their tipsy laughter reached Petty Office Blythe, the yeoman of signals, who was lying on the other side of the bulkhead. He had been trying to read a thriller but was going to give it up because of P.O. Cain's snores from the upper bunk. Good old Starkie. Stoned again. He thought suddenly of the blazing guns, the scream and rattle of cannon fire. Warwick's face as he had come running aft when the order to dive had sounded. Starkie had survived one sinking, though God alone knew how. Just skin and bone. But with him at your elbow and a skipper like Marshall you should stand a good chance.

He switched off the reading lamp. By Christ, we need all the chances we can get, he thought fervently. Then he too fell into a heavy sleep.

6   As Others See Us

WHITHIN two days of her return to Loch Cairnbawn things started to move rapidly so far as U-192 was concerned. Either Browning or Commander Simeon, or both, seemed to have made certain that whatever operation or mission she might be required to execute, her company, from captain to junior seaman, would be able to handle it. Almost hourly, or so it appeared to Marshall, mysterious experts arrived to divide the submariners into small groups, whisking them away in motor boats, or ferrying them ashore where they were met by army trucks and carried swiftly to some new instruction.

Marshall's duties kept him concerned mainly with the progress of work aboard his own command. Paperwork and intelligence files, plus the normal round of seeing men for advancement or punishment held him apart from the others so that he was able to build a mental picture of what was happening. It seemed that the whole countryside was dotted with bleak camps and well-guarded sites where men could learn to shoot with pistols and automatic weapons of almost every nationality. Gullies and steep, crumbling cliffs where sailors more used to the cramped life of a submarine had to master the business of hauling each other up and down in complete darkness while a leather-lunged instructor yelled insults and threats or fired the occasional bullet as close as was prudent to add a touch of danger.

Even the experts themselves lent an air of unreality to the whole affair. Army officers wearing Pay Corps badges and flashes proved to be coldly efficient with portable signalling equipment or in the use of small but deadly explosive pencils. A major purporting to be from the Medical Corps took Buck and his torpedomen on a forced march through torrential rain and thick mud to carry out an attack on a forewarned army gunsite. Some of the kicks and blows were less restrained than had been expected, but as the umpire had dryly explained to Marshall, the Navy seemed to have come off rather better, despite the odds.

The depot ship's engineers had created, rather than constructed, a light folding cover for the U-boat's conning-tower, so that from a reasonable distance she took on the appearance of a British submarine. Once ready for sea it could be dismantled and clipped on to the casing like some weird umbrella.

After the first grumbles and loud-voiced compl‾‾‾ ‾‾ submariners settled down to their hurried training w‾‾ ‾‾husiasm. It was different, and as their bodies becam‾ ‾‾rdened to the exercises and the Scottish weather they discovered they had drawn together as a unit, far more so than when they had gone to seek out the *milch-cow* on the other side of the Atlantic. Partly because of all those others who had come to offer aid and instruction. Most of all because they felt that at last they belonged, if only to be recognised by this small élite of experts.

At the end of ten days the pressure eased. As if everyone had exhausted both ideas and energy. In the limited time available they had taught the submariners all they knew. What happened from now on was up to them. And, of course, the enemy.

Browning was rarely far away from the various training activities. Bellowing encouragement to panting and puffing seamen, or squatting on his shooting-stick like a great bear trying not to miss a moment of it. He was sharing it as best he could, and Marshall often wondered what would happen if he got transferred to some desk job. Worse, if Simeon took over the whole organisation from him.

Browning had come to him on the last full day of training. He had found him working in a borrowed office in the depot ship, coat-off and surrounded by clips of signals, returns of stores and fuel, spare parts and almost anything else which could be gathered into one place.

He had said. "Thought you ought to know, Marshall. The Germans will know today that the crew of U-192 are in our hands. Prisoners of war. We couldn't keep it secret forever. It's not humane. Nor right."

Marshall had considered the news with mixed feelings. In many towns in Germany there would be lighter hearts because of the announcement. Wives and parents, children and girlfriends. Even the people who had merely known the U-boat's last crew as neighbours and workmates in that other world of peace. Browning had been right about one thing. It was the only humane course to take. The Geneva Convention laid down rules, but in war it was about the only one not so far broken by either German or Briton alike.

"They'll know about us then, sir."

Browning had shaken his head doubtfully. "Not so far as I can discover. The German crewmen were taken away by their escort before our people got to the fjord. So far as they know, their boat is lying on the bottom where they left her. We've made certain that the rumour is well circulated. But when you go on your next mission you'll be without your 'cover'. U-192 has ceased to exist. Your guise for each operation will be as you think fit. Visual, rather than having false papers, so to speak."

"I think I prefer it, sir." Marshall had felt some sort of relief without being able to put a finger on it. "I don't mind using our skills against the enemy, our experience and bloody-mindedness. But the other sort of war leaves you feeling dirty inside." He had thought then of Warwick. "You wave to someone, a man you only recognise as an enemy, yet one who is for those last moments your friend in his own eyes. Then you cut him down."

Browning had watched him gravely. "Commander Simeon **might not agree with you. He would** say you were deluding yourself. That a war seen only through a bombsight or periscope is as unrealistic as allowing the enemy to know about our captured Germans. To him the war is everything and anything which can be used."

And people too, Marshall had thought. But he had had to admit there was substance in Simeon's reasoning. The pilots who carried bombs over cities and returned to their bases after each massive raid saw nothing of the pain and horror they left behind. Through the periscope lens you could hear no sound as the scalding steam exploded in the engineroom of a torpedoed freighter or tanker, the screams of those trapped between decks, driven mad with horror, praying for death.

Maybe that had been what Simeon had meant when he had spoken with something like scorn of the contest between torpedo and unarmed merchantman. There was a lot more to it than that of course. There were enough submarines lying on the bottom as proof of the balance. But the other evidence was also there in plenty.

Then, on the last day, some leave had been granted. Local liberty for the bulk of the company. Forty-eight hours home leave for a handful of others. Gerrard had gone south to see his wife. Barely time to kiss her and pay the bills before hitching a ride back again. Knowing Gerrard, it was likely he would find a friendly pilot to fly him to that windswept airstrip. Marshall hoped so for Gerrard's peace of mind.

Two seamen had been allowed home because of the air raids. One had lost his mother in a hit-and-run raid near London. T' seaman was nineteen, but had become the man of the house when his father had been killed at Dunkirk. The other had lost his wife. She had been caught when the bus carrying her home from an aircraft factory had jolted over an unexploded bomb.

Buck had gone off on a lone fishing trip, leaving a telephone number where he could be reached. One of the depot ship's officers had remarked that the inn to which the number belonged was most attractive. As was the landlord's wife. More to the point, the landlord was in Ceylon with the R.A.F.

But as is the way with sailors, most of them remained close by the ship. After craving for ..ave and cursing all and sundry because of the lack of it, they restricted their runs ashore to the naval canteen two pubs and the somewhat primitive hospitality of a nearby farm, where it was rumoured the owner man-ufactured his own "juice."

A twenty-year-old stoker named John Willard went ashore on local leave with no intention of returning at all. His desertion cast a pall of gloom over the rest of the company, spoiling their well-justified pride in what they had achieved together.

Simeon had said of the deserter, "He must be caught and brought back. I don't care how they do it. I don't give a bloody damn if some redcap blows his stupid brains out!"

The young stoker's home was in Newcastle, but he was picked up by two officers of the S.I.B., who had been warned to watch out for him, within fifty miles of the loch.

It was never healthy to keep a man aboard a submarine who tried to desert. There was too much scope for wilful damage or careless inattention when a man hung under a cloud like that. But again, he had to agree with Simeon. It was equally unsafe to let the man pass through the usual channels of court-martial and punishment. In a detention barracks, and afterwards in any ship or harbour where he was sent, the aggrieved stoker might blurt out the secret, or even part of it, which would then filter through to other, hostile ears.

The stoker was brought back to the *Guernsey*, handcuffed to his escort and guarded by the two plainclothes men from the S.I.B. Marshall watched the sorry little procession as it was assisted from the guardboat and wondered what he should say to the man. It was a strange feeling. For once he could do or say practically what he liked. Browning had told him so. Simeon had added his own signature to the report of the man's arrest.

As he sat in the borrowed cabin Marshall considered his new situation. His role, his command, even his company were on the secret list, restricted to a mere two or three hundred people. In a war which involved many millions they were pretty good odds. To the enemy U-192 was written off, one more victim of the Atlantic battle. In the Navy's official records she did not exist. Marshall and his men were listed merely Naval Party so-and-so. On special duties. Top Secret. It could have meant anything.

But in reality he commanded a submarine and was responsible for real people. Stoker John Willard was one of them.

As he sat at the littered desk Simeon stepped into the cabin and slid the door behind him. As impeccable as usual, his face was set in an impatient frown.

"You going to see this chap now?" He threw his oak-leaved cap on to a chair and groped for a cigarette.

Marshall nodded. "Yes. My Number One's still on leave. The navigator will deal with it."

Devereaux would like that. The second time he had been called to act as first lieutenant because of Gerrard's absence.

Simeon blew out a stream of smoke. "Devereaux seems a good type. Proper background. Makes a change these days."

Marshall sighed. It was hard to stay calm, to remain uninvolved with Simeon's likes and dislikes.

"By the way." Simeon was peering through a salt-stained scuttle, his eyes reflecting the grey water below. "You'll be shoving off in about two days time. Your orders will be arriving later this afternoon. Just the bare facts of course. I'll fill you in on *details*."

Marshall was about to answer when there was a tap at the door and Devereaux stepped over the coaming, his features urbane as he reported, "Prisoner and escort, sir." He glanced at Simeon without any change of expression.

Through the open door Marshall saw Starkie, a sheet of plywood under his arm, pinned to which were the details of the stoker's crime. The coxswain looked slightly rumpled, as if he had just been called from his bunk.

"Very well. Remember what I told you. This is not a trial, Pilot."

Devereaux straightened his cap. "As you say, sir."

The stoker was duly marched in and stood between his escort and the coxswain while the latter rattled off the date, time and place of the offence, where he was arrested. None of it seemed to have any effect on the prisoner, nor was it possible to picture him as a deserter.

Willard was small and round-faced, looking even younger than his years. Whenever he had noticed him in the past Marshall had seen him as one more of Frenzel's scurrying, boiler-suited mechanics, usually covered in grease and oil. More part of the machinery than an individual person. Now, in his best uniform, a gold-wire propeller on one sleeve, he presented the perfect picture of innocence and vulnerability.

"What do you want to tell me, Willard?" Marshall kept his voice calm. Willard looked as if he might crack if anyone shouted at him.

"Say, sir? What should I say?" He shuffled his feet. "I mean, sir, what——"

Starkie, who was holding the prisoner's cap, snarled, "Stand still! Answer the captain! 'Old yer 'ead up!"

By the scuttle Simeon breathed out noisily, the sound like an additional sign of their displeasure.

Devereaux said smoothly, "Just *tell* the captain why you tried to desert."

They all waited.

Willard was staring at some point just above Marshall's right shoulder, his face twisted into a mask of concentration.

"I dunno what to say, sir. How to begin." His chin trembled slightly as he added, "It's me mother, sir."

Marshall dropped his gaze to the desk. "Your divisional officer, Lieutenant Frenzel, speaks well of you. You've not been in trouble before. If your mother is sick you should have come to one of your officers and——"

Willard was speaking very quietly, as if he had not heard a word. "Me dad's a prisoner-of-war, sir. He was taken at Singapore. Only heard last year. We all thought he was dead. When I was on me last long leave before I was drafted here, sir, I went home." He swallowed hard. "She was——" He tried again. "She was with this bloke."

Marshall said, "All right, Cox'n. You and the escort can fall out." He looked at Devereaux. "You, too."

The door closed behind them and Willard looked at Simeon then at his own wrist as if expecting to see the handcuff still there.

Then he said, "There are two other Geordies in the crew, sir. I mean chaps from Newcastle. We all joined up together. They know me mother. If they ever found out she was. . . ."

Marshall wished Simeon would go with the others. He asked, "Is that why you went home?"

The stoker nodded jerkily. "She wrote to me, sir. This bloke had been knocking her about. Threatened to carve her if she told anyone. He's a big bloke, with several mates, too. He's been living off her, you see. *Put her on the game.*"

Marshall looked up, seeing the agony on Willard's face, the disgust and the pity. It was all there, like the pathetic determination which had taken him south to put matters right.

He asked gently, "What did you hope to do?"

"All this training we've had, sir." He took half a pace forward but recovered himself. "I've never been no good in a scrap, but those commando blokes taught me *how,* sir. How to fight dirty, to win. The only sort of fight those bastards understand!"

The telephone jangled on the desk, making the stoker gasp with alarm.

Marshall snatched it up. "I said no calls!"

But it was Browning. He was speaking very quietly. "Sorry about this. Is Simeon still with you?"

Marshall said, "Yes, sir."

"How's it going?"

Marshall glanced at the stoker. He was shaking badly and his eyes were bright with tears. Anger and humiliation perhaps. Or the edge of despair at this sudden interruption.

"Fair, sir. Could be a lot worse."

Browning coughed. "Bit awkward. I've got a call on the ship's line from the base. Personal. For you." A pause. "Can you take it? I'm afraid it must be now."

The phone crackled as Browning transferred the call. Then a woman's voice said, "I want to speak with Lieutenant Commander Marshall, please."

"This is Marshall," He kept his eyes on the closed door, hearing her quick intake of breath despite the bad line.

"Steven. This is Gail."

Marshall shifted his gaze very slightly. The young stoker was swaying from foot to foot, his face like chalk. Simeon was standing by the same scuttle, brushing a speck of dust from his cap. He did not seem to have realised what was happening.

"Well?"

"Roger's going to ask you to come over to the house." She spoke quickly, as if afraid he was going to hang up. "I knew you'd make some excuse not to come, so I thought if I—if I said I *wanted* you to. . . ."

Marshall cleared his throat. "Right." What the hell was he saying? "That will be fine." He put down the phone.

Simeon said sourly, "Browning again? Can't it wait?"

Marshall looked at the stoker. "You've been a bloody fool, do you know that? You were going to pick a fight with some local tough and probably cut his throat into the bargain. What the hell good would that do for you or your mother?"

Willard said in a whisper, "Had to do something, sir."

"Right now I'm depending on you, Willard. Your place is here, amongst your friends, people who rely on you as you have been made to do on them."

He was only half listening to his own words. Why had she called him like that? Taking the risk of rousing Simeon's suspicion and worse.

He continued, "I'll get the welfare people to check up on your story. If it's true, I'll do what I can, or rather the Navy will. If not, I'll see you stand trial. But either way, I want you here, under my command, *right?*"

"Yessir." Willard gaped at him incredulously. "Thank you very much, sir."

''You'll be confined to the depot ship until otherwise ordered. Fall out.''

The stoker turned and almost tripped over the coaming as he stumbled through the door.

Simeon opened his cigarette case. ''Bloody hell. His mother's on the game and he wants to save her! I suppose he's afraid she'll have half the Jacks from the Home Fleet ganging on the door next time he's on leave!''

''Is that what you think?'' Marshall leaned back in his chair, watching him curiously. ''I was trying to see our last patrol as it must have looked to that young stoker. His first-ever action. It was probably hell in the engineroom when the supply boat blew up. Like a volcano.''

''So what? We've all been through it.'' Simeon sounded indifferent.

''He must have come back full of it. Then he found that letter waiting for him. All round him his friends were writing to their families, mothers mostly, with a company as young as this one. How do you think he felt?'' He stood up, suddenly sick of Simeon. Of the land. ''What would *you* have felt?''

Simeon raised his hands. ''Fair enough! Keep your hair on! It's your pigeon anyway.'' Then he said in a matter-of-fact tone, ''Come to dinner tonight.''

Just as he had been planning to refuse, the answer came out equally firmly. ''Thanks, sir. I will.''

''Good.'' Simeon walked to the door. ''Any priests in your family?''

Marshall smiled. ''Not as far as I know.''

''You surprise me.'' Then he was gone.

Marshall sank down on the chair again. How easily he became riled. He smiled to himself. Getting past it. He wrote a short note on Willard's folder and closed it. What did it matter what happened to Willard's mother? They were stuck with him no matter what his reason for trying to desert. In the war they were trying to win why did any individual count any more?

Devereaux stepped into the cabin. ''Instructions, sir?''

He pushed the folder towards him. ''Welfare people.''

Devereaux grimaced. ''Great.''

''I suppose it is. People do matter, you know. In the long run.''

He stood up and walked out of the cabin, Devereaux staring after him with unusual astonishment.

Marshall studied himself in the cabin mirror for several seconds. Despite a steward's efforts, his best uniform still showed a few creases in the wrong places. Where it had lain folded in a metal trunk for far too long. But at least it did not feel damp, and the fresh shirt added the right touch of luxury.

"All set?" Simeon appeared in the doorway swinging his cap negligently in one hand. "That's better. You look a proper hero!" He stepped into the cabin. "Or as Buster would have it, a *real* submariner!"

Marshall smiled dryly. "Two a penny around here, I should imagine."

"We'd better get moving then. These roads, as they are laughingly described, are bad after dark."

Together they made their way to the upper deck and then into a waiting motor boat. The sky was very dark but without cloud. It would be a fine day tomorrow, Marshall decided. The first feel of proper spring.

Their shoes rang hollowly on the wooden pier, and Marshall realised with a start that he had hardly set foot ashore since taking command. He had certainly not been outside the base area.

A well-polished car was throbbing at the end of the pier, and a seaman stepped out, holding the door for Simeon to enter the driving seat.

Simeon waited for Marshall to get in and then called to the seaman, "Give her a good polish again tomorrow!"

The rating bobbed his head. "Aye, aye, sir!"

Simeon let in the clutch and said evenly, "I always have the car brought to the pier. Saves groping about amongst the others."

You would. Marshall watched the shielded headlights swinging across hurrying figures, sentries and barbed wire. Simeon had spoken to the sailor like a personal servant. Or the hall porter of a good hotel. As everywhere else, it seemed he had his life well organised.

Once past the gates Simeon pressed on the speed. Again, it was with a practised recklessness, cutting bends, making dark, anonymous figures jump aside for safety. The car was a good one. Expensive.

"It's not much of a house. But I got the admiral to lend me one of his chefs. The food's palatable. But I'll be glad to get somewhere civilised again." He swore as an army lorry hurtled past in the opposite direction, the driver yelling into the headlights. Simeon muttered, "Bloody pongos!"

The journey took about half an hour. During the whole time Simeon hardly stopped talking. About his work with the Intelligence services, his general views of the war, many of them openly critical of both Government and High Command. Marshall was surprised at his frankness, especially in view of their first meeting. Perhaps Simeon regarded him as a mobile extension of his own ideas and strategy, or part of some wider experiment which he had not so far completed. Several times he mentioned important names, men who appeared only in newspapers as far as Marshall was concerned. If he was boasting, Simeon gave little sign of it. It was his world. The arena for power and influence.

They shot through a wide gateway and slithered to a halt beside some parked cars. Simeon consulted his watch. "Took longer this time. Must drive faster in future." He glanced quickly at Marshall. "Let's go inside."

Marshall followed him through a heavy, studded door. It was curious the way Simeon had attached importance to his driving skill, his ability to reach here in so short a time. More importance, or so it seemed, than his place in affairs within the Service. Did it really matter, he wondered, and did Simeon secretly envy him for what he had seen and done in his own world of close combat?

It was a very pleasant house, comfortably furnished. Lived in. A log fire burned cheerfully in an open grate, and the room to which Simeon guided him gave off an air of rural prosperity.

"Few others for dinner, I'm afraid. Can't be helped." Simeon gestured to a cabinet. "Mix yourself something. I'm going to wash." He added, "Not like you. Didn't get time before I left the *Guernsey*."

Marshall smiled grimly. It was just as if Simeon always had to add his little rider. To prove that he was the busy one. A man in constant demand.

He opened the cabinet and regarded the span of bottles with surprise. No shortages here. He selected some malt whisky and half filled a glass. He found that he needed it more than usual. It could turn out to be a tense evening.

A door opened behind him, and he turned, the words ready on his lips. But it was a complete stranger. Not Gail.

She was dressed in a tweed skirt and plain black jersey. In the soft lamplight and the flickering log fire Marshall thought she looked tired, irritated perhaps at his being in the room.

"I'm sorry." She picked up a magazine and dropped it again. "I did not know anyone was here."

She had a faint accent. French possibly.

He said, "I'm Steven Marshall. Let me be the one to apologise."

He watched her as she moved to a chair. Very easily and lightly. Like a cat. She had short dark hair, it was probably black, he thought, and her eyes, which were large and partly in shadow, seemed very steady. Almost too steady.

She said, "Chantal Travis." Then she smiled. It was grave but managed to light up her face nevertheless. "My home was in Nantes."

She crossed her legs and leaned back against the cushions. Relaxing appeared to be difficult for her. She seemed to be listening, and only half with him.

"Are you staying here?" He hesitated, seeing her hands clench slightly. They were small. Well shaped. "I don't mean to be nosey."

She smiled again. "That is all right." But she did not answer his question. "I see you have decorations? More than I expected."

Marshall ginned. Simeon must have told her about him. "There's a war on."

"So I believe." She sounded distant. "A war."

He said quietly, "That was a damn stupid thing to say. I was forgetting. Are your family still in France?"

She nodded slowly, the hair falling lightly over her forehead. "My father and mother are in Nantes."

Marshall remembered her name. Travis. "You're married?"

Again the slow nod. "An Englishman." She looked at the glass in his hand. "If I may have a choice, I would rather have a drink than any more questions." She smiled at his confusion. "Pardon me. That was unforgivable."

Marshall held up some sherry and she nodded.

As he poured her drink she said softly, "Commander Simeon's wife told me something about you. What you did in the Mediterranean."

He handed her the glass, watching the light playing on her hair as she leaned forward. It was black.

"Have you known her long?" He groaned. "God, I'm doing it again!"

But she laughed. "It is all right. But no, I only met her——" She hesitated. "Recently."

Marshall sat down opposite her. It was like some invisible force between them. Holding him back. If only he had more time he would like to stay with her. Just to hear her voice. Watch the stillness in her.

"Getting acquainted?" Simeon strode past them from the door and examined the drinks cabinet with controlled indecision. "Splendid. Dinner in fifteen minutes."

Voices murmured outside and two more figures threw shadows across the heavy curtains. Both were army officers, one Marshall recognised as the so-called Medical Corps major. They shook hands all round and the conversation became general, but, Marshall thought, kept carefully away from the war. Probably for her sake. It couldn't be easy to have your country occupied and under Nazi rule.

He asked, "Is Captain Browning coming?"

Simeon eyed him over his raised glass. "Negative. Flown south to see their lordships in Whitehall."

The other army officer said, "Not that you would have asked him anyway, eh, Roger?"

They laughed.

Marshall tensed as a voice said, "Hello, Steven. After all this time."

She was wearing a flowered dress which left her arms bare. She was exactly as he remembered her.

He said, "You look marvellous."

Her hand felt ice-cold despite the blazing fire, and he thought it was trembling very slightly.

Simeon called, "New dress, Gail? Bit bare, old girl, what?"

She kept her eyes on Marshall. "It's to make the spring come up here. I saw flowers in the village and I thought. . . ."

Simeon remarked, "Good God, you'd think clothing coupons grew on trees!"

The major murmured approvingly. "You make a sight to remember. Don't listen to him."

Slowly the conversation came back again, but Marshall could still feel the tension. Gail was sitting beside the other girl. They could have been sisters, but against the flowered dress, the expensive bracelet on Gail's wrist the French girl looked even more isolated.

Marshall shook himself. It must be the malt whisky. He could not remember how many times Simeon had filled his glass. Or maybe he had been so long away from civilised surroundings he was far out of his depth.

The dinner, served with dignified precision by a naval steward, was excellent, and Marshall found himself wondering where Simeon had managed to obtain not only such plentiful food but also the ample stock of wine.

As the steward poured the brandy Simeon said, "You'll be off soon then, Jack?"

The major shot him a quick glance. "So they tell me. Bangers and mash from now on."

Marshall waited, but there were no questions. No explanations. It was like sharing table with a bunch of conspirators.

"How was Malta?"

He turned to look at Gail who was at the end of the table. She was twisting her wedding ring round her finger, her eyes very bright.

He replied, "Heavy air raids, but you know that of course. The Maltese are making the best of it."

The major called Jack said, "No choice. Poor devils."

The steward bent down beside Simeon and murmured in his ear.

"Despatch rider outside." Simeon stood up dabbing his mouth. "Better go and see what he's brought." He looked round the table. "Make yourselves comfortable. Robbins here will bring you anything you want to drink." He winked. "Anything but schnapps of course!"

The two soldiers were escorting the French girl to the adjoining room. Marshall looked at Gail. They were alone.

She said quickly, "I had to see you. To tell you about Bill."

"I *know* about Bill." He could not hide his bitterness. "Saw him before he was killed."

The other voices had faded and the dining room seemed very quiet. He could hear her quick breathing, see the way her breasts moved under the dress.

She said, "You don't understand. How can you? You don't even *want* to understand!"

"Perhaps I don't. All I know is you married Bill. While he was in the Med. you decided to leave him. To marry Simeon. What else is there?"

She stood up and walked to the fireplace, adjusting a picture, the motion automatic.

He added, "Bill was a good man. The best I know."

She turned and regarded him sadly. "It's not just a man's world, Steven. You are like Bill in many ways. But then you always were. Remember the house near Southampton?" She walked slowly along the room, touching the chairs without seeing them. "I remember when Bill came on leave once. We had had three nights of raids. Non-stop. Portsmouth got it, and Southampton had hundreds killed and injured. It was horrible." She faced him again, her eyes angry. "But Bill didn't even ask about *us*. With him it was always the next patrol, the next target, his men, his submarine." The anger spent itself and she added softly, "You know what he was like."

"Why did you marry him?"

"You know that, too." She met his eyes steadily. "I wanted you, but you were so sure you were going to be killed, remember? Like all the boys we knew, so damned sure."

Marshall stared at her. "D'you know what you're saying?"

She nodded. "I've had plenty of time to think about those days we had together. I've never regretted one of them." She swallowed. "Not one. But the war isn't just for you and men like Bill, don't you see that? It's ours too, every rotten, bloody day of it! Life doesn't stop. I wanted to get married, is that so unusual, I *wanted* a home!"

He said, "I'm sorry. I was very fond of Bill."

"Be honest, for God's sake!" She moved towards him, her mouth moist in the lamplight. "To yourself at least. When I married him you felt guilt too, didn't you? Because of the way you looked at me when you remembered how it was before."

He turned away. "It's hard to say."

She was almost touching him, her eyes searching his face as if trying to discover something.

"Oh, Steven, look what it's done to you, too! I was watching you all evening. You've changed so much."

"It makes you get hard." He thought of his reflection in the mirror when *Tristram* had returned to Portsmouth.

"Not merely that, Steven. You've pushed yourself to the limit. I meet plenty of service people these days. Roger is

94

always entertaining them. Discussing his ideas. They're not like you, can't you see that?'' She reached out and took his hands, her grip insistent. ''It's turned you into a machine!''

He looked down at her, his defences crumbling, the anger gone.

''Try to see it my way, Gail. I *have* to be the way I am. I'd go out of my mind otherwise.''

His arms were around her shoulders and he could feel her face against his chest. He could not stop. The words seemed to burst out like a flood.

''You don't know what it's like. On and on. No end to it. Always telling others to keep going, to remember the ship, the fight, the target, *anything* to hold the whole show together! I couldn't have let you share that sort of life, that kind of separation.''

He could hardly hear her as she said, ''I would have. Willingly.''

He held her away, his hands on her bare shoulders. ''What about Simeon?''

She did not lower her eyes. ''It's different with him. He gives me assurance. In his own strange way he needs me.'' She shook her head. ''But *we* had something else again. Now tell me I'm a liar.''

The door creaked and Marshall saw her eyes fill with sudden alarm. He turned quickly, an unreasonable anger rising inside him. But it was the other girl, Chantal Travis. She stood very still, looking at them in silence.

Then she said simply, ''I am sorry. The wrong room, I think.''

The door closed behind her and he said, ''I thought it was. . . .''

But Gail was staring at him with something like dismay. ''What is it?''

She stepped away from him very slowly. ''Steven, your face, just then when the door opened. I thought it was Roger. I was afraid and a bit ashamed.'' She shuddered. ''But you. You looked as if you wanted to *kill somebody!*''

He shrugged helplessly. ''Maybe I did.''

He started around the deserted table. Lost. A man apart. Exactly as she had described him. It was unnerving. Frightening. If you let it be so.

Marshall heard her say, ''One day, Steven. If we could meet

somewhere. No recriminations. No comparisons. I must hold on to that memory. I have to.'' She was pleading.

He thought of Frenzel with his photographs. Stoker Willard and his mother. Gerrard, who at this very minute was probably suffering the same torment as Bill had done. The need to go. The longing to stay.

Perhaps she was right. Maybe his anger at her marrying Simeon had been because of himself and not caused by Bill's loss. Whatever the true reason, it was too late now. For any of them.

''It's no use.'' He watched her face. Her eyes. ''It's over.''

''Only if you want it to be, Steven.''

He heard voices in the hallway. Simeon's visitor had gone. It was just as well.

''It's not what I want. Nor you either, for that matter.''

The door swung open again.

Simeon looked at them blandly. ''Old confidences, eh? That's the ticket.'' He strode over and put his arm round her shoulder, showing his teeth. ''Ah well, the party's over, children.''

Marshall nodded. In more ways than one, he thought.

7 Second Time Round

THE day after Simeon's dinner-party Marshall received a sudden change of orders. The time had been brought forward twenty-four hours. He would slip from the depot ship at 2000 that evening.

As the sides of the loch dipped into shadow Marshall sat in his cabin making a last-minute check, his mind momentarily too full to consider what might lie ahead.

Gerrard waited in the cabin doorway, arms folded as he watched Marshall putting his signature to his readiness report. In the passageway and along the casing above the constant comings and goings of feet were a reminder, as always, of the need to be sure.

Marshall looked up. Gerrard had fortunately arrived back that forenoon. The change of plans might have left him stranded.

He said, ''Can't think of anything else. Stores and fuel,

ammunition and fresh water. Have you inspected the other new gear?''

Gerrard nodded. He looked tired. "Yes, sir. It was a struggle, but we've got the extra stuff stowed just about everywhere. There'll not be room to breathe until we live off some of the rations." He gave a sad smile. "Back to the Med. Would you believe it."

Buck peered in at them. "Commander Simeon is coming aboard, sir."

His voice was still thick from his fishing trip. But the shadows under his eyes, his expression of spent satisfaction had not been caused by a rod and line, Marshall thought.

"Very well." He winked at Gerrard. "You can carry on. We'll be slipping in about thirty minutes. Better get ready with the sliderule."

The stale joke brought a brief grin.

Gerrard said softly, "With the load we're carrying I hope you don't want to do any crash dives!"

He moved away as Simeon appeared in the doorway.

He said crisply, "Buttoned up. Ready for business." He ticked off the points on his fingers. "All checks confirmed. Last mail ashore and censored. Twice. I don't think we've forgotten anything."

"Why was the sailing time brought forward, sir?"

"Oh, this and that. There's a westbound convoy gathering at Greenock, and the minesweeping boys are doing their stuff down channel tomorrow. Don't want you to get bogged under with that lot." He glanced round the cabin "Or with this boat's previous masters if they're hanging around after that convoy."

"Captain Browning's not back yet?"

"What's that got to do with it?" Simeon stared at him, his face set in a frown.

Edgy. Marshall watched him calmly. It was as he had suspected. Simeon had brought the time forward so that Browning would not be here to see them go. It was going to be *his* show.

"I just wondered, sir."

Simeon regarded him suspiciously. Then he said, "You will be picking up three agents from one of our launches. I've already had their gear sent aboard, but their presence must be kept secret to the last minute."

"I see. Are you worried?"

"Just careful. You check and check again. Intelligence work is like taking a submarine into a deep dive for the first time. Risk nothing, or you'll not live long to regret it." He sighed. "More room in this boat than my last one."

Marshall eyed him thoughtfully. It was odd he had not noticed it before. Aboard the submarine Simeon was the one who was out of place. He was feeling it, too.

Wires scraped on steel and he heard P.O. Cain bawling at his casing party. Soon now. More bodies squeezed down the passageway and he heard snatches of conversation as they discussed their recent runs ashore. Relaxed, unimpressed as yet by the task they were being given.

One voice said incredulously, "You went with that bloody woman again? Gawd, Fred, she's the ugliest party I *ever* laid eyes on. You must have flipped yer brains out."

The second voice said defensively, "What the hell! You don't look at the bleedin' mantelpiece when you poke the fire, do yer!"

Simeon smiled. "Don't change, do they?"

"I'm relying on it."

Marshall stood up, patting his pockets to make sure he had all he needed for the next few hours.

They walked into the passageway and on to the control room. Again Marshall noticed the contrast between the immaculate Simeon and his own men. Heavy jerseys and leather sea-boots. Patched trousers and a variety of woolen hats. It might help to remind Simeon of his own responsibility when they were endeavouring to translate his schemes into hard facts.

Frenzel was leaning over his panel in close conversation with Keville, the chief electrical artificer. He glanced up as they passed, but Marshall doubted if they even registered. If it were possible, Frenzel had given more of his energy and time to his engines since Browning had told him the news.

He led the way up the ladder to the bridge, wondering how Simeon would make his departure. Wish them luck. Add some comment about risks involved. Mention Gail.

They stood side by side watching the men on the casing slacking off wires and chatting to their opposite numbers on the little submarine alongside. Buck was there, pacing back and forth with Warwick. On the bridge the yeoman was testing the voicepipes, the hand-lamp and safety harnesses. He was whistling quietly. Absorbed.

A voice rattled up one of the pipes and Blythe came instantly alert.

"Captain, sir. W/T office reports, ten minutes to go. *Lima* is on station to lead us out."

"Acknowledge." He looked at Simeon. "Are you staying a while, sir?"

Even in the gloom it was possible to see Simeon's rare indecision. Then he said curtly, "No. Better get over to *Guernsey*'s W/T department. In case anything goes wrong at the last minute and I have to make new decisions."

Marshall relaxed slightly. That was more like the man.

Simeon held out his hand. "Good luck then." He swung himself over the side of the bridge and dropped quickly to the deck below.

Marshall smiled and buttoned the collar of his oilskin coat. He moved to the voicepipe, hearing the brow being hauled away as Simeon strode across the other boat.

"Control room. This is the captain. Prepare to get under way. Main motors ready."

The bridge quivered as the motors purred into life. There was no point in bothering with the diesels if they had to manoeuvre against some small boat in total darkness.

He peered over the screen. "Stand by!"

Buck waved his fist. "Singled up to bow and stern ropes, sir!"

The lookouts stepped up on to their respective gratings and made a big show of adjusting their night-glasses, knowing Marshall was just behind them.

Blythe said, "There's *Lima*, sir. Just coming round *Guernsey*'s bows."

"Good."

He thought suddenly of Gail. The feel of her skin under his fingers. The smell of her hair. *It's turned you into a machine.* He found he was clenching his fists. Damn her. What the hell could he do about it?

A light stabbed from the *Guernsey*'s bridge and Blythe was shuttering his acknowledgement with the hand-lamp before the signal had died.

"*Proceed when ready,* sir." He turned and looked at him. "*Good hunting,* sir."

"Very good. Inform the control room." He hesitated, knowing Blythe was waiting. It was expected. The thing to do.

99

"Make to *Guernsey,* Yeoman. *Thanks for your help.*"

The depot ship would probably be embarked on a new scheme within a day or so. An experimental submarine, some new underwater device, a floating pier which the army had been asking for since he could remember. He watched Blythe's light reflecting from the ship's pitted plates. He doubted if they would ever tie up alongside her again.

He shook himself angrily. "Let go aft!" He waited, keeping his mind empty as the soft breeze pushed the hull reluctantly clear of their small consort. "Slow astern together." He waved to Buck. "Let go forrard!"

Stern-first they edged clear of the towering depot ship, the water sluicing along the saddle tanks to make a sluggish arrowhead of white froth.

From forward he heard the main hatch clang shut, the scrape of wires being stowed securely for sea.

"*Lima*'s gathered way, sir."

"Very well." He crossed to the voicepipe. "Stop together." He watched the pale blue sternlight and the wash from a passing trawler. "Slow ahead together. Port twenty."

"First lieutenant here, sir. Follow the light again?"

"Yes." He heard the periscope shift in its sleeve. "We will be taking on passengers in an hour's time."

He felt the hull steady as the rudder came round, and knew that Gerrard had her under control.

"Fall out casing party."

He raised his glasses and tested them for night vision. But the shoreline houses were hidden. He thought of the first time he had come aboard. The old lady and her cat.

Buck's head appeared over the side of the bridge. "The conning-tower screen is secured, sir." He sounded doubtful. "Proper Fred Karno's effort that is."

The seamen came swarming into the bridge and down through the open hatch. Then Warwick dragging his feet, his head towards the dark slap of land.

"Keep a good lookout." Marshall glanced at Blythe's outline. "The launch will signal. But check the code."

It would be just like Simeon to send an additional boat to check their vigilance against any trick.

But he had to hand it to their organisation, his and Browning's. It must take a lot to alert coastal patrols and uninvolved vessels to ensure that nobody would stumble on their departure and raise an alarm. And they still had a lot to do. Fuelling arrangements, security screening of those to be employed, a million things.

He said to Buck, "Go below and make sure everything's stowed all right. Don't want any tins of jam rattling about in the fore ends!" He knew it had been done but wanted to be alone with Warwick.

Buck nodded. "Right, sir." He probably understood.

Marshall looked at the *Lima*'s sternlight, the blue froth of her small wake.

"I'm going to the after casing to see our 'umbrella', Sub." He saw him stiffen. "Number One has the con, but you keep an eye on *Lima*. She will sight any other craft before we do."

He lowered himself down the ladder, feeling the blown spray tapping against his oilskin as he groped along the handrail. The depot ship's mechanics had done a good job with their harbour disguise. He tested the folded screen with the heel of his boot. But the first near miss from a depth-charge would rip it away in a second.

He returned to the bridge and said, "Not like our other departure, Sub." He waited, feeling Warwick's uncertainty.

He replied, "It seems no time since we got back, sir. And now—" He did not finish it.

"I know. Can't be helped." Marshall twisted round to watch the last of the light fading above some hills. The loch was lost in complete shadow. "I wasn't expecting to go back to the Med." The words just seemed to come out. "Not after fourteen bloody months of it."

He clenched his fists into his pockets. Saying it was enough. *Fourteen months.* How long would it be this time? What were the odds now?

Warwick asked, "Was it that bad, sir?"

He remembered his own words to Gail. Was it only last night? *Anything to hold the show together.*

"No." He felt the sweat under his cap. Ice-cold. "Nothing we couldn't handle."

He had to move away. *Liar. Liar.* Why don't you tell him?

He added harshly, "Tell the helmsman he's too far on *Lima*'s port quarter! For God's sake, Sub, you're supposed to be able to stand a watch, so *do* it!"

"Yes, sir. I'm sorry." Warwick groped for the voicepipe. Blythe watched them and sucked his teeth. Warwick was a

101

good kid but wet behind the ears. The lads called him Bunny, but not unkindly. Thank the Lord it wasn't one of the other officers on the bridge, he thought worriedly. That tough egg, Buck, or old *Snooty* Devereaux. They would have recognised the skipper's trouble in a flash. He massaged his hands against the chill air, thinking of his wife in Gosport. He looked quickly at Marshall's vague outline against the bridge screen. Poor bastard. He's got to carry the whole bloody lot of us. But it's him who needs help.

On and on down the loch, following the light, with only a gentle swish of water against the hull to break the stillness.

Then, "Control room to captain." It was Gerrard. "Should be making the pick-up at any minute now, sir."

"Very good, Number One. Tell Petty Officer Cain to get his men on deck at the double."

A pause and he heard feet hammering on the ladder behind him.

Then Gerrard asked, "Everything all right up there, sir?"

"*What?* Of course it is!" He wiped his face with the back of his glove. "Sorry, Bob. Didn't mean to take it out on you."

Blythe called, "Signal from *Lima*, sir. *Boat to starboard.*"

He raised his glasses. There it was. A black blob on the water.

"Stop together. Tell Cain to stand by."

He watched the armed-yacht steering purposefully on her set course. Any unseen watcher would assume that all was normal.

A small torch flashed across the loch and Blythe said, "It's the proper signal, sir. On the button."

"Acknowledge."

He climbed on to the starboard gratings to watch the little launch as it chugged towards the idling submarine. It had to be fast.

A shout, a heaving line, and the jolting groan of timber against steel. He watched the scrambling figures as they were hauled unceremoniously on to the casing, the boat already backing clear. Less than a minute.

"Slow ahead together." The deck began to quiver again. "Increase the revs until you're on station."

He heard the seamen and their passengers groping and stumbling through the hatch, wondered briefly what sort of men volunteered for such dangerous missions. He had carried several in the past. But he had never got to know any of them. It was just as well when you thought what might happen to them. He

Warwick turned. "Did you say something, sir?"

He stared at him. *I must get a hold of myself.*

"Just thinking aloud. Forget it."

A light showed very briefly, far away, like a small yellow eye. Somebody opening a door to look at the night sky perhaps. All at once he had a craving to be over there near it. To feel the grass under his feet, to touch stone and brick instead of wet steel.

He peered at his luminous watch. Thirty-five minutes before they made their dive to trim the boat and leave *Lima* to her own affairs.

He trained the glasses over the screen, hoping to see the light again. But it did not reappear. The land had merged with the sky.

"Good lookout all round." He let his words sink in. "When we leave *Lima* astern, every ship you see will be an enemy."

In his mind's eye he could picture their lonely journey as clearly as if he was looking at a chart. During the night they would slip out into the Atlantic, past those jagged, unlit islands with names as old as time itself. Then south through the Bay and further still around the untroubled coastline of Portugal and Spain. Gibraltar. The gateway. Back to the Med. How they would all have laughed if they had known he would be coming back commanding a captured U-boat. If there was such a thing as an afterlife, perhaps they would still be laughing. While they waited for his return. To put the record straight.

Then he thought of the girl in the wardroom below his feet. Her feelings would be worse at this moment.

He said, "Send for some coffee. We could all do with it."

He could almost feel their reaction around him. Relaxing. Getting back their confidence. He smiled bitterly. The cool, calm captain. Nothing worried him but the job in hand. The super-being. Unbreakable. He heard Churchill clattering up the ladder with his pot.

So be it, he thought. The second time round.

The first three days of the passage south towards the Bay of Biscay were marred by incidents and troublesome faults within the boat. With rest periods broken and interrupted and the urgent demands made on every department, many of the company wondered if they would have to return to base.

Marshall was of the same opinion more than once, although he said nothing of his doubts to the others. After all the training and effort, and the fact they had already crossed the Atlantic to sink two enemy submarines without damage or loss to themselves made these unexpected setbacks irritating and worrying. Like a crude omen. As if the boat was telling them she was not completely tamed and obedient to her new masters.

On the first day the forward periscope gland developed a leak. It could not have come at a worse moment as they were still manoeuvring in busy and dangerous waters and would pass through the approaches to the English Channel later that same day. Frenzel's men were able to clear the fault with just an hour to spare, but the next day the officer of the watch called Marshall to report that one of the torpedoes was leaking in its tube, the air bubbling through the bow cap at an alarming rate. At periscope depth it could have been seen even by a partially-sighted lookout.

To top it all, the starboard main motor bearing began to run hot, so that it became necessary to remain on the surface when still within range of local patrols and fighter aircraft.

Curiously enough, the most worrying fault of all was when one of the suction valves jammed. Even Frenzel's mechanics were about to admit defeat when a stoker discovered it was caused by a lump of waste left behind by some careless engineer from the depot ship. The fact that it was a simple error added to their frustration.

But then, it seemed, the submarine decided to give them a break. They increased speed and surfaced to charge batteries without further incident.

During most of the time Marshall had had little opportunity to speak with his passengers, and the girl he had seen only a few times. Each time it had seemed as if she had not moved. Always sitting in the cabin chair, wide awake, looking into space.

On the morning of the third full day he sat in the wardroom drowsing over a cup of coffee while Churchill removed the dirty breakfast plates and laid a fresh place for the next officer to be relieved from watch. The motion was sickening and uncomfortable for the boat was running on the surface, the diesels thundering and making every piece of furniture and fittings rattle in an insane chorus. The sea was rough and visibility very poor. He had been on the bridge at first light and had marvelled at the sudden change in weather. It was not cold, but the waves which cruised up and over the low hull to smash against the conning-tower were more like those of winter than now.

The coffee helped a lot. Gave him confidence when demands, endless interruptions to even the briefest snatches of sleep had played havoc with his reserves. They had, in spite of everything, done well, he thought. Whatever had gone wrong, they had mastered it. On their own. He hoped the less experienced men would appreciate that point.

Around him, behind their various curtains, others slept, for the present free of responsibility or the need to strain their minds and bodies.

It was surprising how much he had missed his own cabin. On the occasions when he had tried to sleep he had been conscious of the silence beyond his curtains, as if the others were afraid to speak freely or resented his intrusion. It was quite ridiculous. Even if they had hated him they would have been too occupied in the past three days to care one way or the other.

He grabbed his cup as the deck rolled heavily across another deep trough. He felt the hull fabric shake violently as a screw came dangerously near to breaking surface, the attendant oaths from men trying to work in the control room.

When he looked up again he saw her standing in the open doorway, clutching the swaying curtains to support herself.

"Here, let me help you."

He reached over the table and took her wrist, piloting her to one of the bench seats below the bunks. She looked very pale and her skin felt damp.

She said, "It's terrible. I've just been sick."

Churchill padded into the wardroom and placed a cup between the table fiddles.

"Wot would you like, miss?"

Marshall shot him a warning glance, knowing how cruel experienced sailors could be about seasickness. He need not have troubled.

Churchill said, "Drink the coffee while I think." He rocked easily to the motion, his face set in a frown. "Scrambled egg and some nice toast." He grinned down at her. "For you, miss, *anything*." He hurried away to the galley without waiting for a reply.

She said weakly, "I don't know. It might be disastrous." She looked up at the curved deckhead. "The smell of that oil! The noise!"

"Yes." He watched her trying to swallow the coffee. In the dim lighting her face looked very young. "I'm sorry about the weather. The Bay is often like this, I'm afraid."

She stared at him. "Biscay? Are we there already?"

"Allowing for error, we're now about two hundred miles southwest of Brest. We're pretty safe out here if we keep our guard up."

"Brest. I've been there several times." Her eyes had become distant. Wistful. "How soon will it be before we get out of this—this awful weather?"

He smiled. "All being well we will be rounding the northwest of Spain tonight. Cape Finisterre. Then we'll follow the coast, just outside Portuguese waters. It should be calmer there."

"I'm glad." She lapsed into silence, lost in thought.

He asked carefully, "Your husband? Is he in France?"

She shook her head. "Italy. We were working together. But I cannot talk about it."

"I hope my lads are looking after you?" It was pointless to try and draw her out.

"Thank you, yes." She looked around the untidy wardroom, the watchcoats hung up to dry, the pistol rack, the pile of tattered magazines. "It is like being with friends." She shivered. "I will miss this security."

He said gently, "They'll miss you, too. As I will."

The girl stood up, her features alert again. "I imagine that you will have much to fill your daily lives, Captain."

He watched her as she moved unsteadily round the table. "You were wrong about me, you know. It was something which happened a long while ago. It's over now."

"It's not my concern!" She swung round and looked at him with something like anger. "I don't care what you do!" The deck tilted and she almost fell. "Just leave me alone."

"All right."

He saw Gerrard in the doorway, his eyes questioning. "Everything in order, Number One?" His tone was clipped and formal. His only protection.

Gerrard nodded and slid into a seat. "Course two-zero-four. Twelve knots." He rubbed his bristly chin. "God, I'm starving."

Churchill came in with the plate of scrambled eggs and Gerrard exclaimed, "What's this then? The Savoy or something?"

It had all taken less than a minute. He could feel the hull beginning to dive, hear the air being forced from the ballast tanks, but everything seemed confused and drowned by the oncoming aircraft.

A great wave burst over the conning-tower, drenching and choking them, knocking them about like flotsam. Even as he dragged the girl back on her feet he heard the sharp, impersonal rattle of machine-guns, the clang and whine of metal on metal all around them.

A huge shadow swept across the bridge. The plane could only have been a hundred feet overhead.

Despite the din, the urge to get below, Marshall could only stare at the seaman on the edge of the hatch. He had been hurled backwards, his hands like claws as they dug into his chest, the blood mingling with the spray and running down the man's legs.

Someone pulled him below, and Warwick almost fell after him, the girl's hand in his as he stopped her from pitching straight down the tower.

Marshall jumped on to the ladder, seeing the sea spurting up over the screen even as he slammed the hatch and spun the locking wheel over his head. Down the ladder, his boots treading on the other lookout, his fingers slipping on blood. It was still hot. Like oil from a fractured pipe.

He had to shut his ears to the man's terrible cries, to everything but the need to get the boat away.

"One hundred metres! Group up, full ahead together!" He pulled himself to the periscopes and wrapped his arms around the nearest one. "Shut off for depth-charging!"

He saw Gerrard watching him, egg around his mouth and chin. He added between breaths, "Liberator. Must have extra fuel tanks."

They looked at the depth gauges and then at the tell-tales as the planesmen fought to pull her out of the dive.

"Hundred metres, sir."

Something creaked violently while the hull took up the pressure. A man jerked with alarm, as if it had been a depth-charge.

But none came, and he guessed the airmen had been as surprised as he had been with the sudden encounter. It was suddenly very quiet, and Buck said, "He's dead, Captain."

Marshall turned and stared at the little group below the

conning-tower hatch. The dead seaman flat on his back, eyes blank and staring, mouth wide, frozen in that last desperate scream. Buck and the girl on their knees beside him, and the other lookout vomiting helplessly on to the deck. Warwick was standing slightly apart, his hands at his sides, one of them splashed with the man's blood.

The girl looked up and said huskily, "It was my fault. I shouldn't have gone up there." She reached out and touched Warwick's hand. "You couldn't help it." There were bright tears in her eyes.

Marshall recalled the darting shadow in the lens. It was always the unexpected.

"It was nobody's fault." His voice souded flat and without emotion. "You must always anticipate enemy bombers even when they're not expected to be around."

What was he saying? It was a Liberator. One of their own. Probably winging back to base to report they had jumped a U-boat and gunned down some of the deck party. But it was somebody's responsibility. His. Waking or sleeping, nobody else could share that.

He continued, "Open up the boat, and take the body to the torpedo space. We'll bury him tonight." He heard her sobbing quietly, her head bowed over the dead seaman.

Gerrard asked, "Periscope depth again, sir?"

"Fifteen minutes. Then we'll take a look." He tried to smile. "Thanks for being here so quickly, Number One. It was a bad moment." He saw Blythe and one of the telegraphists coming aft with a folding stretcher and added quietly, "Our first casualty."

Then he swung round and took the girl's arm. "Come on."

She tried to pull away, her eyes dull with shock. "Where?"

"Wardroom." He stepped between her and the stretcher bearers. "We need some more coffee." She had stopped resisting and was watching his mouth like a lip-reader. "Both of us need it."

Fifteen minutes later they returned to periscope depth, and after a careful examination Marshall found that once more they had the sea and sky to themselves.

"Stand by to surface." He looked at Frenzel. "You can start charging again, Chief."

Buck asked, "Shall I take over the watch, sir? I'm on after the sub anyway. It won't matter to me."

112

Marshall turned to Warwick. "It matters to me. You can manage, can't you?" He kept his voice very calm.

Warwick nodded dully. "Yes, sir."

"Good. Change the lookouts and keep on your toes." He lowered his voice, excluding the others nearby. "Put it behind you. It could have been any one of us."

Warwick said haltingly, "But you came up to get us, sir. You didn't have to."

"Standing by to surface, sir." Gerrard looked at them impassively.

Marshall nodded. "Right. Let's get on with it then, shall we?" He forced a smile, feeling his mouth cracking with the effort. "Number One wants to finish his breakfast!"

He glanced at the brass plate on the bulkhead, U-192, built in Kiel. Perhaps he had been wrong after all. She was not beaten, but was biding her time. He shuddered.

"And when you get a moment, Chief, have your people take that bloody plate down. I don't think any of us need reminding what it's all about." He looked at the smudge on the deck where the dead seaman had lain. "Not any more."

8   Three Strangers

MARSHALL stood by the chart table watching Devereaux's fingers as they skilfully managed parallel rulers and dividers. The chart looked stained where they had rested elbows or rubbed out calculations and pencilled bearings.

Around him he could feel gentle vibrations from the electric motors, the absence of unnecessary movement. The depth gauges showed they were cruising at forty metres, but otherwise there was little to identify with the navigator's neat lines and figures.

It was a week since that brief, nerve-jarring confrontation with the patrolling bomber. Marshall let his eyes move back along Devereaux's course, seeing each small cross or pencilled fix as a separate memory. Getting through the Strait of Gibraltar had been the most testing moment. Two British destroyers had been sweeping back and forth, probably carrying out their normal patrol of the area, or perhaps investigating some unexplained echo. Their presence had again reminded him of the need for speed and timing, and he had cursed Simeon and the other planners for cutting the arrangements so fine.

Fortunately, an ancient, long-funnelled freighter had come to their rescue, albeit unknowingly.

On one of his frequent searches through the periscope Marshall had seen a dense pall of smoke long before the ship had topped the western horizon and had headed for the Strait. He had examined her with growing interest, seeing the Turkish flags painted on her rusty hull, the careless indifference with which she had steamed towards the destroyers. It had been possible to see washing flapping from her derricks, the master himself on his bridge smoking a large pipe, his uniform cap at odds with a dirty singlet and shorts.

Cautiously they had turned to follow the unsuspecting freighter, keeping so close astern of her that the grating rumble of her single screw had sounded as if it might burst through the forward bulkhead at any moment.

The Turkish ship had obviously been so familiar to the patrolling destroyers that she had not even slowed down. Just an exchange of waves from bridge to bridge. It was unlikely that the Turkish ship would bother too much with formal signals.

Unseen past Gibraltar and along the Spanish coast, north-east to leave the Balearic Islands abeam and further still towards Corsica. Men came and went about their duties, or slept to preserve the air supply, to restore their own private reserves of strength which were tested watch by watch.

Several times they had been made to run deep as fast-moving vessels had pounded overhead, or some suspicious ship had been sighted nearby. There had been plenty of shipping in the area, Italian and neutral, and Marshall had watched one fat oil-tanker pass through his sights with a feeling of impotence. What would her crew have thought, he wondered, if they had known they were steaming within lethal distance of a full salvo? For this was enemy territory, patrolled by aircraft from Italy and Sardinia, warships from a dozen harbours, a backwater which usually lay undisturbed.

Devereaux straightened his back and laid down the pencil.

"That's it, sir." He sounded pleased with himself. "We will be at the rendezvous point in thirty minutes."

Buck had joined them by the table.

"Are you sure, Pilot?"

Devereaux glared at him. "I'm not stupid!"

Buck grinned. "Oh, it's an act, is it?"

Marshall ignored them and studied the chart more closely. Depths and distances, the place to run and hide if things went wrong. The area to avoid, where the risks of driving aground were all too obvious.

He rubbed his eyes, trying to hold back the tiredness. They felt painful, as if they were filled with grit. His mouth and tongue tasted stale. Like the air, the smell of men penned too long without freedom of movement.

"Captain, sir?" A messenger hovered by his elbow. "Major Carter asked if you'd mind joining him in the wardroom."

"Yes." Marshall pushed his fingers through his hair. "I'll come now."

He had hardly seen any of the passengers since the Bay. Getting all the rest they could, going over their plans for their mission. For *now*.

He glanced up at the vacant space on the bulkhead. They had used the builder's brass plate to help weight the dead lookout's corpse for the long journey to the sea-bed. It had been a bad moment for all of them. Unable to surface fully and open the fore hatch, they had been made to drag the canvas-sewn body up the same ladder down which he had been dragged screaming and dying. Marshall and two lookouts, Petty Officer Cain and one other man who had been the dead sailor's friend. With the dark water surging towards the hull and breaking over it in great clefts of white foam it had been an unnatural experience. Five oilskinned figures huddled together, shining in the half darkness like seals on a rock, while amongst them, propped upright on the side of the tower, the dead man's paler outline had been an additional onlooker.

Marshall had not dared to use his torch to read from the prayer book. What, he had asked himself, was the point anyway? The others had watched him, embarrassed, not knowing how to break the moment.

Marshall had said, "Right then. Let him go, lads."

The lookouts had turned swiftly to lend a hand. It did not take long. A quick slither, the grate of metal against the saddle tank as the weights carried the corpse clear and down.

The dead man's friend had craned over the screen as if the truth had finally touched him. He had shouted, "Good-bye, Jim!"

115

Marshall had touched his arm. "That was a better epitaph than anything written," he had said.

Down the ladder again. Diving stations. Back to business. *Put it behind you,* he had told Warwick. He had really been speaking to himself. It had been about then he had seen the girl watching him from the bulkhead doorway. Searching his face, her expression changing again as he had looked at her. He still did not know what she had discovered in those few seconds. Perhaps fear. Of him? Of what he had become?

He shook himself from his thoughts. He was tired. Bone weary with the job of getting the boat to this pencilled cross on Devereaux's chart undiscovered. Intact.

He strode to the wardroom and then paused in the doorway with surprise. Gone were his three passengers. As he had first met them. The girl was wearing a black coat and sat on one of the bench seats, a suitcase on her lap. The man called Moss had changed into a leather jacket and wore a jaunty beret on his head, a half-smoked cigarette protruding from behind his ear. As for Major Carter, he could have been any businessman anywhere in the warring countries of Europe. The overcoat, once well-cut and respectable, was neatly darned around the cuffs. His hat, even his shoes, wore all the marks of privations, shortages, the lot of civilians at war.

Carter asked slowly, "What d'you think, Captain? Good enough for first night at the Duchess Theatre?" He grinned. "Take care of my army clobber, won't you? Otherwise I'll have it docked from my pay."

Marshall nodded, unhappy to see them go. "I've told Petty Officer Cain to have your gear taken to the fore hatch."

Carter sighed and looked at his companions. "Come on, Toby. We'd better check it before we leave." He winked at Marshall "You know what these navy lads are like. Light-fingered lot."

They strolled out of the wardroom, two strangers in an unreal world.

Marshall said quietly, "I hope everything goes well for you."

She stood up and buttoned her coat. "Thank you. Are we at the proper place?"

He watched the shadows below her eyes, wanting to touch her. Keep her from going away.

"Yes. Mid-way between Corsica and the island of Elba. We

came round the north of Corsica during the day. It sounds quiet enough up top." He hesitated. "Is it difficult? I—I mean, will you be able to get there all right?"

She faced him gravely. "That part is no secret. Once we have left you we will be taken to Elba. When the time is right we shall cross in the same boat to the mainland."

Marshall pictured it on the chart. She made it sound so simple. Yet it was over ten miles from Elba to the Italian coast. Patrol boats, guards on the shore, who could tell?

She continued quietly, "We will pick up the train and make our way south. To Naples." She shrugged. "Then we shall see."

"The major seems a pretty competent chap."

"Yes." She opened her handbag and studied the contents with a wry smile. "Good. One must be sure about little details." She shut it with a snap. "Yes, he's good. We will travel together, but separately, if you understand me. If one gets——" She looked away. "You know what I mean. If that happens, the others keep going."

A voice called, "Ten minutes, sir."

He did not turn. "You've done a lot of this sort of thing."

"Some."

He moved closer and took her hand in his. "I wish to God you were staying here."

"So you said earlier, Captain." But she did not take her hand away.

"Or that I was coming with you."

She smiled. "They would sniff you out in five minutes!" She gently removed her hand. "But thank you all the same. I am sorry for some of the things I said." She gave a small shrug. "In war. . . . Well, I can understand how men are."

Feet padded past the curtain and he heard the murmur of voices through the control room. Everyone would be there to see them go.

He said, "I hope we can meet again."

She moved to the door. "You'll soon forget about me. That is good." She made as if to go and then said quickly, "But maybe we *will* meet some day." She picked up her suitcase and he followed her into the control room.

Gerrard said, "All ready, sir."

He glanced at the clock. It was two o'clock in the morning.

"Very well. Pass the word. Silent routine in the boat."

He hung on the moment, watching the girl as she waited for a seaman to guide her towards the rest of her party. She turned as if to watch the transformation. From a man who wanted, needed her to stay. To being a captain again.

He said, "Slow ahead together. Group down." He watched Frenzel's hands moving across the flashing panel. "Periscope depth."

When he looked again she had gone.

"Fourteen metres, sir."

"Up periscope."

He snapped down the handles and swung the periscope in a slow circle. No distinction between sea and sky. The stars were as bright on the water as they were above. He stopped and brought the lens to full power. There it was, the small fishing fleet, their lanterns flickering on the unbroken water like additional fragments from the sky. They looked about right. Some five or six miles away. It was not easy to tell at night.

"Down periscope. Stand by to surface."

Devereaux asked, "Do you want the machine-gunners, too, sir?"

"Negative." He adjusted his night-glasses. "If we're tumbled it's no use hanging around."

He crossed to the ladder, grateful for the dimmed lights as he relaxed his eyes in readiness for those first testing seconds.

"Surface!"

It was surprisingly warm on the open bridge, and as he ran for the fore gratings he felt the breeze across his face, delicate and clean.

A hurried look round. At the distant lights where the little boats floated on their untroubled sea. On either beam. Nothing. He stooped over the voicepipe. "Open the fore hatch."

He peered over the screen, watching anxiously as a lazy swell broke on to the saddle tanks leaving a trailing wake of glowing phosphorescence. But they were moving as slowly as they dared. To reduce still further would mean adding to the risk of drift. They would never make the rendezvous then.

Marshall heard boots on the casing, a swishing sound as the rubber dinghy was hauled through the big fore hatch. It was always a bad time. With the hull trimmed right up, the hatch open. Unable to dive if the worst happened.

He held his breath and then steadied his glasses on a small shadow on the water.

A lookout confirmed it. "Boat, sir. Starboard beam."

He snapped, "Stop together."

The shadow was moving now, the silence broken by the throaty chug of its engine.

He leaned over the screen. "Make the signal!"

Buck was on the casing in charge of things. He flashed his shaded torch towards the shadow, holding it low down by the dinghy.

Marshall waited. It seemed to take an age, and he could almost feel the tracer bullets which would come shrieking out of the darkness to rip aside their deception. Instead he saw the equally brief stab of light.

He let out his breath and called, "Cast off the dinghy!" He was going to add, *as quick as you can*. But they would need no urging.

A short splash and then the small spurts of phosphorescence as the seamen got busy with their paddles. The dinghy was suddenly clear, merging with the night and with the fishing boat which had slewed round to meet them.

He could even hear the fishermen talking, caught the smell of their catch, of tarred rigging and nets. How could they be so sure, he wondered? Then he recalled what Simeon had said. About using anyone who could help. Partisans and patriots, or just people who wanted to be rid of the Germans. And those who took such terrible risks merely for money.

"Dinghy's shoved off, sir."

"Good."

He lowered his glasses and watched the sudden froth from the fisherman's propeller. She was already swinging away, creeping back to join her consorts. As if nothing had happened.

Miles off he heard the vague drone of an aircraft, and he thought of the girl who would be landing amongst the enemy. She had spoken so calmly about it. South to Naples. That was over two hundred miles, but how many checkpoints, examinations of passes, questions to which she must have the perfect answers?

"Dinghy's secured, sir!"

"Very well. Close the fore hatch." He moved to the voice-pipe. "Slow ahead together."

His mind had registered the fore hatch shutting. But he was still thinking about her, the immensity of her loneliness. Of his own.

He dropped over the rim of the hatch and slammed it shut.

Gerrard met his gaze. "Get off all right, sir?"

"Yes."

He looked at the open watertight door, as if expecting to see her there. Watching him.

"Take her down to twenty metres. We'll work clear of the fishing boats and then turn on to the new course."

Gerrard sighed. "Very well, sir." He looked at Frenzel and gave a shrug. "Group up. Open main vents."

Marshall rested his hand on the chart table, listening to the sea forcing the air from the saddle tanks.

Later, when they rose to periscope depth again there was no sign of the fishing fleet, and in the sky there was already a hint of dawn. Another day.

"You wanted me, sir?" Gerrard stepped into the cabin and looked down at Marshall.

"Yes." Marshall sat at his small desk which was strewn with papers, as was the top of his bunk. "It's time you knew a bit more of what we're doing."

Gerrard moved some files and squatted on the edge of the bunk. Like the rest of the crew he looked pale and strained, his chin hidden in stubble.

Since watching the three agents transferred to the fishing boat they had continued on a southerly course, skirting the Sicilian coast as close as they dared before turning north-east towards the heel of Italy. It was maddening to see the dazzling sunlight whenever they had crept up to periscope depth, the empty expanse of inviting sea. Like blue glass. Then, when you removed your eye from the periscope you had to turn and look at **your own men, with their worn faces, their bodies starved of** fresh air and the sun's warmth.

At this moment in time the submarine was steering due north some sixty miles from the Italian coast.

Marshall touched the intelligence pack. "You'll have to know what's happening anyway, sooner or later." He looked at Gerrard and smiled. "There may not be too much time *later*."

Gerrard nodded. "We're going right into the Adriatic, I know that much."

"There's a whole lot more, I'm afraid." Marshall cocked his head to listen. The boat was like a grave, with just the gentle purr of motors and an occasional movement from the control room. "From all our reports it looks as if the Germans will have to throw in the towel in North Africa any time now. The Allies will be getting ready to invade their territory for a change, and the Germans will be well aware of that, too. They will have seen the build-up of landing craft, support ships and all the rest of it, and spies will have kept them informed about shipping entering the Med."

Gerrard said, "Well, you can't very well hide it, can you?"

"Captain Browning seems confident that the Germans believe we're going to invade through Greece and up into the Balkans."

"Not what I'd do if I was the boss-man." Gerrard grinned. "However, as that isn't likely. . . ."

Marshall looked at him. "I know. If I was a German staff officer I'd expect the invasion to come smack through Italy or the south of France." He shrugged. "But Browning was certain the enemy has been fooled in some way to believe in the Greece idea. A ruse, or some arranged leak of plans. We have no choice in the matter anyway." He pushed the file towards him. "Our job is to add to the general idea that we *are* invading through Greece. Intelligence reports that the enemy are moving a floating dock down the Adriatic to Bari. So on the strength of that it looks as if they're sold on the same idea."

Gerrard breathed out slowly. "The dock would be ready to repair any large units which might get damaged in our invasion, eh?"

"Right first time. We're going to blow it up. Make it look as if we're doing everything we can to make it easier for our side when the big day dawns."

Gerrard shook his head. "I'd have thought that one of our submarines for Alexandria could have coped. You and I have been into the Adriatic in the past. I remember we surfaced to shell the railway line along the coast, and that was further north than Bari."

"This has got to make a real bang." He leaned back in the chair, his fingers behind his head. "So that we appear desperately keen on our work."

"I see." Gerrard was still puzzled. "But if we have to show ourselves, our future prospects are a bit grim."

"Yes."

He looked away. Gerrard still did not understand. Any one of

121

their missions could be the last. Simeon had hinted as much, and the written orders filled in most of the gaps. It would be a pity, of course, but each operation was quite separate and could end in disaster or pave the way to the next one, and the one after that.

"We'll attack in the usual way." He looked up again and added calmly, "But if things go wrong we'll use every bluff in the book."

Gerrard turned over a page, his face tight with concentration. As he shifted slightly Marshall saw the small bag below the bunk. The one she had left behind. It contained very few things, but amongst them were the clothes she had been wearing when she had come aboard. And at Simeon's dinner-party. It was six days since she had packed them in the bag, here in the cabin. Changed her identity. Prepared her mind and nerve for whatever she was required to do. Where was she? How far had she got?

Gerrard asked, "Can we believe all this guff about the dock?"

"Can't be sure." He pulled his mind back again. "The sailing time is supposed to be right. Though God knows what sort of escort they'll have."

"Not much." Gerrard yawned hugely. "They'll keep close inshore, in easy reach of aircover at all times. That's my guess." He chuckled. "It's not a bad scheme, I must say. The Jerries will probably blame their Italian allies and move more naval units to the area. They might even send more troops to Yugoslavia and Greece on the strength of it."

"That's the general idea."

Like tiny parts of some huge machine. In the occupied territories bridges would be blown up, ammunition trains derailed, to tie down more and more troops who would soon be needed elsewhere. In Sicily, Browning had said. Perhaps it was as well not to consider the more personal cost. Hostages lined up and shot. Resistance men and women tortured to death by the Gestapo. He glanced at the bag again, sickened by his own thoughts.

"How are our lads taking all this, Bob? You are closer to them than I am." He smiled gravely. "And no flannel. Not from you."

Gerrard replied, "Better than I'd have thought. They were getting a bit jumpy after that chap was killed. But seeing those three agents go off like that." He sighed. "I think it makes them feel they ought to be doing something, too." He added quietly.

122

"But after reading that secret file I don't think they need worry on *that* score."

Feet thudded on steel and Marshall heard Buck's voice in the control room. Being relieved by Devereaux. Nothing changed. Routine.

He said, "We'll be pulled out sooner or later. Even if it's only for a rest period. I'd like to recommend that you be transferred home." He saw Gerrard's face stiffen but continued, "You've done more than your share to knock this company into a team. You're overdue for promotion anyway. A good commanding officer is valuable too, you know."

Gerrard smiled. "You're not fooling me. You're thinking of my wife, aren't you? Valerie knew what the job was like when she married me."

Marshall dropped his eyes. She only thinks she knows. It's what they all say. Like Gail.

Gerrard added, "Besides, there's something else. We've come this far together, so why not finish what we started?" He forced a grin. "The war'll last for year and years. Plenty of time for promotion."

"I expect you're right." He stood up, feeling his muscles protesting, the ache of dampness and strain, "You usually are."

"In that case," Gerrard was also standing, his head bowed under the criss-cross of pipes and wiring, "you won't mind my speaking frankly?"

"Shoot."

"You've been pushing it too much. Driving yourself into the deck."

"So you're at it too, are you?"

Gerrard shrugged. "Someone has to tell you. Most people only see you for short periods. First class C.O., they say. Nerves of steel. God almighty, what do they know?" He was speaking more quickly, his voice suddenly angry. "I've seen what this game can do to people, what it's done to you. These smug bastards ashore have no bloody idea they're born. Submarines to them are just so many hulls full of men. Like cans of **sardines!**" He controlled himself with obvious effort. "I've been with you for eighteen months. You get to know a lot about someone when you've been as close as we have."

"Have you finished?" It was hard to shut him up. It always was.

"Just about. I'm like the rest who depend on you, and I'd do my damndest to help in any way I can. I think you know that. So don't carry all of it yourself. Warwick was right, you need not have risked your life to rescue him from the bridge when we both know it was his fault for not seeing that damned Liberator.'' He held up his hand. ''Maybe if that girl had not been there too you'd have dived and left the bridge party to fend for themselves. I know some who would. But I don't think so. I saw it all happening in *Tristram*. Watched you getting involved with every bloke in the crew. Carrying them when they should have been driven. Had we been given leave before getting another command you might have been all right, but I don't know. You're doing it all over again. Squeezing yourself dry.''

He gave a slow grin. ''Now you can ball me out, *sir*. I suppose I had it coming.''

Marshall thrust his hands into his pockets. He could feel them shaking against his hips.

''I'll try and bear what you've said in mind.'' He wanted to display anger or laugh it off, but nothing came. It was like watching someone else, an onlooker in a dream. He heard himself say, ''But like it or not, we're going through the Otranto Strait tonight. After that we'll find the dock.'' He swung round and stared at him coldly. ''Unless you have any further objections, Number One?''

''Very well, sir.'' Gerrard's eyes were hurt.

As he made to leave Marshall called him back. ''It doesn't help to *know*. There's nothing I can do about it.''

''I understand.'' Gerrard watched him sadly. ''And I'm sorry.''

Marshall sat down again. ''So am I.'' He began to stuff the papers into his safe. ''But you know what they say. You shouldn't have joined if you can't take a joke.''

Gerrard stepped out into the passageway. ''Some joke, eh?''

''Yes.''

He waited until Gerrard had gone and then leaned his head on his hands. It had been a near thing. He had felt it boiling up inside him like a dam bursting. He had actually wanted to tell Gerrard everything, blurt it out, try and share the strain which was twisting him apart.

As he had done that night to Gail, as he had wanted to with the girl who was now somewhere in Italy. Gerrard with his new-found happiness had almost seen through his guard, but not quite. Gerrard who might never see his wife again and was more often than not worrying about their separation, had more than he had.

Frenzel peered through the door, wiping his fingers on a piece of waste.

"Spare a moment, sir? I'd like to discuss the fuel situation and a few other things."

Marshall nodded slowly. There was never any time for regrets.

"Park yourself, Chief. Now, what's the problem?"

Thirty-six hours later found them creeping around the Gargano Peninsula, one hundred and twenty miles into the Adriatic. It had been easier than Marshall had dared to hope to slip through the Otranto Strait between Italy's heel and the opposite coast of Albania. They had sighted one partroling destroyer, and had picked up some fast-moving H.E. on the Asdic which had suggested the enemy had also got some E-boats in the area. They were probably more worried about the comings and going of the countless small craft than they were about a solitary submarine. That was someone else's problem.

The Strait had been very busy with these coastal craft. Schooners and caiques, tiny steamers which looked as if they had been built at the time of Victoria's jubilee, the sea abounded with their haphazard movements. It must be a nightmare for the enemy to keep track of them all. Marshall knew that some of them were used as supply vessels for Yugoslav partisans, others for the mysterious operations of the Navy's Special Boat Squadron. Unlike his own mission, their task was to avoid open confrontation with the enemy. A war of stealth and cunning with little hope of quarter if they were caught.

Marshall stood by the conning-tower ladder, arms folded as he watched Devereaux working on his chart. The regular ping of the echo-sounder was a constant reminder of the sea-bed. The water was shallow here. Shelving to a mere twelve fathoms close abeam. But they must stay inshore as long as possible. He pushed the thought that the dock had already reached Bari from his mind. Or perhaps it had not even sailed yet? They had crept towards Bari the previous day. Quite a lot of activity, but no sign of the dock. Something that size, and it was the largest in the

Mediterrranean, should have been visible.

Devereaux twisted round to look at him. "The Tremiti Islands are about thirty miles ahead, sir. Do you want a course to seaward?"

"No. We might miss the target if we go round them."

Devereaux pursed his lips. "Not much depth in the main channel, sir. Twenty-one fathoms at the most."

The echo-sounder pinged in the background as if to back up his warning.

"I'll bear that in mind, Pilot."

He saw the quick exchange of glances, the way Petty Officer Cain was watching him as he waited to relieve the helmsman.

He had to think. Empty his mind of everything else. If they did not meet with the floating dock in the next few hours, what would he do? Keep going all the way to Trieste where it was supposed to have started from? He seemed to hear those same words again. *It's your pigeon.*

Then there was what Frenzel had told him. The matter of fuel. The arrangements for taking more on board. Fresh water might become a problem, and then there was——

A voice said sharply, "H.E. bearing three-one-zero." A pause. "Slow reciprocating, sir. Still very faint."

Marshall thrust himself from the ladder. "Periscope depth." He tried to relax his limbs. It did not sound like the target, but worse, the newcomer might mean they would have to alter course in order to avoid meeting her in Devereaux's channel.

"Fourteen metres, sir."

Marshall said, "Very slowly." He ducked down and waited for the periscope to hiss smoothly from its well. He could feel his palms sweating on the handles, the pain in his jaw as he clenched it to steady his nerves.

The sunlight was searing, and he had to blink to clear his vision. A quick look around and overhead and then on to the bearing. He licked his lips, tasting oil. There was a lot of mist about and the sunlight on the gently undulating water was almost blinding. Then he saw the other vessel.

He said, "A motor-yacht." He brought the lens to full power. "Painted grey." He watched the distant vessel twisting and extending in the haze. It was just possible to see the tiny flag on her mast. "Italian. Anti-submarine patrol."

Behind him he heard somebody murmur, "Thought it was the old *Lima* coming to look for us!" Someone laughed.

126

He snapped the handles inwards. "Down periscope." He looked at Gerrard without seeing him. "That's a bloody nuisance."

The Asdic operator called, "Getting more H.E., sir, same bearing. Heavier but very faint."

Marshall watched the back of the man's head. "Warship?"

"No." The head shook. "Too slow."

Gerrard said quietly, "One of the tugs maybe. How many would a dock like this one need?"

The Asdic operator interrupted. "Getting jumbled H.E. now, sir. Could be back echoes from the shallows." It sounded like an accusation. "Might be another ship."

"Up periscope."

Marshall swung it round and then brought it back on the little yacht. The haze was making it very difficult. He edged round slightly and saw the far off strip of green coastline. The hump of hills further inland. It looked very peaceful.

Something picked up the sunlight and he steadied the lens, following the little shining dot until it had drifted out of sight.

"There's a plane, Number One. Probably nothing, but it might be some sort of escort."

He was just talking to delay the decision. It was too dangerous to attack anything here. The yacht would soon pick them up with her Asdic, and in these shallow waters would hold the contact until help arrived. What should he do? Wait for dark? That was too long. He might lose her while he manoeuvred out of their way and lost valuable time in taking up another position.

He felt his heat thumping against his ribs. It was like looking at a giant building which had somehow got swept out to sea. It loomed through the mist, half shrouded in haze and the smoke from a tug, although the latter was completely submerged in vapour. He couldn't lose it now.

"Action stations, Number One." He straightened his back. "Down periscope." He looked at the clock, shutting his ears to the grating klaxon. Then he said, "Tell Warwick to get ready. We're going in surfaced."

They might just get away with it. They would have the sun behind them in those first precious seconds. He had told himself in the past, it was always the unexpected which caught you. Well, the same went for the enemy, too.

He snapped, "Stand by to surface. We will start the attack."

127

9   A Bad One

AFTER the cool damp of the enclosed hull the heat was un-
expectedly fierce. Even before the last of the receding water had
surged clear of the casing and gurgled through the bridge
scuppers the sun had raised a thin curtain of steam from the
dripping plates.

Marshall trained his glasses on the distant yacht, his eyes
almost level with the screen. He found he could ignore the
figures who were still clambering through the open hatch or
running towards the deck gun below the conning-tower. But as
he watched the other vessel he was vaguely conscious of other
things, like the growing warmth across his shoulders, the strong
fishy smell which greeted his starved lungs after being so long
submerged.

"Escort bears Green one-five." He dropped his glance to the
bridge sight again. "Range oh-one-five."

He lifted the glasses and held them on the yacht's low hull.
She was zig-zagging slowly, her raked stem making a show of
spray in the bright sunlight. Whether it was a normal practice, or
some additional cover for her massive charge, it was impossible
to tell. But it could make things more difficult.

He felt Buck beside him, heard him adjusting the sights, his
breath coming fast and uneven.

From below the screen Warwick shouted, "All guns closed
up, sir!"

"Good." Without lowering the glasses Marshall said, "The
escort's skipper's not even seen us yet. When he does, be
ready."

Then he glanced at Buck with something like surprise. In his
German cap and leather coat he was like a stranger. He shifted
his gaze to the casing below. There too it seemed as if the boat
had been returned to her original owners. Warwick in his cap
and shorts, a Luger hanging prominently from one hip, and
beside him the gun's crew similarly attired, their lifejackets
making bright patches against the grey steel and armour plate.

When he looked again at the yacht he saw the towering shape
of the dock looming astern of her, its outline still halved in
sea-mist. But there was heavy smoke mingling with the haze,

128

and more beyond the slow-moving huddle to betray the presence of another tug. The latter would be needed to act as a sea-anchor if the dock was caught in a sudden squall or in some offshore current.

Buck had his chin almost on the voicepipe. "Dock bears Green three-oh. Range oh-five-oh." He glanced at Marshall. "What d'you think, sir? Shall we fire a full salvo right away?"

Marshall shook his head, wondering if the Italian lookouts were all asleep. "No. We'll need minimum settings on all torpedoes. Otherwise they might pass right under the dock. There's no telling what it draws. If we fire now we might hit the yacht and waste the whole thing."

Behind him he heard the yeoman snap, "They've seen us, sir!"

Seconds later a light blinked from the yacht's bridge. It was almost invisible in the sunlight.

But Blythe seemed satisifeid. "The same old challenge, sir." He lifted his hand-lamp. "Reply?"

"Not yet. Let 'em sweat for a bit."

Marshall tried to regain a mental picture of his boat as she would look to the oncoming vessels. The U-boat's number had long since been replaced by a large Iron Cross. It too had been badly scored by sea and slime, but should appear authentic enough. There were said to be three or four U-boats operating with the Italians in the Mediterranean. Not enough to be that familiar.

"There is is again, sir."

"Very well. Make the reply."

Through a voicepipe he heard one of Buck's team intone, "All tubes standing by, sir."

Marshall licked his lips, tasting the salt. "Depth setting of three metres. But we must close the range still further. We have to be *sure*."

He ignored Buck's quick instructions and concentrated on the yacht. She was still zig-zagging back and forth, and her course was bringing her slowly towards the submarine's starboard bow. He could see a few figures in white uniforms on her deck and more grouped around a businesslike looking gun just forward of the bridge.

He said, "Tell the control room I want a constant lookout for aircraft on the main periscope. Put a good man on it. One who won't be tempted to watch what we're doing."

Blythe asked, "Shall I hoist the Colours, sir?" He chuckled. "It seems the thing to do."

Marshall nodded. "Yes. We'll go the whole way."

He heard the squeak of halliards and saw the flag's dark shadow flap over the motionless gun's crew as it rose to the periscope standards. When he took a quick glance at the big scarlet flag with its black cross and swastika he was again surprised, even though he knew what he was going to see.

The girl was right. He could no more do her sort of job than fly. You had to be ready for everything. Deception, guilt, suspicion.

Buck said, "Pilot says that we should alter course to starboard soon, sir."

"Negative."

He wiped the spray from his glasses and trained them on the dock. About two miles away now. Devereaux was right to warn him. There were shallows somewhere to port, but they had to keep between the land and their main target. Any change now and the enemy might realise what was happening. There was probably an airfield within ten miles of where he was standing.

Buck shrugged. It was not his concern. "Bridge to control room. Steady at two-seven-eight degrees. Both motors slow ahead."

Marshall heard the slender attack periscope stir in its sleeve and knew Gerrard was watching the approaching vessels, too. Sizing them up, comparing his own calculations with those of the attack team.

The armed-yacht was less than a thousand yards away now, and he could see someone tipping gash over her side where some attendant gulls circled and dipped expectantly.

Blythe said, "Damn! They've got some lighters tied to the side of the dock, sir." He lowered his glasses and swore. "Bloody mist has come down again. Lost 'em!"

Marshall looked at him gravely. The yeoman was not one to imagine things. It now seemed likely that the enemy had lashed the lighters to the dock's sides as some extra protection. It was a good idea for catching any long-ranged shot. A single torpedo, even a pair, might explode against the lighters without allowing the real damage to penetrate further.

"Keep watching." He leaned over the bridge screen. "Sub! Get ready to do your stuff if they draw closer! Answer them in German. But if it gets difficult come up here with me."

130

He saw Warwick turn and wave, and wondered if the Italians would notice how pallid the submariners' skins were, or that they were not wearing white uniforms like themselves. It was unlikely. Submariners were a law to themselves in most navies.

Beside him Buck kept up a steady stream of orders to his men below. Bearings and ranges, courses and estimated speeds. It was a pity they could not fire a fanned salvo. But if this was going to work they had to hit with most, if not all, of their torpedoes.

He looked up, shading his eyes against the fierce glare. There were no aircraft about, just two gulls gliding level with the periscopes, probably in hopes of better fare than that offered by the Italians.

"Yacht's signalling, sir." Blythe wiped his face. "Eye-tie this time."

"Make, *not understood*." A German U-boat commander would doubtless be very correct, if not openly contemptuous towards his Latin ally.

The flag lifted and curled lazily in a freak breeze, and when he looked again Marshall saw the dock fully for the first time. In the powerful lenses it rode above its reflection like a pale cliff, its outline etched against the sky by a spidery upperworks of derricks and gantrys. He saw the lighters, long low craft, four of them. So there were probably the same number on the other side. The towing tug was a great brute of a thing, no doubt an ocean-going salvage job in happier times. The second one was still hidden astern, her presence marked by a thin plume of smoke.

Buck muttered, "Big. That's the sort of dock you'd use for heavy cruisers. Maybe even a battlewagon." He nodded. "Very useful."

Marshall did not reply. The armed-yacht should soon pass clear of her charge to lead the slow procession across the submarine's starboard quarter. The range of the target would be just right. With nothing but a clear, bright horizon behind it, it should be perfect.

"Get ready."

He stepped on to Buck's grating and lowered his eyes to the sights. He saw the yacht's jaunty green and red ensign rippling across the wires, and then as he adjusted the bar he held his breath as first the tug and then the overlapping mass of dock moved ponderously into the sights.

131

"Stand by One to Six."

He stood up slowly and removed his cap. It would be stupid to invite trouble by crouching over the bridge sights for the whole time.

He heard Buck exclaim angrily, "Christ! The bloody yacht's going about!"

What the hell was it doing? She was turning in a sharp arc, and would cross the submarine's bows if she maintained the same course. Curiosity, bloodymindedness, it made little difference now.

He snapped, "Tell Warwick to get ready."

He glanced aft to make sure that the other gun crews were also watching the yacht. The Vierling pointed stiffly at the sky, but he saw the gunlayer's fingers on the grip like a claw, his small team lying hidden by his feet below the steel coaming.

Blythe said fiercely, "Sir, there's a Jerry aboard the yacht!"

Marshall made himself turn casually towards the other vessel, the effort of appearing calm almost painful. As he moved his glasses over the yacht's bridge he saw a solitary whiteclad figure framed in the wheelhouse door. He should have guessed. Expected it. Many Italian vessels carried German personnel. To inspire confidence, as insurance. Either way it was all too obvious that this particular German was showing great interest in the submarine.

"Control room to bridge." It was Gerrard. "Coming on *now*."

Marshall tore his eyes from the motionless figure and lowered his forehead to the sights. Now or never.

"Get ready." He felt the sweat running from beneath his cap, stinging his eyes. "Easy now." He was thinking aloud but could feel the tension around him like part of himself. In the wires the dock appeared quite motionless. Docile.

"Fire One!"

He felt the hull buck as the compressed air was vented back into the boat.

"Torpedo running, sir!"

Buck held his stop-watch as if he intended to crush it, his sharp features contorted against the glare.

"Fire Two!"

Blythe said hoarsely, "Yacht's calling us up again!"

"Fire Three!"

Marshall heard the sudden shriek of a siren and knew they had been discovered.

"Open fire!"

The Vierling swung its four muzzles downward and then settled on the careering yacht. One of the bridge machine-gunners was already taking aim, the trailing ammunition belt glittering in the sunlight as he took the first pressure on his trigger.

Marshall shut them all from his mind and vision as he concentrated on the patch of water beyond the bows. But nothing happened. No telltale froth to mark where the third torpedo had left the tube.

He groped towards the voicepipe and then felt himself hurled backwards as a deafening explosion shook the bridge, followed instantly by a blinding blue flash directly below the bows. Water cascaded all round them and he saw a machine-gunner falling and kicking, his weapon swinging impotently towards the sea.

Buck was yelling, "Bloody fish must have nose-dived an' hit the bottom!" He ducked wildly as a stream of red tracer ripped over the bridge and hammered against the steel.

Marshall dragged himself to the voicepipe. "Carry on with the attack!"

He waited, expecting to hear frantic cries, to know the boat was mortally damaged. He heard instead the sounds of breaking glass and someone yelling for emergency lighting.

Then, "Ready, sir!"

"Fire Four!"

When he looked for the yacht it was swinging across their line of advance, with two machine-guns firing from the bridge while the deck gun groped steadily towards him.

A dull boom echoed across the water, echoing and then expanding into a louder explosion. He swung his glasses on the dock and saw smoke drifting above the lighters, or where two of them had been. Another explosion slammed over the calm water, and more smoke, this time filled with darting orange flames, marked the arrival of their second torpedo.

Warwick had at last got his own gun to fire, but the first shot screamed over the yacht to plummet into the sea a mile beyond. The Vierling had better luck. Like converging tongues the four narrow lines of tracer lanced across the yacht's bridge, steadied, and then ripped down across the hull with the sound of a bandsaw. Pieces of wood and steel, fabric and rigging were hurled in all directions, but above it all Marshall heard the siren still wailing, with probably a dead man clinging to its lanyard.

"All torpedoes fired, sir!" Buck's strained face lit up as another one struck the dock and erupted against the side in a violent explosion. The lighters had vanished, and from the big tug's angle it seemed as if she had either cast her tow adrift or was endeavouring to swing it towards the shore.

"Report damage below!"

Marshall felt himself cowering against the steel plates as more bullets whined viciously nearby, striking sparks from the metal, richocheting over the water and into the drifting smoke.

"God, we're not hurting the bastard!" Buck wiped his eyes and peered at the dock's smoky silhouette. "Bloody hell!"

Blythe called, "Two men wounded on the casing, sir!" Without waiting he bellowed, "Stretcher party to the bridge!"

The yacht was in a bad way, the Vierling's cannon shells had battered her slender hull into a pitted shambles, with smoke and daring flames showing from scores of holes. One of the machine-guns had been brought to bear, and that too had cut down the yacht's main armament, hurling the crew out of sight like so many tattered bundles.

An internal explosion flung a complete length of the deck into the air, and before it had fallen the yacht started to roll over, her bilge displaying another gaping hole where Warwick's crew had scored one fatal hit.

"Aircraft, sir!" The lookout was yelling like a madman. "Port beam!"

Marshall tried to control his reeling mind. The aircraft was far away, probably over the land which was now completely hidden by a rolling wall of smoke. Very tiny. Remote.

Buck yelled, "Another hit!" He was waving his cap in the air. "Look at it!"

The torpedo had struck the dock some two thirds along its tall side. A column of smoke flushed upwards and then froze against the sky as if turned into something solid, whilst below the dock's side Marshall could see tiny white feathers to mark where parts of the superstructure and machinery had fallen into the sea.

A figure blundered through the bridge, carrying a bag with a red cross on it. Through the crouching gunners and drifting smoke Marshall saw it was the young stoker, Willard, the one whose mother was "on the game." The boy looked at him for just a split second and then grinned before leaping over the side and down the ladder to the casing. Others followed him, faces puckered up as they came in contact with the sunlight and the closeness of death.

Marshall cupped his hands. "Cease firing! Shift target to the tug!"

The yacht had nearly disappeared, and yet the gunners seemed unable to stop, pouring round after round into the splintered, burning hulk, ripping the sea into a maelstrom of spray.

The sixth torpedo hit the dock within yards of the previous one. Another tall column of smoke, but no flames. Marshall stared at the dock's square outline, unable to believe that anything could survive such a battering. He felt his nerves jump as the deck gun reopened fire on the big tug, the first shell slamming down hard under her high stem.

"Aircraft's turning, sir!"

Marshall swung the glasses abeam, seeing the small bright chip in the sky, how it seemed to hang motionless as it altered course towards the silent battle far below.

Buck was shouting, "Shall I clear the bridge?"

Marshall gripped his arm. "No! We must make sure of the dock! We'll get alongside the bloody thing and engage with gunfire!" He shook him savagely. "Tell the Vierling gunners to stand by to repel aircraft! There's only one so far!"

Blythe looked up from a voicepipe. "No damage to hull, sir."

Marshall nodded, unable to speak. If the hull had been holed by their own torpedo they might just as well go ashore and surrender right now.

"Aircraft closing, sir!"

Buck yelled, "Shall I use the two stern tubes, sir?" He sounded wild with shock or anger. It was hard to tell

"No. If five won't do the job then—"

He pivoted round as a low, sullen rumble came across the water. It did not stop, but went on and on like some piece of massive undersea machinery.

Buck gasped, "Got her!" He seemed unable to grasp it. "She's done for!"

The dock was tilting towards them, very slowly, as if it was all part of a set plan. Only the surge of froth along the waterline betrayed the sudden inrush, the final collapse of one or more of the great ballast tanks. A tall derrick fell outboard and then hung downwards above the sea like a dead stork, and other fragments could be seen splashing along the full length of the side. The towing tug was burning fiercely, the hull outlined with sudden clarity by the falling waterspout of Warwick's last shell.

Marshall snapped, ''That's it! Clear the casing first! Prepare to dive!''

He looked for the plane but it had dipped out of sight into the smoke. It could be anywhere. He heard the klaxon screaming, suddenly loud through the hatch as the guns fell silent. Men clambered over the bridge, some dragging the wounded with them, others limping and cursing as they felt their way to safety.

The aircraft's engines roared through the smoke, cutting a bright path as it burst into view just two cables abeam. Marshall saw the bright stabbing flashes from its guns, the creeping pattern of splashes as the hail of bullets ploughed across the water, over the casing and away to the opposite beam. The Vierling followed round, the sharp cracking explosions and darting tracers making some of the running seamen falter and crowd over the hatch, too stricken to move.

Buck shouted, ''Get below! Move your bloody selves!''

More bangs, and the attendant clang of steel on steel, before the plane had streaked out of range to begin another turn.

Marshall seized a man's arm and pulled him into the bridge. The aircraft did not carry depth-charges, but one more attack like that and they might be crippled. Unable to dive.

He thrust his mouth against the voicepipe. ''Hard astarboard! Full ahead, group up!''

Buck was hanging over the screen calling, ''Here's the last of 'em!''

It was the stoker, Willard, his round face as white as a sheet, but apparently unmoved by the rattle of cannon fire, the oncoming roar of engines.

A lookout pointed wildly. ''Hold on! There's a bloke down there by the gun!''

Willard gasped, ''Dead! Couldn't help. Dead.''

But the lookout shouted even louder, his features twisted into a mask of despair. ''Saw him move, for Christ's sake!''

Marshall snapped, ''Take over the con, Number One.''

He raised his eyes from the voicepipe and saw the man in question. He was lying spreadeagled below the gun's long

136

muzzle. He noticed vaguely it was still smoking from the last shell. But the man should have been dead. Willard was right about that. He seemed to have lost one leg, and there was blood all round him. Everywhere. Then he saw the man's hand move. Very slightly. As if detached from its owner.

The plane had gone again and was grinding round inside the wall of smoke. It had to be now.

"Cease firing!"

He saw the gun crews tumbling towards the bridge, the machine-gunners already dropping their weapons through the hatch and leaping after them.

"Clear the bridge!"

Buck swore savagely and then croaked, "Come back, you bloody fool!"

Marshall ran to his side and saw Willard was already halfway along the casing, his red-cross bag bounding on his hip like a schoolboy's satchel.

He pulled Buck away and said, "Get below! That's an order!" When he looked again the bridge was empty.

He heard Gerrard calling to him up the voicepipe, his tone desperate. "What's happening, sir?"

But Marshall was watching the stoker as he reached the man by the gun. He paused for just a few seconds and then turned to face the bridge. He opened his mouth, but the words were lost in the sound of the plane's approach, and yet they still seemed to reach Marshall despite everything.

In the smoky sunlight he saw the brightness in his eyes; fear, tears, or just the sudden acceptance of death.

The enemy pilot had misjudged his attack, caught off guard perhaps by their alteration of course and speed. As the aircraft burst out of the smoke it was well astern, but the machine-guns were firing as before, some whipping through the German flag overhead, others whimpering away towards the pall of dense smoke above the blazing tug.

But some straddled the casing. Marshall saw the boy stagger sideways and then jerk violently through the safety rail to roll out and over the side.

Marshall shouted, "Take her *down*, Number One!"

When he reached the side he saw the stoker's body being washed along the saddle tank, arms and legs moving languidly, his face still towards the bridge, until the racing screws sucked him down and out of sight.

The deck was tilting and the air full of noise. The plane's engines, the roar of water in the tanks, the sea surging up and over the casing, carrying the other dead seaman towards the bridge in its path.

Marshall was aware of all these things but still could not move.

He knew someone had come to the bridge, and that his feet were on the ladder, the sky very clear, framed in the oval hatch above him.

Then he was in the control room, which was cloaked in brittle silence as the boat glided down as deep as she dared. He watched the depth gauges, listened to the regular reports from the echo-sounder. He knew exactly what was happening, yet felt no part of it.

They all seemed to be talking around him. As if instead of being here he was still up on the bridge, or drifting with Willard, out of reach, beyond pain.

Gerrard said, "Hold present depth for twenty minutes. Course zero-eight-zero."

A deep echo rumbled against the hull. The dock coming to rest on the bottom of the channel. Marshall had heard such sounds many times. Now he did not even notice it.

Gerrard looked at him. "I've got her, sir."

"Thank you." Marshall flinched at the sound of his own voice. "We should be all right now for a bit."

He could feel his stomach contracting, the clamminess of his skin. As if he was going to be sick. If he could get to his cabin for just a few moments. It might restore something. Give him the strength to go on.

Petty Officer Blythe strode past, his boots crunching on glass from shattered lights and gauges. The sounds dragged Marshall back to reality. He could take no time for himself. No matter what.

"What about damage? Are the wounded settled down?"

He gripped the coxwain's steel chair as the hull swayed slightly in some deep cross current.

Blythe called from the bulkhead door, "Three wounded, sir. But I'm told they're drugged well enough. Nothing serious."

Marshall nodded. "Good."

The yeoman's chest and legs were soaked in spray. It must have been him who had come to the bridge. To look for him.

He tried again. "Get the broken lights replaced and start

reloading the bow tubes.'' He looked at Frenzel. ''Chief, you'd better double check your department again. We shall make for the Otranto Straight tomorrow. Don't want any oil leaks to invite trouble.''

Gerrard crossed to his side. ''It's all right, sir.'' He spoke very quietly. ''I've taken care of it. I'd be happier now if you'd try and rest. You've done enough.''

Marshall removed his cap and stared at it for several seconds. The German eagle clutching the swastika in its claws, just as the last moments were tearing at his nerves until he wanted to scream aloud.

Gerrard added, ''Why did you do it, sir? You could have been killed.'' When Marshall remained silent he said, ''It was Willard, wasn't it?''

He nodded wearily, ''Something like that. He was looking at me. Trying to show me what he could do. What it meant to him.'' He crushed the cap under his arm.

''There was nothing you could do for him.'' Gerrard's eyes flickered across the control room, making sure everyone was occupied. ''You know that.''

''I suppose so.'' Marshall recalled the boy's face as he had stood quite alone on the casing. The link between them for those last few seconds. ''But I had to make him understand. To know that someone cared. Even if it was too late.''

Gerrard smiled sadly. ''I guessed as much.''

More glass crackled on the steel deck, and Warwick stepped over the coaming and leaned against the door.

Frenzel asked, ''You okay, Sub?''

''Yes. Thanks.'' He looked at Marshall and shivered. ''I don't feel anything.'' He sounded surprised. ''Not yet.''

Marshall walked slowly up and down the control room, only partly aware he was moving. He saw Devereaux bending over his table, but noticed that his hands and instruments were still. When he got closer he saw that his eyes were tightly shut, like someone in prayer. Buck was in the passageway beyond the bulkhead door talking to some of his men. Already engrossed in the whys and wherefores of the faulty torpedo. Warwick still standing limply beside the door, dressed in his shorts and wearing the heavy pistol. No matter how he felt, he had behaved like a veteran. Marshall tried to think back, to piece the events together in some sort of order. Buck and Warwick. A garage manager and a student who had been a pacifist.

He watched Frenzel, arms folded as he waited by his panel while an E. R.A. fiddled with a screwdriver to repair some of the damage caused by the faulty torpedo. Was he thinking of Willard, he wondered? Or had he already been written off, pushed away like so much waste?

Marshall said, "You can fall out diving stations. As soon as you've got things cleared up, tell the cook to prepare a meal." It was just as if he had to keep talking, keep giving instructions, if only to hold his other thoughts at bay.

Gerrard walked with him to the door. "I'll call you if anything happens, sir." He tried to smile. "As always. You get some rest."

This time Marshall did not fight back. He replied quietly, "That was a bad one. It seems to get worse every time."

Gerrard watched him go and then returned to his place behind the coxswain. Somehow he must get Marshall out of himself, he thought grimly. Not merely for him, but for all their sakes.

Far astern, where they had last dived, the remaining tug had begun a cautious search of the area for survivors. Not that her crew had seen much beyond the fog of blazing ships and gunfire. By nightfall she had given up and had turned once more towards the land.

Marshall lay on his bunk staring up at the deckhead, picturing the scene as if he was still there. There would be no survivors. Somehow he was quite sure. U-192 had not changed in that respect. They should have known. Understood. Now it might be too late.

Outside his cabin he heard someone sweeping up broken glass, whistling in time with each thrust of the broom. He was still trying to put a name to the tune when he fell into an empty, dreamless sleep.

10 Urgent Mission

MARSHALL clenched his teeth against the chill night air and steadied his glasses across the forepart of the bridge screen. With the electric motors held down to minimum revolutions there was barely any sound but for the gentle swish of water along the saddle tanks, the occasional creak of metal as the boat swayed in an irregular offshore swell.

They had been on the surface for nearly half an hour, but everything was dripping wet and icy to the touch. After the bright sunlight they had seen during the day's searches through the periscope, it seemed an additional strain on everyone's nerves.

There was a loud clang below the conning-tower followed by a stream of savage cursing from Petty Officer Cain.

Buck, who was standing beside Marshall, lowered his night-glasses and said, "That bloody makeshift screen got a bit buckled when the faulty torpedo nose-dived." He groaned as more clanks and scrapes echoed over the slow-moving submarine. They sounded deafening after the silence.

Marshall said sharply, "Tell them to be quick. Keep the noise down."

He lowered his eyes to the luminous gyro repeater. They were steering due south, the bows pointing directly into the Gulf of Sirte and the coast of Libya. Buck's angry comment about the faulty torpedo was a reminder that time and distance still had meaning.

It was very dark, with only a sliver of moon and some high, misty stars to throw any reflection on the black undulating surface around them. For over a week after sending the great floating dock and its escort to the bottom they had been made to endure the frustration of uncertainty, while Frenzel's fuel levels had continued to drop, and all but the most basic of food supplies had become exhausted. It was like being forgotten by that other world to which they had listened on the busy radio waves, or discarded in the face of some new crisis elsewhere. Then at last, as they had opened their special radio watch, the signal had come. When it had been decoded, and the brief references had been marked on Devereaux's charts, Marshall had headed towards the North African coastline without delay. Someone had at last remembered them, and with any sort of luck would have the precious fuel and supplies waiting to be loaded. And rest.

It was strange to realise that the great curving mass of land which now lay hidden somewhere to port had seen some of the most bitter fighting of the North African campaign. Benghazi and Derna, and farther to the east the battered but defiant port of Tobruk. When he had last been here in *Tristram*, prowling along these same shores in search of enemy supply ships, it had looked very different, even at night. There had always been the far off mutter of artillery, the sounds softened by the vast wastes of the desert, the occasional gleam of a drifting flare and the instant pinpoints of small-arms as patrols stumbled on one another and fought it out with rifle and bayonet beneath these quiet skies.

Buck came back rubbing his hands together. "It's been rigged, sir. Looks a mess in this light, but I suppose from a distance it will do."

The light metal screen which the depot ship's mechanics had constructed in such a short time was clipped around the after part of the conning-tower, altering the submarine's sparse outline just enough to hide her German lines from anything but a really close inspection.

Marshall replied, "Probably a waste of time anyway. The enemy may have marked our card by now."

Gerrard's voice echoed up the tube by his elbow. "Should have made a sighting by now, sir. We're ten minutes overdue."

"Yes." He moved his glasses slightly to starboard again. Nothing. Nor was there a sound above their own stealthy approach. "Maybe something's gone wrong."

Buck said, "I was thinking. Suppose the Jerries have made a comeback? We might run smack into one of their patrols."

Marshall smiled. "I'm getting so that I can't remember which side I'm really on."

How could he chat to Buck as if it did not matter to him? Every second dragged at his nerves, and even the placid sea appeared to be full of moving shadows and menacing outlines.

He snapped, "Ask the Asdic to check their gear again. They may have miscalculated because of the depth or the back-echoes from the shore." He gripped Buck's wrist. "No. Belay that. They'll be doing it without my badgering them."

Buck grunted. "God, I bet they'd laugh like drains if they could see us back in Blighty now!"

Marshall lowered the glasses and massaged his eyes. The casual remark brought back the memory of England with sharp clarity. It was May now, with all the colours beginning to show again, despite what the bombs could do.

He remembered too that other time in the house near Southampton. Gail in his arms, their passion which had often pushed away caution. Suppose he had married her? Would things have been different?

"Sir!" Buck was leaning over the screen. "Boat! Port bow!"

Marshall pushed past him, hearing the machine-gunners training their weapons into the darkness, a man's quick intake of breath, his own heart beating urgently.

He said harshly, "No wonder we couldn't hear them. They're drifting."

It was little more than a darker blob against the sea's face. Buck certainly had good eyesight.

Marshall saw the quick stab of a torch, very low on the water, and heard one of the machine-gunners give a noisy yawn of relief.

"Reply, Yeoman."

Marshall gripped the wet metal and waited impatiently while Blythe shuttered off their recognition code. Instantly a boat's engine coughed into life and the dark shadow lengthened slowly before edging closer to the submarine's hull. It was a very old boat with the high bow and stern posts of a Portuguese fisherman. But the voice which boomed through a megaphone was British enough.

"Just follow me, Captain! The Jerries were thoughtful enough to make a bit of a breakwater with some sunken ships when they were last here." He chuckled tinnily. "They make a good jetty, provided you watch out for the jagged edges!"

Buck muttered, "Stupid sod."

A bobbing sternlight presented itself beyond the U-boat's bows, and without more ado they set off again towards the invisible shore.

Marshall said, "Tell the casing party to get on deck. They'll need a good handlamp. Too bad about security, but I'm not ripping the guts out of her at this stage."

He was surprised at the vehemence in his tone. He touched the cold plating. Was he actually growing fond of her? He turned away. Even Buck had sounded angry at the words from the motor boat. It was stupid of course. All the same. . . .

He saw something loom past the starboard side. A ship, or part of one, like a buckled, rusting reef, man-made, and left by men to rot. If and when the war ended, would they ever be able to clean up the débris of it? Or would generations to come see these pitiful remains as marks of their sacrifice, mementos of men's stupidity?

A bright beam of light probed from the darkness and moved slowly along the submarine's hull. Marshall saw his men on the casing, caught in the hard glare, like gaunt statues, or parts of some forgotten tableau. More beams peeped above the uneasy swell, and he saw the nearest wedge of makeshift jetty quite clearly, the lights glittering on a line of partly submerged scuttles and one jagged gash through which the water eddied and gurgled unhindered.

"Stop starboard." He saw a heaving line snaking into the lights, heard someone slip and fall splashing into the water as he tried to catch it. "Slow astern starboard. Stop port." The submarine's bows were right above the nearest lights now, and he saw bobbing figures hurrying with crude fenders to ease the first contact. "Stop starboard." He felt the hull lurch slightly, and watched Cain's deck party dragging more wires aft to secure the boat against the motionless wreck.

There were quick exchanges through the darkness, and somewhere a man burst out in a fit of laughter. He sounded as if he could not stop.

A pale figure was being helped up and over the saddle tank, and even as Marshall ordered Frenzel to ring off the motors a head and shoulders rose above the bridge screen and said calmly, "So you made it, old son. Good show." It was Simeon.

In the poor light it was still possible to see his white smile, the relaxed way he held his head.

Marshall said, "This is quite a place." He did not know what to say. It was all so unreal and vaguely absurd. Two men meeting out here in the black wilderness. Like the middle of a darkened stage. In a moment the lights would come on, and then. . . .

Simeon said, "Let's go below, eh? It's a bit parky up here. I'm not dressed for it."

As they clattered down into the brightly lit control room Marshall was again forced to make comparisons. His own men, tired-eyed and in filthy sweaters as they hurried about the business of opening up hatches and the fuel intake valves. Others were being mustered with empty boxes and stowage cases, their faces so weary that hardly one gave Simeon a glance. He, on the other hand, was perfect. He was wearing pale khaki drill and carried a pistol at his hip, as if he was expecting to quell a riot.

He followed Marshall into the wardroom and stared round at the untidy interior with ill-disguised amusement.

"Really, you chaps have been roughing it!"

Marshall opened the cupboard and took out a bottle and two

glasses. He said shortly, "We sank the dock. Cost us two men——" He faltered, remembering Willard. His face across the table as he spoke of his mother. And along the length of the fore deck while he had waited to die. "I'm still not sure about our damage. A faulty torpedo—" He broke off, seeing the emptiness in Simeon's eyes. He didn't care. Didn't give a bloody damn. "It's all in my report."

Simeon took the proffered glass and replied, "We heard about the dock. From other sources. Good show. The enemy still don't seem to know about *you* though. I said you had the capacity for causing chaos." He lifted the glass. "Cheers."

Marshall sank down on a bench seat and ran his fingers through his hair. It felt gritty. Sand from the shore probably. He swallowed the whisky in one mouthful.

Simeon said, "Now don't you worry about a thing. This place is a dump, literally. There are some engineers ashore sorting out captured weapons and other enemy gear left behind in the rush. They'll come in useful for partisans and so forth. I've managed to get two old German fuel lighters brought here. I'll give you full diesel capacity before daylight. Water too, and almost anything else you want." He sounded pleased with himself.

"Thanks." Marshall could not help feeling admiration for him. "How is the war going?"

Simeon's eyebrows rose slightly. "Of course, you wouldn't know much. The Germans are almost gone from North Africa. Still a few troops here, but most have already skipped by way of Cape Bon in Tunisia. General Rommel flew out some time back, so that shows it's all over bar the shouting."

Gerrard appeared in the doorway. "Look, sir, the shore party seem to have things moving. Could I let some of our unemployed hands ashore? They can start taking our gear to wherever Commander Simeon has earmarked for us while we're here."

Simeon eyed him coolly. "That's the stuff, Number One. Look after the lads first, eh?" He smiled. "But it's not on, I'm afraid. This boat will be out of here by dawn, or I'll want to know why." He was still smiling, but there was no disguising the coldness in his eyes.

Gerrard stared at him and then at Marshall. "Is this true, sir?"

Simeon snapped, "Look, I don't intend to discuss my arrangements with every Tom, Dick and Harry in the company, right? I will tell your captain. He will tell you." He leaned back and eyed Gerrard for several long seconds. "If he feels like it."

Marshall stood up slowly, the sides of the wardroom fading and shivering like a mirage. "Carry on, Number One." He waited until Gerrard had backed into the passageway and then said, "Didn't you see my people when you came aboard just now, sir? They're worn out. Some of them have been on their bloody feet for days and nights on end!" He could feel his limbs shaking, the pressure in his throat like something solid. "What the hell are you asking of them now?"

"*Do* sit down." Simeon regarded him calmly. "In case you hadn't heard me properly, I'll explain. The war out here has reached a climax. The Army, the Navy, the Commander-in-Chief, *and* the enemy, they all know it's a vital time for everybody. Like them, I don't feel inclined to order a halt while you and your company sit on your backsides!" There was a new edge to his voice. "Everything's geared for an invasion through Sicily. Why we've even got most of the recaptured ports in service again. Sousse was operational within days of the Afrika Korps pulling back. That was where I got your damned fuel from!"

A generator grumbled into life, and Marshall was vaguely aware of other sounds outside the hull. Heavy crates being dragged along the casing. The squeak of tackles as more supplies were lowered through the fore hatch.

He sat down and stared at the empty glass. "What is it you want?"

Simeon reached over and poured two more large drinks. "That's more like it, old son." He smiled. "No sense in going at each other, eh?"

"Just tell me."

"Very well." Simeon took out a fat notebook and flicked through the pages. "With the Jerries pulling out so quickly things have got to move even faster. With luck the invasion will be within—" he looked up sharply, "—within two months of now."

Marshall nodded heavily. "So?"

"Something's come up." He held his glass to the light. "The Intelligence people have got word that the Germans have invented a new weapon."

"Not another one, surely?" Marshall did not hide his bitterness.

"This is real enough." Simeon closed his book with a snap. "A radio-controlled bomb. Once dropped from an aircraft it can be 'homed' by radio on to any large target." He nodded slowly. "I see that you are already grasping the possibilities."

Marshall asked, "Where do we come in?"

He did not reply directly. "If this invasion is to have a chance of success then the troops must get maximum support from the Navy. Until airfields are captured and proper fighter and bomber cover can be provided round the clock."

Marshall stood up again and moved restlessly round the table. "This radio-controlled bomb? Would it be easy to use?"

"A child could drop it." Simeon pressed his hands on the table. "No heavy capital ships or cruisers would be safe. They would be incapable of maintaining their sectors for bombardment. The army would have to hit the beaches on their own."

Marshall paused and looked down at him. "So secrecy wasn't enough after all?"

"It never is. However, now that we know a bit about the enemy's intentions we can do something about it. But first——"

The curtain jerked aside and Frenzel thrust into the wardroom, his face lined with anger. "Is it true, sir?" He did not wait for an answer. "I'll not answer for my department if we have to shove off again without a proper inspection! Just what the hell do they think we are?"

Marshall said, "I shall tell you what I think when I've got my orders, Chief."

Frenzel looked at him dully. "You've already agreed then?" He swung round and left the wardroom without another word.

Simeon sighed. "Give them an inch." He continued evenly, "I want you to lift off some agents. They'll know, if anyone does, what the Germans are up to. If this invasion is going to work, we must be sure we know what we've got against us."

"A sea pickup?" Marshall looked away. "Or one of the offshore islands?"

"Neither. You must lift them off the Italian mainland. There's an alert out for them. Even now, we might be too late. Either way, *we must know*!"

Marshall stood quite still, listening to a motor chugging busily from the makeshift jetty as fuel was pumped from the captured lighters. Fill her up and get her away by dawn. That was all that mattered to the men on the shore. It was so unfair. More than that, it was dangerous to push the boat beyond its limit.

He heard Simeon say quietly, "One of the agents is that French girl. You brought her out here, remember?"

Marshall swung round, but there was nothing in the other man's eyes to give anything away.

"Of course I remember."

"I could ask for a conventional submarine, of course. But under the circumstances, and in view of what may follow on, I think this is best."

"Yes. I understand."

"I knew you'd see it my way." Simeon stood up and reached for his cap. "There'll be a few Intelligence chaps coming with you. Just in case." He did not elaborate. "But your decisions on the spot are what count."

Marshall looked at him impassively. "My pigeon again."

"Would you have it any other way?" Simeon smiled. "I think not."

He added, "Your friend Buster is at Gibraltar. He'll be flying out here tomorrow. If all goes well he'll get a nice pat on the back, I shouldn't wonder."

"And if it doesn't?"

"Ah, well." Simeon flicked some sand from his jacket. "That's something else again."

Marshall followed him out of the wardroom and saw Warwick standing by the conning-tower hatch, his eyes drooping as he watched some seamen stowing tinned food in nets which they would then lash in spare corners of the hull.

"Officers' conference in the wardroom in one hour, Sub." Marshall watched Simeon vanish up the ladder and then walked to his cabin. He stared at the bunk, fighting back the desperate urge, the craving to lie down and let darkness sweep over him. Then he saw the small bag and felt the same chill he had experienced when Simeon had casually mentioned that she was somewhere on the enemy coast. Waiting for help. For him.

Later, when he returned to the wardroom, he was conscious of the heavy silence, and saw several of his men lying half asleep or stretched out on the deck where they had finished work.

The assembled officers listened to him in the same silence. Buck lolled against the bulkhead, his eyes red-rimmed and almost closed. Devereaux was little better, and young Warwick could not stop himself from yawning repeatedly. Frenzel stared at his logbook, his eyes blank and unseeing as they moved back and forth across the pencilled calculations. Only Gerrard seemed to be holding on.

When Marshall had finished Gerrard said quietly, "We don't have any choice, do we, sir?"

"No."

Buck lurched to his feet and began to button his stained jacket. He saw them watching him and said thickly, "I'm going to rouse my lads and get the spare torpedoes shifted from their containers on the after casing. While we're still tied up to something steady. They'll come in handy, I shouldn't wonder." He picked up his heavy torch and looked round the table. "If we *are* bloody going, we might as well make the best of it!"

Frenzel also stood up. "I reckon he's right." He looked at Marshall and smiled. "Pity Commander Simeon's not coming along for the ride. If you see what I mean, sir." He foll.. nd Buck through the door.

Devereaux rubbed his eyes and murmured, "Just tell me where, sir. I'll find the right chart for it."

"I will, when I know."

Marshall looked away, feeling the pain behind his eyes as one by one they left the wardroom like men walking in a trance.

Then Gerrard said simply, "Good bunch, sir."

Marshall touched his arm, unable to face him. "Best yet, Bob. Best yet."

As Marshall crossed to the door Able Seaman Churchill peered in and said, "Fresh coffee, soon anyway." He closed the curtain and added quietly, "'Ow does 'e do it, sir?"

Gerrard stared at the empty doorway, remembering Marshall's eyes. "I'll never know."

Churchill grimaced. "Be an 'elp to you when you're a C.O. of yer own sub, eh, sir?" He hurried away to his pantry, whistling to himself.

Gerrard leaned back, his hands behind his head. C.O. of his own boat. Something Marshall had mentioned often enough. How could he tell him now? That he hated even the thought of it. That each time the depth needles crept round their dials he felt the nausea rising in him like fear.

He stood up and stretched, his head touching the deckhead as it always did.

Valerie had said nothing about it. She didn't have to. After this commission was completed it would be the end of submarines for him.

Starkie peered through the door, his wizened face made older by the grey bristles on his chin.

"First lieutenant, sir? Got a moment to check stowage?"

Gerrard smiled. "Fair enough, 'Swain. We must remember the *trim*, eh?"

Together they walked forward through the boat. As men struggled to their feet and went through the motions of preparing for sea it was like an awakening. A rebirth of something stronger than mere flesh and blood. Gerrard recalled Marshall's last words. *Best yet.* He smiled despite his own anxieties. With men like these they could do anything.

He thought too of Simeon. And for him, they might have to do just that.

"Captain in the control room!"

Marshall threw his legs over the side of the bunk and hurried from his cabin. He could not recall if he had been asleep or if he had merely been suspended between active thought and exhaustion. One second he was lying on his blankets, the next he was here, at Gerrard's elbow.

Gerrard grimaced. "Sorry. Thought it best to call you, sir. Just picked up some fast moving H.E. at two-six-zero. Might mean we're getting near trouble."

Marshall nodded and walked to the chart. It had been three days since they had left their makeshift harbour. Three days of unnatural quiet, as if the whole Mediterranean was taking a brief rest after the months of battle. The strain had been all the greater because of it, he thought. Impossible to relax. Just lying there staring at the deckhead. Eating and watchkeeping automatically. Without any sensation but apprehension.

On the surface dawn would be lending colour to the sea again. Down here it was as usual. Dank and clammy, with all unnecessary fans switched off to conserve power and minimise noise. For they were now heading towards the well-known bottleneck between Sicily and Cape Bon on the Tunisian shore. Eighty odd miles over which the struggle for mastery had swayed back and forth without let-up. Air attacks on British convoys as they ran the gauntlet in their attempts to carry supplies to Malta. Submarines of both sides which hunted ceaselessly and tried to cut Rommel's lifeline to the desert or smash the British convoys with equal determination. Well known to Marshall and those like him, if not to the newer hands at the game.

"We'll take a look. Periscope depth."

Marshall left the chart table and stood by the well, ignoring the carefully controlled inrush of compressed air, the gentle tilt of the deck as Gerrard took the boat towards the surface.

They did not want any trouble now. Not from either side. It would take another two days to reach the pickup point on Italy's west coast, more valuable time to get into position, sift the facts before committing all of them to a plan of action.

He thought of the three passengers in the wardroom. No doubt sleeping while they still had the time. What self-control they must have. And a capacity for sleep. They were a mixed trio, yet in some ways very like all the others Marshall had met who fought that remote, secret war.

The senior one was a Major Mark Cowan. Slightly built, with a clipped, matter of fact manner, he looked anything but a regular soldier. From the little he had said, he did not seem too hopeful at the success of the mission.

A radio message had been sent to the agents to tell them about the pickup times and exact rendezvous point. But no acknowledgement had been received and none expected. Cowan had said that the Germans had discovered the agents' hiding place, and any sort of radio message from them would most certainly kill their last chance of rescue. More than that, the major had left unsaid. He was probably waiting until they got closer to their objective. Preserving secrecy unless required to share further details.

Marshall lifted his hand slowly and crouched down beside the well, his fingers on the twin handles and locking the periscope on to the last bearing.

Here was the sunlight, pale green, strengthening to blue as the lens cut through the gentle swell. He shivered. How inviting it looked. So clean.

He gripped the handles tightly and said, "Full extent."

His back ached as he straightened it. He saw a vague purple hump far away on the horizon, still holding the shadows, merging with the dawn sky. That would be the island of Pantellaria. They were right on course. *Naturally*, as Devereaux would have said.

Further still. The periscope moved soundlessly as he edged round. Hold it. There it was. He saw the first sunlight reaching out to touch the glass screen on her bridge, a white moustache of foam beneath her bows. But even at full power the shape was indistinct for exact recognition. He tensed. Probably a second ship on the other one's port quarter. Destroyers.

"Down periscope." He looked at Gerrard. "We'll alter course ten degrees to starboard. Steer three-two-zero. Take her down to thirty metres." He walked to the chart again. "But watch the depths. We're running across the Adventure Bank. No more than thirty fathoms hereabouts."

Gerrard licked his lips. "Very good, sir." He turned away, his hands gripping the helmsman's chair as if for support.

Marshall watched him thoughtfully. "At least it might take the weed off the keel."

He turned and saw Major Cowan by the bulkhead door, a cup in one hand.

"Bother?"

"No. Two destroyers on patrol. Well away from us."

Cowan studied him and then replied, "Not what I imagined. Thought there'd be bells ringing, men dashing about. That sort of thing. This is like damned church!"

Marshall smiled. *Stick around a bit longer, my friend.* Aloud he said, "I'm just going to have some coffee. How about joining me?" He followed him to the wardroom and then said quietly, "Now, suppose you fill me in on some more details?" He pushed the coffee pot across the table. "I don't like going in blind."

Cowan smiled. "Quite so." He glanced round at the bunk curtains. A few snores showed they were occupied. "I get the point. No harm now, I suppose. What exactly do you want to know?" He was offering nothing in advance.

"Mrs. Travis. What is her part in all this?"

Cowan sighed. "I was against her getting involved. Again."

Marshall waited, remembering her words when he had asked her if she had done this sort of thing before.

Cowan added, "She worked in Paris the last time. Being French, her services were invaluable. But her cover broke and the *Milice* caught her. They may be French police, but they work for their new masters, and they're worse than the Germans in some ways. I suppose they see the Resistance as a threat to their own power. And their lives.''

"Caught her?"

He nodded. "Held her for two days outside Paris. Waiting for the Gestapo to pick her up. They'd been after her for some time, although of course they did not actually know who they were chasing."

Marshall thought of the way she moved and listened. Like a hunted animal.

"Anyway, our people managed to get her out of it just in time. A close thing." He shrugged. "But when she was asked to do this job, she agreed without hesitation. Her husband's in Italy. Just inland from Naples."

"I see. So he's working for you, too?"

Cowan watched him sadly. "Actually, no. He's an engineer. A collaborator. Doing the same sort of work as he was doing in France. A construction job. Top priority."

Marshall felt dazed. "And she agreed to see him? Just like that?"

The major refilled his cup. "Did she mention her parents? Well, her father works for the Resistance. He's with the French railways. Very useful contact. I don't have to spell it out to you. We heard that Travis is getting cold feet. Wants to change sides again. Come home and be forgiven. She is the only one he might listen to. He'll know she despises him, but he trusts her. Know it's no Gestapo trap."

Marshall looked at his cup, suddenly sick. "And your people let her go back to him. Knowing the Germans might suspect her. Might even have been told by this Travis, or whatever his real name is!"

Cowan shook his head. "Unlikely. There's not much contact between the German occupation forces in France and those in Italy. It is a risk of course, and in any other circumstances I think we'd not have taken it. But on the face of it, this was worth taking. She is his wife, and was coming to join him at his new location. She had the right papers, and she knows her job." He added quietly, "Travis knows about the bombs. If we can get him out alive we might save countless of our own people later on."

"And if she's failed?"

":Then we'll just have to get what we can from the agents. If you can lift them off."

Marshall stood up, his mind racing. "But the Germans know about her *now*!"

"Perhaps. We can't know for sure until——"

The rest of his words were lost as the deck gave a sudden lurch and from the control room came a cry of alarm.

Marshall staggered and almost fell as the hull jerked violently, and he heard a new sound, like a saw on metal, screeching along the submarine's casing until it seemed to fill the wardroom with its intensity.

He ran towards the control room, cannoning into awakened seamen and startled watchkeepers. He saw Gerrard clinging to the periscopes, his face like chalk as he yelled, "Blow all main ballast! *Surface!*"

Marshall gripped his arm. "Belay that order!" He glanced quickly at the gauges, at the helmsman's back as he struggled with the wheel. "Klaxon!" He could hardly think because of the screeching which seemed all around him. "What happened?" He had to shake Gerrard's wrist to make him react. "What was it?"

Gerrard stared at him. "The hull plunged. Then that noise!" He looked round as the sound suddenly stopped. "I thought we'd hit a wreck. That we were going to take a dive."

Men scurried past to their stations, and Marshall said, "Check the trim." To Frenzel, who had just appeared at his panel, he added, "Report damage to hull."

One of the planesmen said hoarsely, "Can't hold her, sir!" He twisted round on his stool his eyes wild. "She's going mad!"

Marshall stood motionless in the centre of the control room. "Anything on the Asdic?" He looked at Frenzel. "The after planes are jamming. We must have picked up something."

"Asdic reports no H.E., sir."

Marshall nodded, seeing Cowan and his two companions in the bulkhead doorway, yet not seeing them. They were all here now. At their proper stations. Waiting for him to act. To perform a miracle if so needed.

Frenzel's E.R.A. reported, "No hull damage, sir." He was gripping his telephone like a club.

Marshall made himself wait for several more agonising sec-

154

onds. When he spoke he expected to hear a break in his voice. He glanced at Gerrard. Like his had sounded.

"Take her up slowly, Number One. Periscope depth. If she starts to dive, blow everything." He forced smile. "Just like old times."

"Group up. Slow ahead together." Gerrard gripped the coxswain's chair.

Starkie cursed quietly. "She's weavin' about a bit, sir." He eased the spokes and then brought them back again. "Bloody cow!"

The sound came suddenly as before, like a jarring whine, ending just as abruptly with a violent clang across the casing.

"Fourteen metres, sir." Gerrard sounded very tense.

"Up periscope." Marshall snapped down the handles. No time for caution now. A quick glance to either bow and into the sky overhead. How pale the sky was. Almost silver in the sun's early glare.

He brought the lens towards the stern and depressed it slightly. There was no sign of the wire or cable, but there, bobbing close astern, was a mine.

It was covered in green slime, and could have been in the water for months. Years. It had probably broken adrift from a field elsewhere until its severed cable had caught something. An old wreck. Anything. All this time it had waited. He saw the pointed horns twisting slightly against the U-boat's headway. It was as deadly as the day it had left Germany. Or England.

"Down periscope."

Starkie said, "She's steerin' a bit better now, sir."

"She would, 'Swain." To the control room at large he said, "It's a mine. We are towing it about fifty feet astern of us." He saw their stunned expressions, the way some of them looked at the after bulkhead door as if expecting to see something different.

Major Cowan was the first to speak. "Can you handle it, Captain?"

Marshall looked at him, suddenly very calm. "What I'm paid for."

He crossed to the chart. "How about it, Pilot?"

Devereaux wiped his mouth with the back of his hand. "It's a bad place to surface, sir."

"I didn't choose it." He leaned over the table. Shutting them all outside his thoughts. "Smack in the middle of the Strait.

155

Alter course and steer due north.'' He restrained their movements with a sharp warning. ''Slowly! Take your time. The
cable is caught under the bandstand and then down and around
the after planes. I don't want that mine veering into the screws!''

Cowan asked quietly, ''Couldn't we wait until dark,
Captain? If you surface you might be spotted.''

''We've a whole day of sunlight, Major.'' He studied him
gravely. ''To wait until sunset would take too long. We'd be
right up by the enemy's coast. And anyway, if we tried it in the
dark we would most likely get blown up.''

He turned away. ''Up periscope.''

Another look. Empty sky, but the mine was still with them. It
seemed to gleam in the sunlight like something malevolent.

He said quietly, ''Starboard ten.'' He heard the trimming
pumps thudding quietly. Gerrard was watching the boat's
stability all right. What had happened to him? Had he been
thinking of those other boats? Of Bill Wade? He swung the
periscope once more and imagined he could see their own
shadow beneath the surface. ''Steady.''

Starkie called, ''Steady, sir.'' He leaned back slightly to
watch the gyro repeater quiver to rest. Due north.

''Down periscope.'' Marshall thrust his hands into his
pockets. ''Chief, get your men and all the gear you need. As few
hands on deck as possible.''

Buck said, ''I'll take charge, if I may, sir.'' He forced a grin.
''Chief knows his onions where engines are concerned. But I
reckon I've cut up more bloody cars in my Wandsworth garage
than he's had hot dinners. This is right up my street.''

Marshall nodded. ''That makes sense.'' He sought out Warwick. ''Automatic-weapon crews close up on surfacing.'' He
looked down at the chart table, fighting back alternative
thoughts, challenges which still lay behind his hazy plan.

Tools clanked in the background, and he heard Buck say,
''I'll want that, and that big cutter over there.'' He sounded
satisfied. ''Ready when you are, sir.''

Cowan asked, ''Anything I can do?''

Marshall smiled. ''Pray.''

He looked at his watch. What a bloody thing to happen. Now
of all times.

Gerrard moved closer. ''I'm sorry, sir. I should have kept my
head.''

Marshall eyed him thoughtfully. "Not to worry."

Men pushed past them towards the ladder. It seemed to be full of them. Deck party in lifejackets and carrying Buck's tools. Gun crews with their ammunition belts. Warwick wiping his binoculars with a piece of tissue. They all looked very tense, but none seemed to show any doubt in what they were being ordered to perform.

The captain had spoken. That was it.

Marshall licked his lips and looked at Gerrard. "Shut off the boat once we're on the surface. If this thing explodes, do your best to get our lads out the escape hatches." He paused, seeing the doubts crowding Gerrard's face. "If you get clear and we don't, Major Cowan will tell you where to go and what to do. It'll be up to you to get those people off." He gripped his arm. "All right, Bob?"

"Yes." Gerrard nodded jerkily. "But watch out."

Marshall walked to the ladder and said to Devereaux, "Go forward before you shut the watertight doors." He dropped his voice. "If the worst happens, you'll be needed up here to sort things out."

Devereaux glanced at the massive steel door. "Yes, sir."

Marshall watched him grimly. "Stop any panic. You know the score. If they have to ditch, tell them to watch out for the jumping-wire and the gun barrel when they pop through the escape hatch." He made himself smile. "No sense in getting a headache for nothing!"

The lower hatch clanged open and he began to pull himself up the ladder. It was slippery, or perhaps his hands were sweating badly. He gripped the locking wheel, feeling someone taking hold of his legs.

His voice rang hollowly in the tower. "Surface!"

He had learend quite a lot in the last few minutes. About himself and about Gerrard. He had even discovered that Buck came from Wandsworth.

He heard Gerrard's shrill whistle and swung the wheel over his head.

11   Secret Weapon

LIEUTENANT Colin Buck tugged his cap down over his eyes and stared at the mine. He was standing right aft at the narrowest part of the casing, and with his back to the conning-tower he felt strangely detached, as if he was poised on the surface itself, being followed by the slime-covered sphere with its bobbing horns.

What a beautiful morning. Not a cloud in the sky, and only a hint of haze to mask the dark blue horizon. After the cramped hull, the constant comings and goings of other human beings, being made to stand aside in passageways or duck through watertight doors, it was like a dream world.

A stoker petty officer, naked but for a pair of patched shorts, crawled awkwardly along the edge of the casing above the hydroplanes. Buck watched him, his mind unusually relaxed. Despite the dangers of being on the surface in bright sunlight, the need to rid themselves of that ruddy mine, he felt quite calm.

"Well, Rigby, what d'you make of it?"

The petty officer sank down on the wet steel and sighed. "It's a bastard, sir. A real, second-to-none bastard."

Buck grinned. "It's a start anyway."

The petty officer leaned over the edge and pointed into the U-boat's gentle wake. "I did what you said, sir. Followed the wire from where it's caught round the bandstand." His filthy arm moved further aft and down again. "The cable seems to go round the saddle tank and through the port hydroplane." He squinted up at Buck. "Trouble is, there's a bloody great bight in the cable. It's wrapped tightly round the plane, so that the drag is further aft across the rudder."

"I see." Buck seized the jumping-wire and swung out over the narrow, pointed stern. The sea was so clear he could pick out trailers of weed on the hull, the reflected glitter of sunlight from a spinning screw. "You're right. It is a bastard." He turned and looked at the bridge, an uneven black shadow against the sky. He saw the restless muzzles of the Vierling and machine-guns and Marshall's silhouette at the rear of the bandstand watching for some sort of progress.

Buck cupped his hands. "Wire's fouled round the plane, sir!

No good trying to cut it up here. It will have to be done under water.''

Rigby muttered, "Don't fancy that job. Not with a bloody screw buzzing round my arse."

Buck shouted, "If you stop the motors, sir, the weight of the cable will pull the mine into our stern."

Marshall called, "Any ideas?"

Buck looked at Rigby and winked. "A few."

Marshall waved one hand. "Tell me if you need any extra hands then." He turned away towards the forepart of the bridge, his unruly hair rippling in a small breeze.

Buck banged his palms together and looked at his small group of helpers. "Right, lads. Four of you get ready to boom that mine clear if it comes any closer. Petty Officer Rigby will take charge on deck." He was already stripping off his shirt. "I'll do the cutting."

He took off his watch and handed it to a seaman. "Take care of it. I won it at poker." God, they had only been surfaced for ten minutes. It seemed an age since they had stumbled out into the sunlight.

He saw the men laying out the tools, the big wire-cutter, and a bowline to tie around his waist.

Rigby grimaced. "Watch out for the undertow, sir. There's always a nasty tug under these boats."

Buck nodded. He had sounded as if he cared. He fixed some goggles over his eyes and sat down gingerly on the edge of the casing. The metal was already warm, but felt slimy, repellent.

He eased himself outboard and down, holding his breath as the sea explored his loins. It was like ice. A shock after the sun's warmth.

He thought suddenly of the publican's wife in Scotland, the sheer wantonness of their passion together. It had gone on and on, neither of them willing to allow a climax of their need, each striving to break the other's last defence. Once, she had lain on top of him, moving deliberately to the tuneless piano in the bar below. That time, he had given in first.

Buck held his breath and ducked under the water, peering at the wire. It was coated with rust and growth, and as jagged as some relic of the trenches. His father had often gone on about the First World War. The tingling horror of night raids, armed with clubs and sharpened shovels. Hand-to-hand, waist deep in mud. Yet he often spoke of it with a kind of nostalgia, a sense of loss. Buck had been very young when his father had died. It had been that same war which had finally killed him. Gas, which had eaten away his lungs. He could still hear him coughing in the small back bedroom. Cough, cough, cough. Day and night. But when it had stopped, the silence had been all the more terrible.

Buck dragged himself into the warm air again and pushed the goggles on to his forehead.

"Never do it with these tools. Tell the Chief to rig a power cutter and be bloody quick about it."

He looked up at the sky. He could push himself away from the hull and swim. Go on and on.

He heard Marshall questioning the man who had gone forward with his message. He was a good bloke. Not a bit like some of the stuck-up sods he had first encountered. He remembered when he had enlisted with the peacetime R.N.V.R. Just to get away from Wandsworth with its dirt and teeming houses. The constant bicker and shrill cries of children. The noisy arguments and worse on a Saturday night when the fathers came home drunk from the pubs, spewing in passageways or knocking their wives about. And the coppers who had come from the nick at Lavender Hill, pushing and shoving, jovial but deadly. *Come on, mate, what's all the fuss then?* A few thumps and silence before the old police van dragged their haul off to the cells for the night.

The temporary Navy had been the only way for Buck to get away from all that. With his father dead, he had become the breadwinner, working at that stinking garage off Battersea High Street. The owner had been on the crook. Cutting up stolen cars for spare parts, or selling them whole with false plates outside London. But jobs were hard to come by, and he had three sisters as well as his mother to support.

When the war had started, Buck had been a leading torpedo-man, and although his part-time training had been carried out on obsolete equipment, and given by instructors, many of whom had learned their trade in his father's war, he had had the edge on many of his fellow recruits. He had learned the hard way in that crooked garage. Not only when to look the other way, and pocket a small share for doing so, but how to take a bit of wire and produce heat or power. It had lifted him well above better educated men, as it had in peacetime.

Buck was twenty-eight, but when he had been twenty he had

become his own boss, manager of the garage, which if it was still spared by the bombing, would be waiting for him. A foothold. A stepping stone.

He had a thick skin, too. Even the thinly-veiled hostility from some of the regular officers when he had been granted a temporary commission, some of which amounted to contempt, had failed to shake him. Quite the contrary, he knew that on several occasions he had been deliberately revolting, just to get his own back. To see their noses go up in the air.

It all seemed a long way back now. The Navy was over-whelmingly officered by men like himself and peacetime sailors. The old hidebound types were being forced into their shells. He grinned to himself. Or promoted, like that twit Simeon.

But a few of the other sort, men like Marshall, had made it all worthwhile. Anyway, it was different in submarines. He never grew tired of them. Sometimes he wondered if he really could face going back to any garage after this.

The seaman called, "Cutter's being rigged, sir." He shaded his eyes to look at the sky. "Nobody about yet."

Rigby snapped, "Too bloody early, I s'pect."

Buck ignored them, thinking of the Scottish pub. His fishing rods had never left their case. Christ, what a woman she was. She had matched him. Drained him. Left him weak but still wanting more. She had cried when he had left. Funny that. He had not thought she would cry.

He heard Warwick calling something to his gun crews. He'd never had a woman in his life. It was bloody obvious. Buck's first conquest had been, he frowned, trying to remember. Outside the school? Or on that church outing to Brighton? He shrugged and rubbed the spray off his skin. He'd have to find one for young Warwick. *Bunny.*

Rigby said, "Here comes the cutter, sir."

Two seamen were dragging the electric cable aft, the power-ful cutter between them like the head of some forgotten monster.

Buck nodded and leaned out to watch the screw. One slip. Just one, and it would be his lot.

Rigby said anxiously, "Watch out for your legs, sir."

Buck adjusted his goggles. "It's my family jewels *I'm* worried about."

Rigby grinned despite his doubts. "If you lose them, I'll get the Chief to run you up something in his machine-shop. No woman'll ever know the difference!'' But Buck had already ducked under the surface. He said, ''Keep a tight hold on his lifeline. Check that cable, too.''

From his position on the gratings Marshall saw Buck's head vanish below the surface, and half expected to hear the sound of the electric cutter at work. But there was nothing. The cutter was a useful piece of gear. Most U-boats carried one so that a diver could work on deck while the hull was submerged to hack through anti-submarine nets and booms across harbour entrances.

Warwick asked, ''How long will it take, sir?''

He shrugged. ''Half an hour. Hard to tell.'' Despite the risk, he was glad Buck had gone himself. If anyone could do it. . . .

He swung round as Warwick said, ''From control room, sir. Fast-moving H.E. at one-five-zero. Closing.''

Marshall ran to the rear of the bridge and levelled his glasses. There was some more haze now. Rising with the sun's mounting glare, masking the darker line of the horizon.

''Keep a good lookout. Maybe it'll go away.''

Warwick said, ''Lieutenant Buck, sir. Shall I pass him the word?''

''Negative. I don't want him to get flustered. He's enough on his plate at the moment.'' He glanced at the mine. Hating it. Fearing what it could do.

Warwick followed his gaze and said, ''But for that thing, we'd be safely on our way, sir.''

Marshall did not answer. But for running deep to avoid those other destroyers, they would have hit the mine squarely instead of getting entangled with its cable.

''Tell the control room to keep us informed.''

He saw Buck emerge gasping beside the hull, sucking in air and shaking his head like a dog.

What would he do if this unknown ship found them? It was almost certain to be British or American. With the Germans out of North Africa, it seemed unlikely there would be any other vessels about. He could not dive with the mine still in tow. It would hamper their movements, and even a badly aimed depth-charge would explode it and rip off their stern like the tail of a shark. But if he stood his ground and tried to exchange signals, it was equally unlikely any destroyer captain would be inclined to postpone battle. U-192 did not exist, and any German submarine on the surface was too good to miss. He toyed with the idea of rigging their false screen again. But that too was pointless. There would still be the risk of misunderstanding. Worse, it might foul the mine's jagged cable which was clearly visible around the bandstand. A quick jerk, some unexpected slackening, and the mine might surge ahead and touch them, or at best pitch Buck into the whirling propeller blades.

"H.E. steady on same bearing, sir. Still closing. Range approximately twelve thousand yards." Warwick raised himself from the voicepipe and added quietly, "*Two* ships, sir. Speke thinks they may be destroyers."

Marshall rubbed his chin, trying to picture the chart, their change of course, the nearness of the Sicilian coast. The same two destroyers? He pushed them to the back of his mind. It did not matter much whether they were the same ones or not.

A lookout said, "Lieutenant Buck's gone under again, sir. That's five times."

Marshall peered up at the main periscope. It was raised to full extent and trained away across the starboard quarter. Soon now, it had to be.

"Tell the yeoman to come to the bridge. We may have to make a signal."

Blythe appeared in seconds, his eyes like slits against the harsh glare.

He looked at the mine and said, "Pity we can't take a pot-shot at the bugger." He sighed. "It's too damn close."

Marshall looked away. Thinking of Bill Wade. What it must have been like. The sudden explosion. The inrush of water, pressing men higher and higher, until their lips were against the deckhead, sucking those last morsels of air even as the hull nose-dived for the bottom.

He heard Gerrard's voice quite clearly from the other end of the bridge. "Control room to bridge. Ships in sight. Bearing Green one-four-five."

A lookout yelled, "I've got 'em, sir!" He was crouched over his glasses, like a hunter watching the approach of his quarry.

Marshall waited, holding his breath as he allowed the gently heaving water to glide across his lenses. A dull patch of grey, almost lost in the horizon mist. But no doubt about it now.

Warwick said between his teeth, "Coming out of the sun. We'll be sitting ducks!"

Marshall held his glasses on the same bearing. The two ships were probably in line ahead. They might even have made contact with their R.D.F., or the new radar scanner with which some of the ships were fitted.

He knew that Rigby was staring at him from right aft. It did not take a genius to know something was happening.

He said to Warwick, "Go and find out how they're managing." He gripped his arm. "Easy now. Don't start a minor revolution!"

Warwick stared at him blankly. He seemed to be searching for something in Marshall's face. Something he could recognise and share.

Blythe snapped, "They've opened fire, sir!"

Marshall tensed, watching the far off haze swirling like smoke in some 18th century sea battle. Seconds later he heard the echoing crash of gunfire, and twisted round to see waterspouts burst skywards directly in line with the hull, but well clear. The hull gave little more than a shiver to mark their explosions.

"Out of range, but not for long."

He lowered his glasses and wiped the lenses with his shirt. When he looked again there were two enormous white rings to show where the shells had dropped.

Blythe said, "Two together. They'll try for a straddle next."

Marshall pictured the other captain as the reports started to come in. A U-boat on the surface. Hasn't dived, therefore damaged. The chance of a lifetime. All the months of fighting off attacks. Seeing ships burn under U-boat attack. The pitiful survivors too stricken to speak. No, he would not hesitate now. Marshall tightened his jaw. Any more than I would.

Two more columns shot up from the blue water, hanging in the sunlight like glittering crystal curtains before dropping reluctantly as before. Closer. Those two had been a bare half-mile clear. The destroyers would be working up to full speed. Charging through the sea like the thoroughbreds they were. Marshall had been a sub-lieutenant in one. He knew what it felt like, even if it had been in peacetime.

Warwick came back, panting hard. "Nearly through, sir. Just a few strands more and the bight will be easier to free from the plane." He winced as two more shells burst. Wider apart. Feeling forwards. Getting the range.

Blythe muttered, "To think they're our own blokes out there!" He cursed and waited for another pair of shells to explode. This time the hull gave a sharp jerk. "It's not bloody fair!"

Marshall lowered his glasses. It was madness just to wait for a straddle. The mine would explode anyway. They would all die for nothing.

"We'd better try a recognition signal, Yeoman."

He took a quick glance with the glasses again as Blythe went for his lamp. The two destroyers were visible now. In line ahead, the leader cutting through the surface haze like a powerful scythe through corn. He saw more flashes, heard the abbreviated whistle as her shells smashed down into the sea barely four cables away. The leading ship had edged round so that she was almost dead astern. With two guns firing in unison she could drop shells on either beam, and then, if the U-boat still tried to dive, she would be ready to start her run-in with depth-charges.

"Aircraft, sir!" The lookout seemed to come out of a trance. "Starboard bow!"

It was moving desperately slowly, and shining so brightly in the sunlight it was impossible to identify it. Marshall heard the Vierling pivot round. It was all they needed. An air attack to finish their deception once and for all. No matter what higher authority might say, you could never keep a secret like this, even if they were still alive to argue their case.

Warwick said urgently, "German, sir. Đornier 17Z. Turning towards us." He was thinking aloud. "God, I thought the old 'Flying Pencil' was a thing of the past."

Marshall watched it fixedly. About four miles away, he could easily recognise the plane's narrow outline. It was a fair nickname, he thought. Twin-engined bombers, these Dorniers had borne the main share of the Luftwaffe's early probes into Allied territory. But now they were too slow, their bomb loads too small for the war's new sophistication. He ducked involuntarily as more shells exploded. One was dead abeam. He heard splinters sighing into the sea nearby. Spent, but still dangerous.

Blythe swore savagely. "Bloody lamp won't work, sir!"

Warwick stared at him. "I forgot to mention it. The cutter's cable is connected to that circuit. It was the only way it would reach."

Blythe said in a flat voice, "Now, he tells me."

Marshall watched the "Flying Pencil" as it swept purpose-fully towards them. Through the twin arcs of the propellers he could see the black crosses on wings and fuselage, the reflected glare from its bulging perspex nose.

The pilot had weighed up the situation. A friendly submarine, a German one at that, was being pinned down on the surface by two powerful destroyers. He would do what he could.

The Vierling hovered and then steadied on the slow-moving bomber.

"Hold your fire!" Marshall looked at the gun crews. "He might be able to give us time."

Blythe said, "No chance of that, sir. With their firepower the destroyers will blow that kite right out of the bloody sky!"

The Dornier roared sedately overhead, its bomb doors open, the forward machine-guns already swinging from bow to bow as if to sniff out the enemy. The pilot was starting to climb, and even as he swung slightly to port the air around the plane erupted in several blobs of dirty brown smoke. The short-range weapons would be even deadlier, Marshall thought grimly. Any destroyer which hoped to survive in the Mediterranean was well equipped. A floating gun-platform. The bomber was still climbing. It seemed like a great effort, as if it could hardly be bothered despite the growing pattern of flak bursts all around it.

There was a hoarse cry from aft. "Wire's cut, sir!"

When he lowered his gaze Marshall saw the mine spiralling away and Buck being hauled aboard like a corpse, the cutter still in his slime-covered hands.

"Diving stations!"

Marshall winced as another shell exploded. Very near. But for the Dornier's appearance he guessed it might have been right alongside.

Men were tumbling down the ladder, hurling tools and equipment through the hatch while others unclipped the machine-guns. Only the Vierling's crew stood fast.

Marshall watched the bomber. It was rocking dangerously, and he imagined it had been hit by fragments. The German pilot had unwittingly sacrificed himself and his crew, but had given them time to get rid of the mine. The destroyers would still close in for a depth-charge attack. Their thirty-odd knots against the U-boat's best underwater speed of nine would soon begin to tell. But at least they would have a chance, if only—— He stared as a bomb detached itself from the Dornier's belly and plummeted into the sunlight.

Blythe said hoarsely, "Lost his nerve. Don't blame him. He's too far away even to frighten 'em off!"

Marshall saw Buck being dragged into the bridge, his hands and body running blood from a dozen grazes and cuts from the rough plating.

"Vierling crew below!"

He felt the shockwave of a shell overhead, saw it burst directly beyond the bows. The next one would be on deck.

"Clear the bridge! *Dive, dive, dive!*"

But Warwick clung to his arm, dragging him round as he yelled, "That bomb, sir! It can't be!" He sounded wild. "But it's tracking the destroyer, *following her round!*"

Even as he found the bomb with his glasses, Marshall saw it hit the destroyer just abaft her bridge. There was a tremendous flash, followed by a mounting pall of dense smoke, and with stunned surprise he saw the charging destroyer begin to turn turtle, the impetus of her speed thrusting the raked stem into the sea like a ploughshare.

In those few seconds, while the U-boat tilted into the turbulence left by that last shell, he saw it all. The destroyer going over, the second one slewing round to avoid a collision and firing every gun which would bear at the circling bomber. The Dornier was also in trouble, with a long smoke trail streaming from one engine as it turned north, towards the land.

Then he was on the bridge ladder, dragging the hatch over his head, his feet kicking someone just below him as he heard the sea surge hungrily over the conning-tower.

He said sharply, "Hold her at periscope depth, Number One!" He blinked to accustom his eyes to the control room. The normally bright lights seemed dim after the sun.

"Ship breaking up astern, sir." The Asdic operator sounded very calm. The realisation had not yet reached him.

"Periscope depth, sir."

Marshall looked at their strained faces. "Slow ahead. Group down."

He saw Major Cowan by the chart table, as if he had never moved. "It was a British ship, Major." He let the words drop like stones. "Sunk by one of those radio-controlled bombs which were *supposed* to be secret. In half a minute. By a bomber which can barely do much over two hundred miles an hour." He turned to the periscope, his voice bitter as he signalled for it to be raised. "Take a look for yourself."

"The ship has sunk, sir." Speke was very quiet.

Above the purr of motors and fans they all heard the grating mutter of breaking steel as the destroyer went down. At that speed it was unlikely many of her people would get away.

Marshall retrieved the handles from Cowan's grip and took a long look astern. One ship where there had been a pair. Stopped to lower boats. No sign of the bomber which had saved them, and by so doing had laid bare the Germans' first line of defence. It had probably hit the sea some miles away.

"Down periscope. Resume course and depth." He waited, knowing that his strange calm which had stayed with him for so long would soon go and leave him naked to their contempt. "Open up the boat and fall out diving stations."

He nodded to Gerrard and walked quickly to the wardroom. What the hell had happened to him? He felt like ice. Unreached by anything. He saw Buck slumped on a seat, eyes closed as Churchill dabbed at his scars and cuts with a wad of dressing. He said, "Open the cabinet, Churchill." He took the dressing and wiped some of the muck from Buck's shoulder. "Whisky for the torpedo officer."

Buck seemed to realise he was beside him and peered at him painfully. "Whisky, sir? But I might be wanted."

"You are." Marshall held up his hand until Churchill had all but filled the glass. "By me, and the rest of us. I'll see you get some recognition for what you just did back there."

Buck gaped at him, for once at a complete loss. "Whisky will do for me." It was all he could manage.

Marshall stood up again. "Stay with him, Churchill." Then he left the wardroom and walked to Devereaux's table. Cowan was still there, as were most of the hands who would normally have gone to their messes. As he studied the Italian coastline he was conscious of the silence around him, and in his mind he kept seeing the destroyer as she had staggered brokenly on to her side. Simeon had stressed the importance of the mission, but he did not yet know the half of it. The enemy not only had the new weapon, they were also ready to use it. It would make mincemeat of any normal amphibious invasion.

He made two small marks on the chart. "Lay your course to allow for my alterations, Pilot. If we are to get these people off it has got to be perfect. No second tries, right?"

Devereaux swallowed hard. "You're asking a lot to get that close, sir."

"No, I'm *telling* you." He thought of the girl who had been sacrificed in order to reach the one man who had, and most likely still was, betraying her and his country. He added coldly, "And it's going to work. It has to."

He thought about the man they would try to bring back for questioning. It hardly made sense. An Englishman who had betrayed his country. A German bomber pilot who had saved their lives from their own people.

Without another word he turned on his heel and walked to his cabin.

When Buster Browning's staff had put the captured U-boat back into service they had only the haziest idea of what they were starting. He sat down at his desk and opened the captain's log. It was to be hoped they would know how to finish it.

The air in the wardroom was clammy and unmoving, and even the anti-condensation paint on the deckhead was shining wetly and dripping on Marshall's chart which he had placed on the table.

The others crowded round him, their breathing very loud as they stared at the chart and its criss-cross of pencilled calculations.

Marshall tapped it with his dividers. "This is where we are." He saw Cowan and his two companions peering at it doubtfully. "We are in the Gulf of Gaeta." The dividers moved slightly. "Naples is down here, sixty miles to the south-east of our position. We are about three miles south of this cape. Cape Circeo."

Cowan nodded. "Seems all right to me. There's an old ruined monastery just inland. Used to serve the villages of the Pontine Marshes once upon a time." He jabbed it with his finger. "Our people will be here. All being well."

Marshall waited and then asked, "Anything we ought to know?"

The finger shifted on the chart. "Nearest place of any size is Terracina. About ten miles east of where we'll be." He shrugged. "Mostly Italian guardposts in the past. But now, with this flap on, the Jerries will probably have brought their Panzer troops up from Naples. We'll just have to see."

Marshall straightened. Just have to see. It sounded easy.

He looked at each of them in turn. Buck, still strained and hollow-eyed after his struggle to cut away the mine. But he was listening and watching, his thin mouth turning slightly at the major's words. Devereaux seemed fairly calm. His had been almost the worst part. For during the two and a half days since the episode with the mine he had been made to alter his calculations again and again. Once past the Bay of Naples they had been forced into a long detour to avoid two small groups of islets. It was reported in the secret files that the enemy had laid some sort of underwater detection cables on the sea-bed. It might be false intelligence. But they could not take unnecessary chances on the inward journey. Other times they had to run deep when air and naval patrols had come dangerously near. But they had kept at it. On and on up the Italian coast, groping like men in the dark. Taking quick glimpses through the periscope only when a fix was really needed, or some unidentified echo was picked up on the Asdic.

Now it was almost time to play the last part. Marks and diagrams on a chart would become sand and rock. Intelligence reports could be changed into savage gunfire and cold steel.

Marshall said, "Number One will give you landing instructions." He glanced at Gerrard. "We will surface in fifteen minutes. If it all seems quiet I shall get closer inshore and watch for the signal. Then, and only then, we'll open the fore hatch and launch the boat. Questions?"

Cowan shook his head and then dragged a heavy automatic from his belt. "None from me." His companions seemed satisfied, too.

Gerrard said, "If the signal is satisfactory, sir, we can point the boat to seaward. In case we have to run for it. Otherwise we'll be bogged down in those shallows. It would take time to work clear. On the surface." He was speaking quietly but very fast. As if he expected an interruption.

Marshall replied, "Can't do that. If we were fired on from the land, I wouldn't be able to use the gun to cover the rescue. We'll try and lie parallel." He smiled, keeping his eyes on Gerrard's tight mouth. "Best of both worlds."

Buck stood up. "I'll get forrard and check the dinghy again." He glanced at the three passengers. "Good luck. I hope you get 'em safely."

With most of the fans off to minimise noise, the foul air was

170

making them sweat. In the yellow glare they looked like a group of frightened men, Marshall thought.

He said, "We've tried to think of everything. So let's get on with it."

They followed him to the control room, and while Gerrard made his checks with Frenzel and the other watchkeepers, Warwick gathered his gun crews in readiness below the conning-tower. Nobody spoke except in whispers. It was almost unnerving.

Marshall looked at Devereaux. "You've done a good job, Pilot."

The navigator was already reaching for another chart, a pencil between his teeth. But he managed to smile. Pleased with his captain's thanks, or relieved to be handing over his responsibility for the next phase.

Cowan said, "I'll go up to the front, Captain." He licked his lips. "God, this part gets you down." Then he was gone.

Marshall looked at his watch, then at the bulkhead clock. "Ready, Number One?"

Gerrard's eyes glittered in the dimmed lights. "Yes, sir." His face was shining with sweat, and it was running down the stubble around his chin.

Marshall nodded gravely. "If we get a hot welcome we'll head out to sea. Fast." He tried not to face up to it. "There'll be no point in waiting if that happens."

He walked to the ladder. "Open lower hatch." He checked over the assembled men. Making sure they would emerge on deck in the right order.

"Time, sir."

"Very well."

He walked to the periscope and waited until it had risen to eye-level. He felt the trickle of sweat on his spine, the way his palms slipped on the handles. He concentrated on the small, soundless picture. The few stars, the small spurt of spray from the slow-moving periscope. There was a tiny light stabbing the darkness. Miles away.

Devereaux, who was watching the brass ring around the periscope, breathed out slowly, "Right bearing, sir. That's the temporary buoy the Eye-ties laid earlier this year." Surprisingly, he chuckled. "Perfect, if I say so myself."

"Down periscope." Marshall looked at him. "I didn't think you ever had any doubts about it."

He walked to the ladder, and this time did not turn back.

"Surface, Number One. We're going in."

As usual, the noise seemed unending and deafening, and as Marshall and Warwick clambered out on to the slippery gratings he found it hard to believe nobody ever seemed to hear. Yet inwardly he knew that a submarine's antics as she broke surface were barely audible beyond half a cable.

Two lookouts followed through the hatch, and he knew the yeoman was on the top of the ladder, waiting to call out the gun crews if the way was clear.

Warwick had opened the voicepipes. "Control room reports nothing on Asdic, sir."

"Good."

He moved his glasses very slowly to port. The small flashing buoy had vanished around the great cape at the top of the Gulf. It was very dark. But the air was like wine. After enforced diving stations for days on end it got better each time they came up. Cool and sweet. It made your head swim. He tensed and held the glasses on a long dark shape, but relaxed just as quickly as the sluggish offshore swell smoothed the shadow away.

Warwick whispered, "Control room say five minutes, sir."

They both turned to stare at a blink of light far away across the starboard bow. A car with unmasked headlamps perhaps. A citizen taking down his blackout ready for tomorrow's new day.

How quiet it was. Just the easy murmur along the saddle tanks, the gentle pulsing of the motors through his leather sea-boots.

Warwick raised his head from the voicepipe. "We're now in twenty fathoms, sir."

"Right."

He could distinguish the land now. It was an uneven edge below the stars. As if some of them had been painted out by a giant brush. It was damn shallow just here. But against that it was a safer approach than coming in at right angles hell for leather. He thought of Gerrard and wondered. Concern, too much strain. But not fear. No more than they all endured at times like these.

"Come up, Yeoman." He heard Blythe gasping thankfully in the clean air. "We can do with a few good eyes."

"Eighteen fathoms, sir."

"Thank you, Sub." He tried to sound relaxed. "Keep it up."

Blythe said, "*There*, sir! Starboard bow!"

In the pitch-darkness the signal seemed incredibly bright.
N . . . N . . . N . . . N . . . N.

Blythe whispered fiercely, ''Acknowledge?''

''No. They should know the drill. They'll stop in a minute.
Wait for another set period.''

He had to clamp his teeth together to restrain his sudden
anxiety. The light was too brilliant, and even though it was
pointing seaward . . . he relaxed as the darkness closed in again.

''Open fore hatch. Gun crews close up.''

Warwick passed the orders and then said, ''Pilot says we're
about one thousand yards offshore, sir.'' He hesitated.
''Suggests you start your turn now.''

''No. Must get closer. Another cable at least.'' He waited,
hearing stealthy feet on the hatch and round the sides of the
bridge. ''We have to give them a chance, Sub. Imagine what it
will be like. Paddling that damn dinghy there and back.'' He
tensed. ''There's the signal again!'' He touched Warwick's
arm. ''Get down to your gun and train it on the light. Be ready
for anything.''

''Fourteen fathoms, sir.'' Blythe had taken his place at the
vacant voicepipe.

There was a brief clank of steel, and through the gloom
Marshall saw figures moving around the big fore hatch as they
hauled the dinghy on to the casing.

''Ten fathoms, sir.''

There was another light. It must be an inland road. So safe
that the locals had become careless, he thought vaguely.

''Standing by forrard, sir.''

''Thank you.'' He moved slightly to the voicepipe.
''Starboard fifteen. Stop the starboard motor.'' He held his eyes
against the gyro repeater. ''Midships. Slow ahead starboard.''

He looked over the screen. How black the land was. Yet in
daylight it would be one great panorama of depth and colour. He
saw the gun's long muzzle pointing across the beam, like a
finger above their tiny wash. ''Stop both motors.'' He touched
Blythe's hand. ''Pass the word forward. Slip the dinghy.''

''Nine fathoms, sir.''

Marshall ignored the regular reports. He watched the little
boat bobbing clear. Just one more shadow. They had the paddles
out now. Fully armed and dressed in their combat gear, they
would find it warm work.

N . . . N . . . N . . . N . . . N.

Blythe swore under his breath. "Bloody hell! Must think we're blind!"

Marshall said quietly, "They don't even know if we're here. That anybody's coming for them."

Blythe stared at him, his face pale against the sky. "Sorry, sir. Forgot. It was a stupid thing to say."

Marshall looked at his luminous watch. Wait for the major's own signal and then get under way. By the time they had made a full circle to arrive back here again, the dinghy should be ready and waiting. He found he was clenching his fists with sudden desperation. She had to be safe. After getting this far, and enduring anguish he could only guess at. She just had to be here.

"Signal, sir." Blythe licked his lips loudly. "The major's made contact."

Marshall lowered his mouth to the voicepipe. "Slow ahead both motors. Take her round again, Pilot."

"Aye, aye, sir." Devereaux could not resist adding, "We are now in six fathoms, sir."

The deck shivered as the submarine swung slowly towards open sea, the gun pivoting to cover the land until it was masked by the conning-tower.

Marshall removed his cap and ruffled his hair. It was wringing wet. Yet still he felt nothing more than he had endured in the past. Building up inside him like water behind a dam. Biding its time. He waited, testing his reactions. Perhaps he really had become a machine. Feeling nothing.

Then he thought again of the girl out there in the darkness, and knew it was a lie. And for once, he was grateful.

12 Out In The Open

"THERE'S the dinghy, sir!" Blythe pointed over the screen, his voice hoarse with excitement.

Marshall held his glasses very steady while the submarine lifted and plunged lazily in an isolated trough. Blythe was right. He could just make it out now, its shape defined by the busy splash of paddles.

He heard Warwick passing his orders on the casing, and knew the deck gun was already swinging round to cover the boat's slow approach.

"Casing party, stand by." Marshall lowered his glasses and massaged his eyes. After staring so long into the darkness they felt twice their proper size. To Blythe he added, "Can you see if they're all there?"

The yeoman did not reply immediately. "Hard to be sure. But I think I can see ten heads. God knows how they all got in!"

Marshall watched the seamen gathering by the fore hatch. *We made it*. He turned sharply as a flare exploded in the sky. It was far away. Well inland. An exercise perhaps. Or a signal to close the net around escaping agents.

"Stop both motors."

He trained his glasses on the boat. Blythe was right. It was crammed with dark figures, and he recognised Petty Officer Cain's silhouette sitting on the rounded hull as he waited to catch a heaving line.

He saw the dinghy begin to slew round obediently to the tow as the first line was made fast, heard Warwick shouting to a seaman to assist the passengers aboard. He felt his heart thumping against his ribs. Strange how the tension was more apparent now. Maybe because of the complete silence. Or——he stiffened as a figure was lifted on to the casing. Dead or injured, it was impossible to say. Others were following, and he heard brief snatches of questions and answers.

Then Major Cowan came running aft, his rubber-soled boots squeaking on the ladder as he hauled himself up the side of the tower.

He said tersely, "They've had a bit of bother, Captain." He gestured towards the shore. "Been running and hiding for days. The whole place is swarming with patrols." He sucked in long gulps of air. "But we've got Travis." He paused. "The bastard."

"What about the others?" Marshall knew that she had not returned. "I thought the dinghy was full."

"Yes. We lifted off some of our chaps. A lieutenant in the S.A.S. who has been working with an Italian sabotage group. Also a wounded Italian. Communist, to all accounts. And Moss, the only one of the original party."

"And the rest?"

"Major Carter and Mrs. Travis went inland, up towards the canal. It was the only way they could draw off the nearest search party. Moss was shot in the thigh, so he couldn't help." He sighed. "I'm afraid there's nothing we could do to save the others."

Warwick's head appeared over the side of the bridge. "Lieutenant Buck's asked if he can close the fore hatch, sir."

Marshall said, "Tell me, Major, do you think they've been caught?"

Cowan nodded. "They intended to be captured. Nothing else would have convinced the enemy. If they'd taken Travis too, we might never have got our information."

Marshall thought about the drifting flare. It must have been to call off the hunt. To inform the searchers they had captured the enemy agents.

He said swiftly, "Get the first lieutenant up here immediately. I'm going forrard."

He flung himself over the side of the bridge and hurried along the wet casing, with Warwick and the major close behind him.

The dinghy was still in the water. As if they had anticipated his reactions.

Buck said, "This is bloody bad, sir."

Marshall sought out the figure he had just seen speaking to Cain.

"Are you the S.A.S. officer?"

"That's right, sir. Smith's the name." He was a very small man.

"Do you know this area well?"

The lieutenant glanced at Cowan, but the latter merely snapped, "Tell him."

"Fairly well. I wasn't involved with *this* affair." He added bitterly, "I'm afraid I'd have shot that Travis character."

Marshall tried to control his racing thoughts. "I'm going ashore."

The little man froze, his arm in mid-air.

Marshall continued sharply, "Do you think we could find them? Get them away?"

Smith shrugged. "Not much chance. But the Eye-ties are in this sector. They've got strict orders to hold prisoners until their German allies arrive. The Gestapo, I would think." He nodded slowly. "I'll come with you." He turned slightly. "How about it, Major?"

Cowan replied dully, "I've got to start the investigation on Travis. I've got my orders. I'm sorry." He moved closer. "Look, Marshall, I don't know about your motives, I'm not sure I want to. But I'd advise you to drop it, here and now. It's a risk *we* have to take in this game. Today, them. Tomorrow, well, who knows?"

Gerrard appeared on the casing, his thin figure stooping as he groped along the guardrail.

Marshall said, "I'm going ashore, Number One. You will assume command and rendezvous here in four hours."

Smith muttered, "It'll take all of that, Captain."

Marshall ignored him. "If I fail, you can go all out until you reach safety. It'll be an easy run. Make as many detours as you like. Send our private signal when you're well clear, and Simeon will tell you where to dock, right?"

Gerrard exclaimed, "It's madness. You'll never stand a chance. I—I can't allow you to do it."

Petty Officer Cain called softly, "Five volunteers be enough, sir?"

Marshall looked at him. "Thank you. Machine-pistols and grenades. Just like they taught us in Scotland."

He turned to Lieutenant Smith. "Are you sure you can manage another trip?"

The little man chuckled. "Actually, I've been resting up in the old monastery for close on a week. Sipping wine and taking it easy, until this lot tumbled in on me. I guess that bit of cover has been blown for good."

Gerrard said harshly, "For God's sake, sir! What shall I say if you get caught?"

"Apologise, Bob. Say I'm sorry." He gripped his arm. "This is important. To *me*."

"I've mustered the men, sir." Cain was already in the dinghy again. "I had a feelin' you might try some trick or other."

Marshall looked round at the silent figures. "Close the fore hatch and stand well offshore." He turned to Gerrard. "Dive if you like. It'll be your decision."

He saw him nod jerkily. "Take it easy, Bob."

Then he felt Warwick strapping the heavy holster around his waist, heard him whisper fervently, "Take me too, sir."

"No, Sub." He slithered over the side of the casing, feeling the spray on his legs and feet. "My party, this time."

He gripped a paddle. "Shove off. Let's see how fast we can move this thing!" When he turned his head he saw the submarine looming above him, and felt a sharp sense of loneliness. Then as it slid slowly into deep shadow he said, "It'll probably do us good to stretch our legs.'' He heard someone chuckle, and marvelled at the way he could find such stupid remarks to sustain them.

Smith said, "I know a likely place. The only one where the local patrols would hold them until the Jerries arrive. If I'm wrong, we can forget it. It'll be dawn in four hours. After that. . . .'' He left the rest unsaid.

As the shoreline took on a more definite shape nobody spoke, and Marshall was conscious of the tension all around them. Only when he looked at the men crouched in the dinghy did he feel any sort of doubt. What right had he to endanger their lives?

Cain said suddenly, " 'Ere's a bit of beach, sir. We'll 'ave to wade the last part.''

They scrambled into the water, and Marshall felt the gentle undertow pulling at his feet like an embrace. But the touch of land, the absence of steel and busy machinery, helped to steady him, and he said, "Two stay with the dinghy. If we don't come back you will rendezvous with Lieutenant Gerrard. I'll leave the choice to you, P.O.''

Smith murmured, "Quite a bunch, sir. They seem eager to get their heads shot off!'' It appeared to impress him.

Cain squelched through the damp sand. "Told 'em, sir. We're ready when you are.'' He drew the heavy machine-pistol from its holster and cocked it.

Smith held a wrist compass to his eyes. "Follow me. Keep quiet, and freeze when I do.'' He seemed even smaller amongst the sailors. "If you have to fight, then fight. No fancy stuff, or you're dead before you start. Just get in and kill the bastards.'' He grinned. "Try and think of them all as senior officers! Makes it easier!'' Then he turned on his heel and strode up a steep bank, away from the water's edge.

Only once did he pause, and that was to whisper in Marshall's ear. "You know, Captain, it might just come off. After all, nobody but a raving lunatic would attempt this sort of caper!''

"Better rest up for a bit.'' Smith sat down on the ground, his machine-pistol in his lap. "Get our bearings.''

Marshall knelt beside him, every muscle groaning in protest. They had been on the move for about an hour without any break. Smith certainly knew his territory, and had guided them along a

178

small coast road before striking inland through rough and deserted countryside. Occasionally he had pointed into the darkness, describing an invisible village, or some local track which led to isolated dwellings which he had gathered in his mind like a map.

He said, "I've been working north of Terracina. There's a railway cutting in the hills. The local guerrillas want to blow it up. I had to *dissuade* them." He chuckled. "To explain that it might be needed by us one of these fine days." He rolled on to his side. *"Hold it!"*

They all dived into the grass, hearing the dull rumble of vehicles growing and then fading just as quickly into the stillness.

He said calmly, "They've taken the other road. Probably troops called off from the hunt." He looked at Marshall curiously. "This is an odd way for a sailor to fight a war, if I might venture an opinion?"

"It's an odd war."

Smith stood up. "Quite. Time to move, boys. About two miles farther. There's a police post on the road junction. Two storeys and a couple of small outbuildings. Used to belong to the Caribinieri. Now they have a permanent squad of soldiers."

They walked on in silence, feet kicking up dust and tiny stones at the roadside, their weapons probing the darkness.

"There's a light, sir." Cain stood on a pile of discarded logs. He sounded excited.

Smith nodded. "That's it." He looked at the three seamen. "I'll want you on the opposite side of the road from the police post." He peered up at the sky. "There should be a telephone cable somewhere. That can be cut as soon as we move in. Just in case it takes longer than we've planned."

They moved forward more cautiously, each man holding himself low as if to avoid a sudden burst of gunfire.

The police post was very easy to see. It was white-walled, so that the double gates were equally visible, like a gap in a perfect set of teeth.

Smith gestured to Marshall. "One sentry. Just inside. See his cigarette?" He waited and added patiently. "You're new at this, eh?" He sighed. "I'm sure you're a damn good submarine commander, but this is something different." He dropped into a crouch. "The guardroom is directly opposite the gates. Usually about ten men and a lieutenant. He lives in the village, but tonight it's my guess he'll be right on the spot, ready to boast to the Jerries."

"Car coming, sir!"

"*Down!*"

They flopped into the long, coarse grass as the engine grew louder along the road.

Smith said, "Small and fast."

Marshall felt the dust on his face, the grass pricking his chin. Then he saw the headlights sweeping across the front of the white wall, heard a startled challenge, which was followed immediately by a string of angry words. In German.

Smith murmured, "Bad. The Krauts are here now. That makes it a bit naughty."

Doors slammed, and after more muffled shouting the solitary cigarette reappeared by the gates as the Italian sentry recovered from the interruption.

Smith snapped, "Right. Here we go." He prodded the men nearest him. "One of you at each end of the wall, but this side of the road. That'll give good cross-fire." He handed something to the third seaman. "Up that pole and cut the wires. Then be ready to move." He restrained him roughly. "Not yet, man! Where are your manners?"

Cain whispered uneasily, "That leaves us then, sir."

"S'right." Smith was examining his grenades. "Rather like the Wild West. No finesse. You just go in and let rip." He seemed satisfied, and reached down to pull a commando dagger from his boot. "Okay?"

They nodded.

Smith rolled slowly across the road, as if he was being blown over and over by some silent wind. Against the wall his small figure was clearly etched, but he looked more like a distorted shadow than a man.

Marshall gripped the heavy pistol, trying to remember what he had been told about the safety catch. When he lifted his eyes he realised Smith had vanished, and for an instant longer he imagined that he had started back across the road.

Cain exclaimed, "Christ! 'E's done for 'im!"

There was not even the slightest sound. But the glowing cigarette was moving very slowly, lower and lower, until at length it was a tiny red spot on the ground.

Marshall sprang to his feet. "Cut the wires!"

With Cain beside him he ran across the road and almost fell across the spreadeagled corpse of the dead sentry. Smith was kneeling beside it, wiping his knife carefully on the man's coat before replacing it in his boot.

He stood up and gestured towards the main building. They followed him very slowly, aware of the buzz of voices, the smell of petrol from the small car which had just arrived. It had a German cross on its canopy, and had been driven hard.

Smith's head showed briefly against a lighted slit in some shutters. Then he whispered, "A good dozen in there. Swilling vino." He rubbed his chin. "No Germans, and no Italian officer either." He reached up and gently tested the corner of the shutters. "Careless bastards." He drew two grenades from his pouch and added, "Two each. Pull out the pins, release the levers, count two, and then pop them into the window." He slung his pistol over his arm. "Just pray to God there's no unbreakable glass. If there is, we'll have six grenades for company!"

Marshall pulled the pin from a grenade, and holding the lever flat with his fingers, jerked out the pin from another. He saw Cain following his example, and wondered if they could hear his heart pounding.

Smith had only withdrawn one pin. With his free hand he took hold of the shutter:

"Ready? Right, release 'em!" As the five levers clattered in the yard Smith dragged back the shutter with all his strength. *"Now!"*

The smash of breaking glass, the attendant shouts of surprise and then terror, were almost drowned by Cain yelling, "Jesus, I've dropped one of 'em!"

Smith bent down and scooped the live grenade off the ground, and hurled it after the others. He had barely time to pull the pin on his own grenade and throw himself beside Marshall and Cain before the front of the building erupted in one great burst of fire and noise. Glass, woodwork and stones flew across the yard and clattered against the wall and on to the road beyond, and from above came a deluge of broken tiles and huge lumps of plaster.

Smith yelled, "Inside!"

He kicked open the sagging door and dashed into the room. The light had been broken, but enough filtered from a passageway at the rear to show the devastation and death left by the grenades. In a dark corner someone was screaming and

181

choking, the sounds inhuman. Smith aimed a short burst of automatic fire, the flashes lighting up staring eyes and gleaming wounds before hiding them once more. The screaming stopped.

Smith was already in the passageway, his pistol cutting down a terrified man in a cook's apron who had come careering round a corner at the far end. He reached another door and threw his weight against it, falling almost flat as the catch collapsed, allowing the light to spill into the smoke-filled corridor, momentarily blinding them.

A single shot came from the room, cutting plaster from the wall by Marshall's shoulder. He saw an Italian officer staring at him wildly, an automatic in his hand as he aimed for another shot.

Smith screamed, "*Get him!* "

Marshall did not feel any pressure, just the gun jumping in his grip, and saw the officer spin round like a puppet, the wall beyond him splashed with patches of bright scarlet.

Cain shouted, " 'Ere's the major, sir!"

He was still wearing his shabby businessman's suit, but there was dirt all over it, and he had lost one of his shoes. He must have been shot several times at the moment of capture, and his face was barely recognisable.

Smith barked. "That door! Cover it!"

The door in question was at the other side of the room, narrow and heavily studded. A cell. It was opening very slowly, and after the horror of the grenades and the sight of Carter's riddled body it was all the more unnerving. Marshall could feel himself gritting his teeth and panting like a wild animal, and his eyes watered with frantic concentration. Further and further, until a long slit of light played across the room, over the dead Italian and on to Cain's boots. After a slight pause, a hand appeared. It was holding a white handkerchief.

Smith said tersely, "A truce, eh?" He was grinning, but his face was a picture of cold determination.

He yelled, "Come out with your hands up!" In a quieter tone he added, "If they so much as blink, let 'em have it!"

There were two of them. Both in black uniforms, and so much alike they could have been brothers.

Smith gestured to the floor. "Down! Hands behind your heads!"

The Germans understood well enough and laid down without a word beside the dead officer.

Smith said quietly, "Watch 'em, Cain." Then very gently he pushed the door wide open and danced nimbly around the frame.

Marshall followed, the gun almost slipping from his fingers as he saw the girl. She was lying on a heavy table, her arms and legs tied to its corners. She was naked, and in the overhead light looked like a small broken statue.

Smith snapped, "Don't touch her!"

He moved swiftly to the table, while Marshall stood motionless by the door. There were wires connected to the girl's breasts and thighs, they in turn were attached to a small metal box beside the table. The box was humming gently. Like something alive.

Smith dropped his pistol and ran his fingers over a line of controls. The humming stopped, and he said quietly, "Now give me a hand, for God's sake."

Marshall took her head in his hands, his eyes smarting as he saw the raw marks on her body, the blood on her mouth where someone had punched her.

Smith held his breath and unclipped the wires one by one. Only then did she open her eyes, her tongue touching her lips, her stomach contracting as if to resist some new torture.

Marshall whispered, "It's all right. *Please, it's all right.*"

Smith was struggling out of his long leather coat. "Here. Get her into this." He held Marshall's eyes. "Fast as you like." He shouted to Cain, "You all right?"

"Yes." A pause. "But I think I 'eard voices at the rear."

"More sentries."

Smith watched as Marshall eased the girl from the table. Just one movement made her cry out, and then she fell limply against him.

"Carry her." Smith jammed a fresh magazine into his pistol. "Let's move."

As Marshall carried the girl through the adjoining room, Smith called, "You two. In here. *Schnell!*"

The two Gestapo men scrambled to their feet, one darting a quick glance at Marshall as he passed. Smith backed out of the cell, pausing for just a moment to study the two Germans as they stood awkwardly beside their table with its electric box.

He took the last grenade from his pouch and threw it at their feet, before leaping outside and dragging the heavy door behind him. He heard them scream, felt their frantic fists against the door before the grenade exploded. He watched the dust and smoke spouting around the edges and said, "Sleep well, you bastards!"

Outside on the road it seemed very cool, even cold. Smith snapped, "Give your captain a hand." He watched their figures start to melt into the shadows and then said to Cain, "Just one last thing." He trained his machine-pistol on the left-hand corner of the wall. "Then we'll follow along."

Bent almost double, their silhouettes grotesque against the pale wall, the two sentries from the rear of the post edged cautiously towards the gates. They did not want to go inside. The explosions and gunfire, the stench of the shattered corpses told them clearly what had happened. But they had to go just the same. To know. To be sure.

Smith took aim and fired a full magazine, the rasping clatter of gunfire echoing back from the wall like some additional marksman.

He looked unwinkingly at the two inert humps below the wall and then said, "That's it then." He jammed in another magazine. "It should give us an hour or so."

Cain stumbled after him, his mind cringing, the pistol dangling at his side. It was not real. It could not happen to him. In a moment he would awake. Snap out of it.

Smith fell in step beside him. "Here. Have a cigarette." He lit his own calmly, then stooped to pick up a small round stone. Before putting it in Cain's pocket he said, "There. You've got a piece of enemy territory all for yourself. More than some ever get."

Cain sucked on his cigarette and coughed hoarsely. He thought of Major Carter, all bloody and broken. Not a man any more. Just a thing. A nothing. And that poor girl, what they were doing to her. He thought too of Marshall, the way he had carried her from the post. No sign of weariness. He had marched out as if he was carrying the most precious thing in the whole world.

Cain recalled his own wife in Harwich. What would he have thought if it had been her on that table?

Smith halted and waited while Cain vomited against the roadway. "All right now, P.O.?"

Cain wiped his mouth with his sleeve. "Sure thing. Just takes a bit of gettin' used to."

Smith smiled and glanced at the sky. It looked lighter already. "You never do that, my friend. Not in a million bloody years."

Lieutenant Victor Frenzel stood loosely by his control panel watching the chief electrical artificer checking gauges for the umpteenth time. Around him in the control room it seemed extra quiet as the submarine continued circling offshore at periscope depth. They were still closed up at diving stations, supposedly ready for anything, the dimmed deckhead lights throwing gaunt shadows from bowed heads, and arms reaching out to make the usual adjustments.

Buck was at the periscope, his left arm draped over one of the handles as he made a slow, unhurried inspection. Number One and Devereaux were in the wardroom for some reason.

Frenzel glanced impatiently at the bulkhead clock. It must be getting light up top. Soon time to get the hell out.

Warwick was whispering with his senior gunlayer below the conning-tower hatch, nodding every so often as the leading seaman explained some technical point or other. It helped pass the time. Deaden the anxiety.

Frenzel hated such moments. It had not always been so. Just since Captain Browning had sent for him to tell him the news. Poor old Buster. He had not known how to say it. He did not even seem to know there was no way of saying it. Not then. Not ever.

He clenched his fists as her picture came back again. And the kid. Such a little chap. Just like her.

They had been very lucky. He had married her early, when he had been a leading stoker. But for her he might never have got down to his books, never have discovered what she had seen in him. When he had been commissioned she had shared it. All the others had been on the outside. It had always been like that. He stared moodily round the control room. Fifteen years he had been in the *Andrew*. Since he was a boy. Apart from Starkie and a couple of others, he was the oldest one in the boat. But before, in other submarines, he had somehow managed to feel quite the opposite. He shivered. How long would it last?

Buck murmured, "Down 'scope." He walked to Frenzel's side. "Nothing."

"Is it light yet?"

"I can see the headland. Getting a bit dodgy." He shifted uneasily. "It's not the same without the skipper, is it?"

"No."

"D'you reckon he was right?" Buck seemed to want to talk. That was unusual enough.

Frenzel looked away. "What's *right* anyway?" He sighed. "He's full of surprises, that one."

"They'll crucify him for what he's doing."

Frenzel thought of the men he had seen brought aboard. "The Jerries will do that if they catch him."

Buck's remark had brought it home to him. It *was* different without Marshall. The captain was always close, ready to deal with things, make decisions, right or wrong. It was like losing a limb, or some essential part of the boat.

Keville, the artificer, turned in his seat. "All gauges checked, sir." He grinned. "Build good boats, the Jerries do."

Buck whispered, "Can't wait much longer, Vic. What the hell will we do?"

Churchill padded across the deck. "Pardon, sir. Number One'd like you in the wardroom." He was speaking to Frenzel.

Buck grimaced. "Sounds like a decision."

"Maybe." Frenzel turned on his heel. "Indecision more likely."

He found Gerrard and Devereaux sitting on opposite sides of the table below a solitary deckhead light. He heard someone moaning softly behind drawn curtains, and guessed it was Moss, the wounded agent. The place stank of disinfectant. The Italian was in another bunk, snoring fit to burst. He knew that the man Travis and the three agents were in Marshall's cabin. Talking, threatening, he did not know or care.

Devereaux looked up, his sleek head shining under the light. "Ah, Chief, just the man."

Gerrard said, "Pilot thinks it's time to move out." He looked terrible. Gaunt and lined with worry. He seemed to have put on years in the last few hours.

Frenzel sat down but kept his eyes on Gerrard. He could not believe it. He replied flatly, "You're in command. What do *you* think?"

Devereaux interrupted. "Fact is, Chief, I'm not sure we should stay here a second more. The C.O.'s decision was beyond the widest interpretation of his orders. It's obvious."

Frenzel said, "Not to me." He looked at Gerrard again. "Well?"

"I can understand perfectly. The captain did what he thought was right, but. . . ."

Frenzel groped for a cigarette and changed his mind. Those words again. *Right. But.*

Gerrard said sharply, "What about your department, Chief?" He sounded as if he was forcing a decision. "Are you satisfied with fuel and so forth?"

Frenzel stood up abruptly. "A good engineer is never satisfied with anything." He looked at each of them in turn. "Christ, I must be getting old. I should have realised. You want *me* to make it easy for you. Provide a let-out."

Devereaux said, "It's not like that. Number One doesn't seem to know what——" He got no further.

Gerrard said harshly, "When I want your opinions, I'll bloody well ask for them!" He swung on Frenzel. "You don't understand! I'm not trying to shirk responsibility!"

Frenzel stared at him. "What the hell has responsibility got to do with it?" He walked round the table. "He's your friend, isn't he? Wouldn't he do the same for you? At least have a *try?*"

Gerrard looked down at the table. "I know. It's not that."

Frenzel added quietly, "I thought you had more guts."

"What d'you know about it?" Gerrard was on his feet, too. "You haven't got a wife! It's easy for you to make snap decisions which might kill all of us!" He saw the expression on Frenzel's face and said hoarsely, "God, I'm sorry, Chief. That was unforgivable."

From the control room Buck's voice broke the sudden silence between them. "Dinghy in sight! Just saw the signal!"

Gerrard blundered between them, his feet carrying him automatically to his station for surfacing the boat.

Frenzel thrust out one arm and prevented Devereaux from following. "D'you know, I've always thought you were a deep one. But I never imagined you were such a bastard."

Devereaux faced him, his mouth clamped in a small smile. "I suppose *you* know what you're talking about."

"So do you." He dropped his arm. "You want to break him, don't you? Just so that you can beat your little drum in the right quarters."

He followed him towards the control room. If Buck had not

broken the tension he would have said or done something which might have smashed their world forever.

He saw Gerrard slinging his glasses round his neck as he watched the lower hatch being opened. Devereaux had taken over as first lieutenant, and was apparently engrossed in studying the gauges above Starkie's head.

"Blow all main ballast!"

Frenzel threw down his switches and half listened to the air roaring into the saddle tanks.

Marshall was coming back. And not a moment too soon.

13   Where No Birds Sing

"IF you'll wait in here, sir." The orderly held open a door and waited for Marshall to enter the spacious room. "The captain will see you in just a moment."

Marshall walked slowly to the one wide window which overlooked the harbour. Outside it was blazing hot, the glare throwing up shimmering reflections from the many anchored ships and broad expanse of blue water. Alexandria. He smiled wryly. "Alex." But for the dazzle-paint on some of the ships, the neat lines of small buoys and floats which marked the underwater booms and nets, it could have been peacetime. There were awnings spread on most of the vessels, and he saw a marine band marching and counter-marching on the quarterdeck of a massive battleship. The bandmaster must be a real tyrant to keep them at it, he thought.

He turned and looked at the room. Its fine mosaic floor and domed ceiling gave it an air of calm, and after the passage from the depot ship where U-192 had secured just an hour earlier it felt as cool as a tomb. There was a solitary, marble-topped table, bare but for an old copy of the *Tatler* and a dog-eared card which explained "what to do in an air raid." Someone else who had waited here had scrawled, "Take cover in a bottle of gin" underneath it.

Although the building was now classified as part of the naval command set-up, there was little else to show a change of ownership. It had once belonged to an Egyptian government official, but it was said that it was used more often than not by the King to entertain some of his friends. Marshall studied the huge murals which decorated the walls. Voluptuous dancing girls in every imaginable stance. Even the table legs were carved like nude women.

He turned away, recalling with sickening clarity the girl strapped to the table. A week ago. It could have been yesterday. He remembered her twisting in his arms, fighting him without strength or purpose, not knowing she was conscious or even alive.

When they had sighted the surfacing submarine and Cain had stood upright in the dinghy to wave his arms like a madman, she had not given any hint of understanding.

Once on board, with boat submerged and heading out again into open waters, he had made sure she was comfortable in his cabin.

Major Cowan had protested, "But I'm trying to interrogate Travis in there!"

Marshall had snapped, "Do it somewhere else. Stick him in a torpedo tube, for all I care!"

For by then, within minutes of resuming command, he had discovered something else about Travis. He had not come willingly to help his own country. There had been a small attempt at sabotage at the site where he was employed, and quite unbeknown to him the wheels had started to turn. The Italians had panicked and informed the German Military Intelligence, who had immediately telephoned Gestapo headquarters. Most of the labour working on the site was recruited locally, or consisted of heavily guarded wretches from a concentration camp in the north. The Gestapo had begun to check more individual records, and Travis's had been one of them. Their Paris office had sent details of Travis's wife, of their suspicions about her connections with the Resistance.

The girl's unexpected arrival had sprung the odds against Travis, and with moments to spare he had been smuggled through a tightening cordon. As the small party had moved through the countryside, resting briefly in "safe" houses, or sleeping rough in fields, Travis had probably seen his wife as the main cause of his own destruction. But for her he would still have been working safely for the Germans. It was a well paid appointment with more to come. He had travelled widely before the war, and knew that in the unlikely event of the Germans losing the last battle, he would be well placed to disappear into a neutral country, to bide his time until the moment was ripe for

189

his return. They always needed good engineers, especially after a war. And he was very good at his work.

Over and over again Marshall had tried to imagine the sort of man who would knowingly let his wife, no matter what had changed between them, go straight into the hands of the Gestapo. Just to give him time to get away. To allow men like Cowan and Simeon an opportunity to discover the full extent of the enemy's strategy.

Having no doctor on board, Marshall had done all he could to make her feel safe, even if he could not share her inner reactions. Churchill had proved to be a tower of strength. Waiting on her. Seeing she was left undisturbed. Guarding her like a watchdog.

Day after day, hour after hour, while the boat had felt her way clear of enemy-patrolled waters, Marshall had waited for a sign. But she kept in the cabin, with just a small light above the bunk for company.

The S.A.S. lieutenant had said, "Let her be, Captain. It'll take time. And a whole lot more."

They had surfaced to send their private signal, and just as quickly the reply had come back to them. Destination—Alexandria. Maximum security as before.

Only that morning they had surfaced at the exact time arranged, to be met and escorted into harbour by a motor gunboat of the Special Boat Squadron. With her false screen rigged once more, the U-boat had been led to a moored depot ship, and within minutes, or so it had seemed, had been additionally camouflaged with canvas dodgers, painting stages, and anything else which might avoid interest. Not that there was much likelihood of that. The harbour had plenty of evidence of repair work and hasty overhauls. One more veteran would excite little attention.

He recalled the first time she had actually spoken to him. He had been standing just inside the cabin, watching as Churchill had held a cup of soup to her lips. How small she had looked. Lost in a submarine sweater and somebody's best bell-bottom trousers.

She had suddenly pushed the cup away and had said huskily, "Where *were* you?" Her eyes had filled with terror, like those of a trapped animal. "You didn't come!" Then she had fallen back on the pillows.

Churchill had said, "She ain't makin' sense yet, sir." He had been genuinely worried. "But we don't give up where I come from."

Marshall thought too of her body as it had looked when she had been brought aboard. The angry marks on her skin, the blood around her mouth. He had never known such unreasoning fury as at those moments. If he could have got his hands on Travis he would have killed him.

Once alongside the depot ship things had moved swiftly. Grimfaced officers had come for Travis and the three agents. Medical staff had looked after the girl and the wounded agent, Moss. The Italian, who had apparently enjoyed the passage to Alexandria immensely, had walked up the brow without assistance, waving to the watching sailors like visiting royalty.

Smith had been the last to leave. In the searing sunlight, in his filthy boots and leather coat, he had looked for all the world like another Peter Lorre.

"I wish you well, Captain." He had held out his hand. "You are a brave man." He had tapped his heart gravely. "But too much of this, I think."

The door opened silently. "The captain will see you now, sir."

Marshall followed him into a deserted corridor. In his white shirt and shorts he felt out of place. Flowing robes, the scent of strong coffee and young girls would have been more suitable.

It was a similar room to the one he had just left, except that it was crammed with cabinets, telephones and littered tables. Even the dancing girls were hidden by maps and charts which hung from every wall.

Captain Browning was silhouetted against the window, his head shining like a chestnut in the reflected glare.

He turned and said, "By God, Marshall, you never fail to astound me." He gripped his hand and shook it slowly. "You look well, despite what you've been doing."

Marshall placed his cap on a table and sat down. Browning's grip had changed. It was almost shaky. Like someone with fever.

"I'll say no more." Browning settled himself in a chair. "Danger seems to agree with you."

He did not offer him a drink. Nor did there appear to be any in the room.

"Commander Simeon will want to speak with you shortly." He lowered his gaze. "He's with our Intelligence chaps. Checking what Cowan has discovered from Travis. I've read your report too, of course. About the destroyer being sunk by a guided bomb.'' He shook his massive head. ''Terrible. All getting beyond me.''

''Which ship was she, sir?'' He saw her again. Charging in with her consort for the kill. His own command.

''The *Dundee*.'' Browning turned as if to look out of the window, the swivel chair creaking under his weight. ''My son was midshipman in her.''

Marshall stared at him. All the time. It never stopped. While they had been at sea, as Smith had directed their efforts into one savage attack on the police post, others had suffered.

''I'm very sorry, sir. Were there any survivors?''

Browning took a deep breath. ''A few. He wasn't one of them, I'm afraid.'' He looked at Marshall, but his eyes seemed to go right through him. ''I'll miss that lad, you know.''

He cleared his throat noisily and turned over several sheets of paper on his desk.

Then he said, ''I'm afraid there'll be no leave for your people. I've told the depot ship to make 'em as comfortable as possible. Baths, a few film shows, that sort of thing.'' He looked at Marshall again. ''I'm sorry I can't do more. Security.'' He lingered over the word, as if he was examining it for himself.

''I was wondering about the girl, sir.'' Marshall watched for some reaction. ''What will become of her now?''

''Back to U.K., I imagine. Her department will deal with it. Brave girl. I'd like to have met her.'' Something of a smile puckered his mouth. ''By God, that was a fine thing you did. Some people take a different view.'' He shrugged. ''Still, can't have it both ways. Either this is the real Navy or it's a special section. I'm beginning to wonder what the hell we *are* doing some of the time.''

The door opened slightly. ''Commander Simeon is here, sir.''

Browning nodded. Then he said urgently, ''Leave this to me.'' He leaned forward in his chair. ''I may be old, but I've a few cards of my own!''

Simeon strode into the room and threw his cap on to a chair. He was dressed in perfect white drill which showed up the flush on his face as he snapped, ''I heard you were here! God damn it, Marshall, I've just about had all I can take from you!''

Browning said. "Sit down. I'm not having a row in my room!"

Simeon sat down and adjusted the crease in his trouser leg before continuing in a calmer tone, "When I heard what you did. How you jeopardised the mission, the submarine, *everything*, for your own amusement, I could hardly credit it."

Marshall replied, "You told me the decision on the spot was mine alone. The submarine stayed to the precise moment arranged. As laid down in your instructions." He studied him calmly. "Sir."

"I didn't tell you to go off like a madman on your own!" Simeon's face was getting more flushed. "Mrs. Travis had her job to do. We all have."

Marshall realised he was on his feet, the others watching him with mixed expressions.

He said, "She was being tortured. Not sitting behind a desk. She and the major, Carter, or whatever his real name was, went inland alone, knowing they would be caught. Inviting it, just to save that gutless traitor you've been talking to." He swung round, his eyes cold. "Your people sent her into that mess without even knowing what might go wrong. You didn't even care, did you?"

Simeon replied angrily, "Suppose they'd caught *you*? They'd have got it out of you, too. What you were doing. About the U-boat anything they wanted."

Marshall smiled gently. It was Simeon's one weak spot. Criticism, a hint that any part of his planning might be at fault.

"That seems to apply to everyone in this department, from what I can see of it, sir."

Browning stood up and said, "Now I'll have my say, gentlemen. I've been with the Chiefs of Staff, British and American, and we've done a lot of work in the last few days."

Simeon had momentarily forgotten Marshall. "What's this, sir? I've not been told."

Browning eyed him blandly. "I'm telling you now, aren't I?" He went on, "The last details are all but fixed. We're going into Sicily in the first two weeks of July. It fits. It's more or less final."

Simeon took out his cigarette case. "Oh that, sir." His hand was shaking as he lit one. "I know about *that*."

"Good." Browning smiled. "But before then, there is something more we in this section must do. It will cut corners, and with luck, save lives.''

Simeon sat bolt upright but said nothing.

Browning continued in the same unruffled tone, ''These radio-controlled bombs are brought down through Italy and assembled at the site where Travis was employed. From there they go by rail and road to the various airfields. Mostly to the east and the Adriatic coast, thanks to our false leaks about a proposed invasion via Greece and the Balkans. But some will go by sea to Sicily to await despatch to the Luftwaffe.'' He shrugged. ''A good supply is already in Sicily, of course, but nowhere near the amount there would be if the enemy knew our exact intentions.''

Simeon said curtly, ''Well, that's pretty obvious, sir.''

''I'm glad. But what you probably did not know, Commander, was that the Sicily storage point is under one command, that of a certain Italian general. Am I right?'' He gestured towards the chart. ''I knew him well before the war, and during the last one. We were both out here then. On the same side.'' He glanced at Marshall. ''But for the present circumstances we would still be firm friends.''

Simeon had recovered his composure. ''Well, I shouldn't talk too much about *that*, sir!'' He laughed.

''Oh, but I did. To the Chiefs of Staff, as a matter of fact.'' He allowed his words to sink in. ''They all agree that we will get the Italians on our side once we invade. Those on our side of the lines, so to speak. The general I spoke of is intelligent. He is also shrewd enough to know that if he co-operates *before* the invasion, his future will be secure, and there will be no piecemeal destruction of his men and his command.''

Simeon half rose and sat down again. ''*Before* the invasion, sir?''

''That is what I said. Given a solemn promise, he would be able to take over the whole system of bunkers. Seal 'em off. By the time the Jerries got more supplies of bombs brought from elsewhere. . . .'' He swept a beefy hand across the chart. ''Bang! John Bull and Yankee Doodle will be enjoying the sunshine in Palermo and Syracuse!''

He turned to Marshall, who had remained silent. ''Well, what d'you think?''

Marshall nodded slowly. ''If it can be done, then I agree with you.''

Simeon exploded, "*If* it can be done! And who would be entrusted with such a mission, if I might be told *that*, sir?"

Browning smiled, the effort smoothing some of the lines. "Me."

"But, but——" Simeon looked round the room wildly. "You have no experience of this sort of work, sir!"

"No? Too old, eh?" Browning sighed contentedly. "Well, some think otherwise." He regarded him calmly. "If you hop over to the C.-in-C.'s office, his flag captain will fill you in on operational details."

Simeon groped for his cap and stood up very stiffly.

"Very well, sir. If it's all settled, then—"

"It is." He smiled. "Definitely."

As the door closed Browning hurried to a cupboard and produced an unopened bottle.

"Bourbon. Was given it by a chap on Eisenhower's staff. Never tried it myself. But today, anything would be just right." Some of the spirit slopped across the desk. "I've waited a long while for this. Just to see his face, damn his bloody impertinence!"

"You'll be needing my boat, sir?"

He nodded. "Who else?" He looked away. "I'm fond of you. You're very like David might have become. I'd like to think so anyway."

Marshall said quietly, "Thank you. I appreciate that, sir. Perhaps more than you know."

Browning beamed at him. "I'm glad. After this I think we can pay off U-boat 192. Give her a proper name and allow her more conventional work to do."

"What about you, sir?"

"Well, Simeon is right about one thing, of course. I am getting on a bit." He sounded very casual. "There has been talk, just talk, so keep it dark as they say, that I will be made up to rear-admiral." His eyes sparkled. "In charge of a submarine base somewhere."

"I'm pleased for you, sir. You've more than earned it."

"I'm a blunt man, Marshall, so don't take my next remarks too badly. You've had a bad war so far. Too much in too short a time. The strain is showing, but I expect you know that well enough."

Normally Marshall would have felt himself rising to his own defence. But this time nothing happened. It was almost like having a great weight lifted from his shoulders.

"I'll need a good chap to run the base for me until it's just as I want it. An *operational* man, not some stuffed shirt from the Admiralty. And later on, I think we might get you an escort group. Let you fight on the surface for a bit. Teach 'em how to kill submarines, instead of the other way round. Think about it. Right now, we've one hell of a lot to do."

Marshall felt dazed. "I will, sir."

"It'll be a while yet before I can get my little scheme moving, so I've arranged for you and your first lieutenant to be quartered ashore. As you are both on an extended commission, I think it's the very least I can do. How is he, by the way?"

Marshall wrenched his mind back to Gerrard and the submarine. How he had felt the tension during their return passage. The unspoken barrier between Gerrard and Devereaux. Even Frenzel had been in some way involved. But for the girl he might have had it out with them. He was not sure about that either.

"He's fine."

"Good. He did a fine job in getting you off. I've put him in for a decoration." He grinned. "Too."

Before Marshall could speak he added, "Now be off with you. I'm going to have another drink, maybe several, and bask in my petty victory."

As Marshall left the room he saw that Browning was staring out of the window, his eyes moist, perhaps from looking too long at the sun. But he doubted it.

The army fifteen-hundredweight jerked to a halt, yellow dust enveloping the cab in a dense cloud. The driver, a bronzed youngster, wearing only his shorts and steel helmet, gestured towards a white-walled building at the roadside.

"That's the place you want, sir. Sorry I can't wait to give you a lift back to Alex."

Marshall climbed down and slapped some of the dust from his shirt. The soldier was somehow typical, he thought. Homely and reliable. Young, but not young any more. The Eighth Army desert rat insignia on the dented door told its own story. He and others like him would soon be fighting ashore in Sicily if Browning's information proved final.

He tossed him a packet of cigarettes. "Thanks, soldier. I'll have to manage on my flat feet."

The man grinned. " 'Duty Frees', thanks a lot." He looked at the sky. "The flies'll eat you alive before you get fifty paces, sir!" He let in the gears and roared away along the road, dust and sand spewing from the wheels in a miniature tornado.

The road was very straight, so that the isolated building looked even more remote. Marshall stared at it thoughtfully. It was not unlike the police post, except it was larger. He remembered Cain's sudden alarm when he had dropped his grenade. The sightless eyes staring into the gun flashes. Smith screaming at him to shoot. And the girl. Motionless under the light.

An army Redcap sauntered through a gateway and saluted. "Can I help, sir?" He ran his eyes over Marshall's shoulder straps.

He was not unlike the provost sergeant on that terrible airstrip in Scotland, Marshall thought. So much had happened. So short a time.

He held out a pass. "I have permission to visit a patient in the hospital."

"Ah, that's different, sir." The man turned back into the shadow of the wall. "We don't get many visitors out here. They're not encouraged, as you might say." He pointed up a driveway. "Inside the double doors. Ask again."

Once, when he glanced back, Marshall saw the Redcap was on the telephone beside the gates. Security. That word again.

Inside the cool entrance it was much the same. Pass and identity card. Polite, yet giving a vague hint of irritation at having their solitude disturbed.

It was no ordinary hospital, nor had he expected it to be. It was kept for those who had been hurt, physically or mentally, in the unseen war of espionage.

"Follow me, sir." A messenger marched along a polished corridor where some Egyptian orderlies were working with brooms.

He said, "Look at 'em. Bin polishing that bit for an hour, to my knowledge." He opened a door. "This is the doctor, sir."

"What can I do for you?"

The doctor was like a small, neat bird. As he opened and closed the front of his white coat beneath an overhead fan he

197

could have been ruffling his feathers.

"Mrs. Travis. I'd like to see her. If I can."

"Yes. I see." He waved to a chair. "You must be the submarine commander who. . . ." He grimaced. "Well, we mustn't discuss it."

"Is she going to be all right?"

The doctor looked up at the fan. "We can but hope. Of course, it's nothing physical in the usual way. I won't bore you with a mouthful of technical jargon, most of which is pure supposition anyway, but just let me say this. She should never have been sent on that job. But now that's behind her, and it's no use adding recriminations."

"You mean she needs rest? Time to recover?"

The doctor eyed him searchingly. "This is not merely a visit in the name of duty? I had a feeling. But one cannot be sure in such matters." He shrugged. "To be frank, I don't know what she needs. She might rally. She could slip right under, like so many I've handled here." He stood up and walked to the window. "Come here." He pulled down the slats of the sunblind. There was a small courtyard below, partly shaded, and made colourful by several large stone jars of flowers. A solitary figure stood beside one of the jars, staring at it with fixed concentration. He wore an army battledress blouse and pyjama trousers. He was about twenty years old.

"Lieutenant er, well never mind his name, of the Long Range Desert Group. A good brain, and before the war he was getting started as an architect. Now, he doesn't speak, nor does he react to anything I tell him about his home and background. It is as if he has inwardly rejected everything. Ceased to exist."

Marshall watched the figure with something like despair. "Wouldn't it be kinder to fly him to England, get him away from here?"

The doctor looked at him and dropped the slats into place. "I dare not. Those flowers are the only link I've found with him. I don't know what they mean, or even if he sees them. But it's a start. After three months, it's all I've got." A telephone buzzed impatiently and he added, "I'm just warning you. Preparing you." He picked up the telephone. "The room at the far end. Number twenty."

Marshall walked to the end of the corridor, but as he hesitated outside the door it opened noiselessly and a severe looking nursing sister examined him for several seconds.

"I'm Lieutenant Commander Marshall," he began.

She nodded. "I know. We've been informed. Good show." She looked at her watch. "Don't stay long. She may want you to go immediately. They do sometimes."

Marshall stared at her. Hating her. *They do sometimes*. It made it sound as if she had already been condemned, like the man in the courtyard. Looking at the flowers.

The sister added, "I'll be out here if you need anything." She stood aside and closed the door behind him.

She was lying in a white cot, her head and shoulders propped up on pillows, her arms lying straight down her sides on the sheets. She turned slowly towards him, but her eyes were completely hidden by dark sun-glasses. Like a blind child, he thought.

"It's you." One hand moved upwards, pulling the sheet closer to her throat. "They told me you had come." There was no emotion in her voice, nor any expression on her lips.

Marshall moved to the bedside and sat down on a chair. It was still warm from the sister's occupation.

"I wish I'd had time to buy something for you. But I had to rush like mad to get a pass, and find some transport." He wanted to reach out and hold the hand nearest him. "How are you?"

"I can watch the window from here." She made as if to point across the room but let her hand drop again. "There's a tree. I keep looking to see if there are any birds, but—" She lapsed into silence.

He leaned forward slightly and saw her flinch. Like that other time.

He said, "You look marvellous. Even in service pyjamas." But she did not smile. "It's like an oven outside." He felt the despair crowding through him. He was useless. Clumsy and useless. A *machine*.

"How are the others?" She turned towards him. "That nice sailor. From London."

"Churchill?" He forced a smile. "Still complaining. He misses having you to look after. I think the officers will suffer from now on."

She nodded slowly. "It all seems a long time ago."

Marshall thought of the doctor's warning and then said

quickly, "I wish I could take you out of here. Right now."

The sun-glasses caught and held the filtered sunlight, and for a moment she remained quite still.

"But it is impossible." Her shoulders made a small shrug. "And where would you take me?"

Marshall watched her as she turned again to look at the window.

"Somewhere away from here. Where you could be free of war." He did not know if she was listening. "We could look at the pyramids at Giza. Have dinner by the Nile. You could ride on a camel if you wanted to. Be like tourists."

He leaned forward and laid his hand on hers.

"It might help. . . ."

She pulled her hand away and thrust it under the sheet.

"It is only a dream." She seemed drowsy and he wondered if she was under some sort of drug. "Pyramids."

He tried again. "Yes. By moonlight."

Her head came round again. "You have been there before? With one of your girl-friends perhaps?" Her French accent was more pronounced.

He shook his head. "Actually, I've never seen them." It sounded like an admission of defeat.

Outside the room he could hear voices, the slap of feet in the corridor.

She said, "The usual inspections." She gave a long shudder. "Touching me."

He said, "They're only trying to help, Chantal." He started. He had used her name without knowing it.

"You have *never* seen the pyramids?"

She moved under the sheet, using her elbow so that she could turn more towards him.

He grimaced. "Only in the films."

Fascinated he watched her hand emerge again from the sheet. It hesitated, very small, like an animal coming from its hiding place.

She whispered, "But they would never allow it." Her hand lay beside his. "Regulations."

"Maybe." Marshall watched her hand. The wedding ring had gone. "But I could try. I know I'm not much in the way of company, but—"

She fastened her fingers on his hand, gripping it hard.

"Do not say that! You are a fine person. When I think how I

once treated you. What you did for me, how we—'' Two tears ran unheeded from beneath the sun-glasses and she said, ''No, it is all right! Do not get distressed. I find I cry a lot here.''

She did not draw back as he dabbed her cheeks with his handkerchief.

He said, ''I'll speak with the doctor.'' He stood up very slowly. Unwilling to lose the precious contact.

''You promise?'' Her lip quivered. ''You called me by my name just then.''

''Of course.'' He smiled. ''It's a beautiful name.''

''And you are Steven.'' She frowned. ''Ste-ven.'' Then she nodded. ''Nice.''

The door opened and the sister called, ''Time's up, I'm afraid. How are we doing, eh?''

Marshall took the girl's hand in his and turned to face the sister. ''*We* are doing fine, thank you.''

He added, ''I'll be back.''

The sister was still staring after him when he reached the doctor's office.

He listened in silence to Marshall's hurried explanation and request. Then he said, ''How long have you got?''

''I'm not certain. A few days.''

''It might work. I don't see there's too much against it. Unless. . . .''

''Unless what?''

''If you try to force a recovery she might crack up completely. Any sort of real human contact is like opening a door on hell at the moment. You saw what they were doing to her? You, better than most, should know. It's a risk. But a worthwhile one.'' He held out his hand. ''Fix it your end. Leave the rest to us.''

Marshall opened the door, his thoughts in a whirl.

''I'm sure I'm right, Doctor. She needs a complete break.''

The doctor waited until the door had closed and then reached for a telephone. She's not the only one, he thought wearily. But the sailor could be right. They might help each other.

He made his phone call and then walked to the window. The man was still beside his jar of flowers. Only his shadow had moved.

14 Something Worthwhile

CAPTAIN Browning dabbed the back of his neck with a handkerchief. "Bloody hot." He gestured vaguely across the litter of folios and signal clips. "Much more of this and I think my head'll burst!"

Marshall sat opposite him, thinking of his visit to the remote hospital. Yesterday. He had spoken to Browning about his idea immediately on his return, but the captain obviously had a lot on his mind. It might not seem so important to him.

Browning added, "I'm just waiting to tie up a few loose ends. After that, I'll expect you to give me a ride." He grinned. "A meeting has been arranged. It sounds more like a gathering of city stockholders." He became serious again. "But this could be hugely important. A definite arrangement within the enemy's camp, so to speak, would save countless lives. And time."

Marshall nodded. He had been out to the depot ship, and had been surprised to find that most of his company appeared quite cheerful in their enforced isolation. Time to get things in their right perspective perhaps.

He had found Gerrard in a cabin, writing letters.

"I thought you were going ashore, Bob?" He had not expected Gerrard to remain in the depot ship when the maintenance party and all the facilities of the big vessel were at the U-boat's disposal.

Gerrard had replied, "Just got a letter from Valerie." He had sounded worried. "She's expecting a baby."

"That's good news, surely?"

"She seems pleased." Gerrard had stared at an unfinished letter. "It's what we wanted, of course."

"I wish you luck. After this next job is finished, it sounds as if we will be paid off. That's unofficial, of course, so keep it under your hat."

But it had made no difference.

"D'you think it will be worse than the last one?"

"For God's sake, Bob, you were the one who was telling *me* to take things easy. Don't tell me you've got the shakes now?"

202

He had expected a quick retort, or some well-worn joke. It had always been like that before.

Gerrard had said, "I nearly went under on our last job. The others haven't said anything, but they must be wondering. Scared I'll drop them right in it if we have another dicey mission."

So it was that bad. Marshall had sat down beside him and had asked, "Do you want me to ask for a relief, Bob? I'd not blame you. It was because of me that you got roped in in the first place. You've earned a break, and a lot more besides." He had tried to get under Gerrard's guard. "Now, with Valerie having a baby, I can understand how you feel."

"No. If it's only one more job, I'll make it. Anyway, I'd never live with myself if I broke up the team now."

Marshall dragged his thoughts from Gerrard's unspoken anxieties as Browning said, "I can get you four days. If that's what you want?"

Marshall stared at him. "Four days, sir?"

Browning beamed. "I can *see* you want them!" He gestured to the window. "Doctor Williams, the chap you met at the hospital, has fixed it from his end. He's got a house of some sort in Cairo. I was just speaking to him on the blower. He started off with Mrs. Travis about an hour ago." He grinned. "I'd not let the *Department* take too much of the glory, so *I've* laid on transport for you."

"I don't know what to say, sir. I'm not even sure it will help her."

"Can but try." Browning creaked from his chair and walked round the desk. "It might help *you*, too."

"Then if you don't need me any more. . . ."

Browning propelled him to the door. "I've wangled the Chief of Staff's driver for you. If he gets a move on, you'll be in Cairo before dusk." He cocked his head to one side. "Four days. Less if things go wrong. So make the most of 'em!"

Within half an hour Marshall had found his car and threw his small grip into the rear seat.

The driver said, "Ready, sir?" He gestured to a covered flagstaff on the bonnet. "Covered or not, sir, the wogs'll get out of our way when they see it. They'll think it's some top brass coming through." He chuckled and edged the car into the busy roadway. "So hold tight, sir!"

Marshall sat back in the seat, watching the panorama of

jostling figures and little carts sweeping past on either side. What the Chief of Staff would say if they wrote off his car, and how Browning would explain it, seemed totally unimportant.

It was a small but very pleasant looking house on the outskirts of Cairo, and close enough to the Nile to see the crowded masts and furled sails of some local craft. Deep shadows painted one side of the house, and it was peaceful. Marshall stood beside the car and stared at it. Timeless. Like the moored boats, the hint of desert beyond.

The driver smiled. "I'm off to the N.A.A.F.I., sir. I reckon Captain Browning will fix other transport for the return trip." He patted the wheel. "My guv'nor might not like us to make a habit of it!"

Marshall watched him drive away and then turned towards the house. The birdlike doctor called Williams came down some steps to greet him.

"Here, let my houseboy take your bag. He'll get a bath ready. You've been damned fast." Without his white coat and formal surroundings he looked more like a respectable solicitor's clerk than one whose work it was to repair shattered minds. "But first, a drink." He led the way to a cool, book-lined room. "Gin suit you?"

Marshall sat down in a cane chair, feeling strangely relaxed. Like the times when he had been committed to action. No sense in detours or hesitations.

Williams smiled. "Cheers. Fact is, I want to put you in the picture, as you naval chaps say. She's upstairs, by the way. With Megan, my wife. Nice here, isn't it? I'll hate to part with it when I get posted back to U.K."

He seemed to be assembling his thoughts, gauging Marshall's ability to understand.

"Chantal met her husband in England just before the war. She was a student, and he was doing something or other at the university. He's a first-rate engineer." He looked away. "I can imagine he would seem very attractive to any girl. Anyway, they got married and went straight to France. He was working there when the collapse came. Dunkirk, fall of Paris, all the rest of it." He looked hard at Marshall. "Chantal had by that time gone home to Nantes, to her family."

Marshall started. "Left him?"

"Yes. She had discovered he was not the man she thought he was. I don't know how deeply his beliefs went, but he acted like a dyed-in-the-wool Nazi. The German military authorities were suspicious of course, but damn glad to get him all the same. When our armies eventually invade Northern Europe, some of them will have to fight their way through heavy defences designed and built by *friend* Travis."

"I see." Marshall asked quietly, "Then why did she go back to him in Paris?"

"Partly because she was afraid for her father. He is a Resistance chief in Nantes. A good man. I think she thought Travis would get at her through the father. Shop him to the Germans." He sighed. "She started to work for the Department herself when Travis betrayed ten Frenchmen to the Gestapo. He had found out something about them. I am not sure what. I am not even certain they were proper Resistance workers. But the result was the same. They were tortured by the Gestapo, and the lucky ones were shot. From that moment Chantal was determined to find out what she could. Warn the Resistance, or inform them if any chance of sabotage was likely. Travis moved from one important site to another. After he betrayed the Frenchmen, he was trusted. He had proved his *loyalty*."

"Thank you for telling me."

"The rest you know. She was smuggled to England when the Gestapo were almost on her neck. Travis thought she was visiting her parents and never knew a thing about it. So when the Department got news of these new radio-controlled bombs, and that Travis was in charge of the construction work in Italy, she stood out as an obvious choice for making contact. A terrible risk to her, of course. But the faceless men at the top would place far more value on the information required and the lives it might preserve."

Marshall looked at his hands. They were quite relaxed, but felt as if they were shaking.

But for the girl being a passenger aboard his submarine, he would never have known about her, what she was doing, or that she even mattered. She would have died horribly, either on that table, or in some other hideous place of torture. Now, looking back, it seemed almost too incredible that their chance of meeting had been so small.

"Ah, I hear them coming." Williams stood up. "Don't forget, just be yourself. But be careful. Any sort of forced contact, and she might turn away forever."

The two women entered the room, and Marshall caught his breath. The girl was in a plain white dress which left her arms bare and made her skin seem gold by comparison. Her short dark hair was partly covered by a red scarf, and she was wearing the same sun-glasses.

The doctor's wife, Megan, beamed at him. "Quite a party. Pity we can't entertain you in proper Welsh style!"

The girl held out her hand. "I'm glad you could come." Her voice was very quiet. Husky.

Williams said, "We'll do the round tomorrow. Have a look at the pyramids." He winked. "I understand that you've never seen them, Commander?"

Marshall looked at the girl. So she had been speaking about him. Had remembered his clumsy attempt to make her smile.

She said, "I expect you can do with some leave after what you have—" She stiffened and then added, "I am sorry. No *shop* talk."

He saw the others exchanging glances and replied, "Just four days, I'm afraid. But far better than I'd dared to hope."

She smiled for the first time. "You sound as if you mean that."

"He does!" Williams strode to his cabinet. "Now we'll have a couple of drinks while *he* hops off to a shower and some dust-free clothes."

Marshall followed an impassive houseboy towards the stairs, and heard the doctor's wife say, "What a nice fellow, but he looks so tired, poor lamb."

Then he heard the girl say simply, "His name is Steven. We must try and make his leave a happy one."

He groped his way up the stairs. *We must try.* For *his* sake. It was a beginning.

The first two days passed only too swiftly. Each was crammed with incident and colour, with cheerful companionship and only a few moments of tension. It was like living in a private hotel, sharing every hour with guests who had somehow chosen the same moment to spend their holiday.

True to his word, Williams took them across the river to Giza and the pyramids. Panting after a nimble-footed guide they had climbed the great Pyramid of Cheops, all four hundred and fifty feet of it. Williams and his wife had stopped halfway, protesting it was too much at their time of life. Marshall suspected Williams had other reasons, and was grateful.

Once at the summit they had looked at the spectacular view with pleasure and awe. The city of Cairo sprawled on the other side of the river, and turning westwards across the great wastes of Africa, the deserts. Far below, the coloured sails of the little *feluccas* made them conscious of the breadth of time, as well as distance from the ground.

She had said, "I feel free up here. I really do." She had been wearing a big, floppy hat which hid her face in shadow, and she had added, "Are you happy?"

He had touched her arm. "Very."

She had not drawn away, but had looked down at his hand, as if to test her own reactions.

Williams had been busy with his camera when they had returned to the foot of the pyramid for one more camel ride. Marshall could appreciate why they were called ships of the desert. Getting on the beast's back was easy enough, but when it rose to its feet in four separate lurches, it was all he could do to hold on. Watched by grinning handlers, and directed by Williams with his, "Lean back, Steven! Now forward! *Back again!*," he had felt as if his spine would snap in two.

When he had found time and breath to turn towards the girl he had seen her watching him, clapping her hands like a delighted schoolgirl.

He did not think much of what they had shared before, and his mind rebelled against going back to that other world of wet steel. This was all he wanted. This and the girl. Especially Chantal.

On the third day Williams had gone into the city with his wife to visit someone at the hospital there. Without their noisy presence the house seemed very quiet, so that as Marshall sat opposite the girl at lunch he could feel a barrier growing between them. Like guilt. Uncertainty.

He said, "Can I ask if you are staying in Egypt for a while?"

She pushed a lock of hair from her forehead. "I believe it may be so." She looked at him searchingly. "What will you do? Next?"

"Another job." He found he could hardly bear to face it.

"After that, who knows?" He hesitated, toying with his fork. "You will go to England sometime. I'd like—" He rejected the word. "I *want* to see you again. Very much."

"You hardly know me."

He watched her gravely, seeing the quick thrust of her breasts under the dress. Was she pleased or just startled? Was it the beginning of some new strain?

He said, "I want to know you, Chantal. I need to."

She stood up and walked to the window. "I might be bad for you. Bring you unhappiness as I have done for others."

He moved quickly to her side. "You must not say that. It is not true. Any man would give his life for you. I know I would."

He rested his hand on her shoulder but fell back as she pushed herself away.

"But don't you understand, Steven?" Her voice was shaking with sudden emotion. "I might hurt you! Perhaps I will never be able to—" She turned towards the window again. "Never *feel* anything."

"I can wait." He watched her desperately. "As long as you like."

She relaxed slightly and swung round to face him. "I know that, too." She reached up and touched his mouth with her fingers. "But it would be cruel. I would never hurt you willingly."

"Well, then." He forced a smile. "Trust me."

"I do."

He placed his hands on her shoulders again and pulled her very gently against his chest. He could feel his heart pounding, matching hers as he rested his chin in her hair.

"I mustn't lose you, Chantal. Not after what's happened. I don't think I could go on."

She stood quite still, but he felt her breast pressing against him, the quickness of her breathing.

She said in a small voice, "What about my husband?"

"I don't care about him." Something in his tone made her lift her head. He added, "We'll find a way. He'd better not try to see you again!"

She whispered, "Oh, Steven, I never thought this would happen. I remember when we first met. How I thought you were involved with Simeon's wife. Her lover maybe."

He nodded. "That was over a long time ago. I think I must be a slow developer."

She started to shake, and for a terrible moment he thought she was crying.

But she was laughing without making a sound, her whole body shaking uncontrollably until she gasped, "That you are *not*, Steven!" She patted his face again. "You do say some silly things."

He grinned. The relief spreading through him like the removal of physical pain.

"Maybe. Every so often."

A car rattled past the window and he guessed it was Williams. He came into the room and glanced from one to the other.

Marshall said, "It's all right, Doc, we've not been up to anything." He looked at the girl, and they laughed. Like two conspirators.

"Fine." Williams nodded. "I really am pleased. For both of you." He bit his lip. "However. . . ."

Marshall saw the paper in his and and asked dully, "Recall?"

"I'm afraid so. Sounds urgent. They're sending a car for you." For once he sounded at a complete loss.

He added, "I'll go and console Megan. She's very upset about it. Doesn't want you to go. Either of you."

Alone again, they looked at each other.

She said quietly, "Oh, Steven, your face." She crossed the room and placed her hands by his throat. "I hadn't realised. I am so full of my own troubles." She shook her head. "You have to go back. And I cannot even begin to share it with you. I saw you once. Just before I was rowed to that fishing boat. You were there. At the periscope. All your men around you. Trusting you. Depending on you." She dropped her forehead against his chest. "I would like to do that. But to end like this." She quivered with sudden despair. "It's not fair. Just one more day. It would not have hurt them!"

He lifted her chin with his fingers and gently removed the glasses. "I'll be back." He saw the tears running down her face, as if they had been hoarded for this moment in time. "There will be more than one day then."

She was studying him, the tears pouring down her face quite unheeded.

"I will remember everything. The little boats. The market. The Great Pyramid." She reached up and touched his hair. "And how you looked on that camel. *Everything!*"

Marshall heard another car outside. It was over.

Williams and his wife joined him by the door, watching as he half-heartedly checked the contents of his grip.

"We will take good care of her." The doctor's wife had started to cry. "Till you get back."

"**That'll do, woman!**" Williams picked up the grip. "**You'll have me at it soon.**" He looked at Marshall. "**I'll walk with you to the car.**"

Marshall stooped and kissed the girl gently on the forehead. Then he turned and followed the doctor into the sunlight.

Beside the car he asked quietly, "Well? Can you help her?"

Williams took his hand. "**I think you are the one now, Steven. The only one.**" He opened the door. "Take care, *bach*. We'll be thinking of you and your men."

The car bumped towards the road, and when Marshall looked back he saw that she was waving to him. She was still waving when the car rounded the bend in the road and the little house was lost from view.

Frenzel waited just inside the cabin doorway watching as Marshall put his signature on some papers. Overhead feet drummed on the casing, and from the control room came a steady buzz of conversation.

Marshall looked up. "All ready to go, Chief?"

Frenzel smiled. "The last of the depot ship's engineers have gone, sir. They've made a pretty fair job, considering the shortage of time."

Marshall stood up and glanced at his watch. It was seven in the evening. Browning had set the sailing time for 2100.

Gerrard edged round the door and said, "I've made arrangements for our passengers, sir." He looked tense. "Captain Browning has sent word that he would like to bunk in the wardroom."

"Yes." Marshall smiled in spite of his other thoughts. "He told me. I offered him this cabin, but he'd rather get the full treatment, apparently."

Frenzel chuckled. "He'll be one of the boys again. I can understand him feeling like that."

Buck paused in the passageway. "The main brow has been removed, sir. The last mail has been censored and sent over to the F.M.O." He seemed very relaxed, better than he had looked for a long while.

Marshall nodded. "Thank you. You seem very chirpy."

Buck showed his teeth. "Well, the buzz has it this is the last job, sir. After this, it's back to sanity again!" His grin broadened. "Not that I'm dripping about it. We've had a spate of luck, too."

He strolled off along the passageway, and they heard him calling to one of his torpedomen.

Gerrard said quietly, "I don't know how he does it. He's taken to this life better than many regulars."

A boatswain's mate stood on tiptoe to peer over Gerrard's shoulders.

"Beg pardon, sir, but the O.O.D. reports the first of the passengers comin' aboard." He added as an afterthought, "Commander Simeon."

He hurried away, and Gerrard said bitterly, "Damn. We could do without *him*."

Frenzel stood aside and pulled on his stained engineroom gloves.

"I'm off then. A last look round." He winked. "Make sure there's no lump of waste stuck in anything vital."

Gerrard waited and then closed the door.

"I'm sorry about the other day, sir. I'll be all right. It's just the thought of Valerie having a baby. All those miles a-way." He tried to smile. "I guess I'll have to get used to the idea."

"I can understand, Bob." He thought of the girl pressed against his chest. The way she had looked at him.

He added, "I'd better go and meet Simeon." He shot Gerrard a quick glance. "Just take it easy, will you?"

Gerrard ducked beneath the deckhead. "Yes. Right now I'll occupy myself in examining our conning-tower shield. It's probably rusted solid by now."

Marshall found Simeon in the wardroom staring at a cup of coffee.

"Has your gear been stowed, sir?" He was careful to be formal.

Simeon looked at him calmly. "Yes. Captain Browning will be aboard in about an hour with the others."

"Who will they be?"

Simeon eyed him without expression. "An Intelligence chap from Army H.Q., and of course, er, Travis." His eyes flickered very slightly as he said the name. "All right?"

"Travis." Marshall stared at him. "What the hell for?"

"Browning got his way over meeting this Italian *friend* of his. But apart from the Old Comrades Association, we need some-

211

thing else to bargain with. To impress this wavering Eye-tie brass-hat.''

"You mean you persuaded the Staff to have Travis along. Is that what happened?''

"**Insurance.**" Simeon relaxed. "**If the Italian gentleman is to** understand what might happen if he goes against us on *the day*, or even if he tries to remain neutral, Travis is the man to do it. With his knowledge of the bomb's potential, and how the Jerries intend to use 'em, who better?''

"I see.''

Marshall turned away. Remembering the man as he had last seen him. Dark, with deepset eyes. It was easy to see him as some sort of fanatic in the way Doctor Williams had described. And now he was to be aboard again. Forgiven. With a place in affairs once more. It made him feel sick.

Simeon said, "Can't make choices in wartime, you know. Today's friend is tomorrow's enemy. It's always been so.''

The deck gave a quick tremble as Frenzel tested some part of his machinery. Marshall watched Simeon's reactions. A nervous tightening of the jaw, but it gave something away. He was almost sorry this was to be such a straightforward job. Browning had informed him of the plan's loose outline only that morning. The general had been contacted by British Intelligence agents working in Sicily. He had been given Browning's personal message, and he had not exploded or started an alarm. Phase two would be the rendezvous at sea with some suitable craft which the general would arrange. If he agreed. If not, then nothing would happen, and they would have to report as much to the Chiefs of Staff.

It was a strange way to fight a war, but everything else had changed, so why not that?

Marshall asked slowly, "Will he be under guard, sir?''

Simeon smiled. "*Watched.*" He gestured vaguely. "But he will mess with us. Give him a sense of belonging again.''

Marshall regarded him gravely. You bastard. You know. About Chantal. You're enjoying it. Getting your own back.

Aloud he said, "As far as I'm concerned, he can go to hell.''

Simeon nodded, his features very serious. "Of course, old chap. You run the boat, and leave the diplomacy to us, eh?''

"Thank you.'' Marshall walked past him. "I'm going on deck.''

By the time he had reached the bridge he was feeling calmer.

After all, it was obvious that neither he nor Simeon had anything in common, and if Simeon had some idea of finding an outlet for his hostility, he was hardly likely to make this the moment. Nobody in his position, and with so much at stake, would even consider it.

He leaned over the screen and saw some of the deck party taking lashings off the mooring wires under Petty Officer Cain's watchful eye. Warwick was nearby, one foot resting negligently on the guardrail while he chatted with Blythe, and in the warm bronze light of evening it all looked very peaceful. On every hand ships and harbour craft gleamed dully in the strange light, and as the guardboat swept fussily around the depot ship's buoy, its bow wave shone like liquid metal.

The harbour was full. There were plenty of landing craft, he noticed. Low, chunky hulls with no claim to beauty or a ship-builder's pride. Built for the job. To carry men and tanks to the beaches. They would be gathering all along the North African coastline now. They had waited so long for a chance to start back along the road to victory that now it was drawing near it was hard to accept.

Devereaux pulled himself through the hatch and crossed to his side.

"I've got the charts marked, sir. Just as you told me." He shaded his eyes to watch the guardboat. "Shouldn't be too difficult."

"I hope not."

Marshall waited. Devereaux was not one to waste words. He had no need to explain about the charts. They were his job.

"I was thinking, sir." He smiled casually. "After this one. Any chance of my being recommended for a course at Fort Blockhouse?"

"First lieutenant's course?" Marshall nodded. "Every chance. I've already made the suggestion."

Devereaux pouted. "Well, that's just it, sir. I've done quite a bit of time in submarines now. I was acting Number One in my last boat when the chap in question broke his leg. All practical work."

"But you still have to take the course."

Devereaux hurried on, "And I've acted first lieutenant aboard this boat too, sir, more than once." He took a deep breath. "I was hoping I could go straight in for a commanding officer's course."

Marshall looked away. So that was it. He could feel for Devereaux's impatience. But for this unexpected commission in U-192 he would most likely be halfway to his goal.

"You know how it is, Pilot. You can't buck the system." He smiled. "Not even if you've earned promotion to admiral!"

"I'm afraid I'm not taking it so lightly, sir."

Marshall faced him. "For God's sake, don't start getting pompous with me."

Devereaux said stubbornly, "Well, it's not fair, sir. I was going to make an official complaint, but. . . ."

"What about?"

The sharpness in his tone made Devereaux hesitate, but only for a second.

"Number One's getting rattled, sir. On our last billet he nearly lost control." He added quickly, "You weren't there, sir. But it happened."

"That's enough." Marshall stared at him, seeing the picture as clearly as if he had been aboard at the time. "I'd thought better of you. Not that you'd go bleating about a fellow officer behind his back."

"I see it as my duty. An obligation, sir."

"Well, leave it right there and carry on with your other *duties*."

Devereaux made as if to leave. "I suppose that's good-bye to my recommendation for anything now, sir?" Then he dropped down the ladder.

Marshall looked at his hands. They were clenched into tight fists. He had underestimated the navigator badly. Now, if he tore up his recommendation, Devereaux would scream to the world that it was because he had dared to criticise Gerrard. The captain's friend. But if he did nothing, Devereaux might well end up with a command of his own. In just a few sentences he had shown his true value, or lack of it, and his total misunderstanding of responsibility, of comradeship, which was the very strength of every submarine. If it was to survive.

A seaman in gaiters and carrying an empty sack climbed up the ladder from the casing and saluted.

"Just took the mail ashore, sir." He held out an envelope. "For you. By hand, from a Doctor Williams."

Marshall nodded and almost tore it from the man's fingers. Something had changed. She had broken down. It was to tell him not to—

He stared at the photograph which he had pulled from the envelope, his mind racing with anxiety. There was a small note attached, with the hospital's address in one corner. Williams had scrawled, *"Got it developed as fast as I could. Thought it might help."*

It had caught her exactly. She was looking just as she had when they had been alone together. Sad, happy, wistful. She could not have known he was taking it. He stared at it fixedly, remembering her voice when she had said, *I might hurt you.* After all she had endured, and experiences he could only imagine, she had been thinking of him. Afraid she would be unable to let him hold her. Love her.

He put the picture carefully in his wallet. The little doctor had done far more than he knew. He would be back in his hospital now. Probably looking from his window, watching the lonely soldier by the flowers.

He swallowed hard, and had to restrain himself from taking out the photograph once more.

Warwick called from the casing, "Prisoner and escort coming aboard, sir!"

Marshall shook his head as he watched the little group climbing down from the depot ship's side. "Not a prisoner, Sub." He saw Warwick staring at him with astonishment. "Mr. Travis is to be treated as a passenger, nothing more."

"Aye, aye, sir." Warwick looked at Blythe. "I'll see to it at once."

Travis was dressed in new khaki drill, and carried a briefcase. He was accompanied by an army captain who was staring at the U-boat with obvious dismay. Travis climbed up the ladder and greeted Marshall with a curt nod.

"We meet again." He looked at the open hatch and wrinkled his nose. "Ugh. It's all coming back again."

The soldier said, "I'm not much of a one for ships, sir."

Marshall replied, "It should be calm enough." He watched Travis's deepset eyes. But not so calm inside the hull, he thought. "If you go below, I've arranged for you to be accommodated in the wardroom."

He turned his back on them and stared across the harbour again, watching the shadows creeping away from the anchored ships and touching the water with deeper blue. He was still on the bridge when Captain Browning arrived, panting, but obviously excited by the prospect of his trip in a submarine.

215

Marshall saluted. "You're very welcome, sir." He added quietly, "I've put you in the wardroom as you insisted. I hope you'll find it comfortable."

Browning beamed at him. "I'm looking forward to it!" He tapped a leather satchel which he had clipped to his belt. "I've got it all here. I have a feeling we're going to be lucky. Something *worthwhile*, and that means a lot to me."

"Yes, sir."

Marshall watched him as he touched the voicepipes and peered down the oval hatch.

Browning asked, "All went off all right, I hope?" His eyes vanished into his wrinkles. "I can *see* it did, boy!" The grin spread across his face. "I'm glad. Give you someone to live for."

Later, as the deck picked up the steady quiver of Frenzel's motors, and the line-handling parties stood fore and aft on the casing, Blythe said, "Control room, sir." He was smiling. "Cap'n Browning requests permission to come to the bridge."

Marshall nodded, watching the faces which lined the depot ship's rails. U-192's secret could not last much longer. Too many people knew about her. It was natural enough.

Browning heaved himself through the hatch, his girth almost sealing it like an extra lid.

He said, "Won't be a bother, Marshall. I'll keep well out of your way."

Marshall adjusted the glasses round his neck.

"That'll be fine, sir."

He studied the ripple of a breeze on the water, the way the headrope sagged and tautened away from the ship's side.

"Stand by."

He saw the blink of a light from the depot ship, heard Blythe say, "*Proceed*, sir."

"Let go forrard."

He could feel Browning just behind him, hear his heavy breathing as he lived each separate function and movement.

"All clear forrard, sir."

"Slow ahead port. Let go aft."

"All clear aft, sir."

Starkie's voice now. "Port motor slow ahead, sir. Wheel's amid-ships."

"Slow ahead starboard." He lowered his eyes to the gyro. "Port ten."

Blythe said, "Here comes our guide, sir."

"Good. Make our number to him." It was the same motor gunboat, very graceful in the fading light.

"Midships."

He saw the M.G.B. swinging round with a great show of wash.

Buck called, "All secured for sea, sir!"

"Very well. Fall the hands in for leaving harbour."

He looked at the two swaying lines of seamen on the casing, with Buck right forward in the bows. He saw too the look in Browning's eyes and knew what it must mean to him.

He saluted and said, "She's all yours, sir." He hesitated. "If you'd like to take her out."

Browning stared at him for several seconds, as if he had misunderstood. Then he stepped up heavily on to the fore gratings and tugged his cap firmly over his eyes.

Marshall stood aside, and was glad he had made the offer.

A voice called, "Control room to bridge."

The massive head moved very slightly. "Bridge?"

The other voice sounded surprised. "Commander Simeon requests permission to come up, sir."

Browning glanced aft at the lookouts and let his gaze rest momentarily on Marshall. Then he bent over the voicepipe again.

"Denied," was all he said.

15   The Spark

MARSHALL looked at the control room clock and then at Gerrard.

"Take her up. Fourteen metres."

He shivered slightly in the dank air, and wondered why he was feeling so tense. It had taken six days to reach their present position off the north-west coast of Sicily. A careful, steady run, avoiding all shipping, which had been easy enough, and surfacing only briefly to charge batteries at night. And yet the strain was there, all around him. Like the moment when they had passed through the minefields between Sicily and the North African coast. He had watched Gerrard at his controls, seen the unblinking concentration on his face. Remembering the last time.

"Fourteen metres, sir."

The hiss of compressed air died away, leaving the boat as quiet as before.

"Up periscope."

He crouched low, his fingers snapping the handles into position even as the lens broke surface.

It was evening, the sea was very dark, like moving silk in the fading light. He moved around the well, searching for a light, a feather of spray. Nothing. He swivelled the lens upwards, noticing the first pale stars and one tiny cloud like a piece of jagged metal, holding the sunlight which was otherwise hidden below the horizon.

He swung the periscope towards the land and switched it to full power. The coastline was not much more than a blur of grey-blue, but the nearest headland was prominent enough, and familiar. Like an old friend. Or enemy

"Bearing now?"

Devereaux replied, "One-five-zero, sir."

"It's Cape St. Vito. A good fix."

He heard Devereaux's quick breathing, but nothing was said. The navigator was careful to say very little now. Since their talk on the bridge at Alex.

"Down periscope. Take her to ninety metres again."

He stood back as the tanks rumbled to the inrush of water, and saw Browning watching him from beside Frenzel's control panel. Despite the stubble on his heavy jowls, which was almost white, he looked ten years younger. True to his word, he had done all he could to keep out of everyone's way, but was always ready to offer help in more routine duties. While the army Intelligence captain had moaned and retched through most of the passage, and Simeon had made a great show of going over his folios of secret information, Browning had somehow gained in stature.

If he noticed the tension between some of the officers, and more particularly Simeon's watchful hostility, he made no comment. Instead he dominated the crowded wardroom, eating huge meals at each opportunity, and keeping them interested in tales of *his war*, as he put it.

Marshall said, "All being well, we should be nicely placed tomorrow night for the contact, sir."

Browning sighed. "I hope the old bugger keeps his promise." He smiled. "It takes a lot of guts to do what he's been asked." He ambled to the chart table and pulled out a pair of steel-rimmed glasses. "General Cappello will meet us in some sort of launch, with just a handful of close, trusted men. That part should be fair enough. Most of his officers and the troops under him are from his own city or round about. They'll trust him before they will the bloody Germans." He moved one finger across the chart. "I see you've marked the place."

Marshall nodded. "You said that we've got to take the general on board. For that reason I think we'd better close the land from the north'rd. Give us time to have a good look round." He smiled gravely. "No sense in being *too* trusting."

"Makes sense." Browning glanced at the tell-tales and depth gauges. "God, she's a smooth boat." He sounded vaguely uncertain. Maybe he felt guilty for admiring the enemy's workmanship. He cheered up just as quickly. "Let's get some coffee."

They found Simeon at the wardroom table making notes on his personal chart. The army captain, whose name was Hart, sat at the far end, his face the colour of cheese as he stared fixedly at a steaming cup of coffee.

Marshall saw Travis slumped in one corner, a magazine on his lap.

Simeon asked, "Satisfied, sir?"

"Quite, thanks." Browning seated himself in a chair and watched Churchill with his pot. "Tomorrow night, God willing."

Travis remarked, "Not too soon for me." He appeared totally unmoved by their attitudes towards him. To Marshall it seemed as if he was able to shut them off, as he had his wife.

Simeon looked at him thoughtfully. "What'll you do after this war's over?"

"Go back to work, I expect." Travis watched him calmly. "Why?"

"Just wondered." Simeon looked away, as if to dismiss the matter.

Marshall looked from one to the other.

Travis said curtly, "I know what you think. I couldn't care less. Your bosses appear to know my real value. What you choose to believe is a matter of complete indifference to me."

219

"I'm glad of that." Simeon smiled. "I was merely wondering about your *wife*."

"None of your damned business." Travis's composure was rapidly fading. "I'll decide without any help from you!"

"Yes." Simeon glanced idly at Marshall. "How was she when you saw her in Cairo? Pretty fit?"

Browning interrupted harshly, "That'll do. There's enough to keep us occupied for the next day or so without you snapping at each other!"

Simeon held up both hands apologetically. "Sorry, sir, if I put my big foot in something?" He looked at Marshall, his eyes opaque. "Didn't realise it was like that, old boy."

Marshall felt the anger rising inside him like a flood, but saw Browning's face. Anxious. Almost pleading.

He said quietly, "Well, you know now, don't you, sir?" He turned to Churchill. "I'll take mine in my cabin."

But the coffee stood untouched, and it took him several minutes to cool his anger.

So Simeon hoarded more than mere resentment. He was using Travis to get at him. To needle him into saying or doing something stupid. It was Gail. It had to be. After all this time, Simeon was still brooding over the fact that he and Gail had been lovers. He had taken her away from Bill, but that, in his book at least, was different. To know that Marshall had been first was like seeing a man who had somehow soiled something he owned. His pride was smarting.

Marshall could recall the moment when Gail had telephoned him aboard the depot ship. While the young stoker, Willard, had stood wretchedly to await punishment for desertion. Simeon might have known she was phoning. Might even have planned it to prove or disprove some secret suspicion.

He leaned back in the chair and carefully removed the photograph from his wallet. It helped just to see her. To know she was safe. That she would never be made to suffer again. He thought of Travis's sudden anger and replaced the picture in his wallet. Travis would never touch her again either. Of that he was quite certain.

All that night the submarine steered north-east around the corner of Sicily and into the Tyrrhenian Sea, taking her time, gaining room before turning once more to the south for a gradual approach towards the rendezvous.

Once or twice they detected propeller noises, patrolling

warships some distance away, but otherwise they looked inwards on themselves.

During the morning watch Devereaux stood by the sheathed periscopes, his eyes on the helmsman's shoulders. Thinking about Marshall and Gerrard. And about Simeon. At first he had taken a firm dislike to Simeon, but now he realised he was the one man who could help him. When this operation was done, Browning would probably be relieved for some desk job, and it was even more likely that Marshall would get his promotion to commander. That left him isolated once again. Maybe to be drafted to some other boat, with one more bloody-minded captain who would refuse to see his value. Simeon was obviously destined for important things. With his help he might . . . he saw the gyro needle tick momentarily out of true and snapped, "Watch your helm, damn you! You need a white stick!"

The quartermaster ground his teeth and replied, "Sorry, sir." Inwardly he pictured himself kicking Snooty Devereaux's arse right through the main bulkhead.

In the motor room, his back bowed against the after torpedo stowage space, Frenzel peered at his racing machinery, a gloved hand steadying him against the vibration. What would he do next, when this job was over? Go back to Fort Blockhouse. Another course. Another boat. *Leave.* Suppose they made him go on leave? He felt the pain coming back again. What would he do? Go and stare at a mass grave? Try to remember what she had felt like in his arms? How his kid had laughed when he had made some joke or other?

Aloud he said, "Oh Jesus, why *them*?"

The artificer on watch who was standing less than two yards away heard nothing. Even the muted motors were loud enough to keep Frenzel's agony a secret.

In his bunk, his fingers interlocked behind his head, Warwick stared up at the darkness. They were making for another rendezvous. More danger. He found he was unmoved, and yet he could recall his sick horror on that first time when his men had gunned down the waving Germans, as if it were yesterday. He had changed completely, but for good or bad he did not know. A heavy drip of condensation plopped on his face, and with a grunt he rolled over into the damp blankets and fell asleep.

In the dimly lit wardroom Captain Hart of the Intelligence Section drooped weakly in a chair, his eyes almost shut as he watched Travis by the table. Hart knew all about Travis. Probably more than anybody else aboard. In his earlier days Hart had revolted against men like him. Traitors, double-agents, liars, and those who killed without qualms or even understanding the reason for their orders. Or caring. But as the war had gathered momentum he had been made to share his everyday life with such people. Use them. Make them work. Discard them.

Hart had known Travis's wife. He also knew what happened to agents caught by the Germans.

But despite all this knowledge Hart was conscious of only one thing. He must rest. Lie down and take advantage of the first day he had had free of sickness since coming aboard this terrible boat. He could feel the nausea lurking in his insides, and he had to swallow hard to hold back the lump in his throat. And in the morning there would be another breakfast. Fatty bacon. Tinned sausages. He gulped miserably and wiped his face with his hand.

Travis put down a magazine and said, "Why the hell don't you turn in? You'll be damn-all use to anyone tomorrow in that state."

Hart stood up and groped along the curtained bunks. He did not even trust himself to reply.

Travis watched him vanish behind the curtains and then stood up in the empty wardroom.

In a bunk opposite the door Buck lay on his side and watched Travis through a cigarette hole in the curtain. Something must have awakened him, he thought angrily. Probably that damned soldier. He had been with Travis when he had last looked. He saw the other man standing in the wardroom, opening and closing his fingers and staring fixedly at nothing. He was suddenly another person. Not sulky or arrogant as before. There was something frightening about him. Unbalanced.

Buck waited until Travis had climbed into his bunk and then relaxed slightly. Travis would need watching. Hart imagined he knew about men like him. Buck thought of Travis's eyes. He was way out of Hart's league. Anyone who could do what he had done was not going to change overnight.

A hand jerked the curtain aside and a bearded seaman said cheerfully, "Time for yer watch, sir!"

"I've only just got to sleep, damn it!"

The man waited until Buck had staggered down to the deck.

"Shame, annit, sir?" He walked away, humming to himself.

Buck grinned. Unfeeling bastard. Then he walked unhurriedly to the control room where other members of his watch were taking up their stations.

Devereaux handed over to him, confining himself to the bare details of course, depth, revolutions and trim.

Buck said wearily, "Quiet as a bloody grave, Pilot."

Devereaux paused by the bulkhead door and looked at him dully. "And we're in a damned expensive coffin, if you ask me!"

Buck shook his head.

Then to the control room at large he said, "Right then. All the way to Blackfriars Bridge! Hold tight!"

Several of the men chuckled and Buck felt slightly reassured. He thought about the C.O. Marshall had told him earlier that he had written to recommend him for a D.S.C. for getting the boat free from the mine. His stubbled face broke into a broad grin. What would they say in the Wandsworth Road when they heard about that?

Then with a sigh he went through his usual check of each department. Medals were one thing, but to him machinery came first.

Marshall waited beside the periscope well and watched the busy preparations around him. How many times had he stood in this position, he wondered? In this boat, in *Tristram*, and others before that. You never really got used to it. Not enough to take anything for granted.

All day they had prowled back and forth, well clear of the land, but as evening had drawn near he had ordered a change of course, one which would take the submarine directly south to the rendezvous.

It had been a long day. Long and brittle, and one which even Browning had failed to enjoy. Last minute conferences, but with nothing new to add. Plans for a quick escape if things went wrong. Alternative routes should they run into an unexpected patrol.

But according to all the reports they did not have too much to fear.

There was a regular anti-submarine patrol to the north of the rendezvous area, and by day there were plenty of aircraft on the lookout for intruders. Fortunately, the Italians seemed loath to do anything at night. Which was just as well.

He looked at the clock. Nearly midnight.

Gerrard was speaking quietly to the coxswain, and he saw Frenzel examining his panel with unusual care, his face set in a small frown.

Below the conning-tower the lookouts stood wearing dark glasses so that their vision would not be impaired by the control room lights. They looked like two blind veterans, he thought.

"No H.E., sir."

"Good."

He turned as Browning came into the dimmed lighting. He was dressed in fresh khaki drill and wore his oak-leaved cap at a jaunty angle. He had shaved, and against the others nearby looked like a stranger.

He grinned and said apologetically, "Mustn't let the side down. Want to look my best, eh?"

The seamen by the ladder smiled broadly. They all seemed to like Browning. It was not surprising, Marshall thought.

"Ready when you are, sir."

"Yes." Browning fiddled with his belt. Postponing the moment. Then he said, "Let's get it over with."

Marshall nodded. "Take her up, Number One. Periscope depth."

He knew that Simeon and his companions were in the wardroom. Keeping out of his way. This was his part of it. After that they would take over.

"Fourteen metres, sir."

When he made a quick search through the periscope Marshall was pleased to see that the sky had clouded over since his last inspection. The motion was unsteady, and he thought briefly of Captain Hart's seasickness. One more slow examination. A few whitecaps, very large in the lens. Here and there a solitary star between the cloud banks.

He said, "Open the lower hatch. Surface." He stood back as the periscope slithered down and then said, "Try not to let the general fall in the drink. It would be a bad start."

The responding laughter was lost in the roar of air into the tanks, and Marshall was up the ladder and spinning the locking wheel almost before he realised he had moved. Automatic. A machine. The night air struck him in the face like a wet towel, and he had to grip the streaming metal to stop himself from falling.

Blythe struggled up beside him and opened the voicepipes. "Blowing a bit, sir. Gawd, this place can certainly change its mind!"

Marshall steadied his hip against the wet steel and moved his night-glasses across the screen. He could see the uneven banks of short, vicious waves, the spray cutting past the stem in thin streamers.

"Control room to bridge." Gerrard sounded calm. Too calm. "Midnight now, sir."

"Very good."

He shifted the glasses again, wondering how good the agents' report had been about this Italian general. Then he saw a small stab of light, very low down, almost lost in spray.

Blythe called, "It's the right signal."

"Good. Acknowledge. Then get that Captain Hart up here."

He heard the quick splutter of an engine and guessed the general's boat had been lying motionless until the arranged moment. Rolling about in these troughs could not have made it too comfortable. He knew Hart had joined him on the bridge. He could hear his stomach rumbling even above the sounds of sea and spray.

"The boat's coming towards the port side, sir." Blythe sounded doubtful. "It'll pound itself to bits if they're not careful."

"Yes. Get P.O. Cain and his casing party on deck. They'll need some fenders. See to it." He looked at Hart's outline against the pitching bridge. "You all right?"

The soldier nodded. "I feel better in the open. A bit."

"Good. You'll need to interpret for me."

Marshall saw the other craft lifting and rolling on a cautious diagonal approach. A launch of some sort. With smooth Italian lines which told of a good turn of speed.

Someone was shouting through a megaphone, and Hart said angrily, "The general won't come over to us, sir. He wants us to go aboard the launch."

Marshall trained his glasses on the boat. "Ask him why, for God's sake."

Again the lilting voice, pausing every so often to await Hart's replies.

"He says there are two fast patrol boats to the north of this area, sir. From the mainland. They've been poking about for two days."

Marshall nodded. He could hardly blame the general for not wanting to be left in a submerged enemy submarine while his own launch was caught in the open.

He waited impatiently for Cain's seamen to scramble through the hatch and then said, "Yeoman, go below and tell Captain Browning what's happening."

Blythe stared at him. "*Me*, sir?"

Marshall smiled. "Unless you want to stay up here and run things?"

He turned to watch a heaving line being thrown across, and a dark cluster of figures on the saddle tank with heavy rope fenders to take the first impact.

As the launch surged and groaned into the fenders Marshall saw the helmsman glowing faintly in a compass light as he swung the wheel hard over. There were several figures, but not many. The general was taking no chances.

"Browning here." Marshall heard his voice in the pipe by his elbow. "Seems to me I'll have to go over. I'm taking Travis and Hart with me, right?"

Marshall replied, "I think it's the only way, sir."

Hart said thickly, "Oh God! I've got to go on *that* thing now!"

Browning reached the bridge, panting fiercely.

"I'm ready."

Marshall said, "I'll have an armed party sent with you, sir."

"You won't." Browning tugged his cap firmly over his eyes. "I'm not even taking Simeon. It takes long enough to get out of trouble without having half the bloody Navy in the launch!"

Marshall guided him to the ladder. It made sense of course. And in any case the launch was now firmly lashed alongside. They could sink it with a couple of grenades if they turned nasty. It was just that he disliked the idea of Browning going with only Hart and Travis for company.

Browning lifted his leg over the coaming and muttered, "In any case, I've got my revolver with me." His face loomed against the creaming water like a big fruit. "And thanks, my boy. You know what for." Then he was gone.

Marshall held his breath as the three men were half carried, half pushed across the thin, treacherous pattern of spray be-

226

tween the hulls. He thought Browning waved to him before vanishing into the small wheelhouse, or it could have been Hart.

He heard Simeon on the voicepipe. "Permission to come to the bridge."

Marshall managed to smile. Remembering the last time.

"Granted."

Simeon was hatless, and wore an oilskin with the collar turned up to his ears.

"Gone, has he?" He sounded bitter.

"Yes." He watched Simeon peer down at the pitching launch.

"Bloody waste of time." He seemed to expect an argument. When Marshall stayed silent he snapped, "But he wouldn't listen to me!"

"Control room to bridge. Fast H.E. to the north of us, sir. But it's very faint, and we're getting a lot of interference." A pause. "Nothing to worry about yet."

Blythe, who had returned to the bridge, walked aft and cupped his hands around his ears for several seconds.

"Probably those patrol boats, sir."

Simeon said irritably, "Well, they're not likely to come this way, are they? More likely to sweep as far as Ustica Island. They've done it before."

Marshall said, "The yeoman was offering his opinion, sir."

Simeon said more calmly, "If you say so."

Marshall thought of the far off vessels which the Asdic had detected. Fast and probably small. It was unlikely they would have any long-range detection gear, and in the choppy seas, with the land so near, it was safe enough for the present.

It was probable the enemy had aircraft fitted with radar like the R.A.F. were using. It had spelled disaster to many a U-boat caught on the surface in total darkness. If they had, it was equally likely they would keep them in southern Italy, or nearer the scene of anticipated operations.

A lookout said, "I can just hear 'em, sir."

They all turned. Marshall cupped his hands behind his ears and then said, "A long way off." It was like the combined buzzing of a hive of bees. He had heard the sound often enough when British M.T.B.s had swept out of harbour for nightly raids along the enemy coasts.

Simeon said, "What are they doing, I wonder?"

Nobody answered.

Gerrard's voice came again. "H.E. moving from east to west, sir. Fading."

"Thank you."

Simeon had guessed the truth. The patrol boats were keeping a set course. Going through the motions. They would meet trouble if it came. But they were not looking for it especially.

Simeon was peering down at the launch. "I'll bet they're nattering about old times together." He could not hide his resentment. "I wish I could get my hands on that bloody general!"

"Control room to bridge."

"Yes." Marshall trained his glasses across the screen towards one unbroken crest of white foam.

"Torpedo officer wants to come up, sir."

"Trouble?"

Gerrard hesitated. "I'd rather he told you, sir."

"Very well."

Buck pounded up the ladder and almost fell headlong on the wet gratings.

"Very pistol, sir. Missing from the wardroom." He was breathing fast. "It was just a thought, something that's been bothering me."

Simeon snapped, "For God's sake, Buck, can't you do your stores returns in bloody harbour!"

Buck replied harshly, "We're never in *bloody* harbour, sir!"

The port lookout yelled, "Sir! They're fighting aboard the launch!"

Marshall pushed the others aside and climbed up to the screen. He saw several figures reeling about in the wheelhouse, while someone else was hammering on the door from the outside. A tinkle of breaking glass, distorted shouting, and then a man burst from the opposite side and ran drunkenly aft waving his arm in the air.

There was a dull crack, and seconds later a flare burst high in the air, painting the clouds' bellies in bright silver like a moonscape.

"Travis!" Marshall yelled his name. "For God's sake, Cain, shoot that bastard down!"

More figures tumbled out on the narrow deck, and Marshall saw Browning's bald head shining in the glare as he groped his way towards the figure in the stern.

Travis was bent double, reloading the Very pistol, his hair blowing wildly in the wind.

Cain yelled, "Can't shoot, sir! The others are in the way!"

Marshall watched as Browning paused to steady himself against a ventilator, dragging the revolver from his pocket. Travis was shouting at him, though amidst all the other sounds it was impossible to make sense of it. He raised the pistol once more, his teeth bared as if he was laughing, or screaming.

"Control room to bridge! H.E. at oh-one-oh. Closing!"

Blythe said desperately, "They'd be blind to miss that bleedin' flare!"

Travis pulled his trigger even as Browning dropped on one knee and fired.

It was like a terrible two-part tableau. Crouching figures caught in their various attitudes of fear and anger, and then as Browning's bullet smashed the other man down the second Very light exploded into the rear of the small wheelhouse in a searing ball of fire.

In the next instant the whole of the launch's deck seemed to be on fire. Blazing petrol ran down the scuppers in liquid fire, and Marshall saw two men leap into the sea, their bodies like torches, their screams rising above the growing crackle of woodwork.

Gerrard was yelling, "H.E. closing fast, sir! *We must get out of it!*"

Marshall watched helplessly as Cain and some seamen slithered across the saddle tank, only to be driven back by the spurting flames.

He heard the wheelhouse glass shattering in the heat, saw the helmsman flailing round like a dervish, his agony too terrible to watch.

There was a small explosion and more petrol burst into flames, the fire darting along the deck and licking towards the submarine until the mooring lines caught ablaze and parted like cotton.

Blythe gasped, "The cap'n's had it, sir!"

He pointed wildly as Browning lurched to his feet, hesitated, and then toppled backwards into the flames. He must have fallen through a hole blasted in the deck by an exploding fuel tank. He vanished in an instant, with not even a cry.

The wind and sea were already carrying the burning launch clear, the hull tilting into the water, hiding the last horror in a curtain of steam. One figure was trapped in the bows by the advancing flames, and somehow Marshall knew it was Hart. Then he too was taken, and consumed, as with a great spluttering gasp the launch dived under the surface.

Marshall heard himself say, "Casing party below. Clear the bridge."

He swung round as Simeon shouted into his ear, "Why did he do it?" He was almost screaming. *"Why?"*

Marshall propelled him towards the hatch. "Probably because you triggered him off, *sir*! Now get below!"

Men dashed past him, too numbed by the terrible spectacle even to speak.

Marshall stared abeam, where a patch of steam still showed faintly against the dark sea beyond.

Then he listened to the distant roar of engines and shouted into the voicepipe, "Dive, dive, dive!"

He snapped the cock shut and ran to the hatch. But in his mind he could still see Browning falling into the flames.

His boots thudded on to the control room deck, and he said flatly, "One hundred and eighty metres. Bring her round to two-eight-zero."

He saw Starkie's narrow shoulders tense as he put the wheel over. The hull gave a sharp creak while the boat continued in her dive. Down, down, the depth needles crept round remorselessly.

"Course two-eight-zero, sir."

"Shut off for depth-charging."

He listened to the regular Asdic reports but ignored them. He could feel those fast moving engines even though he could not hear them.

"One hundred and eighty metres, sir."

Marshall looked at Gerrard for the first time. "Group down. Slow ahead both motors."

He stared at the shining side of the control room. Between the packed dials and instruments to the actual skin of their existence. Out there, following their dive, Browning was still with them. He clenched his fists, fighting back the anger and the sense of loss.

"H.E. still closing, sir. Two vessels. Probably F.P.B.s."

"Yes." Marshall watched the expressionless gyro compass. "They'll be slowing down soon. They won't want to drown their Asdic with their own noise.'' He found that he could say it without emotion.

He looked again at Gerrard. His face was in profile, shining slightly in the reflected light bulbs. He was thinking hard at this moment. It was not the last job after all. Marshall listened to the faint mutter of engines. Not unless. . . .

He turned as Simeon said thickly, ''For Christ's sake!''

''Sir?'' He watched him coldly. ''Do you want something?''

Devereaux said, ''You can sit over here, sir. By the chart table.''

Simeon looked through him. ''Shut up! I don't need to be told!''

Marshall gripped the periscope support and stared at him. *You do need to be told. And if we get out of this, I'll tell you, right enough!*

Three minutes later the first depth-charges exploded.

16 Tomorrow

MARSHALL felt the hull buck in protest as the first charges exploded. He saw several seamen exchanging glances, heard someone taking long deep breaths. But he kept his eyes on the depth needles. She was still going down, deeper, deeper. More than she had ever done before in his hands.

Metal groaned along the casing as the pressure continued to mount, and he heard Devereaux clicking his brass dividers together in a small tattoo.

The first attack had been made by one vessel. The second one had no doubt stopped to watch results, keeping her Asdic unimpaired by her consort's propeller noises.

''H.E. closing from astern, sir.''

Marshall watched the needles. Waiting.

Gerrard turned to look at him, his face shining in the lights.

''One hundred and eighty metres, sir.''

''H.E. closing fast, sir.''

How different it sounded at this great depth. *Thrum-thrum-thrum.* He tightened his grip on the support, picturing the charges rolling off their little rails, falling slowly, ten feet a second.

He snapped, "Hard a-port. Group up. Full ahead."

The boat responded immediately, and he saw Frenzel's hands flashing across his levers like an organist's.

"Midships. Steady."

"Steady, sir. Course two-two-zero." Starkie sounded cool enough.

The charges exploded as one, the echoing detonation booming against the hull like a collision. The boat rocked to one side, shook herself and came back again. Flakes of paint drifted through the lamplight, and a man began to cough.

Marshall listened to the subdued roar of engines as the attacking vessel tore away to prepare another sortie.

He looked at Devereaux and saw him staring at the deckhead as if waiting for something to cave in on him.

He said, "Keep a good plot. Don't rely on the echosounder." He waited for each sentence to penetrate. "If we pile up ashore, I'll not forgive you."

Devereaux's adam's-apple bobbed above his sweater and he nodded.

Simeon asked harshly, "What are you doing?" He waited, his eyes fixed on Marshall. "Wouldn't it be better to lie low until they give up?"

Marshall cocked his head as the Asdic operator snapped, "Fast H.E. closing, port side, sir."

He replied, "No, I think not, sir. These boats are most likely M.T.B.s or the like. Their job is to pin us down until dawn. By then they'll have plenty of help." He looked at Simeon impassively. "I'm not waiting."

Petty Officer Blythe took hold of the steel flag locker and murmured, "Here we go again."

The engine noises grew louder, rattled high overhead and then faded again. The charges exploded much nearer, making the hull tilt and yaw from beam to beam while Gerrard fought to regain his trim.

Marshall said, "Take her up to ninety metres. Slow ahead."

Gerrard swallowed hard. "Group down. Slow ahead both motors." He glanced at him quickly. "Take her *up*, sir?"

"Yes. They're getting us fixed." He waited, listening to the compressed air as it drowned out the enemy's engines.

"Ninety metres, sir."

"Hold her so."

He crossed swiftly to the chart. He could feel Devereaux pressed against him. Smell his fear.

The deck rocked very gently as a single charge exploded. It seemed to be a long way off, and somebody gave a disbelieving whistle.

Marshall concentrated on the chart. "Starboard twenty. Steer three-zero-zero." He looked sideways at the navigator as the helm went over. "Must get more sea-room."

He strode back to the periscopes and waited, counting seconds.

A double bang, closer, but still well clear. As the echoing detonations sighed against the hull he heard the vessel's engines joined by another. He did not need the Asdic report to know the attackers were changing their methods.

He glanced at Gerrard. "What d'you think, Number One? How many charges will they carry?"

Gerrard stared at the curved side, his mouth in a tight line. It seemed an age before he replied. "About a dozen each, sir. They've not much room for more." He swung round as a new sound came into the boat. It was like a child scratching a fence with a piece of wire, casual, insistent.

Gerrard said, "Christ, they've made a firm contact!"

Marshall looked past him. "One hundred and eighty metres again!"

He turned towards Devereaux, seeing his sudden terror, bare on his face. "Easy, Pilot." He smiled. "And keep your plot going!"

The attacking vessels must have cut diagonally across the U-boat's track, side by side like a pair of terriers after the hare.

A pattern of six charges exploded in a long and ragged bombardment. The last pair burst with such a roar that the hull tilted its stern too steeply for Gerrard's men to restrain the dive, and Marshall saw the needles flying round, while on every side the boat seemed to be jerking and groaning in physical agony. More paint flaked down, and when a signalman grasped the conning-tower ladder for support he shouted, "Christ, it's *bending*!"

Gerrard appeared to be standing diagonally across the control room as he pushed a planesman's shoulder and yelled, "More, Keenan! Hold her!"

Gerrard turned as the tell-tales flickered into line. The depth gauges stood at a full two hundred metres. Even the air felt different, as if it were being squeezed solid by the tremendous pressure around the hull.

Marshall smiled at him. "Makes our first deep dive seem a bit trivial, eh?"

It was all he could do to speak so lightly, and he felt a nerve jump in his neck as the hull gave a sharp, sickening squeal.

Devereaux cleared his throat, the sound making more than one man jump with alarm.

"We are in six hundred fathoms, sir." He cleared his throat again. "As far as I can see, we've plenty of sea-room now."

Marshall looked at Simeon, and was surprised to see him sitting on the deck, his back against the main bulkhead. He was staring at a space between his feet. Like a man under a spell.

"H.E. closing from astern, sir."

He said to Simeon, "I would suggest you stand up, sir. If this pattern comes too close, the shock could snap your spine."

He turned away as Gerrard said, "This one's coming in more slowly."

They all looked at the deckhead, trying to see through the toughened steel, visualising the great depth of water above, the crushing darkness below.

But there was no scraping echo from the patrol boat's Asdic. Just that monotonous *thrum-thrum-thrum*, it seemed endless.

"H.E.'s speeding up, sir!"

Marshall glanced quickly round the control room, wondering how his men were coping in their various sealed compartments. They would all know why the engines were increasing speed. The charges were coming down . . . *now*. The enemy was haring away to avoid having his own tail blown off.

There were three, although to those who crouched and clung to the wildly bucking hull it sounded like an avalanche crashing about their ears. Lights shattered, glass flew in all directions, and pieces of loose equipment rained down on the sobbing, gasping men as if the hull had begun to break up.

"Emergency lights!"

Marshall skidded on broken glass and heard someone calling for help. He saw the additonal lamps flicker across the dials, and watched fascinated as the depth gauges took another slow turn. They were over seven hundred feet beneath the surface. It was incredible. Unbelievable that they had withstood the pressures of both sea and explosions.

He peered at the clock. After three in the morning. The attack had gone on for over two hours. It seemed like minutes, that was the strange thing about it.

Gerrard croaked, "She's steady, sir." He sounded near to cracking.

"Hold her." Marshall staggered through the chaos and touched his arm. "You can do it, Bob!"

Gerrard nodded dumbly, and turned back to his gauges as Marshall added, "Check all departments now."

A man lurched to his feet and cranked at a telephone handset. Others came out of their stunned attitudes and moved to their stations, like old men, unsure of each and every step.

An artificer said, "No damage or casualties in engine or motor rooms, sir." He gave a thumbs up to his mate.

"Lieutenant Buck reports no damage in the fore ends, sir. But one man's broken his wrist."

And so it went on.

Then they heard the distant revolutions again as the enemy began another slow sweep somewhere to starboard.

Simeon crossed to Marshall's side, seemingly oblivious to the others nearby.

In a fierce whisper he said, "Get us out of this! Increase speed, do what you like, but get me out of it!"

Marshall regarded him coldly, half hearing the slow pattern of muffled engines.

"You said *us* the first time, sir."

"H.E. still closing from starboard, sir."

Marshall did not turn. "I'm going to increase speed very soon now. When I surface, not before."

"H.E.'s stopped, sir."

Even the operator turned in his seat as Simeon exclaimed, "*Surface?* Are you bloody mad? You'll kill the lot of us! Is that what you want?"

Marshall replied quietly, "The enemy's stopped. That means they're sitting up there on the surface like a couple of ducks. Probably using searchlights and looking for flotsam and oil slicks, or bodies maybe." He stepped away from him. "So we'll stay down here. Silent routine until they go away."

Simeon was shouting, his eyes wild. "And if they don't go?"

"Then we'll have to stick it out till tomorrow night."

Simeon gaped at the deck. "Tomorrow night. Another day of this?"

Frenzel said flatly, "By then they'll have whistled up the heavy mob." He was watching Simeon with something like disgust. "We'll have plenty of company."

Marshall looked at him and shook his head. Then he said to Simeon, "I suggest you get a grip on yourself and I'll. . . ."

Gerrard shouted, "They've started up their engines!"

They all looked at each other as the even thrumming beat grew and then began to fade until it was lost completely.

Marshall breathed out very slowly. "Ten minutes and then we'll go up for a look."

He leaned against the conning-tower ladder and found that his legs were shaking badly. He glanced up the ladder. The signalman was right. It was bending under the tremendous hull pressure.

The ten minutes seemed twenty times as long as the attack. Nobody spoke, and apart from the motors' purring hum and the occasional creak of protesting steel, they stuck it out in silence.

Marshall looked at his watch. His vision was blurred with strain, and he knew there would be worse to come when he had got them to safety. Right now, it was all that counted. He thought suddenly of Browning's face above the screen as he had made to go aboard the launch. *Thanks, my boy. You know what for.* What did he really mean? For replacing his dead son perhaps. Marshall hoped it was that.

He said, "Stand by to take her up, Number One. Periscope depth. But first warn all departments. In case we're jumped as we pop up."

But when they eventually rose to periscope depth Marshall found the sea devoid of movement.

He told Buck to take over the periscope and then walked to the intercom beside the wheel. He paused, his thumb on the button, not knowing what to say, or why he was trying to say it.

"This is the captain. You all know about the attack. It's been a noisy night." That would make someone smile. "Some of you still don't know about Captain Browning." He bit his lip and added, " 'Buster' to most of you. Well, he died back there. Doing something he thought was worthwhile, as I did, and still do." He turned to hide his face from the others. "If he was still aboard, I'm sure he'd be the first to compliment you on the way you've behaved. I'm trying to do it for him. Thank you all." He tried again. "Very much."

He released the button and said quietly, "Open the lower hatch. We'll switch over to the diesels and begin charging as soon as I've had another look around."

He saw Frenzel blocking his way to the ladder.

"What's wrong, Chief?"

Frenzel faced him gravely. "I just wanted to say thanks to you, sir. From us." He tried to grin. "The lads."

Marshall walked slowly to the ladder and paused with his boot on the bottom rung. When he looked up at the smooth sides of the tower he wondered if he had really expected to make that climb ever again.

The room looked just the same, yet without Browning behind his big desk it was totally different.

Marshall tried to relax in a cane chair, surprised that he felt no sort of tiredness anymore. He had berthed his submarine alongside the same depot ship in the early hours of the morning. Now, it was evening. It had been a very long day.

There were four others in the room. The Chief of Staff, two studious lieutenants and a most important visitor. He was Rear Admiral Dundas, the top liaison officer with British and American Intelligence. In a neat, lightweight grey suit he looked rather like a retired schoolmaster.

Marshall had made his preliminary report soon after leaving the boat in the hands of the depot ship. Now he was back again for another session.

The rear-admiral pressed his fingertips together and regarded him through heavy-framed glasses.

"It might well have come off, you know." He shook his head. "Captain Browning was a resourceful officer. Always was, even as a young man."

The Chief of Staff looked at him. His face was drawn, as if he had been on the go since receiving Marshall's homing signal and the news of their failure to complete the mission.

He said, "We've had a lot more information since we last met. The Germans are building up stocks of radio-controlled bombs, some are even larger and better than the one Marshall saw at work." He added grimly, "Whatever happens in the immediate future, we can expect to be faced with these bombs from now on." He turned to Marshall. "Once we're in the

237

enemy's territory in strength, with captured airfields, easy supply lines and full R.A.F. and artillery support we can hold our own. . . .''

He fell silent as Dundas said sharply, "But if our Sicily invasion is to have a cat in hell's chance of succeeding, we must minimise the use of the new weapon."

Marshall replied, "Captain Browning believed that, sir."

Dundas eyed him unwinkingly. "You may as well know. After all, it'll be your secret, as well as ours. The invasion, *Operation Husky*, is timed to take place three weeks and four days from tomorrow morning."

Marshall looked at the wall charts which hung across the Egyptian dancing girls. In those few seconds he saw it all. The destroyer, with Browning's son aboard, blowing up and turning turtle in the twinkling of an eye. The blazing launch. Browning shaving before going to meet his old friend the Italian general.

Dundas was saying, "We can forget about the little dump of bombs already in Sicily. The first wave of commando will have to neutralise them. It's the other dump on the mainland which is the real headache. Unless we can do something there we might just as well postpone the invasion. Maybe forever."

Marshall stood up and walked to the nearest wall chart.

He said slowly, "You know about the other place then?"

"Quite a lot. That fool Travis gave us some of the information, and our own agents have confirmed much of it. It's a new port called Nestore in the Gulf of Policastro. It has good rail and road links to carry the bombs to different military sectors once they have been assembled further north, in the place where Travis was last working. By sea it is about one hundred and sixty miles to Palermo in Sicily. Not far. And with plentiful air cover the enemy would soon send over a massive supply once he realised our true intention. All our false information and certain other ruses to make him believe we're going to invade through Greece would be so much smoke in the wind."

Marshall studied the chart in silence. Nestore. He had not even heard of it. It was shown on the chart as a small fishing village.

As if reading his thoughts, the Chief of Staff crossed to his side and explained, "The Jerries have made the place into a strongbox. It's used for nothing but military purposes now, and all but a few local people have been evacuated from the area. We understand the bombs are brought by single-track railway to a new jetty and loaded direct into whatever ship they are using at the time. We don't know a lot about underwater defences, but there is a boom, several observation towers, while to seaward the Italians are supplying a round-the-clock anti-submarine patrol.'' He grimaced. ''Nasty.''

Dundas said wearily, ''If Browning's idea had come off, then things might have been very different. With the Sicily bomb dump out of action from the start, and our lads pushing inland, the Germans would have been hard-put to change things in time.''

''What about a bombing attack, sir?''

Marshall turned to watch his reaction. Outside, on one of the anchored battleships, a marine band was playing Sunset. It could have been for Browning, he thought.

''Out of the question, I'm afraid. For a start it would be too difficult to make a real impression. And almost more important, it would tell the enemy what we were really afraid of, and why, just as if we'd given him the date and time of the invasion.''

Marshall walked to his chair and stood with his fingers locked around its back. He thought suddenly of Simeon and wondered why he had said nothing in his report about what had happened. Up to today he had thought that he was exaggerating his own beliefs about Simeon merely because of his dislike for the man. His contempt. But now he thought differently. If Travis had intended to betray them from the start of the mission, he would certainly have said nothing of his secret knowledge of this new port, Nestore. Simeon's unspoken insinuations about Travis's wife, his crude haste to admit his mistake, they had done the trick, and cost Browning his life. The lives yet to be lost hardly bore thinking about.

''I think we could do it, sir.'' He had spoken almost without realising it. Perhaps he had known all along it was what he must do. As these two men did, but were afraid to suggest it.

Dundas regarded him gravely. ''Do you really know what you're saying?''

Marshall did not reply directly. ''We've had my submarine for months now, and yet perhaps none of us has properly understood how to use her to full advantage.'' They stayed silent, watching him as he began to move restlessly back and forth in front of the desk. Browning's desk. ''This one last job would prove our worth.''

239

Dundas added quietly, "And prove Browning's faith was justified from the beginning."

"Yes, sir. Something like that. I'd like to believe that it all meant something. That we hadn't wasted what we've gained."

The Chief of Staff looked at the little admiral. "What do you think, sir?"

"Think?" He rubbed his chin rapidly. "I think it's all we've got." He looked at Marshall. "What can I do to help you?"

"I'd want a free hand, sir. Once we reach the place. My decision whether we go in, or turn and pull out if the situation's hopeless."

The Chief of Staff's eyebrows rose very slightly, but dropped again as Dundas snapped, "Agreed." He looked at the nearest lieutenant. "Get Saunders on the telephone and tell him I want an interview with General Eisenhower within the next two days."

As the man hurried away he added quietly, "By God, it's quite an idea, Marshall. You'll need every support for a landing party, but my people will deal with that. About thirty Royal Marine commando. You'll have to cram 'em in where you can, make the best of it."

Marshall looked away. Dundas was probably thinking that the marines' journey would only be one-way, so a little more discomfort hardly mattered.

Dundas said, "You can still back out, you know. But after tonight, it'd mean getting someone else. I'd understand, of course."

Marshall smiled slowly. "I want to do it. I feel it has to be done like this."

The admiral rose to his feet and held out one hand. "I don't know what to say. I thought I'd seen and heard every sort of bravery. Yours is a new kind. I'm proud to have met you." He removed his hand, as if confused by his own sentiment, and snapped, "I'll want maximum effort, Charles!"

The Chief of Staff smiled. "I'll get my people on it immediately, sir." He looked at Marshall. "I can fix it for your company to go ashore, but for security's sake they must stay in the naval camp area. My staff will get on with running repairs, and I understand from your chief that the starboard screw is a bit damaged after that last attack?"

Marshall replied, "A flaw in one of the blades. Could be awkward."

The admiral waved his hand. "That's your problem, Charles. Do what you can. Anything you need, call me."

He looked up sharply. "I want you right out of it, Marshall. Clear your mind for the big one." He smiled. "I can't give you more than three days, I'm afraid. But if I let you remain here you'll be be poking round the boat, chasing the depot ship staff, oh yes, I know you submarine commanders. And I want you *fresh* when you put to sea again. If anything goes wrong in Alex the Chief of Staff will carry the can, *not you*!"

"Thank you, sir."

Marshall felt confused. She would know by now about her husband. Some of it anyway. Would she blame him? Would she still feel something for the man, now that he was dead?

He added, "I appreciate that, sir."

"One other thing." The admiral was very casual. "Your promotion to commander has come through. Congratulations. Of course, if the war ends tomorrow you'll drop a ring immediately!" He was smiling broadly. "So be off with you. The staff can fix local comforts for your officers, too. But not a word to anyone about the actual operation until I say so, right?"

"Right, sir." The admiral had sounded like Browning. "And thanks."

The smile vanished. "Thanks? I'm the one to be grateful. As will many others when you've pulled this one off."

At least he had not said "*if.*"

Marshall picked up his cap and walked to the door. There he paused to look around the big room, remembering Browning's pleasure, his pride in his own plan being accepted by the combined Chiefs of Staff. And telling him about his son. Everything.

Dundas said, "He was a fine man. I served under him once, so I should know. The mission you've undertaken is just the kind he would have welcomed in his younger days. He got a V.C. for one like it, but there's not a medal in the world large enough for his courage." He dropped his eyes. "Or his integrity."

"I know, sir. I won't forget him either."

Marshall closed the door and hurried down the passageway towards the dying sunlight.

In the big room there was a complete silence until the remaining lieutenant exclaimed. "Surely, sir, it's not possible, is it?"

Dundas turned from the wall chart and regarded him emptily. "An hour ago I'd have said it was completely impossible. But after meeting that young man this morning, and hearing him speak just now, I'm not certain of anything." His eyes sharpened behind the heavy glasses. "All I do know is, that if anyone can make a go of it, *he* will! So let's have enough of this gloom and get on with the bloody war!"

It was one in the morning by the time Marshall reached the house beside the river. It was a warm night, and very still. After the fast drive in the Chief of Staff's Humber, with dust swirling back from the wheels like the wake of a ship, the contrast was all the more apparent.

Marshall watched the car until it was lost along the shadowed road and then walked towards the doorway. All the way from Alexandria he had been thinking about this moment. How she would accept him. What she might say. It seemed incredible that it had pushed the thoughts of the impending mission to the back of his mind. But it had.

The door swung open even as he reached for it. He had been expecting Doctor Williams, or his wife, but it was the girl. With the light behind her she looked very slim. He could smell the scent of her hair and wanted to seize her bodily. Hold her. Not let go for a long time.

Instead he said quietly, "I'm back. You shouldn't have waited up." It sounded like he felt. Lost before he had begun.

She closed the door and took his arm. As the light played across her face her eyes looked very bright.

She said, "The others have gone to bed." She smiled. "Tact, I think."

There was a meal of cold meat and salad on a small table. A bottle of wine stood in a bucket of ice beside it.

Marshall watched her as she spun the bottle in the bucket, felt his heart beat painfully just to see her.

She said, "The ice has nearly all melted. I will pour you some wine now, yes?"

He sat down and nodded.

"About your husband, Chantal. I don't know what they've told you, but. . . ."

She did not turn away, but he saw her fingers tighten on the bottle.

"They explained. I was so afraid this might happen. Right from the moment I heard, I began to worry."

He replied, "I'm sorry. I thought you might feel like this." He did not know how to go on.

She turned very quickly, her eyes filled with concern.

"No! Not that!" The bottle fell back into the bucket as she ran across the room. "I was afraid for *you*!" She dropped on her knees beside his chair, her eyes searching his face. "You see, I knew him, Steven, really *knew* him! What he was like! When I learned they had sent him with you. . . ." She shrugged. "But it is over now." She touched his hand. "Let us not talk about it. You are back. I have been praying for that. Thinking about everything we did together."

Marshall watched his own hand on her shoulder, felt the strain giving way to a peace he had never known.

He said quietly, "To hear you say that. To know. . . ."

She looked up at him again, her mouth trying to smile.

"Do not look so sad, *please*. You are back. It is all I care about. When Doctor Williams told me it was over, I. . . ." Her hand gripped his wrist with surprising strength. "Steven, it *is* over? Tell me!"

He replied dully, "It didn't work, Chantal. Something went wrong."

She stood up by his chair watching him soundlessly.

Then she said very softly, "You're going to do another mission? Is that what you are telling me?"

He nodded. "Yes."

"But there must be someone else!"

She moved to the table and back again. Through her light dress he could see her supple body moving in time with her thoughts, the thrust of her breasts which made her calm voice a lie.

"Why must it be you?" The resistance broke with her question and she threw herself down and wrapped her arms around his legs. "Why *you*? You have done enough. Let someone else take over. I can't bear to see what it's doing to you!"

He ran his fingers through her hair, feeling tears on his legs.

"I must do it, my darling. You, of all people, must know what that means. I have to."

She looked at him, her eyes filled with despair and hurt.

"Yes, Steven. I do. That only makes it worse."

He tried to grin. "I've got three days. They want me out from under their feet."

She brushed her eyes with the back of her wrist.

"Three days. Why do the British always think three days is just the right amount?" She was attempting to follow his lead and smiled up at him, the tears still running down her cheeks. Then she said, "You must be dead tired. I will let you eat in peace."

"The wine, please." He put his arm round her waist and felt her tense.

She whispered, "I'm so sorry. Forgive me."

He held her hands and replied, "There is nothing to be sorry about." He raised the wine to the light and added, "Hock. With the compliments of the Afrika Korps, no doubt."

They drank in silence, each watching the other, until Marshall said suddenly, "When I get back. . . ." It was there again. In the open. Between them like a crevasse.

She nodded, biting her lower lip. "You will, Steven. I know it. You must."

He smiled. "*When* I get back. Will you please marry me?"

She stared at him for several moments. As if she had misheard.

He said, "You must know how I feel." He half rose and added, "Think about it, will you?"

She stood up and reached for the bottle. "More wine, eh?"

She tossed her head, throwing the hair from her eyes. But her hand did not touch it. She turned and looked at him, her eyes filling her face.

"You do not have to ask, Steven." She stooped over him and touched his hair. "If *you* are sure. I am so worried that. . . ."

The rest was lost as he pulled her against him. It was all he wanted. To hear her answer. To know she felt as he did, no matter what else came between them. It made all his past attitudes seem stupid and empty. He wanted her. It was physical pain even to think of losing her now.

She said, "Three days."

"Yes. We can get away from here. I'll take you to see places where they've never heard of the war."

She shook her head. "Can we stay here?"

He held her away and looked at her anxiously. "Of course. If that's what you want."

"It is." She smiled. "Thank you."

A houseboy shuffled past the open door, making a big show of checking locks and windows.

She said, "He is waiting for us to go."

He nodded. "Tomorrow. . . ."

She touched his lips with her fingers. "Do not talk about it now."

They walked up the stairs and she left him by his door.

She said, "I am glad I waited up for you. Perhaps you would have changed your mind otherwise?" She moved away before he could answer.

Later, as he lay in bed, half listening to a breeze against the shutters, he let his mind stray again to what lay ahead. He had to clench his fists to steady himself as the fresh realisation came to him. Now that he had so much to lose he must watch himself every foot of the way. An error of judgement, an unguarded moment, and he might destroy all of them. Like Bill had done as he had entered the minefield with Gail uppermost in his thoughts.

He stiffened, hearing the door open and close very softly. Knowing it was the girl. She stood motionless beside the bed, her figure a pale ghost against the darkness.

As he made to move she said quickly, "Please. I had to come. I could not wait for you again, without knowing." She sounded as if she was shaking. "But do not touch me, my darling. Please try to understand."

He lay on his side, hardly daring to breathe as she slipped into the bed. He could smell her hair, her body, her desperate uncertainty, and wanted more than anything to help her.

How long they lay together he did not know. He listened to her breathing until it became steadier, knew she was watching him even though it was too dark to see.

She reached out impulsively and took his hand. "Steven." She pulled it slowly and laid it on her breast. "Steven." She kept repeating his name, as if to reassure herself. To find some inner strength.

He felt her breast in his hand, the fierce heartbeats, the dampness of her skin.

She lifted his hand away and kissed. Then she said, "Love me, Steven. Do not care what I say. *Love me*. I must be yours!"

Very gently he knelt beside her, feeling her muscles tighten as he moved above her, knowing she was fighting everything she had suffered and still harboured in her mind like a scar. He saw her head moving from side to side on the pillow, felt her legs forcing against him, while one hand gripped his shoulder, digging into it until he knew the skin had broken.

For one moment longer he hesitated, his concern and pity matched only by his want of her.

As he came down so did her resistance break, not immediately, but in parts, until only her body remained unyielding beneath him. Then her arms came up and around his neck and shoulders, and he felt her mouth seeking his as she gasped, *"Now!"*

It was like falling a great distance. Down and down, with her body angling to receive him, her skin embracing his until their passions were finally equalled.

When they lay quiet again she whispered, "Do not move away. Stay. Let me hold you like this."

He kissed her shoulder, knowing he already wanted her again. And again.

She added quietly, "This is our tomorrow, my darling."

He reached down and touched her breast. "And it will last for us."

She stirred beneath him, the nightmare gone.

17 Maximum Effort

THE depot ship's operations room seemed unusually quiet and deserted despite the groups of officers who stood or sat around the central chart table. The deadlights were shut across the scuttles, although it was still early evening, and the deckhead lights played down on the assembled men, on the discarded typewriters and signal cabinets which were normally buzzing with activity. Beside a bulkhead door a solitary petty officer sat at a desk wearing a pair of headphones. By this method he could retain contact with the main communications section on the other side of the bulkhead yet be isolated from the meeting about to begin.

Marshall followed the little admiral to the top of the table and nodded to his own officers and the marines who would be carried with them to the scene of the raid.

There were others, too. The Senior Operations Officer, Intelligence experts, the Chief of Staff and, he was surprised to see, the minute S.A.S. lieutenant called Smith. The one who was like Peter Lorre.

Dundas stood looking down at the large scale chart of the objective, and then said, "Smoke, if you like. You might be too busy later on."

Marshall watched his own officers' reactions. Young Warwick grinned at Dundas's wry remark. Buck was masklike as usual. Frenzel was frowning, adjusting his own department to the broad layout of their mission. Gerrard glanced across the table towards him, his eyes very dark. Anxious, resigned, it was all there. Devereaux too looked as if he had found little rest during the four days in harbour.

Dundas said crisply, "You have been given details of the mission. To enter the new port of Nestore and destroy the enemy's bombing capability. Until this morning, most of you only knew it was to be another job for you. *Until* this morning, I was not sure we could go ahead. But now we have the C. in C.'s blessing." He smiled briefly. "This is the big one. The grand slam. Captain Lambert is in charge of a detachment of thirty marines and their equipment. Including their canoes," he shot the captain a quick smile, "or cockles as I understand they are known. Lieutenant, er, Smith will be i/c demolition and general adviser on local matters of defence and recognition."

Several of the officers were writing busily in their notebooks, and Frenzel nodded understandingly as Dundas added, "The submarine's fuel and fresh water intake will be reduced to a minimum to help compensate for the extra load."

The Chief of Staff coughed politely and the admiral snapped, "Yes, Charles?"

"A point on entering the harbour, sir."

The admiral waved him down impatiently. "I have had it inserted in my orders. Commander Marshall's decision *on the spot* will be final. We have compiled a new intelligence pack on net defences and local patrols. But apart from that, we know very little." He looked sternly at Marshall. "You want to add anything?"

Marshall said, "I'm very sorry to harp about security, sir, but. . . ."

"Quite right, my boy." Dundas sighed. "We are doing all we can. The C. in C. has been in close contact, as have American Intelligence. We have tried to keep it as close a secret as possible. Later, if the signs are right, I will inform F.O.I.C. Gibraltar to prepare a covering force, or invent some suitable diversion. However,—'' the word hung in the air, ''it will be mainly up to you.''

Marshall smiled gravely. Before the conference he had thanked the admiral for giving him the right of a final decision *on the spot*, as he had just put it. Dundas had replied, ''You may have little cause to thank me later on. It is often safer to be under direct orders, right or wrong.''

Dundas continued, ''My staff will be with you until you slip from the depot ship in,'' he consulted his watch, ''approximately eight hours. You will embark the marines as soon as it is dark and get them settled in.'' He looked at Frenzel. ''You want something?''

''The damaged screw, sir. Can't something be done to rectify it?''

''No time. My engineering expert and the base engineer have both said it would take too long. A dockyard job.'' He smiled thinly. ''As you are now totally committed, I can tell you. The Allied forces will invade Sicily one month from tomorrow. I can tell you this because if you fail to delay or destroy the enemy's immediate supply of radio bombs there may be no invasion . . . period.''

Marshall heard some of them gasp with surprise, saw the two marine lieutenants exchanging glances and grinning. As if they had just been offered a year's back-pay instead of this vague, possibly suicidal mission.

He pushed the thought of failure from his mind. Remembering the girl's face when he had left her. Despite all that might be waiting in the next few days they had both felt strangely calm. Detached from all reality by their own special world.

As the Operation Officer's voice droned on about enemy shipping and coastal defences he let his mind move back again. The days and nights, all linked together, dominated by their want of each other.

Nothing else had been important. Dundas had been right about that, too. He had returned feeling totally different, and no matter how the first pressures of action touched him, he knew he had Chantal to hold on to.

He realised the voice had stopped and that Dundas was closing his brief-case.

The admiral said suddenly, "I should add that Commander Simeon will be accompanying this mission, to take overall control of land operations."

The others looked towards Marshall, but he was able to remain impassive. He already knew about this additional pressure, just as he knew why Simeon was absent from the briefing.

Marshall had been unpacking his grip in a borrowed cabin aboard the depot ship when Simeon had strode into the doorway, his face cold with anger. He had slammed the door and had said, "So you got your own way, eh? Total control of the raid. The admiral's bright boy at last!"

Marshall had stayed silent, watching the man's anger, only half hearing his flood of words. He had been standing beside an open scuttle, so that Simeon had been unable to see him against the bright sunlight.

Simeon had been saying, "Well, I've had your number for some time. I knew what you'd been up to with my wife. . . ."

Marshall had interrupted at point. "Before you knew her."

"Don't interrupt!" His face had been pink with rage. "And now you've very conveniently stepped into Travis's shoes, and no doubt his bed as well!"

Marshall had felt completely calm, gratified perhaps that not even Simeon's words could hurt him. As the sunlight had touched his shoulders he had seen Simeon's eyes widen even further, and he had said quietly, "Sorry, I forgot to mention my promotion. It hadn't bothered me much one way or the other. Until now."

Simeon had stared at him. "I'll *bet*! If I know you, you've been. . . ."

Marshall had stepped across the cabin and had said gently, "But now, *old chap*, I can't be accused of striking a superior officer!"

The pain had lanced up his arm, and he had seen Simeon sprawled on the bunk, blood running down his chin and over his impeccable white shirt in a steady trickle.

He had lurched to his feet, his face shocked and twisted with pain. All he had been able to say was, "You hit me! *Me!*" Then he had gone, his blood leaving a small pattern along the carpet.

When the admiral had told him about Simeon's part in the raid he had felt like protesting. But Dundas had added, "If anything happens to you, who would take over? Your Number One? One of the others?'' He had given a quick shake of the head. ''Simeon's been a good man in this sort of work. In the past. Once ashore, he should be able to push the raid through to a successful conclusion. But he knows you will carry the maximum authority. There's far more at stake here than personal likes and dislikes.''

It was dusk by the time the briefing finally broke up. Marshall walked to the upper deck with Gerrard and Frenzel, and stood for some minutes looking down at his command alongside. The marine commandos were already being mustered, their weapons and packs passed through the fore hatch by a chain of seamen.

He said, ''The cockles will take up a lot of space, Bob. Tell Buck to stow half of them in those pressure-tight compartments aft. They've been empty since he removed the spare fish.''

As Gerrard walked away Frenzel said quietly, ''This is going to be *big* all right.''

''I think we have a good chance, Chief.''

''Yes.'' He chuckled. ''Only an idiot would expect us to try and bluff this one out!''

The marine captain came over and saluted. ''Ready to embark, sir.''

He was tall and thin and had a bushy ginger moustache, probably to give age to his rank. In fact it made him look like a boy in a school play.

''Nice to have you aboard.'' Marshall watched the first of the little canoes being lowered down the depot ship's side.

The marine remarked, ''I've done two raids in those things. Piece of cake.'' He marched away, barking orders to his two lieutenants.

Frenzel grinned. ''Christ, it's going to be crowded on board!''

Marshall looked at his watch. Soon he would be too involved to blink. He had to find a moment to write her a letter. To leave behind. Just in case.

Frenzel said abruptly, **''Congratulations, by the way. I'm very glad for you, sir.''** He looked away. ''And I don't mean about your promotion either. That should be yours anyway.''

Marshall watched his fingers locking and unlocking around the guardrail. Thinking of his wife. Remembering. How it could have been.

''Thanks, Chief. I didn't know it was general knowledge.''

Frenzel faced him again. "It isn't. But I saw you when you came off shore. It was enough. You'll be good for each other. Bloody fine girl. Brave, too."

"Yes. I've been lucky."

He made to go, but Frenzel called after him, "Stay that way, sir. I have a feeling we're going to need everything we can get!"

Marshall walked slowly along the boat deck, nodding occasionally to his men as they made their way to the catwalk alongside. He saw Starkie and Blythe, each carrying a steaming bag and smoking his pipe, chatting calmly like old salts off on some routine voyage.

The coxswain said, "See you aboard, sir."

The yeoman added, "What's German for *get knotted*, sir? I want to make a private signal to 'em as we sail out!"

Marshall smiled. "Ask the sub."

He stepped through a screen door and walked to his cabin. The writing pad lay open and ready on his table. It was then he felt his skin chilling all over like ice. It got worse and worse, and when he tried to write the date on the letter he could barely hold the pen. He stared at the bulkhead, the despair returning like fever.

Not now. Not now, of all times.

He closed his eyes tightly. Holding on to her face. Her touch. Her warmth. Until eventually he was calm again.

Then, and only then, did he begin to write.

Marshall stepped over a sleeping marine and walked into the control room. Above the gentle hum of motors he heard the regular comings and goings of crew and passengers. The boat was crammed beyond capacity. Everywhere you looked were marines and seamen struggling to sleep, eat and work in some semblance of order.

And they had had a full week of it. Creeping along at a reduced speed, avoiding patrol areas and anything which looked or sounded like a threat to their isolation.

He bent over the chart table and compared Devereaux's calculations with his own. The boat was still steering due west, with Malta's nearest minefield twenty miles off the starboard beam.

He saw Frenzel by his control panel. He was not required for anything but he stayed there just the same. Perhaps he needed to be there. With something he understood. Or maybe he saw in the familiar gauges some kind of privacy. And that was precious indeed.

Marshall had given his own cabin to Simeon and the marine officers. Even with the spare pipe-cot there was barely enough space for the two marine lieutenants to stretch out on the deck underneath. The wardroom always seemed to be crowded, with Churchill coming and going with coffee, cocoa, tea and food to meet the demands.

He heard a man chuckle and turned to see a German sergeant standing in the bulkhead doorway. He was carrying his helmet and a deadly-looking Schmeisser, and Marshall recognised him as Captain Lambert's senior N.C.O.

A stoker called, '' 'Ands up! We've got our first Jerry prisoner!''

The marine explained to Marshall, ''Just trying it out, sir.'' He glared at the sailor. ''Be a bugger if the bloody outfit didn't fit just as we was goin' ashore!'' He strode away in dignified silence.

Marshall smiled. Browning would have loved it. The cloak-and-dagger atmosphere. The embarrassed anger of the marine sergeant who was more concerned with his appearance than the risk of dying.

He walked over to Frenzel. ''Still bothered, Chief?''

''A bit.'' He cocked his head. ''That flaw in the screw. We can't do more than six knots submerged without making a bad vibration. Any good Asdic would pick us up in no time.''

''Then six knots it must be, Chief. If there's a real emergency we'll have to think again.'' He smiled. ''Or take to the cockles!''

Buck, who was O.O.W., called, ''We will be going through the main Sicilian minefield tonight, sir. Is that right?''

''Correct.'' He clenched his fists in his pockets. ''After that we'll head up and around towards the mainland. Should be in position for the raid in four days. Sunday.''

Buck grinned. ''Oh bother. I'll miss church!''

Marshall looked at Frenzel. Were they really so confident, or was it all just for him? To give him the strength he would need to get them in. And out again.

He said, ''Once clear of the coast we'll have a general run through the plan. Time each part of the operation. See if we can cut corners.''

He forced himself to think forward again. Visualise the port as it really was instead of lines and sketches on a chart. If the wind got up, or the weather worsened, it would be impossible to drop the cockles too far offshore. That would mean losing time while the submarine manoeuvred back to her own attack sector. It might cause a delay to . . . he shook himself angrily. If, if, if. He would have to see for himself. Then decide.

Frenzel said, ''I hope everyone appreciates what we're doing, that's all.''

Buck grinned, showing his sharp teeth. ''Knighthoods all round, I shouldn't wonder.''

Marshall returned to the chart. Listening to their efforts on his behalf was unbearable. It also told him just how much there was at stake. What he had got them into.

A stoker said, ''Time to call the watch, sir.''

''Very well. Carry on.''

Gerrard appeared in the control room and listened intently to Buck's report as he handed over to him. Then he crossed to the table and said, ''Through the mines again, eh?''

''Tonight.'' He waited, seeing the nervous tightening around Gerrard's mouth. ''We'll be all right.''

''Yes.'' Gerrard's eyes rested momentarily on his shoulder straps. ''So it seems, sir.''

Marshall stared at him. Surprised. Hurt. ''Is that what you think? That I'm one of the glory boys? I thought we knew each other better than that!''

Gerrard turned away. ''Sorry. Spoke out of turn.'' He moved to the gyro and said no more.

Marshall said curtly, ''I'm going to get some food.''

As he left the brightly lit control room he heard Frenzel murmur fiercely, ''That was a bloody stupid thing to say!''

He did not hear Gerrard's answer, nor did he want to. He might have expected a remark like that under such tense circumstances. From Simeon or Devereaux. Almost anybody. But not Gerrard. He was a friend.

He saw Warwick playing chess with the S.A.S. lieutenant, while Buck sat at the far end of the table wolfing down tinned sausages as if they were the last available in the world. He wanted to turn and leave. Hide. But there was nowhere to go. He said, ''Move up for one more.''

Smith studied him impassively and then winked. ''The sub here may be fine at gunnery. At chess, he ain't!''

Marshall leaned back and watched Churchill pouring his coffee. It was probably just as well Simeon had his cabin. He might have been tempted to take a drink. Not just coffee.

Churchill asked, "Would you like the first lieutenant's bunk, sir? 'E's on watch. A bit of shut-eye does a power of good."

"No." Perhaps he had answered too sharply, for he saw Warwick and Buck glancing at each other. "Not just yet."

Smith smiled gently. "Once, when I did a little job in Southern France, I did not sleep for three days. I fed myself with method and tactics until I nearly burst. Afterwards I slept for a week. It is better that way."

Marshall nodded. "I expect you're right."

"It is why I am still alive." He pushed the chessboard aside. "And why I am plagued with amateurs!"

Marshall smiled. "Thanks."

"For what?" His eyes were mildly questioning.

"I think you know."

"Any coffee available?" Simeon was in the doorway, his face puffy from sleep. He added, "Are you discussing the raid?"

Smith looked at him calmly. "Piece of cake, sir."

Simeon sat down and glanced at Marshall. The bruise was still visible on his chin.

He said, "And what do *you* think?"

Marshall stood up and walked to the door. "You know what *I* think."

Gerrard was waiting for him, his features working in the harsh lights. "I want to apologise, sir."

He looked at him. "Forget it was said." He made to walk past, but when Gerrard persisted he added, "I said forget it. You're not the only one with problems. After this lot's over tell me again. Then I'll listen. But right now I've got some thinking to do, so leave it, will you?"

"I wanted you to *understand*." Gerrard looked desperate. "Maybe I've been at it too long, I don't know."

Marshall took his arm and pulled him into the chart space, dropping his voice as he replied, "We've all been that, Bob. Even one day is too bloody long! I know you're worried because of Valerie and the child, but remember all the others who will be hitting the beaches of Sicily in a few weeks time. Don't you think they've got wives, too?" He saw Gerrard's mouth tighten ing and added brutally, "If that's not enough for you then think about Browning. He lost his son, and got killed trying to save others. Or ask the Chief about *his* family and find out why he doesn't crack up!" He saw him recoil as if he had struck him, as he had Simeon. He added wearily, "I know we didn't plan for this one. I also know it's not going to be *a piece of cake,* any more than the marine captain believes it. But don't tell me, and don't say it in front of the others. If you value anything between us, then do me that one favour!"

As he stepped through the main bulkhead he knew Gerrard was still staring after him.

Marshall glanced around the packed wardroom and waited while the others eased into position where they could see his large-scale plan.

With all but essential fans and machinery shut down, the air was greasy and humid, and clung to his face like another skin. After a slow crawl through the last minefield, across open water to the north of Sicily and towards the mainland, nearly everyone was showing signs of wear. But the eyes were bright enough, lit by that same old excitement he knew so well. Anxiety, tension, fear, the need to get on with it. Over and done with.

He said, "Most of you know by now that the weather has decided not to be on our side."

Marshall remembered his disappointment when they had gone to periscope depth the previous night to raise the antennae for a last radio contact. Randall, the petty officer telegraphist, had reported glumly that the Med. report was bad. Strong winds closing from the south-west. All the ingredients for a rough sea. He could still feel the disappointment, but knew he must hold it from the others.

He said, "But if it's bad for us, it'll be good news for the invasion arrangements. Enemy reconnaissance will be too hampered to see much of the real build-up."

He looked at them slowly. The marine officers and Smith, his own small team, except for Gerrard who was on watch, the N.C.O.s and chief petty officers standing on the seats and clinging to overhead pipes to get a better view. And Simeon. He sat at the opposite end of the table, arms folded, his face devoid of expression.

Marshall continued, "So this is how we'll handle it."

They all craned forward, their faces shining with sweat in the solitary deckhead light.

The port of Nestore looked for all the world like a large pouch, with the narrowest part at the southern end, an entrance barely a quarter of a mile across.

Marshall said, "We know there's a boom here," he reached out with some brass dividers, "controlled by a single vessel which opens and closes it as required. The left side of the port as you enter is almost sheer, and to the right, where the main fishing village once stood, the land has been cleared." He tapped the small coloured circles. "Pillboxes have been constructed to give a good field of fire, although I doubt if they ever expected to use them."

"We'll soon alter that!" The young marine lieutenant who had spoken fell silent under his captain's withering stare.

Marshall smiled. "It may not come to a pitched battle."

Captain Lambert said worriedly, "If you can't drop the cockles clear of the land, we will have to halve the time of disembarking if we're to escape attention."

"Yes. I shall surface and lower the cockles as close to the boom as I can get."

They had had a brief run-through the method of unloading two days earlier and one unpleasant fact had come to light. The cockles on their own were very light and easy to handle. But loaded with explosives, weapons and demolition gear they would break up if an attempt to slide them outboard was made in bad weather. Buck had come up with a simple solution. The submarine's deck gun would be used as a derrick to sway them over the side. He had devised a wooden spar, to be lashed to the gun barrel like a bayonet, which with block and tackle secured at the end would make a fairly reliable crane. When someone had voiced a doubt, Lambert had snapped, "It's all we've got, so let's get our fingers out, eh?"

Devereaux asked, "What about the patrols, sir?"

"We know about some of them, and yesterday we were able to time one of the local boats." He smiled. "I think they must have German advisers aboard, if not crews. They are regular and precise, and therefore predictable." He added sharply, "However, we take nothing for granted."

He looked at Simeon. "Over to you."

It was strange how they had managed to avoid each other, except on matters of duty.

Simeon yawned. "The object of the exercise is to destroy and delay. But we must make sure the enemy is not triggered off into realising our main intention. That is, to deny immediate support to his forces in Sicily." He reached over and took the dividers. "There is a railway which runs north-east across Italy to Bari, the port from which supplies are being sent to Greece and Yugoslavia. An obvious target if we really were going to invade by that route. Captain Lambert will lead half the landing force and carry out demolition. I will take the other party, and with Lieutenant Smith will do our bit above the village itself." His eyes flickered towards Marshall. "And our commander here will of course attack the main loading jetty and so forth at the top of the harbour. It is a concrete bunker construction which enables the bombs to be loaded aboard ship without ever appearing above ground until that moment." His eyes did not flicker as he added, "The engineer, Travis, stated that the construction is formidable, but once brought down would block the whole installation for weeks, maybe longer."

Lambert said, "I think we're all buttoned up then." He plucked at his moustache. "Should be interesting."

Marshall looked at his watch. It was two o'clock in the afternoon.

"It's mostly a matter of timing. The nearest German garrison of any size is sixteen miles north-east of the port, at Lagonegro, so bearing that in mind we have three vital points." He ticked them off on his fingers. "First, the coastal patrols. Second, the boom and the inner harbour patrol, one boat to all accounts. Finally, how soon or late the port defenders will be alerted and thereby call for inland support." He smiled at their strained faces. "Any comments?"

Warwick asked, "Couldn't we cut the boom and slip through undetected, sir?"

"Afraid not, Sub. The port is only dredged for coasters and medium sized ships."

Devereaux added wearily, "About six fathoms."

Buck rubbed his hands noisily. "It'd be like shooting fish in a barrel."

Marshall nodded. "We will approach the boom at the arranged time. Fire our fish into the top of the harbour, and then drift off the landing parties, who with luck will have created their own sort of pandemonium by then."

Simeon stood up and stretched. "And that is your set plan of attack?" It sounded like an accusation.

Their eyes met again. "It is." A pause. "Would you care to offer an alternative?"

Simeon brushed some dust from his sleeve. "Me? Certainly not. Wouldn't think of it." He glanced at him over the table, a smile on his lips. "Your plan. *Your* responsibility, eh?"

Marshall smiled back at him. "That's right."

He folded the plan and added, "We'll go to action stations in four hours. German uniforms and equipment will then be issued, but prior to that moment I want everyone to have a good meal. See to that for me."

The meeting started to break up.

The captain of marines adjusted his watch and remarked calmly, "We go in tomorrow morning as planned. *Splendid*."

Buck grinned. "Sunday. Day of rest!"

Marshall walked out towards the control room with Frenzel beside him.

The latter said quietly, "Pity we can't bash 'em in the dark."

"I know. But it's already cutting things fine. Our chaps would be more hampered at night than the enemy."

Marshall was still beside the chart table when Buck reported that his arrangements were complete, the crew and landing parties had been fed and fully detailed on their particular parts of the raid.

"Thank you." He glanced at the clock. "Silent routine throughout the boat as before." He looked at Gerrard's bent back. "Watch your trim, Number One. Wait until the marines have settled down before you blow any ballast."

More minutes passed, and he could feel the sweat running down his spine and gathering above his waistband like ice-rime.

Frenzel reported, "All systems checked, sir."

"Very well."

He looked at the gauges. They were still running deep, the hull almost motionless but for an occasional tremble.

"Ready, Number One?" He tried to discover what Gerrard was thinking. How he was taking it.

"Just a few minutes, sir." He was watching the senior Asdic operator.

The man called, "No H.E., sir." He gestured to the clock

"Next patrol should be due in about twenty minutes more or less."

Cool, casual, almost indifferent.

Gerrard said, "Ready now, sir."

"Take her up to twenty metres." He watched Frenzel's hands moving, the stoker by his side making notes on a pad.

Long before the submarine had glided up to the ordered level Marshall could feel the growing motion. A pencil rolled from the table, and he saw Blythe put out his hand to steady himself as the deck yawed uneasily.

"Twenty metres, sir." Gerrard gripped the helmsman's chairback and peered at the tell-tales. "Bad cross current."

Devereaux snapped, "More than that, I'd have thought!"

"Still no H.E., sir."

"Good." Marshall rubbed his palms on his shirt. They were wet with sweat. "Periscope depth."

He waited, counting seconds, hearing Gerrard's voice again and again as he ordered the trim to be adjusted. The motion was getting very bad, with the hull floundering so badly he thought it might even break surface.

"Up periscope."

He slammed down the handles, holding tight while the periscope seemed to swing against and then away from him to the violent motion.

For a while he could see nothing but bursting spray and the curling edge of a long breaker. Then, as the periscope edged cautiously to its full extent he saw the banks of low cloud, a panorama of small, steep whitecaps which cruised towards him like a vicious, bobbing army.

He steadied the handles and flicked the lens to full power. Between the spindrift he saw the first sight of the coast, seemingly low down because of the angry sea. There was still some sunlight, but well inland, playing across the hillsides, and blinking faintly on someone's windows.

"Faint H.E. to starboard, sir."

He swung the handles and tried to see the other vessel. By rights it should be well clear, on the first leg of a rectangular patrol. There was nothing in sight, and it was unlikely they would detect a submarine even if the range closed, in all this confusion. The periscope too would be just one more feather of spray should an aircraft come snooping through the low clouds.

He heard someone give a nervous laugh, and guessed that

259

many of those nearby were watching him intently. Trying to see their future in the gleam reflected in his eye.

Marshall tensed as a shaft of watery sunlight probed down towards the coast.

There it was. In the evening light the port entrance was a blur of blue/grey, but he could see the faint silhouette of a moored ship. The boom vessel. And beyond her the narrow harbour, jumbled and indistinct. He imagined he could see something pale at the far end, but could not be certain. But it could be the first outcrop of massive concrete which protected the jetty and the underground bunkers.

"Down periscope." He straightened his back and saw Simeon watching him from the opposite end of the control room. "We're on station."

"H.E.'s fading, sir."

The patrol boat's commander would be cursing the weather, the discomfort, the stupidity of his German allies who insisted on such unnecessary regularity.

Marshall rested his spine against the table. He could feel his legs quivering. As if he had been running.

"We'll give the patrol half an hour and then resume our original position and depth." He glanced at Captain Lambert, already a stranger in his Afrika Korps uniform. "I shall close the land as soon after midnight as I can. We will take it from there."

Lambert, who had been checking his Luger, jammed it back in his holster and said quietly, "And tomorrow. . . ."

Marshall did not hear the rest. He was thinking of the moment when she had said *tomorrow*.

He turned towards the chart and gripped the vibrating table with all his strength. Please God there might still be a tomorrow for all of them.

18   The Victors

MARSHALL wedged his elbows painfully against the bridge screen and levelled his glasses towards the land. The weather was bad, and with a following sea it felt as if the hull was already getting out of control. While the conning-tower swayed dizzily through a steep arc, the gratings under his straddled legs shuddered repeatedly as Gerrard used both screws to assist the helm.

Blythe shouted above the tumult of spray and wind, "All clear on Asdic, sir!" He spluttered as a wave exploded over the bridge. "*Hell*, what a night!"

Marshall said, "Tell Number One to raise her to full buoyancy." He watched a solitary star amongst the cruising clouds before it vanished again. "Open the main hatch."

They had been surfaced for ten minutes. It seemed like an hour. He peered across the bows, seeing the lively ranks of white horses surging ahead towards the hidden land. If they could get the cockles in the water without mishap the wind might at least help them reach the shore without so much effort.

He made up his mind. "First landing party prepare to move off."

The forward hatch scraped noisily, and he saw groping figures emerging like spectres from a tomb.

Warwick and his gun crew were already on deck, and he heard Buck's harsh voice yelling instructions when the first of the little boats was hauled towards the makeshift crane.

From aft came more thumps and bangs as the pressure-tight compartments were flung open.

Captain Lambert joined him by the screen and shouted, "I'm off then." He staggered towards the ladder. "Submarines! You can keep 'em!"

Marshall smiled. "Tell control room to hold down the revs as much as they can. The first boats will be going at any second."

He craned over to watch as Warwick's crew trained the gun slowly over the side, one small cockle, complete with occupants and weapons, dangling from the tackle like an overloaded basket.

Buck snarled, "Easy on the fore-guy! Lower away, lads!"

The cockle touched the tossing water almost shyly, and in a second was free and away, the paddles glinting as the marines took it clear of the U-boat's lee.

"Next!" Buck was clinging to the guardrail, his body black above the wave crests. "Hook on. Take in the slack. Ready. Lower away!"

Blythe whispered, "Come on, you bloody bootnecks! Let's get the hell out of here!"

A lookout shouted, "Light, sir! Starboard bow!"

But it was gone almost before the others had found it. It was miles away. Probably inside the harbour. Guardboat. Or some careless soldier with a handlamp.

"Carry on." Marshall tried to relax. To remember if he had overlooked anything.

"Number Three cockle's clear, sir." Blythe added, "Two to go."

The little canoes were paddling rapidly out of sight. A well trained team. Lambert had remarked just before they had surfaced, "If we're caught, the very worst they can do is shoot us for wearing *their* uniforms!"

Marshall had thought of the dead major in the police post. The naked girl spreadeagled on the table. *The worst they could do.* But he had said nothing. Lambert was no fool, despite his apparent calm. He was the best available.

A chorus of shouts and curses made him jerk round.

Blythe exclaimed, "Number Four's ditched, sir!"

The canoe was already sinking under its weight of equipment, and the gasping marines were floundering against the hull, groping for Buck's heaving lines.

"Get Number Five on the tackles!"

Marshall said, "Lambert has allowed for this sort of thing. He could lose most of his men before they even touch land."

Blythe gave a great sigh. "She's clear, sir. There they go. Paddles flying like bottles in the fleet canteen."

"Good. Close the fore hatch. Gun crew below."

Marshall wiped his streaming face. His skin was sore, his eyes aching with strain.

"All secure, sir."

"Clear the bridge." He groped for the voicepipe. "Bring her round on to the new course."

Somebody panted past him and clattered through the open hatch.

He heard Gerrard report, "Course now three-zero-zero, sir. Pilot estimates that the eastern side of the harbour is about ten miles off the starboard bow."

He replied, "Good. Take her down. Ninety metres." He saw Blythe sitting on the lip of the hatch.

The yeoman said, "All below, sir."

Marshall snapped down the cock on the voicepipe, wondering if, like himself, Blythe was remembering that other time. All those weeks, an eternity ago, when he had dragged his

262

captain below to save him from following a dead stoker into the sea.

He pushed it from his thoughts and scrambled with Blythe down the ladder.

It was a relief to run in deeper water again. The motion steadied, and he felt his cheeks tingling from wind and sea.

Simeon was watching from the chart space, his eyes in shadow as he asked, "How long now?"

Marshall moved to his side and studied the chart. "It'll take Lambert's party all of three hours to get ashore. It will be up to him what he does then. But he knows the area, and he'll not be looking for trouble."

Simeon's lip curled slightly. "*Yet.*"

Then he added, "Pity about the weather." He had raised his voice, as if he wanted to share his opinions with the watchkeepers. "One more day and we might have had better luck."

"I know." Marshall studied Devereaux's neat calculations. "But Sunday is the best day for it. We decided it would be more likely to work this way."

Simeon shrugged. "I didn't."

Marshall ignored him and walked over to join Lieutenant Smith and the remaining marine sergeant.

He said, "I will get close to the boom and drop your party. You shouldn't have too much bother."

The little lieutenant grinned. "I've briefed 'em, sir. I know this part of the coast quite well from way back. When the good people of Nestore caught fish."

Marshall smiled. "Good."

He could barely stand still. It was beginning. He could picture the tiny cockles bobbing over the waves. Lambert and his men peering through the darkness for a first glimpse of land. And then. . . .

He said, "Just remember the arrangements for pick-up, even if you forget everything else."

The hands on the control room clock moved round more slowly than he could recall. One hour. Then two, with men moving automatically to relieve others on watch. A few snatches of conversation. An occasional joke. Quick. Brittle.

"Getting close, sir." Devereaux's fingers were twisting a pencil over and over in short nervous jerks.

"Very well. Pass the word to the second party. Stand by."

Marshall dabbed his face and throat. "We'll go up and have a look when everyone's in position."

"*Sir!*" It was Speke, the senior Asdic operator. "I'm getting some strange back-echoes at Green four-five." He turned his dial very slowly. "There it is again!"

Marshall pushed Blythe aside and put a hydrophone headset to his ear. For a moment he caught only the usual mystifying chorus of squeaks, static and sea noises. Then he heard it. Like water tinkling in a fountain. Someone tapping a delicate glass at gentle, regular intervals.

He hurried to the table and snapped, "Position, Pilot? Exactly."

The dividers settled on a pencilled cross. "That's as accurate as I can make it, sir." He sounded defensive.

Marshall looked at Speke's hunched shoulders. "Still there?"

"Comes and goes, sir. But the bearing's pretty constant."

Marshall thrust his hands into his pockets to stop them shaking. "Bring her round to two-eight-zero. Slow ahead."

He walked to the ladder and back again until Starkie had the boat on the new course.

Then he said quietly, "They must have laid some new detection gear on the sea-bed." He was thinking aloud, and heard someone gasp with alarm.

Warwick said, "The local patrol will be entering harbour in the morning. Couldn't we follow her in through the boom?"

"No." It was an effort to reply. "The patrol boat is *fast*. We'd have to use full revs to keep up. Even then. . . ."

Frenzel said gently, "No go, Sub. Even allowing for the patrol's screws drowning the usual sounds, with our damaged prop going at full-belt we'd be picked up by this new gear on the sea-bottom. They'd have us pinned down in minutes." He looked at Marshall. "You weren't to know, sir. It's just bad bloody luck."

Smith said doggedly, "I still think my party should go. We might be able to do some damage."

Simeon spoke for the first time. "But not enough damage, eh, *Commander*?"

Marshall looked at him. "No."

"Well then." His tone was gentle. Like silk. "You've made your gesture. You can call the whole thing off. With honour. I

264

can see now why you insisted on complete local control of the mission.''

The others turned to watch.

Marshall said, ''Is that what you think?'' He looked at Gerrard. ''You're not alone, it seems.''

He turned his back on them and walked to the table. He tried to discover his true feelings. It was like awakening from a dream, only to find it was real and stark.

Devereaux said, ''It looks as if they've laid a complete detection grid.'' He tapped the chart with his pencil. ''As much as two miles out, if Speke is right.''

Marshall looked at him. If Devereaux felt any satisfaction at seeing his dismay he was not showing it.

''I agree.''

It got them precisely nowhere. To reach any sort of position for attacking the harbour installations in accordance with his plan they would have to be right up to the boom. He felt the anger and despair squeezing his brain like a vice.

For nothing. It had all been for nothing.

Simeon examined one hand with apparent interest and remarked, ''If I could have got my party to the right place on time,'' his shoulders gave a slight shrug, ''who *knows* what we might have achieved. As it is, it would appear that we have missed the boat, if you'll pardon the expression.''

Marshall looked at the clock. ''What time is first light?''

Devereaux said dully, ''Couple of hours' time, sir. Provided the wind has blown itself out.''

Simeon smiled. ''I'm sure Captain Lambert will be glad to know he's got a fine day ahead of him!

Marshall eyed him calmly. Inwardly he felt close to breaking. He wanted to take Simeon by the throat and smash his head against the dripping steel until his smile was gone forever. Like that night at the house when he had found him with Gail.

He replied, ''We will go in *on the surface.*'' He looked at the clock. ''We will retain the landing party until we are inside the harbour.''

It seemed an age before anyone spoke. Then it was several voices at once.

Devereaux said, ''But they'll never open the boom for us, sir! Even if we were a genuine Jerry U-boat they'd check our identity first!''

Frenzel added thickly, "If the boom stays shut, we're helpless."

"Yes," Marshall watched them impassively. "But it will give us time to get nearer."

"And then you'll talk your way inside, eh?" Simeon could no longer hide his amusement. "I think you're deluding yourself!"

"Perhaps. But that is how we will do it, so pass the word to all sections immediately." He looked at Gerrard. "The enemy will most likely keep the boom shut while they send a boat to investigate."

In his mind he could see it. As if it had already happened. An irritated guardboat, the submarine lying surfaced and naked under the eyes of a coastal battery. The boom vessel's skipper being called to his bridge. It would all take time. Not very much of it, but it was all they had left.

He heard himself say in the same expressionless tone, "We have to succeed. It's too late to execute another raid, even if we had the means. You have to balance the value of this boat and our lives against what is at stake in *ten days time*." He paused, watching their faces, seeing the realisation touching them, some perhaps for the first time.

"In a moment I will speak to the whole company. But it's my decision."

Starkie nodded in slow agreement, but kept his eyes on the gyro. He saw Blythe look at his signalman and give a grim smile.

The little lieutenant named Smith said quietly, "Right up to the front door." He whistled. "It's worth a try."

Simeon thrust himself away from the side and stood almost touching Marshall, his face tense and pale.

"If you wreck this one, my friend, I'll see that you never even command a ferry-boat for the *rest of your life*!"

Marshall met his stare. "If *we* wreck this one, I don't imagine anyone will be left, do you?"

He swung on his heel and called, "Right, Pilot, I want a new course for a central approach." He looked at Warwick. "And *you* can brush up your German."

Ten minutes later he picked up the intercom handset and tried to compose himself. Then he said, "This is the captain speaking. . . ."

As Marshall, with the lookouts pushing at his heels, burst through the hatch, he realised that the weather had eased. Most of the waves had smoothed away, and although the wind retained a blustery strength, the sea's face beyond the bows dipped and rose in a succession of rounded troughs.

He heard reports stammering through the voicepipes, the clink of metal as the short-range weapons were freed and brought to the ready, but concentrated his full attention on the sea and sky.

Across the boat's quarter he saw a small hint of paler light, but ahead it was still very dark, with no border line to betray the land or the horizon.

He snapped, "Alter course two points to starboard." He rubbed the slime and salt from the bridge gyro repeater and watched the card ticking round in slow obedience.

Starkie's voice. "New course, sir. Steady on three-four-zero."

Warwick climbed up beside him and adjusted his binoculars against the small patch of paling sky.

Blythe remarked, "Black as a boot up ahead, sir."

Warwick seemed satisfied. "You know how it is, Yeo. Out here in the Med. Dark one second. Full brilliance the next."

Marshall turned slightly and saw Blythe grinning at Warwick's back. How Warwick had changed, he thought. He had just spoken like an old man of the sea.

"Control room, sir." Blythe forgot the little joke. "Pilot estimates outer span of detection grid to be six thousand yards."

"Very good."

He moved his glasses and waited until the stem had sliced noisily through a steep-sided trough. But as his eyes moved beyond the submarine's slow approach his mind was elsewhere, working, calculating. Speed through the water. The nearness of that strange, tinkling detector. And the span beyond that before they were sighted. Or fired on.

He heard feet thumping on the after casing, a sharp scrape of steel and a splash. Moments later he saw Buck's bare head over the rim of the tower. He was grinning.

"Got rid of that bloody screen, sir. I hope the depot ship won't mind us ditching their monstrosity."

Warwick asked, "Don't we need it any more?"

Marshall did not comment. There was no point in denting Warwick's new reserve of strength.

Instead he said, "Ask Pilot if he's found us a number yet. There's not much time."

"Control room, sir. Commander Simeon wants to come up."

"Yes."

He remembered Browning again. It was just as if he was with them. His reply, *denied*, seemed to hang in the air.

Blythe reported, "Pilot says that U-178 is the best he can do, sir."

"So be it." He looked at Warwick and the yeoman. "Remember. We have intelligence reports that U-178 is one of several U-boats working with the Italian Navy. She's not supposed to be in this area, but we can't be certain. However, when we're challenged we'll stick to it, and hope for the best."

He watched their faces. Already they had gained sharper outlines, although the sea was just as dark.

Simeon's voice came through the gloom. "It's bloody cold."

Marshall said, "Tell the Chief to be ready to switch to main engines when I give the word. No friendly boat would come sneaking inshore using valuable battery power."

Simeon chuckled. "My, we are getting cunning."

Marshall moved a few paces towards him. "Do you wish to remain here?"

"Of course I bloody well do!" Simeon glared at him.

"Good. Then remember, one more crack like that and down you go."

"Five thousand yards, sir."

A steep roller curved upright and broke into a gentle rim of foam. Marshall watched it. It was no longer dull grey, but yellow, and when he glanced over the quarter he saw the muzzles of the Viérling were also shining in the first faint daylight.

He saw the machine-gunners standing by their weapons, their heads encased in captured coal-scuttle helmets. Warwick too was in his enemy uniform.

He saw Marshall's scrutiny and grinned awkwardly. "At least I'm a full lieutenant in *this* navy, sir!"

Marshall consulted his watch. Getting close. Time to begin the full deception.

"Tell the Chief to change over."

He waited, but jumped nevertheless as the clutches brought the heavy diesels into use, the exhaust noise spluttering and coughing throatily before settling into a regular pattern.

"Half ahead both engines."

He tried to pitch his ear above the other sounds, to catch some change in the propeller noises. But there was nothing. He raised his glasses and peered ahead. Out there, dozing over his set in some shore bunker, the enemy operator would hear it soon enough. Probably long before the detector on the sea-bed made any direct contact. The uneven swish of their damaged screw. The fault might yet be used to their advantage.

Buck was standing above the open hatch, one foot on either side, his hair dragged across his forehead as the diesels sucked hungrily at the sea air.

He asked, "Time, sir?"

"Yes. Tell your hands to prepare a full salvo. One to six. There'll not be time for a reload."

Buck vanished down the hatch.

Marshall looked up at the swaying periscope standards. They were blacker than the sky now, and he could see the jumping wire and even the thin antennae whipping to the motion.

Gerrard would be taking a look through the periscope at regular intervals. Waiting to alter course once they had sighted the boom vessel. But what would he be seeing right now? His wife? His unborn child? Death?

He snapped, "Run up the German ensign, Yeoman."

Simeon was crouched almost double, fumbling with a machine-pistol. He said irritably, "I hope this thing works!"

The scarlet flag flapped and then blew stiffly in the wind above their heads. Marshall glanced at it. Hating it. Depending on it.

"Have the other one ready."

Blythe nodded. "Aye, sir." Under his breath he added, "I'm not getting chopped under *that* bloody flag!"

"Asdic reports echoes from dead ahead, sir."

Marshall sucked in a long breath. Contact.

"Tell your deck gunners to prepare, Sub. One up the spout, but keep the ready-use ammunition hidden."

A seaman ran along the casing, his helmet bobbing up and down like a pot.

"And tell him to take that damned lid off. Only the A.A. gunners would be at a state of readiness."

He tried to clear his mind. *Would be. Are. Ought to be.* It was like some crazy puzzle.

"Echoes getting stronger, sir."

"Very well."

A complete patch of water glowed suddenly along the port beam. He saw the fore casing catching the fresh light, even a crude tattoo on the gunlayer's forearm as he checked the ammunition.

"Your cap, sir."

Marshall took it and pulled it over his unruly hair. He wanted to go below. Walk through the full length of his command. Make sure. One more check. It was stupid even to torture himself.

He said, "Any second now, I should think."

The light seemed to grow and spread with each turn of the screws. It was like two equal curtains being dragged away on either beam, laying them bare and vulnerable. Across the sharp stem he saw the first blunt outline of land, and crouched over the compass to compare the bearing with what it should be. Right on. The darker wedge to port was the western side of the harbour. In half an hour there would be no room to manoeuvre if the plan misfired. Even now some battery commander might be passing his range orders, gauging the moment to blast them to fragments.

A piercing blue eye blinked over the undulating water, its reflection touching the offshore swell like the tail of a comet.

"The challenge, sir." Blythe licked his lips. "I'd better get ready." He held up his lamp, but seemed unable to hold it firmly.

Marshall turned deliberately, his back to the land.

"Now listen. All of you. Don't get jumpy. We've just had a bad time of it and we're trying to get into the first available *friendly* port, right?"

All but Simeon nodded in time to his quiet voice. Like puppets.

He touched Warwick's hand. It was like ice. "You've got the signal ready. Read it to the yeoman." He looked at Blythe. "All right?"

He forced a grin. "As I'll ever be, sir." Then he became serious and trained his lamp over the screen.

Marshall turned to watch the land as it grew and gained new life from the receding shadows. Deep clefts, marked here and

270

there by a moving necklace of white spray as the wind drove the sea against the beach. He heard the lamp clattering beside him, and hoped Warwick had made a proper translation.

The signal read, *We require assistance*. Nothing more. What any submarine commander rattled by some running battle or depth-charge attack might send if he was at last within sight of safety.

The blue light blinked out again.

There was a pause and Warwick said, "They require our number, sir."

"Then make it. U-178."

This was the first vital moment. Or the last.

"Asdic reports that echoes have faded, sir."

"Thank you."

He watched a brief stav of light from the shadows.

"Acknowledgement, sir."

He bit his lip. Someone out there was trying to make a decision. To rouse higher authority for advice. On a Sunday morning, and at this hour, it would take a very brave man, he thought grimly.

When he raised his glasses again he saw the full breadth of the harbour mouth like a blacker line between the headlands, and poised just to the starboard side of their approach, the boom vessel, her bridge windows already glinting faintly in the watery light. He moved the glasses slowly, noting the lines of dots, the buoys which held the anti-submarine boom in position. Against the sky he could just make out a thin wisp of smoke from the boom vessel's funnel. She had steam up already. Probably to open the boom for the first returning patrol boat. He looked at his watch. In about two hours' time. He felt a droplet of sweat fall across his wrist, and made a fresh effort to steady himself.

"Tell Lieutenant Buck to stand by. Tubes One to Six. Minimum settings."

He was studying the boom vessel when Gerrard's voice came up the pipe by his elbow.

"Bridge? There's a ship moored in the harbour, sir! I just saw it on the main scope!" He was almost shouting. "We won't be able to hit the installations!"

Blythe said, *"Jesus!"*

Simeon crossed the bridge in three strides. "Sunday, eh? A quiet day, you said!" He spoke in a savage whisper, his face inches away. "Well, you can't damn well fire now, can you?

271

That ship will take the salvo, and the Jerries will have the wreck moved within a week!" He shook his head. "You've really made a cock of it this time!"

"Signal, sir." Warwick was listening to Blythe's slow voice. "They want us to heave-to. They're sending someone out."

"Slow ahead both engines. But retain course."

He had to force the words out. Simeon was right, he had misjudged it. He should have thought of this last detail. That a ship might be resting in port. Sunday. It seemed to rise up and taunt him.

"Boat's crossing the boom, sir. Small affair. Harbour launch."

Simeon said fiercely, "Well? Are you just going to stand here and be killed? For God's sake, man, let's get out while we still can!"

Warwick said, "Captain Lambert's party will be coming back by now, sir, if they've not been caught." He held up his wrist. "The charges on the railway are set for one hour's time. We can't leave them. . . ."

"Hold your bloody tongue!" Simeon waved his arm towards the land. "Are *you* going to explain to this boat what we're doing here?"

Marshall said, "He's right, all the same." He looked at Warwick and added, "Thanks, Sub."

He turned away before Warwick could reply.

"Tell Smith I want him on the fore casing. He'll know what for."

Blythe had some glasses trained on the boat as it swung fussily towards the slow-moving U-boat. He said, "Eye-tie launch, sir. But there's a Jerry officer in charge!"

Simeon snapped, "What did you expect, a priest?"

Marshall felt strangely calm. As if he had been suddenly injected with a drug. He watched the launch, his foot tapping slowly on the gratings as he studied her frothing wake. If the German came directly to the starboard side they were done for. But if he was naturally curious he would go right round the U-boat first. And they had to get between him and the watching boom vessel, and God alone knew how many others.

Some of the seamen on the casing were waving at the launch, and he saw an unfamiliar sailor just below the bridge. It was Smith. He had had no time to get a proper uniform, but had stripped to his shorts and wore a German forage cap rakishly over one ear. He too was waving, and as the boat turned to cross the submarine's stern he shouted something in German.

Blythe murmured, "He's coming round t'other side, sir!"

Marshall watched the boat's bow wave fall away, and saw a white-clad lieutenant clinging to the small wheelhouse, a megaphone in one hand. Now for it.

"Was ist los, Herr Kapitan?"

Marshall took Warwick's arm. "Tell him we've got engine trouble. That we were bound for Taranto." He licked his lips as Smith climbed down to the saddle tank. "And ask him aboard for a drink. He'll like that."

Simeon muttered, "It'll never work."

But it did.

As willing hands took the launch's lines, and the German lieutenant clambered up the slippery bulge of the tank, he was met by Smith. For those few seconds as they were hidden below the conning-tower Smith wrapped his arms around the surprised German and seized the safety rail at the foot of the tower. He pressed him against the steel, still talking to him soothingly until with a sudden wrench he jerked a knife from his waistband and drove it upwards into the German's stomach, holding him there like an impaled animal.

Other figures were already scrambling down into the launch, and in minutes it was over.

Marshall said harshly, "Quickly now. Second landing party in the launch. Take cover until we're through the boom. Make the Italian seamen understand that they'll live only if they do as we say."

He heard men hurrying along the casing, the occasional clatter of weapons.

Simeon stared at him and then said, "I will take the launch. We'll move that ship and get clear as best we can."

Their eyes held.

"I'll pick you up when the job's done." Without conscious thought he thrust out his hand. "Good luck."

Simeon stared at his hand but made no effort to take it.

Instead he said, *"Go to hell!"*

Marshall watched him leave. Just minutes. It was incredible. He felt like cheering. Or screaming.

"Cast off the launch."

As it idled clear he had to shake himself to accept it had happened. The boom vessel lay unmoving in the strengthening

273

light just as before. The launch, with two or three Italian seamen on deck, was steering towards the harbour. Only when he looked over the screen and saw something pale sinking deeper and deeper in the water did it become real.

Blythe explained thickly, "Mr. Smith weighted the Jerry with some mooring wire, sir. Quick as a bloody ferret he was!"

Marshall gripped the cool metal with both hands.

"Half ahead together. Follow the guardboat."

He waited, hardly daring to blink as slowly, and then with more haste, the boom vessel began to winch the net.

Nearer and nearer, until all at once the boom vessel was gliding abeam, an officer coming out on to the bridge wing to salute as U-192 entered harbour.

"He's closing the boom behind us, sir."

But Marshall was watching the little launch as it increased speed and dashed towards the top of the sleeping harbour and the moored freighter.

"Launch is alongside the freighter, sir."

"Slow ahead together."

Marshall watched the nearest jetty and tried not to think about the pillboxes on the hillside. He watched Cain and the casing party making a great show of preparing lines for mooring, and on the little jetty he saw a handful of yawning Italians, probably sailors from the freighter at the top of the harbour.

Warwick was saying hoarsely, "Come on! *Come on!*"

Marshall snapped, "Watch the freighter. As soon as Simeon's party have cast off we've got to move fast."

He looked at his watch. Not long now. It seemed too bright, too peaceful. Surely something would break soon?

Warwick gripped his arm. "She's moving, sir! Look, her mainmast is level with the pier!"

Marshall sprang to the voicepipe. "Full ahead! Port ten!"

He felt the hull lurch forward, the bow wave mounting powerfully and sluicing towards the nearby jetty and the mesmerised Italians.

"*Steady!*"

He pounded the screen with his fist.

"Get Pilot on deck to lend a hand! We've got to take the freighter's tow-rope and warp her clear!"

As the harbour widened out he conned the submarine round in

one huge arc, while high in the freighter's bows he saw the marines lowering a wire hawser, while others held their machine-pistols trained on the shore.

A rattle of machine-gunfire pattered impersonally across the sheltered water, and Marshall saw the bullets cutting feathers of spray around the abandoned guardboat.

Somewhere in the distance a klaxon blared, and within seconds tracer ripped above the harbour, although it was obvious the garrison had been caught completely unprepared.

"Hard aport! Stop the port engine!"

He gritted his teeth as the freighter loomed over the conningtower.

"Stand by on deck!"

There was no time to rig fenders. No more time for anything. A bullet smashed into the tower and whimpered away over the water.

More machine-gunfire probed into the harbour, and Warwick yelled, "Open fire, sir?"

"Yes." He yelled, "Stop starboard!"

The submarine's starboard bow shuddered and lurched below the freighter's great anchor, the metal screaming in protest as both hulls ground together.

Hands grabbed and hauled on lines, and he saw Devereaux, hatless and wild-eyed, yelling at them to drag the hawser down on to the casing and the forward mooring bollards.

The air seemed to split apart as Warwick's gun crews fired long bursts of cannon shells and tracer bullets towards the nearest pillboxes. From one came an answering volley, and someone on the casing fell thrashing wildly in a pattern of blood. Against the dull steel it looked like black paint.

"Secured, sir!"

"Right! Tell the boarding party to get back here on the double!"

He winced, his mind cringing as the deck gun crashed out for the first time, the shell ripping past the conning-tower.

The shell exploded beside a pillbox and the firing stopped instantly.

There was a short, abbreviated whistle and a violent explosion. For an instant he thought the enemy had brought up a mobile gun, but Devereaux was shouting, "Mortar! Above the bunker!"

Blythe yelled, "Chief reports he's ready to tow, sir!"

The diesels had fallen still, yet in the firing Marshall had not even noticed it.

He thanked God that Frenzel, blind to danger and ignorant of what was happening about his head, had managed to remember his part.

The electric motors were purring smoothly, and Marshall shouted, ''Slow astern together!''

He saw the hawser tauten, felt the towering hull alongside shudder violently as another mortar bomb exploded somewhere on the upper deck.

But she was answering. Slowly and painfully, as the U-boat pulled astern, the freighter began to swing away from her original moorings. Another bomb shrieked down and burst on the ship, hurling splinters and fragments of steel in all directions.

''She's started to sink!'' Warwick was waving his cap like a madman. ''Simeon has opened her cocks!''

It was true, and with the additional damage caused by the mortar, it would not take long before she settled on the bottom of the harbour. A rope ladder had been thrown over the bulwark, and Marshall saw some of the marines clambering down and being dragged bodily on to the casing.

Further round, and still further, with gunfire blasting from every side, although there was so much smoke it was hard to tell friend from enemy.

A savage burst swept from the land, and Marshall ducked as bullets flayed the bridge like a steel whip. When he looked again he saw several of his men sprawled on the deck and others dragging themselves towards the conning-tower. Devereaux was clinging to the guardrail and yelling at a marine who was still dangling from the ladder. Another sharp burst cut the marine down, so that he dropped into the churned water, his weapons carrying him straight to the bottom.

A dull boom echoed and re-echoed around the hills, and Blythe yelled, ''Captain Lambert's charges have blown, sir!''

''That'll get 'em out of bed!''

The lookout who had spoken clutched his chest, and with an amazed gasp toppled against the machine-gunner at his side. He was dead before he hit the deck.

Marshall snapped, ''Prepare to cast off. Stop both motors.'' He could not wait another second.

Firing was heavier along the shore, and Blythe shouted, "Here comes Lambert's mob!"

The returning raiding party were scampering behind the pillboxes, and the air shook and crashed to their grenades. It must have been worse than a nightmare for the Germans in the pillboxes. The sudden awakening, and then the sight of what appeared to be reinforcements running from inland. Then the terrible realisation. The grenades, the lethal clatter of machine-pistols. Oblivion.

Cain cupped his hands and shouted at the bridge, "Two more to come, sir!" He ducked as more tracer slashed overhead.

Marshall shaded his eyes and peered at the listing freighter. He knew one of them was Simeon. It had to be.

The he saw them. Smith clambering down the ladder, with Simeon clutching his body like a drowning man.

Warwick gasped, "Simeon's bought it, sir."

Marshall looked desperately at the dead and wounded on the casing. "Open the fore hatch." To Cain he shouted, "Help those two across!"

He saw Buck and some more hands emerging through the fore hatch and dragging the wounded below, their faces frozen to the clatter of gunfire, the screams of their companions.

A groan went up as Smith lost his hold and fell. As he broke surface a machine-gunner found him, and lashed the water into foam all around. He threw up his arms and vanished, the foam turning crimson before spreading between the two hulls.

He saw Simeon being dragged towards the hatch and shouted, *"Cast off!"*

When he looked again the fore casing was almost empty but for a pathetic cluster of dead sailors. Devereaux was struggling with the heavy eye of the hawser, while Cain tried to help him, one arm hanging at his side, bloody and useless.

Simeon was halfway through the hatch, his shoulder shining in the frail glare where a splinter had cut him down on the freighter's deck. He pushed someone away who was trying to help him through the hatch and lurched back on to the casing. He was shouting and cursing like a madman, most of the words lost in the metallic clatter of machine-guns. As he reached the bollard Devereaux turned and saw him, then he too was down, rolling and kicking, his screams cut short as his life splashed across the buckled plating.

Simeon pushed Cain towards the hatch and then threw himself on the heavy hawser. Once, twice, and then it was free, splashing into the harbour where Smith and others had died.

He turned and stared towards the bridge, and seemed to grin. Or perhaps it was a grimace, for even as he made to follow Cain he dropped to his knees and then toppled very slowly over the side.

Marshall said hoarsely, "Full astern. We'll pick up Lambert's party *now*."

He was still staring at the fore casing. The hatch was shut. Only the dead remained.

It did not take long for the breathless marines to leap aboard. The submarine hardly paused as she slid sternfirst past the small jetty where they had first seen the waiting Italians. Lambert was with them, but he had less than half of his men intact.

Marshall's aching mind registered all these facts, but he felt detached from them. Like a dying man who can hear those about him, yet is incapable of reaching them.

He dragged Warwick to the ladder. "Help those men below. Then clear the deck gun." He had to shake him to make him move. "We must finish what we came for."

"You all right, sir?" Blythe was crouching beside him, his face ashen in the smoky sunlight.

"Stay with me, Yeoman." He watched the stern edging out into the harbour again. "Stern tubes *ready*." He rested his forehead on the sights, watching the boom vessel swimming through the crosswires as if in a mist. "Fire at three second intervals."

He winced as more metal crashed into the hull, and saw Warwick pulling a wounded marine through the hatch like a sack.

"Now!"

The hull kicked very slightly. He counted the seconds, and felt the second torpedo burst from its tube. They were now so near to the boom vessel that the explosions came almost together. When the spray and fragments began to fall he saw the ship toppling on to her side in a welter of smoke and flames. She would soon sink, and with her the boom.

When he staggered to the forepart of the bridge again he felt he was the last man alive. He dashed the sweat from his eyes and saw what they had come all this way to destroy. With the freighter leaning at a steep angle on the opposite side of the

278

harbour, the towering wall of concrete, the black cavernous mouth of the bunker stood out as they had on Travis's neat diagrams.

"Standing by, One to Six, sir."

Marshall could only whisper a reply, but Blythe shouted, "Bridge to control room! Coming on *now*!"

Marshall tried again. There was smoke everywhere. Like steam. He saw an armoured car racing down a cliff road. It was like a child's toy. Even the tiny, spurting flashes from its turret were without threat or reality.

He concentrated on the pier at the entrance of the bunker. A powerful mobile derrick, and beyond some big metal cases. Bombs which would have been in the freighter tomorrow morning, en route for some German airfield.

"Fire One!"

He heard Buck's voice on the intercom, and imagined him with his stopwatch.

"Carry on firing. Three second intervals."

He turned to peer astern as the hull continued to back towards the boom. There was no sign of the boom vessel. Just a great patch of oil and bobbing flotsam.

The fourth torpedo had left the tube when the first exploded against the pier. After that it was impossible to tell one from the next, or night from day.

The torpedoes must have touched off some of the stacked bombs, and in an instant a massive explosion rocked the harbour, sending a small tidal wave creaming wildly towards the submarine as if to seek revenge.

The noise went on and on, fading and then mounting again as the piled explosives detonated far inside the bunker and into the hillside itself.

"All torpedoes running, sir!"

He nodded dazedly, "Clear the bridge."

He coughed in the funnelling smoke which had almost blotted out the harbour. The hull was rocking violently in the tossing water, but he knew he must *think*. Still act. Like a machine.

"Stop port. Full ahead starboard. Wheel hard astarboard!"

Metal cracked into the bridge, and he found himself on the gratings, a terrible pain in his side. He wanted to cry out, but the agony was too great. He felt Blythe pulling him to the hatch, but used his body as a prop to haul himself back to the voicepipe. The bows were swinging.

279

"Full ahead port. Wheel amidships." He moaned as the pain made his eyes fill with shadows.

Then he heard Gerrard's voice and saw him clinging to the screen at his side.

Blythe shouted, "The cap'n got one in the side!"

But Gerrard was holding his arm. He said, "It's all right, sir. I've got her now."

Marshall stared at him. "Clear the boom area, Bob. Then get her down and run for it."

Gerrard watched him sadly. "I can cope. You get below and have that gash cleaned." He watched as Blythe and a lookout half carried him to the hatch.

Then he looked at the sky. It was clearing. Just as Devereaux had predicted.

He crouched over the voicepipe and snapped, "Steer one-five-zero. Maximum revolutions!"

He glanced astern, but there was only smoke and the intermittent boom of underground explosions.

We made it. We made it.

He thought of Marshall, and what he had seen him do. What he had done for all of them. The victors.

Three days later, surfaced, and with both diesels damaged almost beyond repair, U-192 was steering west for Gibraltar.

Marshall stood on the battered bridge, watching the sea, and for once content to leave his command to others.

They had done all they set out to do, and had made their homing signal in accordance with the original orders. Now there was nothing left but to reach Gibraltar before some new failure left them helpless and at the mercy of an enemy attack.

Two destroyers found them on the morning of the third day, and as they ploughed purposefully towards the crawling submarine Blythe muttered, "I hope they've been *told*, that's all, sir."

They had.

As the lights stammered back and forth Blythe asked thickly, "Their senior officer wants to know, sir. Do you wish to abandon or shall he take you in tow?"

Marshall turned and looked up at the flag overhead. The proper one, for once. Then at the full length of his command. Six months he had had her, and now it was all over.

Buck was watching the destroyers as they swung round making a great creaming wash while they took station on either beam.

"Bloody cheek!" He looked at Warwick. "Typical, that is!"

Marshall touched the ache in his side. It was an answer, if he had needed it.

He said slowly, "Tell him neither. *His Majesty's U-boat* 192 *is rejoining the Fleet.*" He hesitated, thinking of those who had been left behind. "We've come this far. I'll not leave her now."

"Signal from escort, sir. *Congratulations.*"

Marshall smiled. "Thanks. I think we've earned them!"